TRUTH ABOUT NERDS & BEES

ANDREA SIMONNE

Liebe
Publishing

Truth About Nerds & Bees

By Andrea Simonne

Copyright © 2023 Andrea Simonne

All rights reserved. Published by Liebe Publishing

First Print Edition, August 22, 2023

ISBN: 978-1-945968-14-3

Edited by Hot Tree Editing: www.hotreeediting.com

Cover Design: LBC Graphics

CHAPTER ONE

~ Gabe ~

Day One

"There's a woman chained to your front porch."

"What's that?" I growled, putting the phone on speaker. I'd just gotten out of the shower and was still dripping wet. Setting my phone on the black marble counter in my bathroom, I reached for a towel from the warming rack and began drying my hair.

"She's been here for at least a few hours now. Just thought you might want to know." The guy's scratchy voice sounded amused.

"I have no idea what you're talking about." I rubbed the towel across my wet body. "Who did you say you are again?" I was expecting a call from my lawyer, Davis, which was why I answered the phone straight from the shower. We were in talks with a major designer about putting out a cologne with my name attached. We planned to call it Beauty Bardales for Men. It would come in an artsy black bottle that looked like a dildo, though everyone kept assuring me it didn't.

"This is Gary, the head contractor in charge of your house construction."

I wiped steam from the mirror until I could see my reflection. Dark hair and eyes. Stern face. Hard chest. The fashion designer suggested I do a shirtless ad holding the dildo bottle while I squirted myself with cologne.

To be honest, the whole thing wasn't working for me. We needed to go back to the drawing board.

"This is about my house in Truth Harbor?" I asked.

"Yes, sir."

I'd bought some property in a small island town north of Seattle and had a vacation home built on it. "All right, Gary. So what you're telling me is there's a woman chained to my front porch."

"That is correct."

"Is she naked?"

Gary chuckled. "No."

I tried to picture this woman, imagining a voluptuous brunette or maybe a sexy redhead with pouty lips and a come-hither expression. I considered my options. It was probably a fan. While most of my female fans were terrific, occasionally there was a nutjob. "Listen, I'm sure she's harmless. Just cut the chain off and send her on her way. In fact, get her address and tell her I'll mail her a signed photo."

"Sorry, that won't work."

"Why not?"

"First off, the chain is too thick. Second, there's the matter of her vehicle, which is also chained to the house." He paused, and I detected more amusement. "This gal means business."

I sighed to myself and frowned when I noticed I'd nicked my jaw shaving in the shower. I had a photo shoot this afternoon. Of course, they'd mostly be taking photos of my ass since the shoot was for my line of boxer briefs called Beauty Bardales Jock Style.

"You want me to call the sheriff?" Gary asked. "The deputy sheriff was here earlier."

I tore off a small piece of tissue for the cut on my jaw. "Let me talk to her first, see what I can do." I did my best to avoid fans who were unhinged, but it sounded like it might be the quickest solution in this case.

There was some noise on the other end of the line. I could hear Gary telling someone they'd be going on break in five minutes.

A break? Seriously? I glanced at the time. It was barely nine in the morning.

I'd paid a fortune to have that house built. There was the main house and an elaborate guesthouse as well. It was all done in a Spanish style that suited me, down to the customizations in every room.

"Here you go, hon," I heard Gary say to someone, presumably the crazed fan. "I've got the owner on the line for you."

I waited. Except no one spoke.

"Hey, sweetheart, are you there?" I crooned softly into the phone. It wasn't a voice I used often. In fact, I couldn't remember the last time I'd crooned. As the starting quarterback for the Seattle Sentries, I was usually barking orders. Mostly at my offensive line during football season.

There was a huff of breath and then a female voice, strong and clear. "So this is what it *finally* takes to get your attention, Mr. Bardales."

I gave a soft chuckle. "It's pronounced Bar-*dallas*, sweetheart, and you've definitely got my attention." I knew exactly how to handle this type of whack job. Flirt a little and make small talk. Soon she'd be eating out of the palm of my hand.

"I've sent you multiple emails and letters and not a single response."

"Well, I didn't mean to ignore you. It's just that I get a lot of letters and emails. Why don't you give me your address, and I'll send you a signed photo? How does that sound?"

"And what would I do with a signed photo?"

"Well... whatever you want." I had a pretty good idea of what some of my fans were doing with theirs.

She snorted. "I don't want a signed photo. That's absurd."

My eyes narrowed. This woman was even more far gone that I thought.

"I'm not leaving here until you meet me face-to-face," she said.

"That's not possible." With irritation, I noticed the nick on my jaw was still bleeding and tore off another piece of tissue. "Look, I'm only trying to help you out. We don't want to get the sheriff involved, do we?"

"Oh heck, yes, we do. Let's get the sheriff involved. The press too. I'd love to explain to the whole world what a jerk you are, and that you're messing with almost a million bees."

I was confused but then realized she must be one of those crazed environmentalists, the ones who'd decided professional sports were to blame for all the ills in the world. I had nothing to do with the NFL's carbon footprint, but these people couldn't be reasoned with.

She began to rant about pollinators and population numbers. "You're nothing but a Varroa destructor in human form," she spat out.

I had no idea what the hell that was. "Listen, you're trespassing on private property," I said in a stern voice. "I suggest you vacate or I'll have the sheriff remove you forcibly."

"Oh, really?" She snorted. "Bring. It. On."

"Let's see if you feel the same after spending the night in jail." I waited, then heard three beeps in a row. "Hello?"

She'd hung up on me.

What a freak, I thought with disgust. *Where do these weirdos come from?*

I wondered if I should call the contractor back.

To hell with it. I've got people for this.

I'd never bothered with an assistant, but I texted Davis, who was far better, and quickly explained what was happening at my vacation home.

Gabe: I need you to handle this. No press.

He responded right away.

Davis: Consider it handled.

CHAPTER TWO

~ Gabe ~

Day Two

"Just thought you'd like to know that woman is still here." It was Gary, the contractor with the smoker's voice. He seemed in a chipper mood this morning. "Her name's Theo, and she's still chained to your house."

I was lying in bed and had just woken up. I wasn't in a chipper mood. Old demons had been haunting me all night.

Glancing over at the clock on the wall, I could see it was almost eight and that I'd missed my seven o'clock workout. *Shit.* I swung my legs over the side of the bed. I rarely woke up this late but had gotten little sleep.

I scrubbed my face with one hand and listened as Gary began

talking, presumably to Theo, the chained woman. "Thanks, hon. These honey cakes are delicious. It was real sweet of you to bring them for everyone."

"No problem," she said in the background. "I'm glad you like them."

What the hell is going on there?

"What's she still doing there?" I growled. "The sheriff should have gotten rid of her yesterday."

"Sheriff's on vacation," Gary said in a muffled voice as he chewed.

Why didn't Davis handle this like I told him to? "There must be someone up there who can get rid of her."

Gary smacked his lips, enjoying his honey cake. "Deputy sheriff came by but then left. Had other matters to attend to, apparently."

I pinched the bridge of my nose and took a deep breath. I didn't need this aggravation. *Don't these people know who I am? That I'm not someone you want to mess with?*

"Do you think I could get the recipe for these?" I heard Gary ask her. "I've been learning how to bake since I quit smoking."

"Of course. Just give me your email and I'll send it to you," she said.

This is unbelievable.

"Put her on the phone," I demanded. *"Now."*

"Sounds like he wants to talk to you," I heard him say.

There was a moment of silence, and then a female voice in a clipped tone asked, "Are you finally ready to meet with me?"

"I want you to listen, and listen good. You need to remove yourself from my property."

"As I stated yesterday, I won't be going anywhere until we meet face-to-face. There's too much at stake."

"Your life's going to be spent wearing an orange jumpsuit. That's what's at stake for you."

She scoffed. "Just the attitude I expected. But you messed with the wrong woman. I'm not leaving until we meet and I get it in writing that you're leaving my bees alone."

I was tired from lack of sleep, but the fog began to clear. "What are you talking about? What bees?"

"Wow. Do you even read your own mail? Actually, *can* you read? You have no idea what's going on up here, do you?"

Damn. The balls on this woman. "Who the hell are you?"

She was silent for a second, and it sounded like she was taking a sip of coffee. "I'm your next-door neighbor."

I scowled. "My what?"

"Neighbor. The one you've been threatening to take to court if I don't remove my beehives. Ring any bells?"

The funny thing was it *did* ring some bells. She began to rant about lawyers and threatening letters, telling me how she'd been forced to hire an attorney of her own.

It was all coming back to me from months ago. "My landscape architect said your bees are a nuisance. They're buzzing all over the swimming pool out by my guesthouse."

"If you're worried about bees, you shouldn't have built a swimming pool right next to multiple beehives." Her tone dripped with sarcasm. "I mean, what kind of overprivileged fool needs a swimming pool for a guesthouse, anyway? Especially in the Northwest."

"It's my property, and I'll build whatever I want! I'll put in *fifty* swimming pools if I feel like it." My breath shook as I tried to control my temper. I couldn't believe this strange woman had gotten me so worked up. It didn't help that I hadn't slept for shit last night.

"How many swimming pools do you have? You might as well just light your money on fire."

"Go to hell, lady."

"I'm sure you'd like that." Her voice turned officious. "But I'm not going anywhere until I have a guarantee in writing."

"We'll see what the sheriff's department and a judge both have to say about that."

"Maybe so. But first we'll see what the public has to say."

"What do you mean?"

"Oh, didn't I mention it? I called the press." There was a deter-mined tone in her voice. "I called them yesterday and again this morning. They should be arriving shortly."

Shit. But then I figured it was probably just the local paper.

"I'm sure it'll make a great story," she continued. "'Millionaire jock hates bees.'"

"I don't hate your bees. But I can't have them swarming on my property."

"They've never swarmed on your property. That's a lie."

"How would you know? What if one of my guests gets stung by a bee?"

"Because none of my hives have swarmed, and my bees were here long before your stupid swimming pool."

I couldn't believe the nerve of this woman. On the other hand, the last thing I needed was for the press to jump on this story. I already had a reputation for being difficult—a reputation that wasn't deserved. At least not for good reason.

"I'm sure we can find a compromise," I muttered. "Unchain your-self and we'll figure it out."

"There is no compromise. I'm not going anywhere until you call off your lawyers and sign a statement saying you won't come after my bees ever again." She paused and then added, "You'll also need to remove your guesthouse swimming pool so it doesn't keep attracting them, or at least drain the water."

I balked at this. "Who do you think you are? You can't just tell me what to do. Are you going to pay for the swimming pool's removal?"

"Of course not. But I'm not the one who put it in such a dumb location to begin with."

I took a deep breath. This conversation was getting more absurd by the second.

"What's that?" She spoke to someone else, then directly to me again. "Gary says he needs his phone back. I'll give you my number, and you can call me to discuss this further."

I didn't want to call her. And I definitely didn't want her having my private number. "Fine. Give me your phone number," I said, humoring her. She rattled off some digits, and I wrote them down in a notebook on my nightstand. I'd been using it to take notes recently after watching film of us playing Chicago last January. They'd beaten us in the wild card game 12–8. I was determined that wasn't going to happen again.

We hung up, but I didn't call her back.

Though, as it turned out, I probably should have.

"MAKE YOURSELF AT HOME," I said to Davis, who had loosened his tie, gotten himself his own beer, and was now handling the remote control for the flat-screen in my living room as if he owned the place.

I noticed the bags of takeout from a nearby Chinese restaurant on the coffee table. At least he'd brought dinner.

Davis had been my lawyer for about five years, and somehow during that time we'd become best friends, though I wasn't sure how it happened. I didn't allow many people to get close to me, except Davis had a way of ignoring personal boundaries.

"You have to see this," he said, navigating the menu on the television over to YouTube. "I just got word."

I crossed my arms and leaned against the arched doorway in my living room. My Seattle penthouse had a spectacular view of Elliot Bay, and I could see the sun low on the horizon. "You need to talk to that damn fashion designer again. I'm serious, Davis. I want the design for that cologne bottle changed."

Of course, he ignored me. Instead, he brought up the search menu on YouTube and typed in my name along with the date. I wondered what this was all about. Before I knew it, he was playing a video that showed a female newscaster talking to some woman in front of a house that looked awfully familiar.

I snapped away from the wall. "What the hell? That's my house in Truth Harbor!"

"I just found out about it. The footage comes from a local area news station up there."

The camera focused in on some woman in her early thirties with curly bright red hair, tortoiseshell glasses, and a freckled face.

I couldn't take my eyes off the screen. "Who is that?" I asked as I strode into the living room and stopped behind the coffee table.

"That's the woman who's chained herself to your house."

"That's *her*?" Listening, I recognized the voice from the phone. She was telling the reporter the same thing she'd told me, that she wasn't unchaining herself until I gave a written guarantee about her bees.

Davis snorted. "Trust me, she doesn't have a legal leg to stand on. No judge is going to allow these crazy shenanigans. She's just digging a deeper hole for herself."

The camera panned over to my large front porch. It showed the thick stone pillar that she'd chained herself to, then out farther to my driveway where a green Jeep I'd never seen before was also chained to a pillar.

My mouth fell open in shock. *What the fuck?* "This is unbeliev-able. Why the hell didn't you get rid of her like I told you to?"

It was odd, but I couldn't take my eyes off this woman. There was something arresting about her.

"I sent the deputy sheriff out late last night, and he said she wasn't there anymore. She must have left for the night and come back early this morning."

"Who is she?"

Davis took a sip from his beer. "Her name's Theodora Stewart. Apparently she's a professor at the university's bee research facility up there."

"A professor?" I continued to watch her on-screen. She had the brightest red-orange hair I'd ever seen in my life.

Davis nodded. "She's a bee biologist. Obviously she's the neighbor we're suing to remove her hives."

I watched as Theodora told the reporter how important bees were to humans and the ecology. Freckles ran across her nose and cheeks.

"She reminded me on the phone yesterday," I said. "I'd forgotten all about suing her."

"That was a mistake, Gabe. You shouldn't be talking to her. Just let the lawyers handle it, and let me deal with the press too."

Theodora smiled at something the reporter said and revealed a gap between her two front teeth. I stared at it. I'd had a thing for females with a gap between their front teeth since my second-grade crush on Maria Arnold.

At that moment, I made an irrational decision. "I'm going up there."

"What? *Why?*" Davis turned to me with alarm. "Trust me, the best thing for you is to stay away and let this story die a quiet death. That's my advice to you as your lawyer."

"Are you kidding?" I pointed at the screen. "There's a circus happening right in front of my house. I can't just ignore it."

"Ignoring it is exactly what you should do."

CHAPTER THREE

~ Theo ~

Day Three

I read the text from my lawyer, April, again and sighed. She told me the same thing everyone else had been telling me, that I needed to unchain myself, unchain my Jeep, and stop all this insane behavior.

The only two people who thought I should continue were my besties, Leah and Claire. "Give him hell," they said, cheering me on, but they both had an independent streak like me.

Some local press had been here yesterday, and from what it sounded like, more of them were coming today. Apparently this football player was a big deal. Everyone had told me he was, but now I realized it was true.

Hopefully that works in my favor.

I shivered a little and zipped up my jacket. It was July and the days had been warm, but it was still chilly at five in the morning. It didn't help having this cold steel chain wrapped around my waist. Luckily, I'd come prepared. My thermos of hot coffee and cooler with food sat beside me. I'd also brought more jars of honey and had baked more pans of honey cakes to share with reporters and the guys working on the house. I needed this football player to feel pressure to call off his lawyers, because if this case went before a judge, April said I'd most likely lose, which meant finding a new home for my beehives.

What a depressing thought.

April told me if I was running a business it would help my case, but I'd never sold my honey, and all the tours I gave were free. I took donations to help pay for glass jars and the equipment I needed, but that's it. Somehow the fact that I had a PhD and had made the study of honey bees my life's work didn't seem to matter.

I sipped my coffee to warm up and glanced around. It was quiet this time of morning. I'd spent two days sitting in front of this large fancy house and had to wonder what it looked like inside. The architecture was done in a Spanish style and had an actual turret that made it look like a castle. Judging by the behavior of the jock ogre who owned this place, I was surprised he hadn't put in a moat and a dungeon.

By the time noon rolled around, the construction crew was here maneuvering their way around me and my vehicle, and Claire also stopped by to say hello.

"Philip says he's sure he can help you out of this situation with Bardales," she said, shifting Amelia, her five-month-old, in the sling on her hip and giving her a pacifier. "Just say the word and he'll make a phone call."

Philip was Claire's husband and ran a successful venture capital firm. I'd become friendly with his younger sister, Eliza, too.

"That's okay. I prefer to handle it myself. Besides, I doubt this guy will listen to reason. You should have heard him on the phone with me the other day. He actually told me to go to hell."

"Really? What an asshole. I know he has a reputation, but I've never believed any of the stories people say about him."

I took out a slice of apple from the baggie I'd brought for lunch and offered some to Claire. "What kind of stories?"

"Well, they're just rumors, but some people say he attends orgies, and I even heard that he once killed a man."

My brows shot up. "Crikey."

"I know. If he killed somebody, he'd be in jail, right? Though as far as the orgies go, who knows?"

I crunched on a piece of apple and wondered if I'd made a mistake chaining myself to this guy's house. But then I remembered my bees and knew I wasn't going anywhere.

"I always thought he seemed like he had a wounded quality to him," Claire mused. "There's something in his eyes, like maybe he's been through some rough times, but I'm probably just imagining it. Obviously he's very handsome. That's why everyone calls him 'Beauty.'"

"Is he really that handsome?"

Claire reached into the baggie for another apple slice. "He is. Haven't you seen pictures of him?"

"Not really. I looked him up once, but he was wearing a football helmet in the photo."

She laughed. "Are you serious? You've chained yourself to his house, and you don't even know what he looks like?"

I shrugged. "It seemed unimportant." I didn't care what he looked like. All I cared about was getting him to call off his lawsuit so I could get back to my normal life.

"You're so funny," she said, eyeing me with affection. "You're probably the only person in the country who doesn't know what Beauty Bardales looks like, even though you're chained to his house."

Claire already knew I didn't pay attention to pop culture. It all seemed like meaningless noise. And professional football seemed like the most meaningless of all. Grown men tackling each other and getting paid astronomical sums of money to do it. The whole thing was absurd.

We chatted some more, and then Claire had to leave to go put her daughter down for a nap. Afterward, I realized I should have asked her to cover for me while I snuck off to go pee. That was the hardest part about being chained to this stone pillar—my bladder. Yesterday, I managed to sneak back to my house before the reporters arrived.

Unfortunately, there was a hive of activity with all the construction guys coming and going. More reporters could show up at any time.

I got my phone out and figured I'd hold my pee a little longer. Maybe use one of the construction crew's porta-potties if I got desperate.

I'd been reading a paper about queen genetics written by a colleague in Oregon, but I kept thinking about Claire's description of Bardales.

Finally, curiosity got the best of me, and I searched for his name and then images. Immediately the page was flooded with photos of some handsome guy with dark hair and eyes. He had a firm jaw, full, even lips, and a straight nose. He looked like a dark-haired version of Prince Charming. His eyes turned down slightly at the corners, and I could see what Claire meant. There was something soulful in his gaze.

"I thought you weren't a fan," said a deep voice above me.

I glanced up from where I was sitting and was shocked to see the same guy on my phone standing right in front of me in living color. He was wearing mirrored aviator sunglasses, but it was definitely him. The jock ogre. And it was clear that he saw me looking at his picture.

"I'm... not," I said, quickly putting my phone down.

He smirked. "Maybe you'd like a signed photo after all."

"No, thank you."

He appeared to be studying me, though I couldn't see his eyes behind the sunglasses. His expression was flat as he took in the heavy chain wrapped around my waist and then followed the second one that led out to my Jeep.

"Damn." He shook his head. "Don't you think this is all a bit much?"

I didn't bother to reply.

Behind him, I noticed some of the work crew had stopped what they were doing and were watching us. Reporters were probably going to be here soon. I needed to do something about my full bladder.

I squirmed a little. "Do you think I could use your bathroom?"

The corner of his mouth kicked up, and I noticed he had a dimple in his right cheek. "Seriously? You think I should offer you my bathroom? You *do* realize you'll have to unchain yourself first."

"I know," I said testily. "But I've been out here since 5:00 a.m."

"Maybe you should have worn a diaper like that astronaut lady."

"Very funny."

"You're both in cuckoo land. Hopefully they'll let you share a prison cell."

"Look, can I use your bathroom or not?" I stood up, taking the chain and padlock with me. I realized the absurdity of my request, but I really had to go.

His mouth dropped open. Not at my absurd request but at my height. It was a reaction I'd gotten my whole life.

"Damn, how tall *are* you?" he asked, scanning down my body. It was rude to comment if someone was short, but if you were tall, nobody cared about rudeness.

"I'll tell you if you take off your sunglasses. Don't you know it's impolite to have a conversation with them on?"

He seemed to suppress a grin, but I watched him place the sunglasses on top of his head, then look me square in the eyes.

Good God.

I tried not to show my reaction.

He was extremely handsome. Claire wasn't kidding. He was

possibly the most handsome man I'd ever seen. The photos online didn't do him justice.

"I'm waiting," he said, crossing his arms while looking me over like I was a side of grass-fed beef he was considering purchasing. "You must be at least six feet."

And that's when I realized I wasn't looking down on him like I did most everyone else in the world. I was looking *up*. "How tall are *you*?" I asked in amazement.

He smirked, and I could tell he was enjoying himself. "Six foot five." He glanced down at the striped sneakers on his feet and turned one to the side. "I suspect these add another couple of inches."

My eyes wandered down from his neck to his broad shoulders, then lower to a chest made of steel and arms corded with muscle. I knew professional football players were big, but I'd never met one in person. I actually felt physically intimidated, and I never felt physically intimidated.

"I'm six foot one," I said.

He grinned. "You're nothing but a shrimp."

My eyes widened. I'd been called a lot of things—Jolly Red Giant, Amazon, Beast—but never *shrimp*.

"Your name's Theodora, right? I'm Gabe."

"I go by Theo."

He nodded, and I almost thought he was going to shake my hand, which was quite magnanimous considering our current circumstance.

Instead, he jingled his keys and motioned toward his front door. "Fine. C'mon, I'll show mercy and let you use the bathroom, even though I shouldn't."

"Really?" I had to admit I was surprised. "I appreciate it."

He stood and watched me as I took a key from my jeans pocket and undid the padlock for the thick chain around my waist, then relocked the chain ends together and let it clank to the ground. My Jeep was on another chain with a different padlock.

"Damn," he said. "If I had a dirty mind, I might find those chains interesting."

I glanced at him, unsure how to interpret that comment.

It was bliss being able to pee after holding it in so long. I was sort of a camel and didn't have to go that often, but this was too much, even for me.

As I sat there on a comfortable toilet seat that wasn't too short, I glanced around the bathroom. It was a smallish powder room decorated in tones of forest green. Everything was obviously brand-new and done in the latest bathroom style.

After peeing, I went over to wash my hands and discovered the sink was also comfortable, quickly realizing it was the height. Normally I had to hunch over to wash my hands, but this was just right.

I could see in the mirror that my curly hair was turning to fuzz, so I squeezed some water into it with my hands. It made little difference. My friends always said they were envious of my hair, but I didn't understand why.

Being a woman who was over six feet tall with curly bright red hair hadn't been easy. I'd been the butt of a lot of jokes in my life.

I left the bathroom and went out to find the football player. His house was a maze, all of it done in a masculine style with dark wood paneling and high ceilings that reminded me of a castle. There was a fireplace in the living room large enough to stand in. *Is he planning to roast a whole boar soon?*

I hated to admit it, but something about this house appealed to me.

Finally, I found him in the kitchen. He was going through the mail that had been piled by his front door. There was a large cardboard box open on the floor. And sitting in the middle of the kitchen's marble countertop, right next to a stack of mail, was a big black dildo.

I stared at it.

He was still shuffling through his mail, occasionally reading something. "You find everything okay?" he asked.

"I did. Thank you." I glanced around the room in confusion. *Is this a test? Is he testing me?*

"So you're a professor, huh? You study bees?"

"I do. Primarily honey bees." I stared at the dildo on the counter. This could be an attempt to throw me off-balance. Maybe a Sun Tzu tactic? It *was* rather generous of him to let me use his bathroom, considering the situation.

Gabe put the mail down, and those soulful brown eyes met mine. "Listen, you and I got off on the wrong foot. What do you say we start over? We're neighbors, after all."

"Um, sure. We can start over." Except my eyes kept going to the dildo on the counter. It made no sense.

"I think if we put our heads together, we can come up with a solution that will make us both happy."

As he continued to talk, I glanced down into the box on the floor and was stunned to discover the whole thing was filled with dildos. At least a dozen. *Perhaps this is normal behavior?* Since I didn't follow pop culture or fashion trends, I was often behind the times. Was it possible celebrities were open about this sort of thing nowadays?

Then I remembered what Claire had told me about his participation in orgies, and the puzzle pieces clicked into place.

"Are you even paying attention to what I'm saying?" he asked with an edge of irritation. "Don't you want to resolve this?"

"Certainly I do. I apologize. I got distracted by your sexual devices."

"My what?"

I motioned toward the kitchen counter and the box on the floor. "Your dildos. Isn't that what they're called?"

His mouth fell open. His expression looked as if a surprise dildo had just serviced him.

"No judgment." I put my hand up quickly to reassure him. "I've always considered myself a tolerant person. Consenting adults and all that."

His face turned redder than the planet Mars.

"Should I not have said anything? I'm not always good with people. Just ignore me. Honestly, I'm better with bees."

"That's *not* a dildo," he managed to say through gritted teeth.

"You must be having quite an orgy later," I mused, glancing down at the box again. I had to admit, the biologist in me was curious. "To require a whole twelve-pack."

"Those aren't dildos! They're bottles of men's cologne!"

I tilted my head. "What?"

He grabbed the dildo from the table and pressed the dick's head, and some kind of liquid squirted out.

"Aaah!" I yelped, jumping back with alarm. *Ew!*

But then I caught a whiff of what smelled like pine and patchouli.

"*See?* It's my new cologne. The bottle is a *prototype*," he said in a voice that sounded like thunder. "I have no idea why they sent me a whole damn case of them."

I laughed a little. "Well, it certainly had me fooled."

He was shaking his head and grabbing for his phone. I watched as he stabbed in some kind of message with his thumbs. He looked highly pissed. "I've *had* it with this shit," he muttered.

"What kind of compromise were you thinking of?" I asked as he continued to murder his phone. "About my bees."

He still wore a scowl when he glanced over at me. "Did you really think I was having an *orgy?*"

I tried to smile. "I probably shouldn't have said that. I made an erroneous assumption. It's just that I've heard stories about you."

He stopped typing. "What kind of stories?"

"Nothing really." I shifted uncomfortably. "I'm sure you've never killed a man."

His brows slammed together.

Uh-oh. I probably shouldn't have said that either.

It occurred to me that I was making a mess of this. For some reason, this guy made me nervous, which was fascinating, and if I weren't so nervous, I'd probably enjoy analyzing it.

"These fucking rumors are never going to leave me alone," he growled. "And no, I *don't* attend orgies. Jesus!"

Interestingly, he didn't refute killing a man, though maybe that was a given.

"I have a habit of speaking my mind," I explained to him. "Try not to hold it against me."

He seemed to have calmed down somewhat, though he was still studying me as if I were a new species of human.

"Do you still want to start over?" I asked with a hopeful note in my voice. "Perhaps find a solution to our problem?"

CHAPTER FOUR

~ Gabe ~

Still Day Three

I had no idea what to make of this strange woman. I'd never met anyone like her in my life. She was both odd and beautiful.

It was the damnedest thing.

Between the height, the hair, the freckles, and the gap-toothed grin, she looked like an overgrown version of Pippi Longstocking. And I'd had a big crush on Pippi when I was a kid.

I couldn't seem to pull my eyes away. She was breathtaking. But clearly also unhinged.

Why are all the beautiful women crazy?

"You shouldn't listen to rumors," I said, forcing myself to look away. "Oftentimes they're wrong."

Theo pushed her glasses up on her nose. "Now, about my bees. Perhaps you could keep your swimming pool covered during the warmer months?"

"Warmer months? You mean like spring and summer?"

She nodded. "Exactly. That would be perfect."

"And when would my guests go swimming? In the dead of winter?"

"Honey bees don't actively forage in the winter."

I still couldn't believe the nerve of her. "You're serious. You expect me to only use my swimming pool during *winter*?"

"Isn't the pool heated?"

"No one is going to want to go swimming outside when it's thirty degrees."

She tilted her head and seemed to consider this as she tapped her chin. "If only you hadn't built it in such a terrible location."

My jaw muscle flexed, and I nearly gave her an earful but then stopped myself. I'd led a team of hardened athletes to the Super Bowl three years ago. Surely I could handle one nutty bee professor.

"I don't know much about bees. Maybe you could explain why they're so attracted to my swimming pool in the first place."

She blinked at me behind those glasses. "Well, isn't it obvious? They need water just like we do."

"So they're drinking it?"

"Of course, and they're also bringing it back to the hive. I have a variety of birdbaths on my property, and there's a pond a short distance beyond my fence, but your pool being so close is an attraction as well." Her face brightened. "Hey, maybe you could turn it into an indoor pool."

"Forget it. The whole thing's already built. It would cost me a fortune to have it redone."

"But you're the one who made the mistake of building it in such a terrible location."

"It's not a terrible location for my own land!" It was in a great location. The guesthouse was just far enough from the main house for privacy. I couldn't believe all the fuss about a bunch of bees. "Why don't you just move your hives somewhere else?"

Her expression grew serious. "My bees were here first. So *you* need to be the one who takes steps."

We stared at each other.

A stalemate already.

Behind those tortoiseshell glasses, her eyes were green and full of intelligence.

Fuck stalemates.

It was time to let her know who was boss. I gave her my hardest glare. It was the same one I used on the field when anyone dared question my authority. I'd seen men the size of grizzly bears buckle under my glare.

Except this woman didn't even flinch. Instead, she glared right back, and I sensed something in her. A steely resolve. When she put her mind to a task, she was probably as pigheaded as I was.

Just great.

Though I had to admit it surprised me.

What surprised me even more was how much I liked it. I liked a challenge. Hell, I *loved* a challenge. It's one of the reasons I played football.

As we continued our staring contest, I tried to decide what made her so beautiful.

It might have been her eyes. Green and gold. Sunshine on wild grass. I imagined her standing naked in a field filled with wildflowers, her long arms stretched toward the sky like a goddess, long-limbed and statuesque. I'd glide my hands over her entire body, and I already knew she'd feel as smooth as silk.

My mouth went dry. I wanted... something. What? To kiss her?

Damn. What the hell is wrong with me?

She must have sensed my interest, because her brows drew together and she seemed confused. Bewildered, even.

In truth, I was bewildered myself. What had come over me? It was like I was under a spell. I'd never had such a visceral reaction to a woman. *Flower-filled meadows and goddesses? Sheesh.* I sounded like a romantic idiot.

I took a breath. "Maybe you should put in your own swimming pool," I suggested in a dry tone.

"Some pollinators would still be drawn to yours. We're talking about almost a million bees. Plus, I have no space or use for a swimming pool."

"I guess we'll be letting a judge decide what happens."

Her mouth drew into a hard line. "Or you could do the right thing."

"*Me?* What about *you?*"

"I've done nothing wrong. You need to fix your mistake."

"You got some balls. I'll say that much for you."

She snorted. "One of us has to have them."

I took this in with amazement. "Do you know who I *am?*"

Except she'd already turned away and was striding down the hall toward the front door.

"Where the hell are you going?" I called after her. "We're not done here."

But then I knew.

She was going outside to put that damn chain on again!

I raced after her. Theo was already standing on my cement front steps.

I loomed over her, casting a large shadow. "Don't you dare touch that chain."

She glared up at me. "You can't stop me."

"I sure as hell can. I have a good mind to throw you over my shoulder and carry you out of here."

She scoffed, but then her eyes widened as they took in my size. Recalculating.

Yeah, that's right, Professor. There weren't a lot of men capable of throwing a woman like her over their shoulder and carting her off.

I happened to be one of them.

"You wouldn't."

I took a step closer. "Try me."

The air sparked between us. There was definitely an attraction, and I wondered if she felt it. Up close, I could see the freckles sprinkled across her nose and cheeks. She bit her pink lower lip. Wild curls sprang out from her hair like a mad scientist.

"Mr. Bardales!" someone called.

I turned to see who it was and discovered it was some female reporter walking alongside a guy with a camera. They were coming up my driveway.

Shit.

Behind them were a couple more news vans with reporters inside.

Dammit. Why are they back?

This was the last thing I needed. I was still dealing with bad press from last year when some paparazzo shoved a camera in my face while I was chatting and signing an autograph for a kid. The asshole wouldn't leave us alone. Kept asking insulting questions, obviously trying to get a rise out of me. After the kid and his dad left, I went after that prick, took his camera away, and smashed it to bits.

I shouldn't have done it. I knew that. It was a mistake. We settled out of court, but some press picked up the story and ran with it. It only added to the rumor mill that said I was difficult.

I plastered a fake smile on my face and put my hand up in a wave. "Hi there," I said, hoping I could make this all go away somehow. "Can I help you guys with something?" I glanced over at the news vans. At least they were just local stations. *Thank God.* Hopefully none of the networks or cable sports stations got wind of this thing.

"We're glad to catch you here, Mr. Bardales. We have some questions for you," the blonde reporter said. She turned and instructed her cameraman to get footage of the professor's vehicle in the driveway and how it was chained to one of the two stone pillars in front of my house.

Spinning back to me, she asked, "Is it true you're trying to bully your next-door neighbor?"

"*What?* Of course not." I glanced down at Theo, who'd taken this opportunity to rechain herself. Her eyes caught mine, and she wore a smug smile. "I'm not bullying anybody."

"What do *you* have to say about that?" The reporter moved closer, addressing the professor. "Why have you chained yourself to the home of the Seattle Sentries' starting quarterback? Are you making a statement?"

Theo sat up a little taller and adjusted the chain around her waist. "Yes, I am making a statement. A statement against all bullies in the world. That's why—"

"No one's being bullied here!" I threw my hands up. "You're the one who's chained yourself to *my* house. If anyone's being bullied, it's *me!*"

Both the reporter and the professor seemed astonished at my outburst, and it occurred to me that I probably sounded like a jerk. Chaos erupted as everybody started asking a million questions at once. More reporters had joined the mix, and there was now a small crowd gathered, which included some of the guys working on my home.

It turned out that Davis had been right. I should have let this whole thing die a quiet death. Instead, I was adding fuel to the fire.

"Someone has to take a stance against bullies," Theo was saying as a separate cameraman dangled a microphone over her head. "Not to mention that some people are *ignorant* about how important bees are for our planet. I'm sure Mr. Bardales is rethinking his position as we speak." She gave me a pointed look.

"Are you rethinking your position?" the reporter asked eagerly, holding her microphone out to me. "Are you against bullies now?"

"Of course I'm against bullies! What kind of question is that? I've always been against bullies."

"Didn't you beat up a photographer last year?" some other reporter asked. "Isn't it true that you gave him a black eye?"

"That's a damn lie!"

The phone in my pocket buzzed, and I yanked it out. It was Davis on the caller ID. "Excuse me," I grumbled. "I have to take this."

I stepped away for some privacy and answered the phone, only to be greeted with Davis screaming in my ear. "*Are you insane? Get out of there and stop talking to those fucking reporters this instant!*"

I glanced back at the growing circus in front of my house and tried to act like I hadn't just lost my temper in front of all of them. "How do you even know what's going on here?"

"I told Gary, your head contractor, to call me if any more press came by. He showed me the whole thing on his phone!"

Meanwhile, the professor had stood up with that chain clanking around her waist and was giving the crowd a lecture on bees. She handed out jars of honey, bribing everybody, telling them that honey lasted indefinitely, how they'd found three-thousand-year old honey in King Tut's tomb that was still edible. There were even pans of honey cake everyone was munching on.

This definitely wasn't going my way.

She discussed bee biology and how important bees were for our environment. Except as I scanned the crowd, I could see their eyes glazing over. Clearly Theo didn't understand how short most people's attention spans were. Some reporters were trying to interrupt her to ask more juicy questions, but with amusement, I noticed she couldn't be deterred from her favorite subject.

Definitely pigheaded.

Just as she was explaining how 75 percent of the world's crops rely on pollinators, I noticed a new vehicle drive up. It had blue-and-red lights flashing on top.

"Looks like the sheriff is here," I said to Davis.

"Good. I called them. Let me do the talking. I'll make sure this woman is removed and thrown in jail."

"Thanks, but I've got it from here." I hung up the phone to the sound of Davis yelling at me not to hang up.

I chuckled to myself. He knew me pretty well.

AFTER CLEARING OUT THE REPORTERS, and after the construction crew finally got back to work building my back deck, the deputy sheriff crossed his arms and stood in front of the professor. I got the impression the two of them knew each other. "What are we going to do about this situation, Theo?"

She shrugged and waved her hand in my direction. "Why don't you ask *him*?"

"I'm asking *you*."

"I can't lose my beehives, Lars. And all because of this jackass's guesthouse swimming pool? Forget it."

The deputy sheriff turned to me. "Is there any compromise you two can reach?"

"I tried, but she won't listen to reason."

"That's not true," Theo said. "You're the one who created this problem, but you won't do anything to solve it."

I shook my head and turned back to the deputy sheriff. "You can see what I'm dealing with here. What are my options?"

"What would you like to do? It's within your rights to have her arrested for trespassing and damaging private property."

"I haven't damaged anything!" Theo exclaimed.

I considered this. "Can't we just cut the chains off her and her vehicle and let that be the end of it?"

Gary, my scratchy-voiced construction manager, was standing with us, popping nicotine gum in his mouth. "I don't see how that's possible, boss."

"Why not?" I asked.

Theo spoke up with self-satisfaction. "Because this is a 5/8-inch Grade 80 steel chain. You can't use typical bolt cutters on it. My Jeep and I won't be going anywhere."

"She's right," Gary said, motioning to the chain. "We don't have anything here to cut that. It could take a little while to get my hands on something."

"How long?" the deputy sheriff asked.

Gary shrugged. "Probably another day or two."

I watched as Theo leaned back against the stone pillar and stretched her long legs out in front of herself. She was wearing jeans, a yellow T-shirt, and a smug smile. She'd obviously thought this through.

"Fine," I said. "We'll wait." Then I turned to her. "Eventually you're going to lose. You know that, right? In fact, I still might press charges and have your ass thrown in jail."

She blinked up at me like I was a monster. I could feel both Gary and the deputy sheriff studying me. Nobody said anything, but somehow I felt their judgment.

How did I become the asshole here?

CHAPTER FIVE

~ Theo ~

Still Day Three

I waited until it was dark out before I finally unchained myself, picked up my cooler and thermos, tucked the empty baking pans inside my backpack, and got ready to walk home. When I came up with the idea of chaining myself to this guy's house, I knew I wouldn't be able to stay here twenty-four hours a day, which was why I'd also chained my Jeep.

"Leaving so soon?"

I glanced over. To my surprise, the jock ogre was standing in his doorway watching me.

"As a matter of fact, I'm going home now," I said, shifting my belongings around so I could carry them more comfortably. "But I'll be back tomorrow."

He sipped from a bottle of beer as he leaned his muscular body against the doorframe. I noticed he was barefoot and had changed from the button-down shirt into a gray T-shirt advertising some sporting goods store.

Everyone who was here before had left hours ago. I mainly stayed because I hoped I was making the jock ogre uncomfortable with my presence, though he didn't seem uncomfortable.

He was studying me again. I had no idea why he was staring at me so much. I'd had this happen with men before, where they wouldn't stop staring, and it was usually because they thought I was a freak. It's like they couldn't get over my height or my hair.

"Do you want a beer?" he asked, holding the bottle up with two fingers.

He had a nice speaking voice. And I'd be lying if I didn't admit that he was easy to look at. Dark hair fell over his forehead, and more of it curled around his neck, framing his square jaw and handsome face.

"No, thank you," I said stiffly.

"Don't want to fraternize with the enemy, huh?"

"That's correct. Unless you're ready to end your lawsuit, we have nothing to say to each other."

"Are you sure? Maybe you should come inside and... educate me about bees."

I paused and considered this. Did he really want to learn about bees? There was a note in his voice, almost seductive. I remembered then how he'd offered me a signed photo of himself. He was probably hoping I'd succumb to his appearance like so many other females.

"If you want to learn about bees, all you have to do is open a search engine and type in the word *bee*. I'm sure you can manage that."

"Why should I do that when I have an expert right here to teach me?"

"B-e-e," I said. "I hope it's not too big of a word for you to handle."

He raised a brow.

"See you tomorrow," I said cheerily as I turned to walk away.

"You're going to lose this little game you're playing, Professor," he called after me. "I hope you know that. Because when I play, I play to win."

I glanced back at him. Our eyes connected, and for an instant, I felt a peculiar buzz of energy between us.

Ignoring it, I continued to walk down his driveway. Of course he'd frame everything in terms of a game. His whole life revolved around one.

It was a warm summer evening as I made my way back to my house. We were neighbors, but it was still a bit of a walk since the jock ogre's property was so much larger than mine.

When I got home, my intention was to go inside and take a long hot shower, but instead, I left my cooler and backpack on the front porch and headed down to my backyard. My property was built on a slope with the house sitting at the top. It leveled out near the bottom, which was where all my beehives were kept.

It was nearly dark out as I approached my hives. Most of my bees were home and resting for the evening. Bees couldn't see well in the dark and didn't forage at night. I saw a few stragglers returning as I headed for the gate in back.

A wooden fence ran along my entire property, put in place by the previous owner, and for some reason, they'd installed an artsy wooden gate that opened to the land behind it.

Initially, I'd ignored it. I thought it was odd, but there was no reason for me to go beyond my fence since that was somebody else's property.

As the number of my beehives increased over the years, I noticed something. In the early morning, when the bees left for their day's foraging, many of them headed north over that gate. Finally, I got curious enough that I pried open the latch, which had rusted shut from years of nonuse, to see what was back there.

What I found was astonishing. The area was wooded, but if you kept walking past the trees, it eventually opened to a large meadow filled with tall grasses and wildflowers. Purple, orange, pink, and red, it was bursting with color. There was also a pond nearby that attracted its own assortment of plants and animals. My bees, of course, were among them.

Like a fairy tale, the place was bright and colorful and humming with life.

I had no idea how that meadow came to be, but I certainly understood why my bees loved it. It was a pollinator's smorgasbord. I found myself drawn to it as well and began to go there regularly.

Eventually I did some digging and learned the land, which comprised almost fifty acres, was owned by an older gentleman. He and his wife had built a small farm on the northwest corner of the property but, as far as I could tell, had consistently left the southern part untouched. The eastern half bordered the state forest.

The owner died several years ago, and his two sons had inherited the property. Neither of them lived in Truth Harbor. They'd put the whole fifty acres up for sale, though so far no one had bought it.

And I hoped no one ever did.

I dreaded the day and prayed land developers wouldn't buy it.

This place had become my refuge, and even though I wasn't supposed to be out here, I couldn't stop myself from coming often.

It was so peaceful. Like a different world.

As a quiet observer, I'd seen a fair amount of wildlife, including deer, elk, coyotes, and even a black bear with her offspring last summer.

The animals never bothered me, and I never bothered them.

At other times, I simply relaxed, taking in the colors and smells. Appreciating this meadow almost like a bee would. At night I sometimes came out here with binoculars and stargazed.

Tonight I just wanted to relax. At the beginning of summer, I'd brought out a comfortable lightweight chair and some blankets. I spread the blankets on the ground and lay down.

I'd loved reading *The Secret Garden* as a child, and this meadow had become *my* secret garden. I'd never told a soul about its existence.

Gazing up at the night sky, I let all my worries and stresses slip away. There wasn't much light pollution in Truth Harbor, so on a summer night, the stars were dazzling.

I thought about the day I'd just had. Apparently I'd made a good impression on the local news—at least that's what Leah and Claire told me. Some colleagues from work and a couple of beekeepers had also texted. They told me the football player hadn't come across well, and nothing could have made me happier than hearing that. I needed to pressure this guy into doing the right thing.

My biggest worry was that I'd seem like a crazy kook. I already knew some people would think that upon seeing this story.

Am I crazy for doing this?

Probably.

I mean, let's face it. I'd taken time off from my work at the university to chain myself to a football player's house.

How I spent my summer vacation...

I wasn't someone who typically did rash or impulsive things. I'd always lived an orderly and private life, but I'd been pushed into a corner and had seen no alternatives.

I had to admit, Bardales wasn't exactly what I'd expected. Not quite. I mean, in many ways, he was. He seemed like an overconfident, overly privileged jock who probably wasn't too bright and had everything handed to him on a silver platter.

Just look at that house. A Spanish castle built for one person to live in alone.

I shook my head. *So wasteful.*

His size was a surprise. It shouldn't have been, and I hated to admit it, but I'd found it interesting. Oddly exciting. I think it was why I'd felt nervous in his kitchen. I wasn't used to men who were so much bigger than me. My boyfriend, Clement, was a couple of inches shorter than I was, not that I minded.

I was thirty-two and hadn't dated much, but I'd always been more interested in an intellectual companion than a sexual one.

In truth, I'd never understood the fuss over sex. It was just one more way I was out of step with modern culture. Sex was enjoyable, certainly, but often I could take it or leave it. Clement and I usually had sex when he came into town, and that was an adequate amount for me.

I'd bet it was quite different for that football player. If I had to guess, sex dominated his existence. One could only imagine how many women were throwing themselves at him. Even though it was obvious that he stomped on anyone who got in his way, many people admired a man like that.

Not me.

I snorted to myself. I didn't care how many people kissed that jock ogre's ass. I intended to put as much pressure on him as possible.

Gabriel "Beauty" Bardales was getting the fight of his life.

CHAPTER SIX

~ Theo ~

Day Four

"What do you think of this one?" the jock ogre asked as he sat beside me on the front steps of his house. He held up his iPad. "Though I'm worried the bottle looks like it's giving me the middle finger."

"I don't have an opinion," I said stiffly.

"Oh, come on, Professor. I'll bet you have an opinion about everything."

I sniffed and turned my head away. Unfortunately, he was right. I *did* have an opinion about most things.

"Let's see the dark purple one again," Gary said, munching on some honey cake and sipping a Diet Coke. The guys from his crew had come over, and I'd offered them some honey cake as they sat around eating lunch.

The jock ogre fiddled with his screen and held up his iPad to show everyone the purple prototype bottle for his men's cologne. Apparently his agent had sent all these photos this morning straight from some Italian designer's work desk.

"That one looks like a pair of tits to me," one of the workmen said, pointing at it. "Not sure if you want to use that."

"Tits are better than the one that looked like a turd," another guy said, and they all laughed, the jock ogre laughing right along with them.

I didn't know what happened between last night and today, but this football player had clearly changed his strategy.

A few reporters from local stations had stopped by an hour ago, and he'd charmed everyone. It hadn't looked good for me that I was chained up but sitting next to the same guy I was protesting against. Unlike the reporters from the past couple of days, I could tell these weren't taking me seriously.

It was a nightmare. All my hard work was going up in flames.

Things had started off fine this morning. After checking on the chain to my Jeep, I'd settled myself down on his front steps, enjoying the quiet. I could sense the football player alone inside his Spanish castle. At one point, I'd even caught him watching me through one of his turret windows.

Lurking had been more like it.

I'd smiled to myself when I saw him. He definitely seemed uncomfortable.

But then a couple hours later, he'd come outside with a bottle of water and sat down right next to me on the steps. He wore a pair of faded jeans, a dark blue T-shirt, and those same striped sneakers that probably cost more than my monthly grocery bill. He acted like we were the best of friends. Such arrogance.

The jock ogre studied his iPad again. "I agree that brown one does look like a turd, though I think it's mostly the color." He picked up his water bottle, took a sip, and eyed my honey cakes. "You sure I can't have one of those? I'll bet it would really hit the spot."

"Don't even think about it," I said tersely.

Gabe patted his hard, flat stomach. "Training camp starts in a couple of weeks. This is my last chance to indulge."

"Aw, come on, bee lady," the tits-are-better-than-turds guy said. "Give Bardales some of your cake. You catch more bees with honey, don't you?"

Gabe looked at me with those soulful eyes, which I now understood were a ruse. In the same way that hover flies tricked other insects into thinking they were bees, those soulful eyes tricked unsuspecting females into thinking he was deep.

Because he wasn't deep. He wasn't soulful.

And he didn't seem uncomfortable or angry that I was still chained to his house. In fact, the only one uncomfortable and angry out here was me.

It turned out the jock ogre was clever. Much cleverer than I'd anticipated.

He'd been jovial with the reporters earlier and had quickly befriended the crew working on his house. They were all crazed football fans.

It figures.

I could sense them watching me like *I* was the ogre for not sharing the honey cakes I'd baked.

"Fine." I shoved the pan in Gabe's direction. "I hope you choke on them."

He chuckled as he reached for it. "Damn, woman. Didn't take you for the violent type."

"Looks can be deceiving. Something *you* should know plenty about."

"I have no idea what you mean," he said lightly, helping himself to some of my cake. "What you see is what you get with me."

I scoffed.

Gary made noises about the time, and he and his crew packed up their lunches to go back to working on the house. Which left the jock ogre and me alone together.

"This honey cake's not bad," he said after devouring a second piece in three bites. He licked his fingers. "Thanks for letting me have some."

"Everybody's gone now," I said. "You can drop the nice guy act and leave."

"What act?"

"The one where you're pretending like you're everyone's best friend."

He smirked. "I don't know what you mean."

Except he knew. And he also didn't leave. Instead, the two of us sat there in silence. Mine gloomy and his crafty. He was probably thinking of more ways to make me look bad.

As he got more comfortable and stretched his legs out in front of himself, a breeze blew past, carrying his scent. Clean, healthy, and male. He smelled like the outdoors. Like fresh air. I tried to ignore it, though I sniffed a few more times, hoping to find it again.

We continued our silence. I refused to speak to him or carry on this ridiculous charade of friendship. Instead, I wondered how things were at the lab where I worked. I'd have to get ready for fall classes soon after my vacation was over.

"Is that one of yours?" he asked, pulling me out of my reverie.

"What?"

He nodded at a flowering bush in his front yard not far from us. Right away I saw the honey bee on it.

"She probably is one of mine," I said. There weren't many other beekeepers in this area, so the likelihood was high that she came from my hives.

We both watched as the bee flew from one flower to another. "How can you tell it's a female when they're so small?"

I turned and took in his handsome profile as he continued watching her. "Because most bees are female."

"They are?"

I nodded. "Male bees only make up 10 to 15 percent of the hive. They're called drones, and their appearance is quite different. They're a bit bigger and have much larger eyes."

He took a drink of his water. "Aren't they the warriors, though? The ones who sting the hell out of you to protect everyone?"

I smiled a little. "That's a common misconception. Actually, drones don't have stingers."

Gabe turned to me with surprise, and it was odd being this close to him. Like a drone, his eyes were also large. A deep brown framed by thick lashes. "The male bees can't *sting?*"

I couldn't help my laughter. He seemed personally affronted by this news. "That's correct. Only females have stingers."

He shook his head. "It figures. No wonder you like bees so much." He turned back to search for the honey bee, which had flown away.

I shifted position, moving the heavy chain wrapped around my waist so it wasn't digging into my pelvis. I sensed the football player's gaze on me as he took in my green blouse, cropped jeans, and yellow Converse sneakers.

"So what's it like being such a tall woman?"

I took out a baggie of baby carrots from my lunch cooler to nibble on. Usually I hated questions like this, but since Gabe was tall himself I didn't take offense. "I imagine in some ways it's the same as being a really tall guy."

He leaned back on his hands and nodded. "You don't fit into anything. My feet hang over the end of a normal bed. I can't buy regular clothes off the rack in a mall. Cars are too small, and airplane seats—"

"Airplane seats are the worst," I finished for him. "At least commercial seats. I've never flown first class."

"First class is better," he admitted. "But not by much. And I always have to get an aisle seat."

"Me too. It's the only way I can stretch my legs and not be tortured."

He chuckled. "Guess if we ever flew together, we'd have to get opposite aisle seats."

I glanced over at him. I couldn't imagine any scenario in this universe where I'd be flying somewhere with this guy.

I bit into a piece of carrot and chewed. "Actually, I noticed something when I was in your bathroom. The sink wasn't too short for me."

He nodded. "That's because I had the whole place designed for my height."

"Really?" I glanced at his Spanish castle. "No hunching over anywhere?"

"Nope." He seemed pleased to impart this information. "Everything you can think of was custom-built. There's lots of space. And my bed's, of course, a California king."

At the mention of his bed, our eyes met, but I quickly looked away. It was weird to be talking with him like this. Like we were friends.

"You should let me give you a tour," he went on. "I bet you'd love it."

I took another bite of carrot. He was right. I probably would love this house, even though I thought it was wasteful and too big for one person.

"Unchain yourself and I'll show you around." He leaned toward me, his voice low and persuasive. "Come on, Professor. I won't tell anyone you've left your post."

I zipped my baggie of carrots shut and put it away. "No, thank you." I'd already decided it was a mistake to use his bathroom yesterday. I didn't know what I'd been thinking, but I'd used the work crew's porta-potties ever since.

"I can't tempt you, huh? If you're nice, I'll even let you make me a sandwich."

"Why would I want to make you a sandwich?" Ironically, there were probably a million women out there who would love to make this guy a sandwich.

"Because you'd get to experience a kitchen where everything is comfortably within reach. It's fantastic, trust me."

Our eyes met again, and this time I didn't look away. I hated to admit it, but there was an odd understanding between us.

"Sorry. As tempting as that sounds, you'll have to make your own sandwich."

He sighed. "All right, fine. I was just doing you a favor."

"Sure you were." I opened my backpack and dug around for my water bottle. I felt his eyes on me again.

"I take it you're kind of a nerd, huh?"

My brows went up. "I suppose you could say that."

"When I was in high school, my best friend and I were such dicks we used to force the nerds in class to do our homework for us."

"Gee, how charming." I finally found the bottle and pulled it out.

He shrugged. "Like I said, we were dicks."

"What happened to being against bullies?"

He licked his lips. "I *am* against them. And I don't bully anyone these days unless they deserve it."

"And do I deserve it?"

He snorted and flashed me a look. "We both know I'm not bullying you, Professor. You're bullying me."

"You can't possibly believe that."

"I know what I see. You've chained yourself to my house and won't leave. You're bad-mouthing me to the press and anyone else who'll listen. What do you call that?"

I was silent, contemplating his spin on things. "You're conveniently leaving out your ridiculous lawsuit. Can't you just call it off?"

He shook his head. "I can't have bees flying around, stinging everyone who visits me up here."

"My bees aren't going to sting everyone!"

"They will if you tell them to."

I opened my mouth in astonishment. *Does he really think bees follow voice commands?* But then I noticed the little grin on his face. "Are you teasing me?"

That dimple showed up again. "Maybe a little."

"Well... stop it. I don't like being teased."

"Are you sure? Because I'm really good at it." His gaze wandered lazily down my body, and a strange electric sensation spread through me.

Why does this jerk have to be so blindingly gorgeous?

"I think you can handle my teasing," he went on in a soft voice. "You seem pretty tough, Theo."

It was a warm summer day with a blue sky above us and birds chirping. I didn't want to acknowledge even the slightest attraction to this Neanderthal. Especially when he said my name.

Besides, I had a boyfriend, so I shouldn't be acknowledging it in the first place.

"Take off your glasses," he said.

"What?" I touched my frames. "Why should I do that?"

"Because I want to see you without glasses."

I fingered the edges of them. *What's happening here? Is he flirting with me? Perhaps it's another strategy to put me off guard.*

I lowered my hand. "My glasses are staying in place."

"That's okay. I like them. They're sexy."

I blinked with surprise. "What do you mean by that?"

I didn't have a chance to hear his answer because three expensive-looking SUVs approached the house and pulled into the driveway. Loud music thumped from at least one of them.

Gabe grinned and waved at the cars.

What fresh hell is this?

The vehicles' doors opened, and a bunch of people flooded out of them. Several were hulking males as large or even larger than Gabe. There were women, too, all of them dressed in heels and short skirts.

The jock ogre unfolded himself from the steps and strode out to greet them. "Hey, I was wondering when you guys were going to show up."

The women swarmed around him, each of them giving him a

hug, while the guys were all admiring the house. "Damn, Beauty, this is some place you got here."

He described the property, and they all listened with admiration, though they'd also noticed me and my Jeep. I could tell nobody seemed to know what to make of me. I wondered how he'd explain what I was doing here.

"And this is my neighbor, Theo," Gabe said as he walked up the steps with the group following behind him. "Just ignore her. She has some strange hobbies and likes chaining herself to things."

The women glanced at me dismissively, parading past me in a glamorous cloud of gold jewelry and expensive perfume. The men seemed more puzzled. My response to all of this was to glare at Gabe.

After they all went into the house, I stared down at my unglamorous sneakers and felt foolish. I couldn't believe I'd thought for even one second that the jock ogre was flirting with me. It was absurd. I didn't have much experience with men, and he was clearly using every tactic he knew against me.

It didn't take long for rap music to start blasting from inside the house, and it was obvious they were having a party. I debated leaving. Did I really want to stay chained to this pillar while these people were partying inside? Was I accomplishing anything at all besides making a fool out of myself?

But then I thought, *I've come this far. He's not chasing me away. And this was obviously another tactic.* Besides, more reporters might show up, and I wanted to be ready for them.

So as the party went on inside the house, I made myself comfortable on the outside. I'd always enjoyed my own company. I got my Kindle from my backpack and adjusted the chains so I could lean against the stone pillar.

When my friend Leah called to see how I was doing, I told her I was fine but wished I had a cup of tea. Both she and my other bestie, Claire, had been incredibly supportive during these past few days.

"Actually, Josh and I are in town right now," Leah said. "If you want, we can pick up some tea from Polly's and bring it to you."

"Really? I'd appreciate that."

"So how's Bardales?" Leah asked. "Do you think he's going to drop the lawsuit?"

I sighed. "It doesn't look like it. And Gary, the head contractor, told me he's bringing an angle grinder tomorrow to cut my chains off."

"I'm sorry to hear that. Has any more press come by? From what I saw yesterday, Bardales looked like a total asshole."

"Unfortunately, things haven't gone as well today. I'm hoping more press will still come by later."

We hung up, and I got back to my book.

As the party went on inside, I decided I didn't feel foolish sitting out here after all. It was never foolish to stand up for something you believed in.

My bees deserved better, and I wasn't going to let them down.

Besides, reading a good book and enjoying a cup of tea were two of my favorite things. My life wasn't glamorous, not like what this football player probably lived, but it suited me perfectly well.

CHAPTER SEVEN

~ Gabe ~

Still Day Four

"You have to unchain that woman," Xavier, one of my offensive linemen, said to me in a low voice against the loud background of rap music. "It ain't right, dawg."

Carson, one of my other offensive linemen, nodded in agreement. "Yeah, dude. You can't just leave some woman out there chained to your house like that. People are going to talk."

"I didn't chain her to my house," I said. "She chained herself."

"Even if it's some kinky sex thing," Xavier continued, "that shit belongs in the bedroom and not on your front steps. You feel me?"

I rolled my eyes. I couldn't believe these two knuckleheads.

"What part of the words *she chained herself* are you not hearing?" I asked.

"Plus, that chain is too big," Carson continued. "A smaller gauge would have been easier to manage, if you want my opinion."

Xavier stroked his chin like a judge mulling over the facts. "I concur. A smaller gauge is for sure the right choice." He looked outside again. "Is she really your neighbor?"

All three of us were standing by the window staring out at Theo, who was, of course, still chained to the stone pillar. I thought for sure my throwing a party would be enough to get her to leave. Most people would be too humiliated to stay. Not this woman.

To make matters worse, she appeared to be reading some kind of tablet without a care in the world.

"Yeah." I sighed deeply. "She's my next-door neighbor."

"She looks tall," Carson said, still watching her. "I've always liked me a tall woman."

"And that hair," Xavier said. "I wonder if the curtains match the wallpaper."

"Don't you mean the carpets match the drapes?" I asked.

"Whatever." He grinned. "You know what I'm saying."

Two of the women they'd brought to the party came over to join us. I'd seen Shawna around. She was a pretty blonde, though I didn't know her friend, a brunette with a curvy body and highlighted streaks around her face.

"This is Brooke," Shawna said, introducing us. "She's been dying to meet you, Beauty."

"Is that right?" I put my hand out and shook Brooke's.

"I'm a huge Sentries fan," she said with a flirtatious smile. "And *you're* my favorite player."

"Thanks, it's nice to hear that."

"And I just love your Jock Style boxer shorts. I wear them to bed every night."

"Really? I didn't know we had a female market."

"Oh, you definitely do. They feel *so* good against my skin."

I chuckled. "Maybe that should be our new slogan."

Brooke kept flashing that smile and telling me how much she loved my men's fashion line.

Carson and Xavier stayed for a little while, then got bored and left to go see what kind of food I had in the kitchen. Shawna went back over to talk with Levi and Tray, a couple more of my teammates. They were across the room chatting with the other women who'd driven up here. All total there were twelve people. Not a huge number, but enough.

I'd talked to Davis last night and told him about my plan to throw this little party today to scare off the professor. The irony was that I hated parties and seldom threw them, but this time I had a purpose. He pointed out that we'd gotten lucky with the press. So far the only news stations that had run the story were local. Some local papers also ran a short piece about it.

"I don't think the story has legs," Davis said. "Nobody's heard of it. It appears to be dying a quiet death, just like we hoped."

I was still standing alone by the window with Brooke as she told me more about herself, how she was a flight attendant for one of the major airlines and worked first class.

"I've always hoped I'd get you on one of my flights," she said, leaning toward me, enveloping me in a cloud of perfume. "But so far, no luck."

"Yeah?" I forced myself not to look outside at Theo. "What would you have done if I were on one of your flights?"

"Believe me, I'd make sure you were treated *very* well." She winked at me. "I'd give you all the extras."

I chuckled. "I might have to find out which routes you're flying next and see if I can get a seat."

Brooke laughed and continued to flirt with me while I mostly tried to avoid looking out the window. I felt my neck visibly twitching from the effort to keep my head still. Finally, I couldn't stand it anymore and had to see if the professor was still there.

To my surprise, not only was she still there, but she was talking to a couple of people who must have been her friends. An attractive brunette and some guy with long blond hair who looked oddly familiar. They were standing around chatting and enjoying themselves.

Is she seriously entertaining her friends out there? On my front steps! She's supposed to be suffering for her cause, not having fun.

I turned back to Brooke, who was telling me how her family lived in Santa Monica. "You're from California, too, aren't you?" she asked. "I thought I read that about you."

"I am." I forced myself to turn away from the window and stop staring at my fiery-haired nemesis. I'd done everything I could to throw that bee professor off-balance today, making it clear she was playing a game that was way out of her league. "I grew up in the LBC or Long Beach," I clarified.

"Oh, wow, there are some nice homes there on the water."

I nodded. "There are." What I didn't say was that I didn't grow up anywhere near those nice homes on the water.

She told me how much she missed California and her family while I nodded politely. One of her brothers had moved up to Marin County, and the other one lived in San Diego.

"It's so hard being on my own and new to the Seattle area." Her glossy lips turned into a pout, dropping a hint for me to ask her out.

"I know what you mean." I glanced outside again and could see Theo was alone. Her friends had left.

"Maybe you could show me some of your favorite parts of the city," Brooke suggested.

"Can you excuse me for a minute?" I asked. "I need to go check on something."

Her eyes widened. "Of course." Her gaze drifted out the window, where obviously my attention had gone. "Is your neighbor a football fan? Is that why she's chained herself out there?"

I snorted. I'd be surprised if Theo knew the difference between a football and a baseball. "No, she's into bees."

"Bees?" Brooke asked, tilting her head. She seemed confused.

Hell, who wouldn't be?

Brooke seemed nice enough, and I felt bad that I wasn't inter-ested in her, but I had more pressing problems. Luckily, Carson and Xavier chose that moment to come over and tell me they were ordering pizzas because my fridge was empty.

"Sounds great," I said. "Make sure one of them is mushroom pepperoni. And make sure Brooke here gets whatever she wants."

And then I left to go outside and talk to that she-devil.

"I can't believe you had the nerve to invite your friends here," I said once I got outside. It had been a warm day and was turning into a warm evening. The crew working on my back deck had left a short while ago. The sky, a mixture of red and orange, looked just like the professor's hair. "I can still have you arrested. You know that, right? This is private property."

She turned and glanced up at me. "They were just dropping off some tea," she said, motioning down at her cup that said "Polly's" with a cartoon parrot on it. "I enjoy a nice cup of tea when I'm reading."

"Don't invite people here again," I said in a stern voice, "or I'll have all of you arrested." I didn't know why I was being such a hardass. Gary already told me he'd be able to cut the chain off her and her vehicle tomorrow. Once that happened, the game was over, and I'd be the winner.

The professor laughed, showing off that sexy little gap between her front teeth. I wished I didn't have such a thing for that. This strange woman had my number, and it only added to my annoyance with her. "My friend Leah is the deputy sheriff's twin sister, so I hardly think he's going to arrest her. Although, if you did try to have us arrested, we'd get to see your true colors, wouldn't we?"

"What's that supposed to mean?" Though I knew exactly what she meant. She'd seen right through my friendly act earlier. I could turn on the charm whenever I wanted. I just usually didn't want to.

I sat down next to her on the steps. "You know this is all going to end tomorrow."

"I know."

She sounded wistful, and I glanced at her as she gazed out at the sky. As usual, her red curls sprang out untamed in every direction. "I hope you don't expect me to feel sorry for you after pulling a stunt like this."

She turned to me with defiance in her eyes. "What I expect is for you to do the right thing and drop your lawsuit, but I guess that's expecting too much."

I didn't bother to reply. We both knew the answer to that one.

Music drifted out from my house. It had been rap earlier, but someone switched it to dance music.

Neither of us spoke, and I figured Theo was giving me the silent treatment, not that I blamed her. This whole thing hadn't exactly gone her way, though I had to admit she'd put up a hell of a fight.

Who would have thought to use a chain that couldn't be removed with regular bolt cutters? It was smart. It may have all been for a lost cause, but I admired the way she didn't back down from anyone, including me.

"Don't you need to get back to your party?" she asked in a snide tone. "I'm sure your female guests are desperate for your attention."

I smiled. "You almost sound jealous."

"Jealous?" She looked at me like I was nuts. "Of what, exactly?"

I shrugged. "My attention, of course. Let's face it, *you're* the one who's chained to my house. No one's ever done that before." I ran the tips of my fingers along the cement steps and grinned a little, enjoying getting a rise out of her. "I have to wonder if you're out here for more than just your bees."

She rolled her eyes. "I can't believe how arrogant you are. Trust me, you're not my type."

"I'm not?"

I let my eyes drift down her long, slender body and wondered what her type was. She wasn't my type either. I liked my women beautiful and agreeable. She might be beautiful, but she was hardly agreeable. Just the opposite. For a moment, I tried to imagine what she'd be like in bed. Cool and collected? Hot and passionate?

Interestingly, I'd put my money on the latter.

"I happen to have a boyfriend," she said. "And believe me, he's *nothing* like you."

"You have a boyfriend?" I sat up and brushed the cement dust off my fingers. This was news. "Was it that guy who was here earlier?"

She shook her head. "That was Josh, my friend Leah's fiancé."

"Who is this boyfriend, then?" I growled. I didn't know why it came out like a growl. Why would I give a shit if she had a boyfriend? I barely even knew this woman.

"His name's Clement."

"What's he do?"

"He's a fellow entomologist."

I leaned back on my hands. It figured. Some egghead scientist. Was that really her type? Theo was fierce and magnificent. Any idiot could see she didn't belong with a guy like that. "You don't belong with some guy who stares at bugs all day."

She seemed perplexed. "What do you mean? *I* stare at bugs all day."

"You're a professor. Don't you teach?"

"Yes. And when I'm not teaching, I'm staring at bugs."

Mostly I was interested in this boyfriend. "So where is this guy? Why isn't he chained to my house right alongside you?"

She picked up her tea and took a sip. "Because he spends most of his time in Central America. He studies beetles. The horned passulus beetle, to be precise."

"So he doesn't even live here?"

She shook her head. "We have a long-distance relationship."

I kept my expression flat, though inside I was smiling. "And how long has that been going on?"

"We've been dating a little over three years."

"Long-distance the whole time?" I sounded skeptical. "That doesn't sound too great."

She put her tea down wearing an annoyed expression. "Who are you to judge? And why are you asking me all these questions? Shouldn't you be inside entertaining your guests?"

I watched as a white Toyota Camry came down the driveway and pulled up behind one of the parked SUVs. "I'm just waiting for the pizza to be delivered."

Some teenager got out of his car and came up the walkway carrying a stack of large pizza boxes. He glanced down with a perplexed expression at the chain around Theo.

I got up and tipped the kid, then brought all the pizzas inside the house, glancing around. People seemed to be having a decent time. A card game had started in the living room, and I got waylaid by Carson and Xavier on my way to the kitchen, asking me to join. They were both young guys in their early twenties. Usually I discouraged friendships, but after discovering we'd grown up in the same area, they'd bonded themselves to me like two puppies. Xavier was from the LBC like I was, and Carson grew up in San Pedro, which was close enough.

"Maybe in a little while," I said. I brought the pizzas into the kitchen, where people gathered around. I stood and made small talk so I didn't seem like too much of a lousy host. Finally, I grabbed a plate and slapped a few slices of pizza on it for myself.

Brooke was smiling and batting her lashes at me from across the room, letting me know she was a sure thing. I should have been pleased. Beautiful and agreeable—exactly my type.

I glanced down at my plate of pizza. And then for reasons I'll never understand, I slapped a few more slices on it and left to go outside again.

Except when I opened my front door, carrying the plate of pizza to share with Theo, my jaw dropped in alarm. Things were *not* how I'd left them. There were lights and camera crews and reporters all over the damn place.

What the hell?

Right away I could tell these weren't local news stations. I felt like a deer in the headlights.

With a groan, I recognized Tara Brady, one of the reporters from ESPN, standing right in front of my house, interviewing the professor.

This is the last thing I need.

With all the music blasting, I hadn't heard a damn thing outside. They couldn't have been here long, but it was long enough.

I wasn't sure if I should duck back inside the doorway, but then I heard someone calling my name.

"Beauty! Would you like to comment on why you have a woman chained to the front of your house?"

I didn't know his name, but I recognized him. He was one of the reporters from CBS Sports. This was going to be plastered everywhere.

Shit.

With dread, I realized I had no alternative but to try to explain my side of the story.

"She's here by her own choice, not mine." I strode down the front steps and stood next to Theo, who had at least three microphones shoved in her face as she calmly eviscerated me to multiple networks.

I was typically great under pressure. Regularly staring into the faces of an opposing team's defense—guys who wanted nothing more than to take me down—had a way of forcing me to stay coolheaded. And if these reporters had been asking about football, I could have talked all night.

But instead, they were asking me about the environment. About the ecology. About *bees*, for fuck's sake. They wanted to know why I was forcing this woman to chain herself to my house to get my attention.

I tried to answer as calmly as I could, though I sensed I was screwing it up. At one point, I glanced down and saw I was still holding the plate of pizza. Grimacing, I could only imagine how ridiculous I looked.

It didn't take long before the partygoers inside my house realized what was happening and began peeking nervously out the windows. The music was still blasting, though someone finally turned it off.

This party had sure backfired. It made me look like the biggest asshole in the world.

When I glanced over at Theo, she almost seemed sympathetic to my situation. Almost. Mostly, she was smiling with glee.

How did it all go downhill so fast?

When I finally escaped the reporters and got back inside my house, the party was over, and I had over a dozen missed messages—at least five from Davis, three from my publicist, and two from my sports agent. None of that was a big deal. The two messages from our head coach and the three from our team's general manager—*that* was a big deal.

Shit.

Xavier and Carson looked worried, and so did the other guys.

"I'll handle this," I told them. "It's on me. You were never here."

I called our GM, Alan Ryan, wondering how pissed he was. He answered on the first ring. "Jesus Christ, Gabe. Tell me it isn't true. Tell me you don't have a woman *chained* to the front of your house while you're inside throwing a party?"

I licked my lips. "It's not like it sounds."

"You've got to be fucking kidding me!" I'd never heard him so angry. Not even after I broke that paparazzo's camera last year.

"She's my crazy neighbor," I said. "She chained herself to my house. I had nothing to do with it." I tried to explain this absurd situation to him, but he didn't want to hear it. His job was to protect the organization, and I was making that difficult.

"I don't care who she is. Get rid of her. *Now.*"

"She'll be gone tomorrow. My head contractor's bringing something to cut the chains off."

I could practically hear the steam coming off him. He'd never liked me, and this only added to his list of reasons why he thought I was a pain in the ass. "If we weren't two weeks out from training camp, I swear I'd suspend you for this."

I remained silent as he continued his rant, figuring it was best not to say anything that could get me in deeper.

CHAPTER EIGHT

~ Theo ~

Day Five

The day began like any other as I chained myself to the jock ogre's house early in the morning with my coffee and backpack. I didn't bother bringing a cooler of food or more honey cakes. I had a feeling I wouldn't be here long. None of the crew working on his house had arrived yet, and unlike last night, which had been a madhouse filled with reporters, today was quiet.

Peaceful even.

I was quite pleased with how things had gone yesterday evening. Sitting on the front steps with my chain today, I knew my time here was coming to an end, but at least I was going out with a bang.

After yesterday, there was no way this football player was going through with his lawsuit. Not unless he wanted the whole world to think he was a jerk.

Friends, family, and colleagues had been sending me links from news sites and YouTube. Initially, I'd watched them with trepidation. It was strange seeing myself on camera. My hair was a fright, and I appeared paler than I would have liked, but otherwise, all my hours in front of a classroom had served me well.

I thought I did a fairly decent job of explaining how important bees were to the environment, our food supply, and how we needed to do more to protect them. My chains, I'd explained, were symbolic of how humans and bees were linked together. Living in harmony. They didn't need us, but we certainly needed them. I explained that this football player's guesthouse swimming pool shouldn't be more important than the work that my bees and *all* bees were doing everywhere.

Fortunately for me, Gabe hadn't been as eloquent.

I watched some of the footage of him, and he bumbled through every question. For some reason, he was holding a plate of pizza. Clearly he'd been blindsided, and if he hadn't created this situation with his ridiculous lawsuit to begin with, I might have felt sorry for him.

"I'll bet you're feeling pretty good about yourself this morning."

I turned. It was the jock ogre, of course. He'd come outside looking especially handsome. His dark hair was damp and wavy. When he sat beside me, he smelled like soap and must have just taken a shower. Instead of jeans, he wore a pair of black athletic sweats and a white crew neck T-shirt that hugged his muscular chest.

I tried not to look at him. Or smell him.

Instead, I gave him a smile. "What do they say in sports circles? 'You win some and you lose some'? And you lost some in a big way last night."

"I agree. Not my finest moment in front of a camera."

"I especially liked it when you said, 'Bees are our girlfriends because most bees are girls.' That was priceless."

Gabe scratched the top of his nose and seemed embarrassed. "You should be proud that I was paying attention to you yesterday."

"At least you're man enough to admit when you're defeated."

He glanced at me, but there was something in his gaze I didn't like. He didn't look defeated. "Gary just called. He said he's on his way here to cut your chains off."

I took a deep breath and nodded. Obviously I was expecting this.

The two of us fell silent. Except I felt him staring at me, staring in that same way he'd been doing since I met him.

"What's your problem?" I asked with irritation. "Stop staring at me. It can't be my height because you're even taller than I am. So why are you doing it?"

Those soulful eyes seemed taken aback. "I'm not staring at you."

"You've been staring at me since the day we met. Is it my hair? My freckles? I know I'm odd-looking, but didn't anyone teach you that it's rude to stare?"

His brows slammed together. "Who says you're odd-looking?"

"Just knock it off. Seriously." I grabbed my coffee.

It'll be a relief to end this thing and get back to my life. We might be neighbors, but I had no intention of ever speaking to this guy again.

As I was thinking about all this, Gary's black Ram pickup approached the house. He waved, and we both waved back. A couple of other vehicles approached as well—the guys from his work crew.

I'd hoped some press might come by for this, but as I peered in the distance, I didn't see any news vans.

"There'll be no more press conferences," Gabe said as if he had read my mind. "I had security placed on the street outside my driveway. Something I should have done from the start."

I shrugged. "Whatever. I said everything I had to say last night."

"Did you?" He smirked.

I shot him a look. What did he have to smirk about?

It didn't take long for Gary to pull the equipment out of his truck and set up a vise grip so he could cut the chain to my Jeep.

"Are you sure you don't want to just remove it?" he asked me before getting started. "Seems foolish to cut through a perfectly good chain."

Meanwhile, Gabe was standing beside him with his arms crossed, looming over everyone like a mountain. "Just go ahead and cut it, Gary. Trust me, she won't leave until that chain is off and I threaten to have her arrested."

I sniffed. He was right. I wasn't leaving until forced to. I believed when you committed yourself to something, you followed it through to the end.

While I sat there waiting for Gary to cut through my Jeep's chain, his work crew gathered around to watch. The noise of metal against metal was loud and abrasive. Eventually he stopped the grinder, and there was a clank as the chain attached to my Jeep hit the ground.

I was still chained to the pillar, of course, but now it was just a formality. My umbilical cord had been cut. Obviously I couldn't stay here forever, and I'd lost my leverage.

"Do you want me to cut that one as well?" Gary asked, motioning to the chain around my waist. "Could get a little dicey."

I sighed. "Don't bother. I'll do it myself."

Everyone watched as I pulled the key out of my front pocket and opened the padlock so the chain fell away. When I stood up, to my surprise, all the guys clapped.

I glanced around and then took a bow while they hooted and whistled.

"We're going to be sorry to see you go, Professor!"

"This is the most entertainment I've ever had on a job!"

"Do you think you could still bring by more of that honey cake?"

I laughed a little. When I turned to Gabe, his arms were still crossed, and he wore a stern expression.

"Guess that's the end of it," he growled.

"It looks that way." I was still smiling. "Once you drop your lawsuit, my lawyer and I will make sure that information gets released to the press."

He snorted. "What makes you think I'm dropping my lawsuit?"

"Come on, haven't you seen the news stories? The whole world knows about this. That's the only way to redeem yourself."

"You made a tactical error, Professor. A big one."

My smile faltered as a ball of dread formed in my stomach. "What do mean?"

"I mean, you're right. Everybody thinks I'm an asshole. But everybody already thought that before this whole thing started. This changes nothing."

"Are you serious?"

"If I drop my lawsuit now, it'll only make me look weak. I can't afford to look weak. Your bees have to go."

Everybody around us had gone quiet at his words. Even Gary seemed stunned. As we all stared at this guy with disbelief that he could be so coldhearted, I had the strangest feeling. I understood why he'd built this Spanish castle to live in alone.

He was guarding himself. But from what, I had no idea.

Looking the way I do, and always drawing attention, I knew a thing or two about guarding myself.

Nobody seemed to know what to say. Some of the work crew turned to me, probably thinking I was going to freak out. Instead, I reached down for my backpack, hoping I hadn't emptied it yesterday.

Luckily, there was one jar left, and I pulled it out and walked over to Gabe.

He unfolded his arms and seemed surprised, even trepidatious, that I was approaching him. "I'm not changing my mind."

"This is for you," I said quietly.

"I don't want that."

I reached down for his hand and felt a warmth spark through my whole body as soon as I touched him. He glanced at me, startled. He must have felt it too.

"Please take it," I said, pressing the jar of liquid gold into his hand. "You never know when you're going to need some totally amazing honey."

CHAPTER NINE

~ Gabe ~

I watched the professor from the window of my study, standing off to the side so she couldn't see me if she glanced up. Gary and some of his guys helped her load the chains into the back of her Jeep. I should have stayed and helped, but I had to get out of there.

Before leaving, she turned toward the house one last time, gazing at it.

I jumped back from the window.

When I looked outside again, she'd already climbed into her Jeep and had started the engine. I stayed and watched her drive off until her car disappeared from sight.

Good riddance.

That's what I told myself.

I was glad the woman was gone. Who'd ever heard of chaining yourself to a house? She was nuts, and I didn't need that in my life.

I glanced at the jar of honey on my desk. I had no idea why she'd given it to me. It made no sense. I'd told her I didn't want it, but being her stubborn self, she shoved it into my hand anyway. Her fingers wrapped themselves around mine, warm and firm. Her touch had sent a strange sensation through me. Like static electricity, except not painful. In fact, her touch had felt good.

I closed my eyes, reliving it.

Better than good.

Was she trying to make me feel guilty? Was that why she gave me that honey? Well, it wasn't going to work. I had nothing to feel guilty about.

I tried not to think about the expression on her face when I told her I wasn't calling off my lawsuit. The hurt in her eyes. *It doesn't matter.* What I'd told her was the truth. I was leading a multimillion-dollar football team to the Super Bowl this year and couldn't afford to appear weak.

My phone buzzed, and I pulled it out of my pocket. It was Davis. I'd talked to him briefly last night after the fiasco with the press but didn't feel like talking to him right now.

Instead, I grabbed the jar of honey and headed downstairs to the great room, my footsteps echoing in the hall. The house was big, and I hadn't fully furnished it yet.

I put the honey on the chunky wood coffee table and then flopped down onto the leather sofa, which faced a large flat-screen television. Flipping through my phone contacts, I found my sister Regina's number and pressed Call. I glanced at the time. It was midafternoon, and she was probably busy getting ready to open. I should have texted first.

"Hey, baby bro," she said, answering on the second ring. "I just saw your face plastered all over the sports page. I didn't know you were so kinky. Whips and chains, huh?"

"Ha ha. Very funny."

"Seriously, what's with your neighbor? Is she really chained to your house?"

"Not anymore." I tucked a small pillow behind my head and lay back. "They just cut her loose today."

"Sounds pretty wild. So, are you dating her?"

"What? Why would you ask that?"

Some glasses clinked in the background as Regina told someone to refill the Pale Ale tap. "I don't know. I saw a picture of her, and she looks like your type."

"I don't have a type." Beautiful and agreeable. That was my type.

"Sure you do. You have a thing for redheads."

"No, I don't. What the hell are you talking about?"

"Uh, yes, you do. Remember Dawn Robbins? Your first girlfriend in high school? I was friends with her older sister."

"Give me a break. The last thing I'm looking for is a *girlfriend*." I overemphasized the word and knew I shouldn't have.

Regina went quiet.

"Besides, that was years ago," I said, trying to hide my blunder and act like we weren't both thinking about all the consequences from the worst night of my life.

"People's tastes don't change that much," she said. "That's all I meant."

I stared over at the jar of golden honey on my coffee table. "I'm not dating my crazy neighbor. Trust me. So, how's Tess doing? Did she get the new job?" Tess was Regina's schoolteacher wife who was up for a new teaching position with better pay.

"She hasn't heard back yet. Hopefully by next week. Oh crap."

"What?"

"I gotta go. There's a delivery truck out back, and Angel isn't here. I'll call you later."

We hung up, and I stared up at the ceiling, wondering what I should do next. I could call my younger brother, Mateo, but he'd probably try to guilt me into talking to my dad.

My days were typically packed with activity, and I wasn't usually at loose ends like this. I didn't like having time to dwell on things. Training camp started soon, and that would be a complete immersion. I couldn't wait. Some of the guys on the team privately complained about training camp, but I wasn't one of them.

I considered going out to play a round of golf. They had a great course in Truth Harbor, which was one of the reasons I'd built a vacation home up here.

Instead, I closed my eyes. Golfing would be too much hassle. I'd have to socialize with everyone and make small talk, and that sounded like work.

Maybe I should take a nap. As was typical during the offseason, I hadn't been sleeping well. But I could hear the work crew outside chatting and hammering away on my deck, so that wouldn't happen.

It also didn't help that when I closed my eyes, all I saw was the professor. Her fiery-red hair and those freckles. Something stirred in me. My sister was right. I did have a thing for redheads. With all the women I'd been with over the years, oddly, I'd kind of forgotten about it. Not that I hadn't had a few redheads, but somehow the women all blended together.

I didn't like anybody getting too close.

Feeling out of sorts, I rolled onto my side and reached for the TV remote. The jar of honey sat there like it was taunting me.

I should just throw it in the garbage.

But I didn't. Instead, I turned the TV on and scrolled until I found the History Channel. There was a documentary on about the Roman Army.

Perfect. I settled myself in comfortably on the couch and watched them discuss the types of weapons used in ancient Rome. Not unlike people today, the ancient Romans were a savage bunch.

I drifted off to sleep as they showed the swords used by warriors. My last thoughts before I fell asleep were the lyrics from the Pat Benatar song "Love Is a Battlefield."

IT WAS early evening when I woke up to the sound of my doorbell. I glanced toward the French doors. The work crew was long gone. Was it Gary ringing the bell? Who else could it be? I'd already sent the security detail away, and I didn't know anybody else in Truth Harbor.

Unless it was Theo.

The thought jolted me. There was no reason for her to come back here, but then again, a woman like that could be as unpredictable as a summer storm.

I scrubbed my face with both hands to wake myself up and then headed for the door just as the bell rang for the third time.

They were persistent, whoever they were. Maybe it *was* Theo.

My pulse kicked up. *Why is this woman getting to me so much?*

I swung the door open, hoping to see wild red curls, green eyes, and a tall, slender body with legs so long I just knew they'd feel perfect wrapped around me.

Instead, it was Davis.

"Could you look a little happier to see me than that?" he said with a laugh. "It took me almost three hours to get here."

"The question is what the hell are you doing here in the first place?" I turned away from the door, and he followed me inside carrying an overnight bag. "I don't remember inviting you."

"That's okay. I invited myself." He glanced around at the house. "Damn, this place has really come together. It's fantastic."

"Thanks." He'd been up here a couple of times with me while it was being built.

We both went into the great room where the TV was still on, and I grabbed the remote from the coffee table to shut it off. I sat down on the leather couch where I'd been sleeping and ran a hand over my jaw that was already getting stubbly. "So seriously, what are you doing here, Davis?"

He walked over to the French doors. "Look at that deck. Shit. I'm afraid to ask what you're paying for all this." Then he came over, dropped his bag on the floor, and took a seat in one of the fat leather chairs. "You got anything to eat or drink? All they had on the ferry was stale coffee and a vending machine with potato chips."

"This isn't a restaurant."

He grinned. "You're in a lousy mood. Shouldn't you be happy that your wacko neighbor is gone?"

I shrugged. "Of course I'm happy."

"You don't look happy."

"I just woke up from a nap. What do you expect?"

He drummed his fingers on the arm of the chair, glancing around, but then stopped when he saw the honey on the coffee table. "What's that?"

"What's it look like?" I asked irritably.

"Is that from the bee biologist? She gave you some of her honey?"

I nodded.

"Have you tried it yet?" He eyed the jar with interest, but when he reached for it, I stopped him.

"Leave it alone."

"I just want to see what it tastes like. Do you have any bread and peanut butter I could eat it with? I'm starving."

"Don't touch it," I said with a growl. "I haven't opened it yet."

He gave me a strange look. "Let's go get some food then. Hopefully this town has some decent restaurants."

It occurred to me that I was hungry myself. "All right, fine. We'll go out."

I got up to find my shoes while Davis took his overnight bag down to the guesthouse. When he came back, we headed into town in his silver Mercedes with him talking the whole time about his ex-girlfriend, Miranda, and how she seemed to have a new boyfriend.

"Who is this clown?" he asked. "I'm tempted to have him checked out. I don't want Petey around a stranger. It could upset him. I don't think he's ready for someone new in his life yet."

The way Davis talked, you'd think Petey was their kid, but no, Petey was, in fact, their dog. A shivering little Chihuahua that both he and Miranda treated like a beloved child. They'd actually had a lawyer from his firm put together a custody agreement when they split up.

"I'm sure Petey is fine," I said.

Miranda had broken up with Davis because he was a workaholic with no social life. I was the same way, which was probably how Davis and I wound up as friends.

Truth Harbor on a Friday night turned out to be a lively place. There were people everywhere. Some club called Walk the Plank had a line out the door. I could hear live music coming from inside. It took us a while to even find parking.

"I saw a place that might be okay," Davis said. "A restaurant up the street called Bijou's. It looks like a nice diner."

"Sure," I said, glancing around. I'd bought the land up here a few years ago, and the town had seemed sleepy. Apparently it wasn't sleepy anymore.

Bijou's was crowded like everywhere else, and Davis and I had to wait for a table. They offered us seats at the counter instead, and we agreed to take them.

After settling in and ordering our food, I felt a few people staring at me, but luckily, nobody approached us. I was happy to sign autographs and be on for fans, but sometimes I just wanted to relax and have a meal.

Davis was still talking about Miranda. I tried to be sympathetic as I listened to his plight. It was obvious he was still hung up on her, though he insisted he wasn't. I'd even tried getting him laid after they broke up, but he'd told me to fuck off, that he didn't need my help getting women.

"Have you decided on a design for that cologne bottle yet?" he asked me, finally changing the subject.

"Not yet." I picked up my beer and took a sip. "To be honest, I'm rethinking the whole thing."

"What's there to rethink? You're going to make a killing." He grinned. "Between your name and that pretty face, it's like robbing a bank."

I smiled a little. He knew how I was, and that I liked to maximize my assets, but I had to watch my brand. I was thirty-two and couldn't play football forever. I had to be sure I made enough money to last me a long time.

As we discussed my options, I let my eyes wander around the restaurant. I nearly choked on my beer when I saw the professor sitting across the room. I couldn't believe it. She was at a table with four other people having dinner. It looked like two couples, and she was the extra wheel.

So much for that long-distance boyfriend.

"What is it?" Davis asked, noticing my expression and following my line of sight. "Holy shit, isn't that your crazy neighbor?"

"Yeah, that's her." I forced myself to turn away.

Davis frowned. "Who's that with her?"

"I don't know. Must be friends of hers." I tried to act indifferent as I reached for my beer again and took a sip. I couldn't believe the professor and I had gone to the same restaurant. With my luck, she'd call a press conference and accuse me of stalking her, and I'd not only get suspended from the team but banned from the league.

"Jesus, I think that's Philip North."

"I don't know who that is."

Davis continued to stare at them like he was trying to solve a math equation. "It sure looks like him. I've heard he lives up here. Is it possible your nutty professor is actually friends with him and his wife?"

"Dammit, Davis, stop staring before they notice us. And she's not *my* nutty professor. I barely know her."

"Too late," he said with chagrin. "They've already noticed us. And now they're staring back. Actually, glaring would be a better description."

"What?" I turned my head around, and sure enough, Theo and the others at her table were giving Davis and me the stink eye. The blond guy looked familiar, and there was some other guy there with dark hair. He wasn't particularly big, but there was something about him. He looked like someone you didn't want to fuck with.

"Dammit." I sighed to myself and glanced at Davis. "Now I'm going to have to go over there. What the hell am I supposed to say?"

He sat there with his brows drawn together.

"Why aren't you responding?"

"Because I'm *thinking*. As your lawyer, my advice is that it's best if you don't go over there."

"So we're supposed to sit here and eat dinner with the five of them glaring at us like we're a couple of assholes?"

"We *are* a couple of assholes."

I chuckled. He had a point.

"On the other hand, if that's Philip North, maybe you should go talk to them and try to smooth things over." Davis grabbed his phone and was looking something up. "I can't believe this. I think that *is* Philip North. *Fuck*."

"Who the hell is Philip North? That name sounds like a brand of cigarettes."

Davis looked at me, and his expression was so solemn that it gave me pause. "He owns NorthStone Capital with his business partner, Gavin Stone. It's one of the most profitable venture capital firms in the country."

"So?"

"He's also well acquainted with Bob Hanson. As I understand it, they're part of a monthly poker game with a few other captains of industry."

I felt my face grow pale. Bob Hanson was the current commissioner for the NFL. "Seriously?" I saw my football career going up in flames right before my eyes.

I glanced over at their table again. I wasn't one to back down from a challenge. But then something occurred to me. "If Theo is actually friends with this Philip North guy, why wouldn't she have gotten him involved? She could have ended this thing without ever chaining herself to my house."

Davis shrugged. "I don't know."

But I did. I knew as soon as I'd asked the question. Theo wouldn't want anyone else fighting her battles. Without even knowing her, I instinctively knew that wasn't her style. She'd want to fight them herself. In fact, she'd be pissed if anyone interfered.

I glanced over at her again. She wasn't glaring at me anymore. She was ignoring me, and in a way, that was even worse. In fact, the entire table was ignoring us.

I allowed myself a few more seconds to study her profile. The way her curls had been pulled into some kind of messy bun on top of her head. The curve of her neck and shoulders. I wished I could see what she was wearing. It wasn't her usual T-shirt and jeans, but something with thin straps that showed off all that sexy freckled skin.

Over the years, I'd denied myself so many things because I knew I didn't deserve them, and gazing at the professor, she was one more item on a long list. One more thing I could never have.

CHAPTER TEN

$\sim$ Theo $\sim$

I woke up to the sound of someone knocking at my front door in the middle of the night. *What's going on?* My heart pounded as I threw a robe on and worried about who could be out there. Was it a friend? Was someone in trouble?

To my shock, I discovered the jock ogre standing on my front porch. I pulled my robe tighter. "What on earth do *you* want? Do you know what time it is?"

"Are you going to screw up my football career? Is that your grand plan?" He wore jeans, a fitted black T-shirt, and a scowl.

"I have no idea what you're talking about."

His eyes drifted down over my robe to my bare legs, lingering for a moment before they met my face again. "I know you're friends with this Philip North guy who plays poker with Bob Hanson. Are you going to end my career?"

There was something off about him. "Are you drunk?"

"No." He glanced around at my porch and then licked his lips. "I've had a few beers, but I'm not drunk."

"I have no intention of ending your football career. And I have no idea who Bob Hanson is."

"Are you sure? Your whole table was glaring at me during dinner."

I had to admit, it was a surprise seeing him at Bijou's tonight. I hadn't even wanted to go out, but both Claire and Leah had convinced me. When we noticed he was there, it had grown awkward. Everybody at that table knew what he was doing to me, though I wouldn't let anyone intervene on my behalf. I'd insisted on it. I could fight my own battles.

Gabe's gaze wandered over my face with those soulful eyes, his expression imploring. "I don't want to be the bad guy. It sucks. Except it's become the story of my life."

It was clear he was in some kind of state. "Are you okay?"

He leaned his hand against the side of the door and put his head down, swallowing. "I don't know."

I wasn't sure what to do. This was a situation out of my normal range of experience. "Do you want to come inside?"

His head snapped up at my question, and he seemed stunned. "Don't you hate me?"

I considered him, this football jock who was suing me, and wondered if I did hate him. I certainly should. But for some reason I couldn't. "I don't hate you."

He shook his head. "I don't even know what I'm doing here. I should go."

Instead of leaving, he went and sat down on my front porch steps. His T-shirt tightened around his muscular back as he covered his face with his hands. There was something lost and sad about him.

I walked outside and sat beside him. It was a quiet night, and I didn't know what to make of this. It was unusual seeing him so vulnerable, and I suspected few people ever saw him this way.

For a long while, neither of us spoke. We listened to the occasional frog croaking and to all the nighttime sounds. I sensed he didn't want to be alone, so I stayed with him.

"Why did you give me that jar of honey?" he asked in a strained voice, breaking the silence. "*Why?* After everything. It doesn't make sense."

"Because it's sweet and delicious. I wanted you to experience it."

Gabe turned to me and seemed uncertain. "That's the reason?"

"What other reason would I have?"

He was doing that thing again where he stared at me, but then he nodded. "Beautiful. *God.* Seriously beautiful."

"What?"

"I'm going to go now. You don't want me here this late. I know you have a boyfriend." He stood up, and I felt dazed. What was all this about?

And before I could say another word, he left. Talk about strange. I didn't know what I was supposed to feel. Except there was something, despite everything. I was as confused and twisted around inside as if I'd just gotten off a carnival ride.

I watched him walk off into the night, his broad shoulders diminishing in the distance, and this whole thing felt like a dream.

THE NEXT MORNING, I woke up to a phone call from Clement. He'd missed our last two scheduled calls. Guatemala was only a couple of hours ahead, but I was sleeping in later than usual. I felt groggy. After being woken up in the middle of the night by that visit, I'd had trouble falling asleep again. I kept thinking about Gabe.

"We need to talk," Clement said.

"Do we?" I asked, still rubbing the sleep from my eyes. He'd been completely absent from my protest this past week, but I knew how obsessive he got with his work. "Did you see the links I sent you? They interviewed me on ESPN."

"I haven't had a chance to look at them yet."

"Really?" I couldn't help feeling annoyed. I mean, how busy could he be that he couldn't watch a five-minute video?

"I'll look at them later."

"Okay. What's going on? You missed our last two calls."

He sighed into the phone. "I know. Things haven't been good here. It looks like my funding is being pulled."

"Oh no." I sat up in bed. "Are you sure?" I reached for my glasses and slipped them on. He'd applied for some grant renewals this year and was worried he wouldn't get them.

"I'm not entirely sure, but the university hasn't been too keen. They seem to think my time might be better spent elsewhere."

"What are you going to do? Are you coming back to Seattle?"

He paused. "I'm going to Belize. I think I may have found a software company down there that's willing to fund me through the college."

"How long will you be there?" Clement was supposed to come back to the States next month.

"I'm not sure. If the funding goes through, it could be another year."

I was stunned. "What about Leah's wedding? When will we see each other?"

He sighed. "I won't be at the wedding. You'll have to go alone. I'm not sure about anything, Theo. I'm sorry, but I've got a lot to figure out."

"What are you saying? Where does that leave us?"

The phone went silent. Too silent. Was I being dense? "Are you breaking up with me, Clement?" I expected him to say no, of course not. That he was just trying to sort things out.

"You know how much I care about you. But I think it's for the best."

"Are you serious?" I jumped out of bed and saw a flash of myself in the bedroom mirror. My hair stuck out like a frizzy orange cloud, and my skin was pale with shock. "It's for the *best*? How is this for the best? After more than three years together, that's all you can say? Can't we at least discuss this?"

"Our lives are moving in different directions. I don't feel a connection with you like I used to." He went quiet, then said, "I want to be free to explore new relationships."

"Have you met someone else?"

"Of course not. I just feel like this isn't working."

"Well, it takes two to make it work."

"I don't think I'm in love with you anymore."

"*What?*" I was shocked. My heart sank, and there was a strange bitter taste in my mouth. "And when did you decide that?"

I could feel him squirming on the other end of the line. Clement hated confrontation. It was one of the most frustrating aspects of our relationship. He never wanted to fight, but sometimes you needed a good fight to clear the air.

"I just don't have those feelings for you like I used to. We can still be friends. I just don't want to continue as a couple."

"Friends? I don't want to be friends with you!" I felt sick to my stomach. This was humiliating.

"I'm going to go now, Theo."

And with that, he hung up.

I stared at my phone in disbelief. *He dumped me. I've been dumped.*

I threw my phone on the bed. I wished I'd thought of something clever to say, something cutting.

My phone buzzed, and I wondered if it was Clement calling me back. Maybe he'd changed his mind.

But when I picked it up, I didn't recognize the number. I answered it anyway. "Who is this? What do you want?"

"Whoa." It was a male voice. "Is this a bad time?"

The voice sounded familiar. "*Who* is this?"

"It's Gabe. I wanted to call and apologize for the way I came over last night. I know that was weird."

"How did you get this number?"

"You gave it to me."

"I did?"

"Yeah, the second day you chained yourself to my house. Don't you remember?"

I nodded. I did remember.

"Are you okay?" he asked. "You don't sound too good."

I swallowed and tried to catch my breath. "My boyfriend just broke up with me over the phone." I couldn't believe I was telling him this.

"Why would he break up with you?"

I bit my lip, embarrassed to admit the reason—that Clement found me lacking. "He says he doesn't love me anymore. That he wants to explore new relationships."

"What an idiot. Seriously. Do you want some company? I could come over."

I glanced at myself in the mirror—flushed and disheveled. "You want to come over *here? Now?*"

"Sure." It sounded like he was licking his lips. "I mean, if you don't want to be alone. That's all."

Have I stumbled into a bizarre alternate universe? "Have you forgotten that you're suing me? You're not the hero in this story. You're one of the villains."

"Yeah, about that...." He lowered his voice. "I've been thinking. I'm going to drop my lawsuit and leave your bees alone."

My jaw dropped as a powerful wave of relief washed through me. "Really?"

"Yeah, really. I've already told my lawyer to call it off."

"I appreciate that. What made you change your mind?" Maybe this jock ogre wasn't so bad after all. Maybe he realized it was the right thing to do. But then I remembered what he'd said last night when he was here. "Wait a minute, is this because you're afraid of Philip?"

"I'm not afraid of anybody," he said heatedly. But then he paused and laughed a little. "Okay, maybe I'm a little afraid. I didn't know you were friends with someone who played poker with the NFL commissioner."

"Are you serious? So you think I'd try to use one of my best friend's husbands to mess up your football career? Wow. Screw you." I hung up the phone. This was turning into a really lousy Saturday.

At least he was dropping his lawsuit. I had to admit that was great. It almost lifted me out of being upset over Clement. Even if he was doing it for the wrong reason, at least I wouldn't have to worry about my bees anymore. *Thank God.*

I got dressed and decided to go down to my hives to tell them the good news about the lawsuit, and the bad news about me and Clement.

CHAPTER ELEVEN

~ Gabe ~

So here I was, standing on Theo's porch. Just like last night when I'd come over and made a fool out of myself. I sure hoped I wasn't making a fool out of myself again.

What is it about this woman? I wondered for the tenth time as I knocked on her door.

Except no one answered. Her Jeep was sitting in the driveway, so she must be around somewhere.

After our conversation this morning, I'd called and texted, trying to apologize, but of course, she ignored me.

Her house was a Craftsman-styled bungalow. I knocked again and then walked across her front porch, peering through the large window in front, but all I saw was her living room with nobody in it. There was a comfortable-looking couch and chairs. A big bookcase and a television. It all seemed normal.

Where could she be?

I decided to check her backyard. Davis would go ballistic if he knew I was here, much less snooping around looking for her.

As it was, I had to sneak out of my own house like a damn burglar while he dealt with some client on the phone. I didn't dare tell him where I was going or I'd never hear the end of it. He'd gotten me freaked out about that Philip North guy last night, but I never should have listened to him. I realized now that I should have followed my instincts about Theo.

Davis still thought I was canceling my lawsuit because I didn't want to get on Bob Hanson's bad side, in case this North guy did talk to him, but that wasn't the reason.

I came here last night with all my demons in tow, and Theo had stayed with me and shown no judgment. She'd been kind. I felt embarrassed for being such an asshole to her. I didn't want her to see me as a bad guy. Even if I was one.

I opened the gate that led to her backyard and discovered her house sat on top of a grassy slope. I walked around to the rear of the house first. There was a flat stone patio with a low concrete wall. Along the edge were flowerpots, the colors standing out against the backdrop of the gray stonework. In the center of the patio was a small table and a few chairs. It was a small house, but overall the place was nice. Cozy. It reminded me of Regina and Tess's house in Santa Monica.

There was no sign of Theo, so I headed into her lower yard, which was larger than I expected. As I got farther down, it leveled out. There was a picnic table and a shed. A short distance away, there were rows of tall wooden boxes that looked like filing cabinets. As I got closer, I saw bees flying nearby and realized these must be her hives.

Interesting. I'd never seen beehives in real life.

I glanced around, but there was still no sign of the professor. I wondered what I should do. Maybe she'd gone out with friends?

Just as I was ready to leave, an ornate gate built into the back fence opened, and she came inside the yard wearing jean shorts, sneakers, and a green T-shirt.

She paused when she saw me, her eyes widening.

I lifted my hand. I hadn't meant to startle her.

"What are you doing here?" she asked, striding toward me. "Do I need to remind you that this is private property?"

I snorted. "*You're* going to lecture *me* about private property. That's rich."

"What do you want?"

"I came here to apologize."

"Really?" She gave a humorless laugh. "This is your idea of an apology? Snooping around my yard uninvited? Not to mention that you don't sound in the least bit apologetic."

"Well, I *am*." I tried to look sorry. I *was* sorry, but I didn't do a lot of apologizing in my life. "And I wasn't snooping. Not much, anyway."

"Whatever. Fine." She waved me away. "You can go now."

I stepped forward. "You're not getting it. I'm apologizing and admitting I was wrong."

"You were wrong. Good for you. Now please leave and don't come back."

I shook my head in frustration. "I swear, you're the most pigheaded woman I've ever met!"

She crossed her arms. "I'm impressed. This apology is getting more sincere by the second. Do you have any more insults you'd like to hurl at me?"

"I'm sure I could think of a few," I grumbled. "Look, I was wrong to think you'd use your friend to try and mess with my career. I know you're not that kind of person."

This seemed to mollify her a bit. "That's right, I'm not. I don't need anyone to fight my battles. I can fight them myself."

"Tell me about it," I muttered. "I've experienced it firsthand, remember?"

Our eyes met, and I thought I detected the hint of a smile.

"C'mon, Professor, I'm waving the white flag here. Let's call a truce."

She gave a deep sigh and uncrossed her arms. "All right, fine. We are neighbors, and you did drop your lawsuit, so I accept your apology."

"Good."

We studied each other, our truce still new and delicate. I nodded toward the filing cabinets. "I take it those are your famous beehives, huh?"

"They are."

"They're not what I expected."

"What did you expect? Round beehives hanging from a tree like you see in a cartoon?"

I shrugged, not wanting to admit that was basically what I'd pictured. "Why do they look like filing cabinets?"

Theo tilted her head and contemplated me. Finally, she seemed to come to a decision. "Would you like to see one of my beehives up close?"

My brows rose. "Sure."

Her eyes roamed the length of me, checking me out. I wondered if I measured up to whatever her standards were. I shoved my hands into my front pockets.

"You're quite large," she said, still studying me, "but I think I have a suit that will fit you."

I was taken aback. "You want me to wear a suit?"

She nodded and began walking toward that white shed, so I pulled my hands out of my pockets and followed her.

"I was just down here earlier telling my bees about you," she said. "I was letting them know they won't be forced to move after all."

"You talk to your bees?"

"Occasionally. When it's important."

I could tell she was serious. The nutty professor was definitely nutty.

She stood in front of the shed door and put in the combination for a padlock to open it. "I know it sounds odd talking to bees," she went on, entering the small structure, which was larger and more refined inside than I expected, "but it's actually an old tradition in Europe, and here in the States as well. It's called 'telling the bees.' People used to inform their bees about marriages, births, and deaths. In some places, they still do."

"I've never heard of that." I entered the shed. Pungent and sweet, the scent of honey was so strong, I could almost taste it. Jars of the stuff lined the walls in neat rows. One corner appeared dedicated to her beekeeping supplies.

"When Queen Elizabeth II passed away, her royal beekeeper let all the bees know she had died and that her son King Charles III was the new sovereign."

"Really? That's an interesting tradition. Do you talk to them a lot?"

Theo shook her head. "The carbon dioxide from our breath stimulates guard bees, so I only do it occasionally. Only when it's important." She handed me a white costume. "Now, let's get you suited up, and I'll teach you about bees."

———————

"You ALWAYS WANT to stand behind a beehive," she said as we approached them. "Think of the front with the opening where the bees come and go like a runway."

We walked over and stood behind one of the hives in the middle of the row.

"This is a hive I haven't inspected in a few weeks," she explained as she opened the filing cabinet from above. She held something in her hand that blew smoke over the bees, explaining that it would help keep them calm. "It's best not to check them too often. Just like people, bees don't like to be interfered with."

We were both wearing one of those white beekeeper outfits with a hat and something over our faces called a veil. It felt weird, and I was amazed it fit me, but she was right. She had a suit that was large enough. Theo looked elegant in hers, whereas I was certain I resembled the abominable snowman. At first I wondered if we really needed all this protection, but when a multitude of bees came flying and buzzing close, I was glad to have it.

"What happens if you check the hives too often?"

"They react in various ways, but sometimes they'll get irritated and abscond. Which is the last thing you want."

"Abscond?"

She nodded. "The whole hive will just leave. One day they're here, and the next day they're gone."

"You're kidding. Just like that?" I stared down at the thousands of bees. "Has that ever happened to you?"

"Rarely these days, but when I was a teenager I had a few hives abscond, which is not to be confused with swarming. It was quite upsetting. One time I got lucky and found the absconded hive and brought it home."

"What happened to it then?"

"It thrived. I stopped making the mistake that had gotten it to abscond in the first place."

"And swarming is something different?"

She nodded. "Very. When bees swarm they divide the colony and create a new hive with a new queen. It's something healthy beehives do as a way of reproducing."

"Huh." I was learning more about bees than I ever thought I wanted to learn. "That's wild you've had beehives since you were a teenager."

"Since I was a child, actually. My parents were always very supportive of my interest in bees."

"It sounds like you had a great childhood."

She nodded and glanced over, obviously sensing something from me. "Your parents weren't supportive of your interests?"

"Not exactly. It doesn't matter though. I did okay on my own."

"They didn't want you to be an athlete?"

"It was just my dad who raised us. He wasn't supportive. He was against me pursuing football the way I did."

She considered me for a moment. "I'm sorry to hear that."

"I'm over it." I peered into the box, hoping to change the subject. "Is it true that bees only have one queen?"

"They do." She turned back to the box. "Let's see if we can find her. We always have to be careful of the queen when we inspect a hive. We never want to damage her."

Theo lifted various frames from the hive and explained what they were, and how some areas were just for eggs and growing young. She called it the nursery.

"There she is." She pointed to a bee somewhere in the center. She carefully replaced the frame and slowly pulled out another. "And these are drones over here." She pointed to some bees that were off to one side on another comb.

To be honest, they all looked the same to me. Still, I thought it was interesting the way bees lived and worked together so efficiently. That was something I could appreciate. You wanted everyone on your team playing to their best potential.

"Has a bee ever stung you?" I asked, watching as she blew more smoke to calm them down.

She nodded. "I've been stung many times."

"It's a good thing you're not allergic."

"I agree. That would be terrible, though I had a classmate when I was in graduate school who developed a bee allergy, so it does happen."

She showed me where the bees stored their extra honey. "Being mid-July, it's still a busy time for them. They're getting ready for the fall and winter."

"What happens then?"

"They stay together in the hive and live off the honey they've put aside. Luckily, they make much more than they need, which is why humans can remove the extra for ourselves."

Eventually Theo closed up the hive, and we both walked back over to the shed and removed our beekeeping suits.

"Thanks for showing me all that," I said. "It was interesting." And, surprisingly, it really was. I could appreciate the industriousness of her bees.

"You're welcome."

After putting the suits away and locking up her shed, we began walking up the slope toward her house. The afternoon was turning to evening, and the sun was still warm on us both. I felt relaxed being out here with her.

"How are you doing?" I asked. "After what happened with your boyfriend this morning?" I never pried into people's business, but she'd sounded upset earlier.

Theo shrugged. "I'm still processing it, but I'm sure I'll be fine."

I glanced at her with skepticism. She seemed way too cavalier. "You don't seem upset anymore."

"Of course it's upsetting. I'll be okay though." She shrugged. "Just one more wedding to attend alone. By now I'm used to it."

"Wedding?"

"It's nothing. My friend Leah is getting married next month. Clement was supposed to go with me."

"You're too good for that guy. That's what you need to remember about all this."

"How would you know? You've never met him."

"I don't have to meet him. If after three years with you, and he's not all in, then he must be an idiot."

She seemed surprised by my words, but didn't say anything more.

We reached the top of the hill where her house sat and then walked around to the front. I was hoping she'd invite me inside like she did last night, but I could tell she wasn't going to.

The two of us studied each other in the early evening light. To be honest, I could have stared at her all day. She was striking. I couldn't recall ever meeting a woman as vivid as Theo. Vivid in every way. A big part of me wanted to see her again, but that wasn't wise.

As I was contemplating this, I heard a vehicle pull up to her house behind me. Turning, I saw a white truck with two women inside.

"My friends Claire and Leah are here," she said. "I told them about the breakup, and they insisted on coming over tonight."

I nodded. "I guess I'd better be going. Thanks again for the lesson on bees."

Both women were getting out of their truck when I walked by them. They seemed shocked to see me, but that quickly turned to glares.

I nodded and smiled at them. "Good evening," I said, continuing on.

When I glanced over my shoulder, I could see all three women were watching me. The two friends of hers were still giving me the stink eye, but Theo—the only one I cared about—wasn't.

Instead, she lifted her hand and waved her fingers. And as crazy as it sounded, that little wave meant everything.

I waved back, and as I walked home, there was a lightness inside of me, a lightness I hadn't felt in a long time.

CHAPTER TWELVE

~ Theo ~

"What did *he* want?" Leah asked.

"I can't believe he had the nerve to show up here," Claire said. "Philip still thinks you should let him talk to his friend Bob. He's certain he could get Bardales to drop his lawsuit."

I watched Gabe walk around the corner and disappear. "He came here to apologize. And he already dropped his lawsuit."

They both spun toward me with surprise.

"He did?" Leah asked. "That's awesome!"

"You must be so relieved!" Claire said. "How did it happen?"

"It's kind of a long story. And I *am* relieved. I know my bees are too."

Claire and Leah smiled. They both knew all about "telling the bees" and that I'd told them when Claire's daughter, Amelia, was born, and also about Leah's wedding to Josh next month.

The biologist in me knew my bees didn't understand a word I said to them. That it was impossible. However, the child in me, the one who'd been talking to bees her whole life, still believed they did.

"So, as instructed, we didn't bring ice cream to commiserate with you about your breakup," Claire said, reaching inside her purse. "But I brought this." She pulled out a bottle of wine. "I'm still nursing, but you guys should indulge."

In the past, when one of us had broken up with a boyfriend, we usually ate junk food, drank wine, and watched romantic comedies together, but I didn't feel like doing that tonight.

Instead, we hung out on my back patio and talked. Leah and I both had some wine, and I also opened a bottle of mead that I'd been saving for Clement. *Good riddance to that waxworm. He doesn't deserve this mead.* Claire had a glass of the honey lemonade I'd made the other day.

"So, how are you doing?" Leah asked, holding her wineglass, studying me with concern. Her dark hair was pulled back into a ponytail that showed off the bold silver streak that ran near her temple. "After dating for three years, this must be hard."

I took a sip of the mead I'd poured myself. It was delicious. A local beekeeper I'd become friendly with from the extension classes at the university made it.

When I'd texted Leah and Claire this morning and told them about the breakup, I'd said it was a mutual decision. I just couldn't admit the truth. That I'd been dumped. It was too humiliating.

Obviously I'd told Gabe the truth on the phone, though I wished I hadn't. Claire was happily married with a new baby, and Leah was getting married soon. Both of them were so normal. Once again I was the freak. The outsider. My whole life had been like this.

"It sounds like the right decision," Claire said, leaning back in her lounge chair. "To be honest, I've always thought you were too good for him."

Her words made me think of Gabe's earlier. "Does that mean you never liked Clement?"

She smiled and seemed uncomfortable. "Don't take this the wrong way. I liked him just fine, but I thought he was too self-involved. It's like he cared more about his bugs than you."

I considered her words. "He's certainly dedicated to his research. His work on the passulus beetle's acoustic signals have been considered groundbreaking by many in the field."

"Maybe so," Claire said, "but he wasn't that great of a boyfriend."

"She's right." Leah nodded in agreement, swallowing a sip of wine. "I'm glad you're moving on."

I should tell them the truth, that it wasn't mutual, that Clement didn't want me anymore, but I didn't want to be the object of anyone's pity. Plus, I didn't want to bring them down. Not when they both had so much joy in their lives right now.

I'd gone out to my secret meadow that afternoon and sat in the warm grass, reflecting on the last three years of my life. I'd met Clement not long after I'd gotten my PhD. He'd been a visiting lecturer at the university, and we'd hit it off immediately.

Claire took a sip of her lemonade. "He was hardly ever here anyway."

"Three years is a long time to date someone and not see any forward movement," Leah said.

I nodded in agreement. "You're both right."

As they tried to be encouraging and continued to discuss all the ways this breakup was for the best, I kept thinking about Clement. *Should I have seen this coming? What did he mean by "explore other relationships"?*

Apparently it means he's done exploring ours.

"What is it?" Leah asked, watching me. "You look upset. You're not just pretending to act tough about this, are you? Because you seem awfully calm."

I shook my head. "I'm fine. Really. It's just going to be an adjustment, that's all."

I gazed down toward my lower yard and thought about the way Gabe showed up here this afternoon. And then about his strange appearance last night. I barely knew this football player, and we had nothing in common. I was used to men staring at me, and never in a good way, but somehow with Gabe today, after I'd shown him my bees, there'd been something different. For a moment under his gaze, I'd felt *seen*. It was the only way I could describe it.

Of course, I wasn't an idiot. I'd seen the women at his party that night. All of them glamorous and beautiful. The kind who'd look perfect on his arm and actually cared about football. They were probably all cheerleaders. Let's be honest, these women were practically a different species from me.

"Are you sure you're all right?" Claire asked with an expression of worry. She leaned forward in her lounge chair. "Because we're here for you, no matter what. You can tell us anything."

I forced a smile on my face and pushed away any thoughts of my jock neighbor. "Really. There's nothing more to tell," I said. "I'm perfectly fine."

Over the next couple of weeks, my vacation came to an end and my regular life began. I went back to work at the pollinator lab, where I continued my research on the effects of Varroa mite infestations on queen laying habits.

I hadn't heard anything from Clement, though a couple of my colleagues knew him, so I told them about our breakup. They offered their condolences, but I made it clear to them that I was okay and no condolences were required.

It was true. I still had moments of sadness and anger, but I hadn't cried. I didn't want to. There was an occasional tightness in my throat, but if I swallowed enough times, I found it went away. More than anything, I was determined to move on from this unpleasantness.

It was all going smoothly until Gerald, one of my work colleagues who was acquainted with Clement, mentioned that Clement was in Belize, living with Kendra.

"Kendra?" I asked.

He nodded. Gerald and I had been up for the same professorship two years ago, and I suspected he still held a grudge that they chose me over him. In fact, I'd heard through the grapevine that he'd gone to the head of the entomology department after I'd chained myself to Gabe's house and been interviewed by all those news stations, complaining about me. He said I was an embarrassment to the university. What Gerald didn't know was that Michael, our department chair, was a staunch environmentalist. I'd already sent him the links of those interviews, and he'd been delighted by them.

"She's his research assistant," Gerald said with relish in his voice.

"I know who Kendra is."

"Apparently they're romantically involved. Sorry, Theo." Though he didn't sound sorry. "I thought you knew."

I went still, trying to hide my shock. "Of course I knew."

But, of course, I *hadn't* known.

So it was all a lie. Clement had broken up with me to be with her. I doubt he'd cheated, but was this really that different?

I felt a strange numbness as I processed this new information.

I'd never met Kendra, but I'd seen photos of her. The irony was that Clement used to complain about her all the time, telling me she was a horrible assistant and that the university had forced her on him. But Kendra was also cute, petite, and blonde. Clement and I had a strong intellectual connection, and I would have thought he was immune to Kendra's physical appearance, but when it came down to it, he was still a man, wasn't he?

It wasn't easy, but I tried not to let this new knowledge drag me down.

I also hadn't seen or heard from my next-door neighbor since that day I showed him one of my hives. Not that I was expecting to see him. Occasionally, I drove by and tried to peer into Gabe's property, but you couldn't see much from the road. It didn't help that he'd recently installed a large metal gate to keep people out.

Leah's wedding to Josh was coming up next month, and Claire and I had started going to dress fittings in town since we were both in the wedding party, along with Isabel. Isabel and I were bridesmaids while Claire was the matron of honor. The two of them had been friends since elementary school, so I understood the decision behind it. Leah talked to me and wanted to check that my feelings weren't hurt, but I assured her I was okay.

Mostly I filled my days like I always had, with my bees and my work. At night, I snuck out to my secret meadow to lie on blankets in the grass contemplating this vast universe we were all a part of.

Look at me, I thought, gazing up at the stars. *I'm doing just great. How can I miss a boyfriend who's never here? Who cares if he's with Kendra?*

Claire and Leah were right. Clement and I had been living in some kind of permanent limbo. It was ridiculous.

It was getting cool out, so I decided to head back to the house. I slipped my hoodie on and grabbed my backpack. I camped in my secret meadow occasionally but always planned for those nights by bringing a sleeping bag and sometimes a tent if rain was expected.

As I headed through the woods toward my back gate, I noticed the way the edge of Gabe's property butted up against my own.

Instead of going toward my yard, I took a detour and walked along the edge of his fence. Like mine, a part of it was quite old, built years ago by the property's original owner.

I pulled my phone out to use as a flashlight, not even sure what I was doing at first, but then I realized I was searching for a back gate in his fence like the one I had.

The night forest surrounded me with the smell of pine and moss, my footsteps padding on the ground. It was mostly quiet out, though I heard the occasional frog croak.

Unfortunately, I didn't find what I was looking for. There was no gate. However, I did notice where the old fence overlapped with the new one, leaving a gap between them.

I stared at that gap and bit my lip.

It wasn't large, but was probably large enough.

Are you really doing this?

Apparently I was, because I tossed my backpack through the gap onto Gabe's property and then squeezed my body through it as well.

As soon as I got to the other side, I picked up my bag and took in my surroundings. I wondered where I was. There was a row of thick shrubbery directly in front of me, and I pushed my way through. Something sticky—probably a spider web—clung to me, but I pressed on regardless. Unlike most people, I wasn't afraid of spiders. Finally, I emerged at the back of a small house.

What have we here?

I wiped my hands on my jeans and brushed the leaves and remnants of web off of me. Everything was still and quiet in the darkness. I crept around to the front. When I saw cobblestones, I realized the house was reminiscent of the larger one, the Spanish castle Gabe lived in, but on a much smaller scale.

The overprivileged guesthouse.

I glanced around at the lounge chairs. Moonlight glimmered on water nearby.

And that must be the overprivileged swimming pool.

I had no idea what I was doing here, but I felt exhilarated.

There was a sidewalk leading away from the area, so I followed it. I wondered if Gabe had security cameras installed and was getting all this on video, though I saw no sign of any. Perversely, I stuck my tongue out and flipped the bird with both hands, just in case he did. Then I laughed to myself. *What has gotten into me?* I never behaved like this.

As I approached the main house, it was obvious no one was home. All the lights were off except for the porch lights, and those were probably on a timer. There were no cars in the driveway. He must have gone back to Seattle.

Standing there, I was uncertain what to do next. *Should I go home?* Instead, I headed toward his front steps, toward the stone pillar I'd gotten so familiar with.

I put my backpack down and took a seat, leaning against the pillar like I had for those five days when I chained myself to it in protest.

I thought about Clement, about how he hadn't called me even once during that time. I should have known something was wrong. In hindsight, I'd probably made too many allowances for him. Neither of us had ever complained about our relationship being long distance. We both accepted it in a logical way. His research required him to be out of the country, and I understood that, since I had my own research to focus on.

We spoke regularly on the phone and were close.

Although apparently not as close as I thought.

Clement and I had a lot in common and seldom argued. It had always been an easy relationship. Last year, I'd traveled back to New York to meet his parents, and though we hadn't discussed marriage explicitly, there was an expectation between us. Eventually, when his current research ended, we'd be together.

How did it all go so horribly wrong? What should I have done differently?

I was so deep in thought contemplating this that I didn't pay attention to the car engine approaching. By the time I saw headlights and realized there was a vehicle driving up to the house, it was too late.

Should I run and hide? But he'd already seen me. A silver Mercedes pulled into the driveway, and my heart pounded. I had no idea how to explain my presence here.

To my surprise, two men got out of the car. One of them was Gabe, but the other guy, the driver, was unfamiliar. He was shorter than Gabe, and his eyes widened in alarm at the sight of me.

Uncertain, I waved at them.

The guy I didn't know strode toward me. "The lawsuit's been

dropped," he said. "You've got no grounds whatsoever to continue harassing my client."

I blinked up at him. "What?"

Gabe followed him and called out, "Leave her alone, Davis."

But Davis continued on. I got the sense that he was nervous about me. "Whatever the problem is, my client has already expressed his remorse. It would be best for all parties involved if you left the premises." He paused and seemed to reconsider his words. "We mean you no ill will, of course."

I could see Gabe rolling his eyes.

"I'm not trying to harass anyone," I said, glancing between them.

"I know that," Gabe said, stepping around this guy. "We *both* know that."

Meanwhile, Davis continued to stare at me as if I were a bomb ready to detonate. He turned to Gabe. "I suggest you let me do the talking. We have no idea what her intentions are, but we both know the type of damage she's capable of."

I scoffed. "I haven't damaged anything. All I'm doing is sitting here."

Gabe shook his head. "Seriously, Davis. Shut the fuck up. I got this."

"As your lawyer, I believe it's best if you escort this woman off your property immediately."

"And as your friend, I suggest you escort your ass down to my guesthouse and let me handle it."

"Fine, but I'm leaving under protest. Call me if she asks you to sign anything."

After he was gone, I glanced up at Gabe to see he was smiling at me.

"Who is that guy?" I asked.

"My lawyer."

"Really? Do you hang out with your lawyer often?"

"He's basically my best friend."

"He seems quite jumpy." I peered into the dark toward the guesthouse where Davis had disappeared. "I think he was afraid of me."

"Davis still thinks you might try and wreck my football career."

I was taken aback. "That's absurd. I would never do that."

"I know, and I told him, but he doesn't believe me."

"Maybe *I* should tell him."

He shook his head. "It won't make any difference. He deals with asshole clients all day and doesn't have a high opinion of humanity."

"But aren't you one of his clients?"

Gabe snorted. "Exactly." He tilted his head. "How did you get in here, anyway? Did you climb over the gate out front?"

I shook my head. "Of course not. I found a gap in your fence behind the guesthouse and squeezed through that."

He chuckled but then considered me and went quiet. "So, why *are* you here, Theo?"

I avoided his eyes. "It's the silliest thing, really. I was feeling sentimental about your front steps and decided to visit them again." I placed my hand on the stone pillar. "I missed Carlos too."

"Carlos?"

"That's the name I gave this pillar while I was here." I patted it a few times. "Good old Carlos. The strong and silent type."

Gabe came over and sat next to me on the steps. "You're a highly unusual woman. Do you know that?"

My pulse jumped as soon as he sat beside me. Normally I'd take offense to a comment like that, but I could tell he didn't mean it as an insult. "I suppose I am."

"How are your bees doing?"

"They're fine."

He leaned in closer, and I caught a whiff of his scent. Warm and male and inviting. "And how are *you* doing?" he asked in a low voice.

I turned to him. This jock ogre. This football player who I barely knew, and who couldn't be more different from me. "Not so great," I admitted.

He studied me with those rich brown eyes, and I could tell he saw me. Just like that day when I showed him my bees. He saw me.

For a long moment, neither of us spoke.

"It's the boyfriend," he said. "That's why you're here, isn't it?"

I nodded, and this time when the tightness rose in my throat, I tried swallowing it away like always, but it didn't work. I kept swallowing, but the tightness only got worse.

And then, to my ultimate horror and shame, I started to cry.

CHAPTER THIRTEEN

~ Gabe ~

Theo didn't cry a lot. It was an instinct I had about her, but my gut told me I was right. The professor wasn't the overly emotional type and probably kept a lot bottled inside. I could tell by the way she acted after her boyfriend dumped her. Too self-contained. Too calm. It was something I had experience with myself.

We sat close, and I wrapped my arm around her shoulders as she put her face in her hands and sobbed. Her glasses were in the way, and she yanked them off in frustration, so I took them from her.

"It's going to be okay," I murmured. I wondered how long she'd been holding this in. The whole time, if I had to guess.

"Why doesn't he want me anymore? What did I do wrong?" she asked, still sobbing. "I haven't even told you the worst part. It was all a lie! He broke up with me so he could be with his research assistant."

I thought about this boyfriend of hers and decided I'd like to have some alone time with him. Trust me, when I was done, *he'd* be the one crying.

"Violence doesn't solve... anything," she said to me through her tears. "Beating up Clement wouldn't change a thing."

Shit. Did I just say that out loud?

"Maybe not," I said. "But *I'd* feel better. Besides, I wouldn't beat him up." A few pressure points would do the job nicely.

She cried some more. "Why didn't he just tell me the truth?"

I shook my head. "Because sometimes men are spineless jerks."

"You can't force someone to love you," she said, her voice shaking. "I wasn't enough for him. I have to accept that."

It was terrible seeing a woman as magnificent as Theo laid low. "Listen to me. You're *enough*," I told her. "Never doubt that. You're more than this guy deserved, and if he's too dumb to see it, then fuck him. He's obviously an idiot."

She turned to me, wiping her eyes. "He's actually a brilliant scientist."

"Yeah, well, he can eat a dick."

Theo burst out laughing, though she was still crying. "You have quite a succinct way of putting things, don't you?"

"It's true. I'm known for my eloquence in many literary circles."

She laughed some more. Her nose and eyes were red from crying, as were her cheeks. Yet she was as stunning as ever. "I didn't know football players were so well-spoken."

"It's mostly just us quarterbacks."

She sniffed and wiped her nose with her hand. "Gosh, I need a tissue."

My arm was still wrapped around her, and it felt good to hold her close. Too good. Which was why I forced myself to pull away. "Do you want to come inside the house?"

Theo reached over and took her glasses back from me. She sniffed again and glanced toward the door. "I probably shouldn't."

I gave her a look. "It's a Friday night. Do you have somewhere else to be?"

"Not really."

I stood up. "Come on then." I held my hand out.

After wiping her glasses, she slipped them back on and blinked up at me. Her warm palm slid onto mine, and I helped her up. Standing together, we weren't eye to eye, but I liked that she was right there. I didn't have to look down far to see her. Occasionally, I felt like an unwieldy giant next to some of the women I'd dated.

I pulled my keys out and unlocked the house, Theo following me inside as I entered.

"Do you mind if I use your bathroom again?"

"Go ahead."

As she went off toward the restroom, I headed toward the kitchen, trying to tidy things along the way. Davis had been coming up for the past couple of weekends, and neither of us was particularly neat, so the house was getting messier than I liked.

When she emerged from the bathroom, I was in the kitchen loading the dishwasher.

She took a seat at the island, watching me. "I'm surprised you don't have a maid."

"Yeah, I should probably hire one."

Theo brightened. "Actually, one of my best friends owns Maids of Truth. It's a successful local cleaning service."

"Really? Text me the number, and I'll give them a call." I closed the dishwasher and then grabbed a towel to wipe my hands. "Can I get you anything to drink?"

She studied the dishwasher, then glanced around the kitchen. "Everything in this house really is built taller, isn't it?"

I grinned with pride. "I told you it was."

"It's quite comfortable." She turned back to me. "I'll have some whiskey. Do you have any of that?"

"Whiskey?" I was expecting her to say wine or beer. "Is that what you usually drink?"

"No, but I want something different from my usual."

"Sure. I guess I'll join you." Davis drank Scotch and had brought his own bottle with him, so I pulled it down from the cabinet along with two glasses. I dropped a couple of ice cubes in each one and then poured in a finger of Scotch.

After I handed her a glass, she took a sip, and I watched the face she made with amusement.

"What do you think?" I asked. It was single malt and very smooth. Davis only bought the highest quality.

She stared into her glass. "I wondered why you gave me so little, but now I understand. It tastes terrible."

I laughed. "Do you want something else? There's beer, or I could open a bottle of wine."

She shook her head. "That's okay. I'm expanding my horizons." And then, to my surprise, she drank the rest of it in one gulp.

"Damn, slow down. Scotch is meant to be savored."

"It is?" She licked her bottom lip, still making a face. "Why?"

"Because it warms you up."

"Give me another one, and I'll savor it this time." She handed me her glass.

I took it and poured in a splash before giving it back. "Are you hungry? I could throw some food together."

"That's okay." She got up from her chair. Taking her glass with her, she wandered over to the great room.

My eyes followed, and I let myself enjoy this. Theo in my house. Her long, elegant body. That fire-engine-red hair. And for a moment, I imagined us together. Not just sexually, because I'd already imagined that, but as someone important in my life. As someone who belonged here.

It was a foolish daydream, but I wanted it. I sensed Theo would be good for me.

Not going to happen, Gabe. You already know that.

I took my glass and followed her. She was wandering around the room, and I took a seat on the couch and continued to watch her.

"This fireplace is enormous," she said. "Why do you need a fireplace this size?"

I shrugged. "Isn't it obvious? I like a big fire."

"This place reminds me of a Spanish castle," she said, running her hand along the edge of the stone mantel. "Is that what you wanted when you built it?"

"I suppose. My family came from Spain, and I've always been partial to the architecture."

After browsing through the room a little more, Theo walked back toward me, and I tried my hardest to resist this attraction to her. She wore jeans, a green hoodie, and sneakers, but it didn't take away from the effect she was having on me.

"I think I'm starting to like this stuff." She held up her glass. It was already empty again.

Shit.

"Do you mind if I get some more?" She breezed past me, and before I knew it, reappeared carrying not only her own glass of Scotch but the whole damn bottle.

"Would you like a refill?" she asked, coming closer.

I put my hand over my glass. "I'm good for now, thanks."

Instead of sitting in one of the chairs, she placed the bottle on the coffee table and then sat on the couch with me. Not close, on the opposite end, but I felt that short distance.

"I do feel warmer," she said, taking another large gulp. She put her glass down next to the bottle and then stripped her hoodie off, revealing a white tank top. The straps from a beige bra showed on her shoulders.

I told myself to look away from her body, from those pert breasts, but my eyes wouldn't listen. Instead, they trailed along the curve of her neck and collarbones, over all that pale freckled skin, and then down to that shadow of cleavage. So lovely. I could stare at her all night.

"Of course, it's not possible for alcohol to actually warm you," she informed me as she placed her hoodie on the couch. "Alcohol is a vasodilator, which explains the warmth you feel, but it interferes with your body's ability to keep its core temperature warm." She pushed her glasses up on her nose. "I was going to inform you of that earlier but didn't want to sound like a know-it-all."

"So you're telling me now?"

She nodded. "I am."

If she were a guy, I definitely would have forced her to do my homework in high school.

I guess this is revenge of the nerds.

She leaned back on the couch and smiled at me. And that smile. *Damn.* It was like the sweetest sunshower.

I put my glass down. I needed to keep my wits about me.

"So what *is* a quarterback?" she asked, shifting toward me on the couch. There was a looseness about her, and I suspected she was drunk.

"Are you asking in a philosophical sense, or do you really not know what a quarterback is?"

Theo blinked behind those glasses and seemed confused. "I have no idea what a quarterback is." She held a finger up. "However, I do know that you throw a football."

I chuckled. This was unreal. I was going to tell her that a quarterback was the offense leader, that we called plays, directed team strategy, and read defenses, but I didn't. "It's true," I said. "I throw a football."

She tilted her head and licked her lips. The professor was definitely drunk. "Now, is that really worth being paid millions of dollars for? Be honest."

I thought of what I put my body through every year. Broken fingers, two bruised ribs, and an ankle sprain last season. A lacerated hand and a fractured foot the year before. Not to mention the pressure to perform and make fast, accurate decisions with the whole world watching.

I shrugged. "Probably not."

"That's just what I thought."

"I *can* throw a football with a high degree of accuracy."

"I'm sure that's true." She took her glasses off and held them up to the light, inspecting for smudges, before putting them back on. "And please don't take this the wrong way, but it all seems so pointless." She began a tirade about millionaire jocks running around tackling each other, and why would anybody watch such a thing, and how football was basically a drug that dumbed down the masses, lulling them into a coma of both idiocy and mediocrity.

It was breathtaking in its scope of insult. I barely knew what to say.

"You do realize this is what I do for a living."

"But *why?*"

I rubbed my forehead. *Am I really having this conversation? How did I get myself into this?*

She reached for the bottle to pour more Scotch into her glass.

"Take it easy," I said. "Slow down. Maybe you've had enough."

"I don't think so. Besides, drinking seems like an appropriate response when my boyfriend dumps me to be with another woman."

I couldn't argue with that, and I felt bad that she was going through such a hard time. But then a thought came to me. "Hey, I have an idea that might help you feel better."

"You do?"

"That's if you're open-minded."

She grew indignant. "Of course I'm open-minded. I've always been *very* open-minded."

I started to tell Theo my idea, but then she took a sip from her glass. Her lips parted as she licked off a drop of alcohol. It was that lush mouth that did me in. I was struck by a bolt of erotic lightning.

God help me. This was too much.

Our eyes caught, and she must have sensed the storm blowing through me. I watched her gaze wander lower, checking me out, and I could tell she felt it too.

This powerful attraction between us that shouldn't exist.

I forced myself to look away. I might be an asshole, but I wasn't the kind who took advantage of a woman when she was drunk.

"What's your idea?" she asked, her voice curious. I couldn't help noticing a breathless quality.

She shifted position on the couch, and when I turned back, to my horror, Theo had moved closer. Much closer.

"I...." *Is the room getting hotter?* I felt like this was a test, one I was going to fail.

Abruptly I stood up. "We have to go outside."

"Outside? What for?"

"I'm going to show you something that might help you feel better. At least for a little while."

Theo seemed skeptical.

"C'mon, Professor. What do you have to lose?"

CHAPTER FOURTEEN

~ Theo ~

"Let's go, Theo. You can do it!" Gabe clapped his hands and called out from about thirty feet away. We were standing in his backyard, and I was holding, of all things, a football. It was the middle of the night, but he'd turned on the backyard flood-lights. "Just throw it to me."

I stared at the ball. "I'm not so sure about this."

"C'mon, do it like I showed you." He'd stood next to me a few moments ago and demonstrated the best way to grip a football in my right hand with my fingers over the laces. "Just go for it. Throw that sucker as hard as you can."

"I don't want to hurt you."

He laughed. "You're not going to hurt me."

"All right, fine." I gave the football a lackluster throw. It veered to the left, though Gabe still managed to catch it.

He jogged over to bring it back, and we did this a few more times.

"You're not taking this seriously," he scolded after my fourth attempt. "I thought you said you were open-minded."

"I *am*, but I dislike football. I've never thrown one in my life."

"That doesn't sound very open-minded. How can you dislike something that you know nothing about? Also, aren't you expanding your horizons?"

I huffed in irritation. This man was infuriatingly good at trapping me with my own words.

"Pretend you're throwing it at Clement's head," he said, handing the ball back to me again. "Maybe that will help."

"All right, fine." This time when I threw it, I used my anger. The ball flew out of my hand with more force and glided through the air toward Gabe, who caught it.

"Yeah, that's more like it," he said. "Now I'm going to throw it back to you."

"*What?* Don't throw it back! You'll probably kill me!"

He laughed some more. "I'm just going to toss it to you gently. I promise it won't kill you."

I waited with trepidation. I was still kind of drunk, but just the right amount. Just enough to feel less inhibited in front of this guy who threw footballs for a living. At least he wasn't making fun of my nonexistent athleticism.

True to his word, Gabe gently tossed the ball, and by some miracle, I caught it. I could barely believe it. I was proud of myself. Typically, when sports were involved, I was all arms and legs. A red-haired tarantula having a seizure.

"All right, now throw it to me again," he said, watching as I got into position. "Bring that elbow up. Put some power into it. Remember that left foot comes forward."

"Stop barking orders at me," I complained. Even though I did what he said and brought my elbow higher and my left foot forward when I released the ball. I also pretended I was throwing it at Clement's head. That image really worked for me.

"That's not bad, Professor. Let's do it again."

He tossed it back, and I managed to catch it. The entire experience was surreal. We kept doing this over again, and every time he encouraged me to throw the football harder. It was cool outside, but I started getting sweaty. I also started getting into it. Finally, I threw that ball as hard as I could every single time, imagining Clement's head exploding like a giant pumpkin on impact.

It was *fun*.

Occasionally, I screwed up, and the ball veered way off, but Gabe never complained. Even when he had to search around in the bushes for it.

After a while, I was rubbing my shoulder. "My arm's getting kind of tired. Do you think we could take a break?"

"Sure, of course." Gabe walked toward me holding the football, and I admired the way he moved. For a man his size, he was extremely graceful. I'd never spent time with any professional athletes, and I wondered if they all had this natural grace.

His hair fell across his forehead in an appealing way. He was the type of man who was so handsome it hurt to look at him.

My mind went back to the moment between us just before we came outside. I'd felt particularly drawn to him. Overwhelmed by it. I guess, now that I didn't have a boyfriend anymore, I could admit to myself that I was attracted to this jock.

How is this possible when there's no reason for it? No mutual intellectual pursuits. No similar interests at all. *It makes no sense.*

Gabe was playing around with the ball, and it looked so natural in his hands. The way he deftly maneuvered it, it was almost like another appendage. He held it up on his finger and spun it around.

I laughed with delight. "How do you do that?"

"Years of practice."

He grinned at me, and my stomach dipped like a roller coaster. And that's when a crazy thought came to me. Was this attraction to him purely physical? Nothing intellectual at all? Just *animal lust*?

I sucked in my breath at such a startling idea. Animal lust was for other people. Not for me. *Never.*

"What?" he asked, glancing over. "You want me to teach you how to do this? Because I think you have natural talent with a football, Professor."

My eyes rolled at such an absurd statement. "I'm just glad I didn't break any of your windows." I'd come embarrassingly close a couple of times. "I appreciate you not making fun of my athletic abilities. Because of my height, people often assume I play basketball or volleyball, but I've never been good at sports."

"Yeah, I get that too. People always assume I play basketball or football. Though in my case, they're right." He stopped spinning the ball. "I wouldn't say you're bad at sports. You seemed to be getting the hang of it. Though I hope you weren't lulled into mediocrity. At least you don't look like you're in a coma of idiocy. Not yet, anyway."

I cringed with embarrassment. "I apologize for saying that. In hindsight, I realize that was quite rude."

He shrugged. "I've gotten worse insults that were far more personal. Besides, I'm glad to see you expanding your horizons. I could tell there was real power behind some of those throws you sent me."

"That's because I did what you told me. I pretended I was aiming at Clement's head. I liked to imagine it exploding into a million pieces."

He chuckled. "Damn, woman, you're bloodthirsty." He gave me a wary look as he fiddled with the football in his hand some more. "I'm going to have to be more careful around you."

"I'm not bloodthirsty! And it was *your* idea!"

"Yeah, but I didn't tell you to imagine it exploding into a million pieces. That's some sick shit."

I shrugged and pulled away a hair the wind had blown into my mouth. "I have to admit, it was rather cathartic."

He was grinning at me again. "Maybe you're starting to realize that football's not so bad after all. Turns out you might even like it."

"I wouldn't go *that* far. I have no idea how the game is even played."

"Damn, seriously?" He shook his head and then sighed like the headmaster who'd found out his prized student was caught cheating on a test. "So I'm going to have to teach you about football? Is that what you're telling me?"

"I don't know." I bit my lip. "It seems so dull."

"It's not dull. And I let you teach me about bees. Learning about football is the least you could do to prove how open-minded you are."

He certainly had me there. But then I realized what this meant—that we'd see each other again. "When would we do this?"

"I'm headed off to training camp tomorrow, and I've also got preseason, but we'll figure out a way for me to teach you."

Another breeze blew past, and I rubbed my arms to warm myself.

"Are you cold?" he asked. "We can go inside."

I glanced up at the sky, sensing it was late. "I should probably be going now. It must be well past midnight."

We went into the house so I could get my backpack and put my hoodie back on.

"I'll walk you home," Gabe said, grabbing his keys off a hook in the kitchen.

"That's not necessary. I'm only next door."

He gave me a look. "It's the middle of the night, Theo. I'm walking you home."

We headed toward his new gate out front, which was as tall and forbidding as a tower.

"This gate is imposing," I said as he held the side door open for me to walk through. "I'm surprised you didn't put in a moat as well."

"I considered it, but it was too expensive."

I glanced at him and couldn't tell if he was serious or joking.

Once again I wondered why he'd built this Spanish castle to live in all alone. What was he guarding himself against?

Neither of us spoke much as we walked toward my house, but I had to admit I was very aware of him beside me. His physical presence. His strength. I wasn't used to being around men who were so much larger than me. Most of the men I knew were work colleagues, fellow beekeepers, or friends' husbands.

When we arrived at my porch, Gabe came with me to the door.

"Thank you for walking me home," I said. I'd already gotten my keys out and stood there awkwardly. I wasn't quite sure how to handle this new feeling of animal lust I was experiencing.

"No problem. I'd better head back now."

But he didn't move. Instead, we gazed at each other. It was a breezy summer night. Clouds had moved in, and it was probably going to rain soon.

"You're the only person who knows the truth," I blurted out.

"The truth about what?"

"About what happened with Clement. I've been lying to everyone, telling them the breakup was mutual. Isn't that terrible? I've lied to all my friends and the people I work with. No one knows my humiliation."

Gabe went quiet, mulling this over. "Why did you tell *me?*"

I fingered the keys in my hand. "I'm not entirely sure. But I'm usually honest about everything. I don't normally lie like this."

"Don't worry, I won't judge you for it." And there was something in his tone, something that told me he had his reasons for not judging.

We were standing a normal distance apart, and it must have been the whiskey swirling through my veins, or maybe it was the way he accepted me, or maybe it was just the *animal lust*, but I took a step closer.

"I want you to kiss me," I announced, looking up at him.

He went completely still. I thought he'd be surprised, but instead, his eyes were dark and complicated. I couldn't tell what he was thinking.

"Just *do* it," I said. It flashed through my mind that maybe he didn't want to kiss me, that maybe I was making a fool of myself. I wasn't always good at reading subtext in social situations. "You don't want to?"

"Theo," he whispered.

And just when I thought this was a disaster, that I was going to have a whole new level of humiliation to experience, Gabe took a step forward and closed the gap between us.

He brushed the backs of his fingers against my cheek. I closed my eyes at the sudden rush of heat burning through me.

It was a soft kiss, tentative, like he wasn't sure how I would react. But as soon as our lips met, it was like something inside me snapped into place. I kissed him back with a fierceness I hadn't known I'd possessed.

Gabe groaned, his hands on my waist, pulling me in tighter.

Everything inside me seemed to shift and melt. I dropped my backpack and keys on the porch and threw my arms around his neck. This kiss was unlike anything I'd ever experienced. Raw and rough with desire. Clement had never kissed me like this. I was certain no man ever had.

When we broke apart, I didn't want it to end. "Come inside the house," I said, breathless. "Stay with me."

"It's a mistake, Theo." He shook his head, swallowing. He wore a troubled expression. "We can't do this."

I drew him toward me, and for a moment he resisted, but then gave in. Solid and warm. His hands tangled in my hair, holding me to him as we kissed some more.

Finally, he pulled away, both of us breathing hard. Gabe's eyes were inky, intense. "I'm going now."

"Don't leave." I sounded wild to my own ears. *What's happening to me? Is this animal lust turning my normal high-functioning brain into a cabbage?*

"I have to," he said, his voice rough. "It's for the best."

"Is it because I'm not like all those other women? Is that it? The ones from your party?"

"What?"

"I know I'm not like them. I'm not glamorous, and I'll never be a cheerleader. And, let's be honest, I *hate* football. But does it really matter?"

A smile crept up on Gabe's mouth. "You're right, you're nothing like them."

I stared at him. It was just as I'd figured. Once again, I was the outsider. The freak.

He put his hand up to my cheek. "The reason you're nothing like them, Theo, is because you're more beautiful than all of them."

My stomach dropped.

It was the one thing he could have said that would make me recoil.

CHAPTER FIFTEEN

~ Gabe ~

Theo pushed me away from her. She looked seriously pissed.

"What's wrong?" I asked, bewildered. "Did I do something?"

"Don't patronize me. Don't you *dare!*"

"What the hell are you talking about?" A second ago, I was passionately kissing a beautiful woman, and now I was dealing with a fire-breathing dragon.

"I know what I am, okay? I'm weird-looking. I'm *odd*. I've had a lifetime to accept that I don't fit into the normal standards of beauty, so don't treat me like I'm an idiot."

I was as confused as if my linemen were wearing tutus and dancing *Swan Lake* before the snap. "I'm not treating you like an idiot."

She pointed at me accusingly. "People may call *you* 'Beauty,' but trust me, no one ever calls *me* that. I've been listening to people snicker about me my whole life. I've been called 'Beast' more times than I can count!"

As her words sank in, I felt a strange rushing in my ears. It was like a vacuum filling with an explosion of air.

What the fuck?

Rage tore through that vacuum. I wanted to pound those mother-fuckers into the ground. Every last one of them. Forget pressure points. I'd beat the shit out of them. Not because what they said was true, but because they'd hurt this woman, and the thought of anyone hurting Theo was enough to make me want to break their arms and legs and eat their bones for dinner.

"Who?" I could barely speak, my voice guttural. "*Who* has said this to you?"

"Everyone. Everywhere I go!" She threw her hands up. "All I get are rude comments about my height and my hair! So don't tell me I'm beautiful. Don't lie to me. I've been honest with you, Gabe. The least you could do is be honest in return."

"But you *are* beautiful."

She swung down and grabbed her backpack and keys off the porch, her movements jerky and angry. Before I knew it, she'd unlocked her front door and slammed it in my face.

I stood there, stunned.

Rage was still coursing through me. At the same time, I felt sick to my stomach because I knew I couldn't protect her, not like I wanted. Not from the whole world.

I barely remembered walking back to the house. I stalked down to my home gym that wasn't fully set up yet. Luckily, I'd done one thing right—I'd put in a punching bag. And I pounded the shit out of it. Every hit was against some fucker who dared to try to bring down a woman like Theo.

"I told you she was trouble. You should have listened to me." It was Davis, standing in the doorway, watching me with a concerned expression. "Just tell me this—how much damage control are we looking at?"

I punched the bag again. "Nothing happened. Just drop it."

He leaned against the doorframe and shook his head. "Who knew this bee biologist would be the equivalent of ten landmines? She didn't ask you to sign anything, did she?"

I rolled my eyes. "Jesus, Davis. You really *are* an asshole."

"I'm just looking out for your interests. Also, who the hell drank all my Scotch? Half the bottle is empty."

"I'll buy you another one."

"You don't have to buy me another bottle. It's the principle of the thing. You don't go drinking another man's Scotch. It's part of the bro code."

I laughed. "Does the bro code include moving into my house without asking me?"

"Yeah, it does."

I laughed some more. *Fucking Davis, I swear.* Sometimes I wondered how we'd become such good friends. Though, to be fair, if he wasn't around, I'd probably be talking to the walls.

"Are you still driving with me back to Seattle tomorrow morning?" he asked.

"Yeah, I want to leave my truck here." I had two vehicles—an Escalade and a Ford 250 pickup. I figured the truck would be more useful up in Truth Harbor, since it was difficult to park it in the city.

Eventually, I was done with the punching bag and went upstairs to take a shower. I tried texting Theo, but she didn't respond. I wasn't even sure what I was supposed to say. *Apologize for telling her she's beautiful?*

Afterward I started packing a bag for tomorrow. I usually looked forward to training camp, but felt conflicted about the situation with Theo. I hated leaving things like this between us. The irony was that I hadn't met many women who I thought were truly beautiful, and it wasn't a compliment I gave often. I understood that Theo's appearance was unusual. But that's what made her so striking. She stood out in a crowd. It pissed me off to think that anyone would give her shit for it, much less call her names. Were these people blind?

Then a strange thought occurred to me.

Is it possible I'm the only one who sees how beautiful she is?

That made no sense.

I finished packing the clothes I needed, along with my iPad and all the notes I'd been taking from watching game film. There'd be even more film to watch during the next couple of weeks. I spent a lot of time analyzing our opponents' defenses, not to mention ways we could improve our own strategy and performance.

I glanced over at the jar of honey on my dresser. The one Theo gave me. The one Davis kept trying to eat on his peanut butter toast every morning. I finally had to hide the damn thing upstairs in my bedroom.

It was just a plain jar filled with golden liquid, but I still remembered the expression on Theo's face when she gave it to me, the feel of her hand over mine. It was the first time she'd ever touched me.

And tonight was the second time.

I could barely believe it when she'd asked me to kiss her. It was like a fantasy come to life.

Except she tasted and felt far better than any fantasy.

I picked up that jar of honey and weighed it in my hand. Then I added it to my bag, tucking it gently to the side so it was surrounded by clothes to cushion it.

Maybe I didn't deserve Theo, and maybe she was already done with me, but I didn't want anything to happen to that honey.

As I COULD HAVE PREDICTED, Davis spent the whole trip back to Seattle talking about Miranda. Apparently he'd been stalking her Instagram page, which was filled with pictures of their dog.

"Petey's wearing an outfit I don't recognize," Davis said. "I keep wondering if this new boyfriend of hers bought it for him."

I shrugged and sucked on the straw from the green smoothies we'd picked up on the way. "She probably bought it herself."

He shook his head. "It doesn't look like something she'd buy. It's too macho."

"Macho?"

Davis forced me to bring up Miranda's Instagram page on my phone so I could weigh in on the dog's clothes. The picture in question showed Petey sitting on some grass wearing a zippered camouflaged hoodie. It even had a little hat attached. The dog looked like he was in the Army.

"Is the boyfriend military?" I asked, putting my smoothie back in the cupholder.

"He works at a bank."

I skimmed through the rest of Miranda's page, which was filled with photos of Petey. I couldn't believe I was analyzing a Chihuahua's wardrobe. Except I had to admit, Davis had a point. Most of Petey's outfits were preppy. Lots of plaid sweaters and scarves. In one photo, he was wearing a pink polo shirt. That camo hoodie stood out from the rest.

Davis glanced over at me. "What do you think? I'm right, aren't I?"

"It *is* kind of macho," I heard myself say.

He slapped the steering wheel. "Fuck, I knew it! Where does this jackass get off buying clothes for *our* dog?"

"He's probably trying to impress Miranda."

Davis shook his head. "That's it. I'm getting Franklin to dig up some dirt on this asshole when we get back to the city." Franklin was his firm's private investigator. I'd met her a number of times over the years when she'd done some work for me. "Miranda needs to know who she's dating. What if he's a maniac? He's probably just pretending to be a dog lover."

"You're only going to piss Miranda off if she finds out," I said, stating the obvious. "Just let it go. It's only some dog clothes. Next time she calls, just ask her about it."

Because Miranda was *constantly* calling Davis. For two people who were supposedly broken up, they were endlessly in each other's lives. Even with this new boyfriend, it seemed like Miranda wanted Davis to handle everything for her. Just this past weekend, she'd called and wanted him to figure out some issue with her car.

I shifted in my seat to look at him. Davis bringing up Franklin had reminded me of something. "Listen, I need you to do me a favor. Theo is going to be at a wedding next month. Can you find out where and when it's taking place?"

He glanced at me. "Theo—your *neighbor*? The bee biologist?"

It was an idea that came to me last night when I was lying in bed, unable to sleep as usual. There might be a way to fix this situation. "It's one of her friends who's getting married. I think her name's Leah."

"Why don't you just ask her about the wedding yourself?"

"Because she won't talk to me." I tried texting and calling Theo twice again this morning. Still no response. I already knew how stubborn she could be. It pained me to think I'd hurt her feelings. I would never want that. None of this made any sense, but the professor was an unusual person.

"Why? What did you do?"

I shook my head. "Nothing." No way was I telling Davis about this. "Can you find out for me or not?"

He snorted. "Of course I can. I can find out anything. You know that." But then he turned to me, always thinking two steps ahead. "Shit, you're not going to leave training camp to go to this wedding, are you? The GM will have your balls in a sling."

I smirked. Davis wasn't wrong. Ryan would go ballistic if I left training camp without permission. Not that I would ever do anything that might hurt the team.

"Just find out when and where it's happening," I said, "and I'll handle the rest."

As LUCK WOULD HAVE IT, the wedding was taking place on a Saturday in August that had been scheduled as a rest day. Not all rest days at training camp were created equal, and sometimes coaches wanted you to stay at camp, but luckily, this wasn't one of them.

"So Coach Mallory gave you the okay to leave?" Davis asked. He was calling me back after he'd found out the wedding and reception were both taking place at a beach near Truth Harbor. The wedding itself was small and private, and I had no intention of crashing that, but the reception was another matter.

"Yeah, it's fine. Some of the other guys are leaving to spend the day with their families. As long as I'm there on the sidelines for the game on Sunday, I'm good."

"That's going to be tight. Maybe you should schedule a flight to get you up there and back."

"You're right. That's a good idea."

Davis told me he'd have one of his assistants set it up for me. "Listen, the reason I'm calling you again is that you're never going to believe whose wedding this is."

I rolled my neck around to get out a kink. It was the first week of camp, and I'd been working out every day along with doing drills and game scenarios. Training camp could be grueling as hell, but I loved it because I slept like a baby every night. "It's her friend Leah's wedding, isn't it?"

"But do you know who this Leah is marrying?"

"Should I?"

"Joshua Trevant."

I sorted through my memory. "That name sounds familiar."

"It should. Joshua Trevant is the lead singer for East Echo."

My brows went up. "No shit." I had three of their albums on a playlist on my phone.

Davis laughed. "You're crashing a rock star's wedding reception. The security's going to be at DEFCON one. Do you still think you can get in?"

I appreciated that he wasn't trying to talk me out of it. He knew me too well for that. "You know what? I've met him."

"You have?"

I nodded, remembering it. "It was brief, but I met him in LA a few years ago after a game." I also realized why that blond guy I kept seeing Theo with looked so familiar. "Hell, he came to my house when she was still chained to it." I wished now that I'd gone outside and talked to them, but obviously I was in a different headspace.

"What I want to know is who the hell is this bee biologist? Franklin says she's got one best friend married to Philip North, and the other one is marrying a rock star."

I smiled to myself. Theo was full of surprises. "She's an unusual person."

He snorted. "You're telling me. She's not just a guest at that wedding—she's *in* the wedding. She's one of the bridesmaids. Dean Kennedy, the drummer for East Echo, is a groomsman, and so is Lane Hart."

"Who's that?"

"One of the most famous surfers in Australia. The guest list for this wedding reception is nuts. It sounds like every famous rock musician in the country is going to be there. I honestly don't know how you're going to get in."

"I'll get in."

"So what the hell is going on with you and this neighbor? Are you involved with her? What are you not telling me?"

I hesitated, unsure how to answer his question. "We're friends," I said finally.

"*Friends?* When did you become friends with her?" He sounded shocked. Or as shocked as someone like Davis could ever be. "And if you're friends with her, why did you need me to have Franklin skulk around and find out about this wedding?"

"It's complicated."

"Damn, Gabe." And then he chuckled. "When is anything with you ever not complicated?"

CHAPTER SIXTEEN

~ Theo ~

"We're gathered here today...," Leah and Josh's wedding ceremony began.

I tried my hardest not to cry.

The problem was I always cried at weddings. I'd never considered myself to be an overly sentimental person, but there was something about weddings that got to me.

I reached up and discreetly dabbed my eyes.

Thank goodness I'm wearing waterproof mascara.

Leah and Josh looked so happy.

It was a sunny day as we stood beneath a white canopy on the beach. Chairs had been placed in neat rows for the wedding guests, with flower-filled vases everywhere.

I wasn't used to being this dressed up and felt out of my element.

Rhys, the guitar player for East Echo, had strummed the wedding march as Dean, their drummer, escorted me down the aisle. He was a large man with thick dark hair and a long black beard. While his appearance was intimidating, I found him to be the perfect gentleman. Josh's twelve-year-old son beamed from ear to ear, standing beside his dad as best man. A guy named Lane with sun-bleached hair, tanned skin, and a thick Australian accent was the other groomsman.

The wedding colors were jewel tones—sapphire and emerald. Isabel and I both wore an emerald dress, and while bridesmaid dresses weren't typically my taste, I had to hand it to Leah. This one suited me. It hugged my waist and somehow gave me more curves than I ever thought possible. Claire looked beautiful in her sapphire gown.

Leah's mom and her two cousins had joined us beforehand at Leah's house to get ready. It felt like a party, all of us chatting and laughing with excitement as we drank champagne and ate chocolate-dipped strawberries. Leah had brought in stylists to do everyone's hair and makeup, and the air was filled with the scent of perfume and hairspray. I'd never felt so glamorous. I was amazed at the shoulder-length ringlet curls the stylist had magically turned my hair into.

While the wedding was small and intimate with only close friends and family, Leah and Josh's reception had become the event of the summer. Truth Harbor was buzzing. A number of celebrities had flown in for the event—not that I knew who most of them were. There was a gauntlet of press and news vans on the street outside.

I'd never been part of such a ritzy event, and my heart raced as I took it all in.

Thankfully, Leah, Claire, and Isabel were still their normal, fun, and down-to-earth selves. Leah's fitted white lace dress was stunning on her, though she'd joked that she felt like a mermaid. Claire made us laugh when she said we looked like a girl singing group. During the limo ride to the wedding, music played on the speakers and we sang to it at the top of our lungs just like an actual singing group.

"You may kiss the bride," the minister announced.

Josh swooped in to kiss Leah, and it sent everyone into a frenzy of cheers and claps.

I wiped my eyes again, so happy for them.

Afterward I rode with Dean, Lane, Isabel, Claire, and Philip to the wedding reception in another limo. There was security everywhere, and it was surreal to be escorted through a corridor of checkpoints and even a metal detector.

The whole day had been such a whirlwind that I tried not to think about how I was once again attending a wedding alone. I'd been to a number of weddings over the years, and Clement had never managed to attend a single one with me.

He always claimed work got in the way, but in hindsight, it should have been another warning sign. A red flag, if you will.

I sighed and took a sip from my glass of white wine. The table I sat at was empty since Claire was dancing with Philip, and some guy had come over and asked Isabel to dance. Dean and Lane had disappeared into the crowd as soon as we arrived.

My feet ached a little, and I slipped my shoes off, wiggling my toes around. I seldom wore high heels. Except I couldn't resist these peep-toed pumps. I almost didn't wear them because I knew I'd tower over everyone. But I'd shown them to Leah and Claire, and they both agreed I *had* to wear them. They were perfect with my dress.

I reached for my glass of wine again, barely recognizing my own hand with its dark red fingernail polish. The wedding party had gone to a salon a few days ago, and we'd all had mani-pedis. I rarely bothered with nail polish but had to admit I was enjoying it, especially on my feet, and might have to start painting my toenails more often.

Sadly, this wasn't the first wedding I'd been to where I sat alone. It was typically like this. Often, I'd seek out the table with all the elderly relatives and join them, but this reception didn't seem to have a table like that.

I was tempted to get my phone out and read. A new issue of the *Melittology & Apiology Journal* came out yesterday, and an article titled "Pesticide Resistance and the Chemical Ecology of Varroa

Destructors" had caught my attention, as it tied in with my own research. Regrettably, I suspected sitting alone reading might seem rude.

As I was contemplating how soon I could leave without insulting Leah and Josh, I noticed something. In the sea of long-haired and tattooed musician types, there was an absurdly handsome guy a head taller than everyone else. He looked familiar.

Oh my God.

It was Gabe!

I could barely believe it. The object of my animal lust.

What's he doing here?

There was no way Leah and Josh invited him. They didn't even know him.

Has he already seen me? Should I dive under the table?

Except it was too late. He wore a funny, almost alarmed expression when he noticed me but then seemed to recover, grinning, as he held his hand up. "Theo, there you are! I've been searching for you. Will you let this guy know I'm your plus-one?"

My mouth opened in confusion as I turned to the bald guy next to him dressed all in black and wearing a Bluetooth earpiece. He was obviously part of the security detail. He asked my name and then wanted to know if Gabe was my plus-one.

"Plus-one?" I stared up at them both.

The object of my animal lust seemed slightly ill at ease, wondering if I'd back up his story.

I nodded toward the guy with security. "Yes, this is my plus-one."

"We have a Clement Woodard listed as your plus-one," the security guard said with a hand on his earpiece. "Am I to presume that he won't be attending and that Mr. Bardales is here in his place?"

"That's correct," I said. "Clement won't be attending."

The guard turned toward Gabe. "Sorry about that, Mr. Bardales. I had to be certain. It's my job. You understand."

"No problem." He stuck his hand out. "And call me Gabe."

The guard shook it and seemed dazzled. "Thank you, Mr.... er, Gabe. It's a real pleasure to meet you. I'm a huge Sentries fan."

After the security guard left, Gabe took a seat at one of the empty chairs next to me and seemed quite pleased with himself.

"Did you really just crash Leah and Josh's wedding?" I asked with amazement.

"Not the wedding, just the reception," he said, as if that somehow made it okay.

"What are you doing here?"

"Holy shit." He leaned forward in his chair. "I can't believe how many famous musicians are here. This is unbelievable."

"You didn't answer my question," I said. "What are you doing here?"

"I'm here for you."

"*Me?*"

He nodded. "I remembered when you'd said you'd be going to this thing alone. Now you're not alone anymore."

I gawked at him. "And so you took it upon yourself to come here as my *date*? That's quite presumptuous of you." Obviously we hadn't left things in a good state between us. There were those remarkable kisses on my porch, but then he had to ruin it with a phony compliment.

"You wouldn't return any of my phone calls or texts."

"So your solution was to crash my friend's wedding reception? That makes a lot of sense."

"I wanted to see you." He lowered his voice, leaning closer. "I didn't mean to hurt your feelings, Theo. I would *never* do that."

"Just be honest with me then. That's all I ask. Don't lie or patronize me."

Gabe opened his mouth and then closed it. He seemed frustrated. He was doing that thing again, too, where he kept staring at me. "I've always been honest with you."

I picked up my wineglass in annoyance. "We both know that isn't true."

He shook his head and then shifted in his chair. "Why the hell are we arguing? I'm here. You're here. Let's go dance and have some fun."

I nearly choked on my wine. "Dance?"

"Yeah." He grinned at me. His hair had been gelled to bring out the waves, and a dark lock fell across his forehead, giving him a roguish appearance. My gaze drifted across those wide shoulders. He wore a dark gray suit and a green tie that set off the brown in his eyes. It occurred to me that his tie matched my dress. We almost looked like we'd planned it and had come together.

That's if you ignored the fact that people called *him* Beauty and *me* Beast for a reason.

I glanced out at the crowded dance floor. A band had played for a short while earlier, the Busy Beavers or something, but now there was a DJ spinning a variety of music.

I rarely danced at weddings. Occasionally, someone would ask. It was usually a husband or cousin who'd obviously been told to, or a kindly grandfather. Never a man I was interested in.

"I don't dance at weddings," I said.

"Why not?"

"No one ever asks me." The music changed, and I heard the intro for The Supremes' "Come See About Me." A song I loved.

Gabe seemed surprised by this. I watched him as he stood up and put his hand out. "Would you like to dance, Theo?"

I sucked in my breath at the realization that, for once, I wasn't the outsider. The one left behind.

I put my hand in his larger one. "I'd love to."

CHAPTER SEVENTEEN

~ Gabe ~

My high school guidance counselor used to have colorful posters on her walls with corny expressions. One of them was about how you should dance like no one was watching. Theo must have seen that same poster, except she took the message to heart.

Because she definitely danced like no one was watching.

Most of the women I'd dated practically turned into strippers on the dance floor. Meanwhile, Theo hopped and skipped around like a bunny rabbit.

I'd never seen anything like it. It was sweet and cute. Definitely nerdy. And, for some reason, oddly sexy.

She wiggled her hips and shoulders, then pointed her fingers around in all directions like she was shooting lasers.

"Come See About Me" played, and she obviously loved this song because she sang every word. She was dancing in front of me, barefooted and swirling in circles, but then I blinked and she was gone. It turned out she'd skipped around and was now dancing *behind* me.

I chuckled and turned to face her again. "So you don't dance much?"

"Oh, I dance all the time! Just not at weddings!" Her face was flushed. She pretended to have a pistol in each hand, shooting me as she continued to wiggle and hop. "I dance in my living room," she shouted over the music.

That explained a lot.

The next song was Lady Gaga's "Born This Way," and Theo graduated from pistols and lasers to pantomiming washing a window with both hands.

To hell with it. Soon I was washing windows and shooting lasers and pistols right along with her.

We definitely worked up a sweat. Mostly I was waiting for a slow song and was finally rewarded when the Rolling Stones' "Wild Horses" began.

Taking a step toward Theo, I wrapped my arm around her waist and pulled her into me, both of us still breathing hard.

"Oh." Her eyes widened as our bodies came together. "That's, uh... oh, wow." She slid her arms around my neck.

I looked down into her face.

She blinked up at me like a baby owl behind those tortoiseshell glasses.

"I'm glad we finally got a slow song," I admitted.

"I can't get over how tall you are. You're a giant." But then her expression turned to horror. "Oh my *God*! I can't believe I just said that! I'm *so* sorry. It was rude! I hate it when people go on about how tall I am."

I chuckled. "Don't worry about it. Coming from you, it's not rude. And besides, next to me, you're a shrimp," I teased.

The truth was I liked Theo's height. The way her body fit so well into mine. I'd noticed it right away when we were kissing on her porch.

It was just one more way she was stunning. I was startled when I first glimpsed her here at the reception. I thought she was beautiful in a T-shirt and jeans, but it was something else to see her in this green dress that wouldn't quit. That dark lipstick against her white teeth when she smiled was almost too much for me. It felt hard to breathe staring at her mouth.

We started slow dancing with our bodies pressed together. Every sway of her hips sent a rush through me. Every brush of her hands against the back of my neck kicked my pulse up a notch.

The lights were dim with soft flecks of light from a disco ball above us. The dance floor filled with other couples, but I only had eyes for Theo.

She gazed up at me, and I realized that when I was with her, all my demons were gone. Lifted away as if by magic. I felt lighter than I had in years. I'd forgotten that I'd once felt this way all the time. Long before everything that happened. Back when my life was an open road full of possibilities instead of a long list of regrets.

If I had met Theo back then, I suspected she might have been a part of those possibilities. My moral compass. Nothing could have dragged me away from those intelligent eyes. From that stubborn, yet kind, heart of hers.

"I really like this song," she whispered.

"Me too."

And that's when I leaned down and kissed her. I couldn't stop myself. This woman was pulling me in at every turn.

She kissed me back with a hunger that surprised me. I pulled her closer, and she moaned into my mouth. *God.* I couldn't get enough of the way she tasted. It was as if the world around us had disappeared.

She's everything you ever wanted.

I deepened the kiss, needing more, but then I remembered where we were—on a dance floor in a public place.

I broke apart, gasping for air. When I looked into her eyes, she seemed stunned too.

"Wow," she said, her voice breathless.

"Yeah," I replied, still reeling from the chemistry between us.

The song was almost over, and all I could think about was getting her out of here, taking her straight to my house, to my bed. I'd strip this dress off, and I'd finally get to see every inch of her. I remembered the fantasy I'd had about her when we first met. The two of us in a field of wildflowers. An erotic fairy tale.

"Come on." I took her hand when the song ended.

She followed me as we both pushed our way through the crowd that had started dancing to Queen's "Crazy Little Thing Called Love."

I wasn't even sure where I was going. All I knew was I wanted to be alone with Theo.

Right after we left the dance floor, somebody stopped us. It was a couple she knew. A short, curvaceous blonde and a guy with dark hair and piercing blue eyes.

Theo introduced them to me as Claire and her husband, Philip. I shook each of their hands. They seemed astonished to meet me. And it wasn't because I was the quarterback for the Sentries, but because I was the villain whose house Theo had chained herself to, and who was now mysteriously here as her date.

"Gabe is my plus-one," Theo said to both her friends, as if that explained everything.

Claire nodded and seemed curious while her husband coolly assessed me. The infamous Philip North, who probably had the NFL commissioner's number on speed dial. I was a head taller and probably had fifty pounds on this guy, but I had an uneasy sense that he could handle himself, and it wouldn't be smart to test him.

"We saw you guys *dancing* out there," Claire said to Theo, glancing up at me. She seemed to be trying to figure me out, just like her husband.

I wondered if they saw us kissing.

This is nuts. Theo and I are adults who can do whatever we want.

"It was never mentioned that you had replaced your date," Philip spoke up. He turned to his wife for confirmation.

Fuck.

It figured that I'd run into the one guy here who could not only get me thrown out of this event but also wreck my career as the cherry on top. I hoped Theo didn't think it would be a funny story to tell these friends of hers that I crashed the wedding reception.

"Well, I wasn't sure if he'd be able to make it," Theo said, to my relief. "That's why I never said anything."

"We're in the middle of training camp right now," I explained. "But luckily, I was able to leave for a day."

"You're only here for a day?" Theo turned to me.

I nodded. "Yeah, unfortunately. I have to head back tonight."

She took this in, but I couldn't tell what she was thinking.

"Crazy Little Thing Called Love" ended, and the music stopped altogether as the atmosphere shifted. I glanced around, wondering what was going on.

"I think Josh is going to sing to Leah now," Theo said with excitement.

Philip suggested we all head back to their table.

The small stage was set up, and it wasn't long before the guys from East Echo appeared on it. Joshua Trevant sat down behind the piano. The first song he sang to his bride was one I knew—"Silver Days." A ballad I'd always liked. The next one was written just for her and was simply called "Leah."

"This is so romantic!" Theo said. She and Claire seemed to be in a state of ecstasy while watching their best friend get serenaded by her rock star husband.

I did my best to seem interested, even though I didn't know any of these people and wasn't actually supposed to be here.

More musicians appeared on stage to perform after Trevant stepped down and went off somewhere with his new wife.

Throughout all this, Philip North still seemed suspicious of me. The guy had the instincts of a shark. I took a sip from my glass of water and tried to appear harmless, though it wasn't a look I pulled off well. I was used to being the one who was intimidating, not the other way around.

He kept texting on his phone until his wife gave him a stern look, and he stopped. I had to chuckle to myself over that one.

Finally, he leaned toward me to speak. I dreaded what he would say. I hoped he wasn't going to tell me he was contacting security, and they'd be over here soon to toss my ass out. The press would love that.

"So, what are your expectations for the team this coming season?" he asked.

The tension inside me loosened. He wanted to talk football. *Thank God.* "Our team's been working hard during the offseason. I have high expectations for us this year."

"I heard Gomez and Holmes were being pulled from the starting roster."

I nodded. "That's true. They're both still dealing with injuries."

"Do you think it'll interfere with your offensive strategy?"

"I hope not. We have a lot of talented players who are committed and focused. I still expect us to be competitive as hell."

North asked me about a few other teammates, and about some of the strategy changes from last year. I felt myself relax in my chair. *Piece of cake.* I could talk football all night.

THE REST of the event went by in a blur. There were champagne toasts and a cake-cutting ceremony. No garter belt was thrown, but the bride and groom both laughed and smashed cake in each other's faces, which told me they had a sense of humor.

Afterward, they came over to join us at our table, still wiping cake off themselves. Theo introduced me to them as her plus-one, and they seemed as surprised by my presence as Claire and Philip had been.

"We've actually met before," I said, shaking Joshua Trevant's hand. "It was after a game in LA a few years ago."

He nodded. "I remember."

"Congratulations on getting married."

"Thanks." He grinned over at Leah, and it was obvious the guy was totally crazy about his new wife. "It's been quite a ride today."

I shook Leah's hand as well, and while she'd been smiling at everyone else, her demeanor toward me shifted. "I had no idea you were replacing Clement. I hope you're an upgrade."

I chuckled, not sure how to respond to that.

"Theo is one of my best friends," she continued. "I suggest you treat her well or be prepared for a shitstorm like you've never experienced in your life."

I blinked with surprise at her warning. *Who the hell is this woman?* I glanced at Trevant with concern. Did he know who he'd married? She was kind of freaking me out.

Everyone at the table sat and talked in the comfortable way that people who are good friends do. I smiled and tried to fit in, but I felt like the annoying new kid no one wanted around.

Eventually, the happy couple announced they were headed out. But first Leah needed to throw her wedding bouquet. A crowd of women gathered behind her as she tossed it over her head.

And guess who caught it? Yep. Theo.

Except she didn't want it. She acted like it was a basket of snakes. I watched with amusement as she tried to get rid of it, handing it off to other women, but they shook their heads and said she caught it fair and square.

Everyone blew bubbles in the air as Leah and Josh finally drove off in a limousine. They were off to honeymoon in Fiji, which I had to admit didn't sound bad.

Despite the married couple leaving the reception, it was barely four o'clock, and the party seemed to be going as strong as ever. As Theo and I walked over to our table, she slipped her hand into mine. The contact sent a jolt down my spine.

"You know, we can leave and do something else," she said.

I turned to her in surprise. "What do you mean?"

"I mean, we don't have to stick around now that Leah and Josh have gone. We could go somewhere more private." She bit her lip, drawing my eyes to that mouth.

I felt my pulse kick up as the implication of her words sank in. "Do you have somewhere particular in mind?"

She considered me for a long moment, as if she were weighing her options. "As a matter of fact, I do."

CHAPTER EIGHTEEN

~ Theo ~

I went over to let Claire know we were leaving the reception.

Philip was talking to Gabe again. The two of them had gone from silent stares to friendly conversation. And it was all over football.

Ugh.

Why is everybody so crazy about a useless sport?

"So, what's going on between you and Beauty Bardales?" Claire asked, grabbing my hand and pulling me close enough so the men couldn't hear what we were saying. "I saw you guys *kissing* on the dance floor!"

"I'm sort of attracted to him," I admitted. I glanced down at the colorful bridal bouquet in my hand that I wished I hadn't caught.

She grinned. "Well, who wouldn't be? Just look at him. I know he was at your house that day, but I thought you guys were still arch-enemies?"

"Not anymore."

Claire glanced over at the men. "I could see that. He seems really into you."

I tilted my head. "He does? How can you tell?"

"For starters, he can't seem to take his eyes off you."

"Oh, that." I waved my hand. "That doesn't mean anything. He's always staring at me. I think it's my hair." That's the conclusion I'd finally come to. "The color seems to hypnotize him. You see the same behavior with insects who are drawn to certain colors. For instance, mosquitos are drawn to red, orange, black, and cyan."

"It's not your hair. It's *you*," she said, laughing. "He's not a mosquito."

"You'd be surprised how often human and insect behaviors align. At least that's been my observation."

"I noticed he was quite attentive getting you cake and champagne."

I glanced over at Gabe, still chatting with Philip. I had to admit, it was true what Claire said. He was mindful of me.

She squeezed my hand, her face growing serious. "You just broke up with Clement. I wouldn't want to see you get hurt. Whether it's true or not, Bardales has a reputation for being difficult."

"He went out of his way to come here today for me when he didn't have to." I bit my lip. "I like him." I wanted to tell her about what really happened with Clement and hated myself for lying to her and Leah, but this wasn't the time or place. "I just want to enjoy myself for a change. To move past Clement. Gabe is surprisingly fun to be around."

"Really? You two seem like such opposites. I'm glad you're having fun. Just be careful, too, okay?"

"I will."

I gave Claire a hug, and then Gabe and I left. It was a good thing I had a ride, because I didn't have my car to begin with. Gabe's truck was parked in the large harbor parking lot that had been cordoned off for the reception.

"So, what were you and your friend talking about?" he asked as we walked to his vehicle. "Was she warning you away from me?"

"Basically."

He got his car keys out of his pocket and seemed troubled. "You should probably listen to her."

"Why? Because you have a reputation for being difficult?"

"Is that what she told you?"

I nodded. "I don't mind difficult. I've had people say the same thing about me." Though usually I didn't understand what they were talking about. I liked things done correctly and didn't see why that made me "difficult."

He laughed. "Why am I not surprised?"

We got to his truck, and he opened the passenger door. I climbed up and slid into the seat. The inside of the truck was stuffy and warm and smelled like leather from baking in the sun all day. There was a water bottle in the cupholder and a travel bag in the back seat.

I held the bridal bouquet along with a small purse in my lap. I didn't normally carry a purse, preferring a backpack, but it didn't exactly go with my dress.

Gabe got into the driver's seat.

"Where are we headed?" he asked. He'd taken off his suit jacket before getting in the truck and put it in the back seat. Now he reached up to loosen his tie and unbutton the top of his shirt to reveal an area of tan skin.

I was mesmerized watching him. His strong hands. The way the shirt hugged his muscular body. It struck me all over again how physically attracted to him I was. This animal lust business was more powerful than I ever gave it credit for, and I suddenly understood why so many people fell under its spell.

"My house," I said.

There must have been something in my voice, because he turned to me. His eyes held mine. Something electric passed between us.

Without another word, Gabe started the truck, backed up, and then drove us out of the parking area. I watched all the reporter and press vans lining the streets with fascination. So many people, and all because of Leah's wedding to Josh.

"What are you thinking about?" he asked as we headed out of town.

"I was thinking about how I don't really follow pop culture. As a result, I don't often know who famous people are."

He nodded. "Yeah, I noticed that about you. I kind of like it. Nobody impresses you."

We stopped at a light, and a pack of summer tourists crossed the street in front of us. "That isn't true. There are people who impress me." I put my hand up to my chest. "There are a few eminent bee scientists who I'd just *die* if I ever met them."

"I guess everyone has their own idea of what's impressive. I've been lucky enough to meet some of my football heroes and definitely felt nervous."

I glanced at him. "I had no idea *you* were so well known when you first bought the land next door. Do you enjoy being famous?"

Gabe shrugged. "Sometimes it can be useful. I don't like being under a microscope or having to watch what I do or say. I can be too blunt, and it's gotten me into trouble."

He told me some more about the pitfalls of fame and how it suited some personality types better than others. He also told me something surprising, that his "Beauty" nickname didn't come from his appearance.

"It doesn't?" I turned to watch his handsome profile. He sure looked like a Beauty.

"Everyone always makes that assumption, but it came from my second year of playing college ball. One of the coaches commented in the locker room after practice that the way I threw a football was a thing of beauty. Some of the guys started teasing me and calling me Beauty, and it just sort of stuck."

We pulled up to my house, and Gabe parked his truck in the driveway next to my Jeep.

"Except you are quite beautiful," I said to him.

"Thanks." He turned, shifting his large body in the seat to face me. "This isn't going to work between us if I can't be myself with you, Theo."

I blinked in surprise. "What do you mean? Of course you can be yourself."

"Really? Because I think you're beautiful."

I turned my head away. "Don't do that."

"You may not believe me, but it's the truth."

"I've seen all the women who—"

"Stop it." His voice was firm. "I don't know what's happened to you. It sounds like you haven't been with enough men who have appreciated you though."

I fingered the bridal bouquet in my hand. I'd already decided I was going to tuck it in the back of my junk closet since it would probably hurt Leah's feelings if I threw it away.

"This isn't some fetish thing, is it?" I asked. "Like, you're not into tall women who'll dominate you?"

"Uh, *no.*" But then he got a disturbed expression. "Why? Have you had to deal with that?"

"Let's just say I've encountered it. I mean, it's fine if that's your thing. But I'm not interested."

His mouth kicked up at the corner. "If I wanted a woman to dominate me, she'd need to be a lot bigger than you."

"True."

He went quiet. The late afternoon sunlight came through the windshield. "What are we doing here, Theo? Tell me what you want."

I let my gaze drift over him. I'd never had sex with someone I wasn't in a relationship with. It would never even have occurred to me in the past. I thought about the way he showed up for me today. I hadn't experienced that with a lot of men. The showing up part. I remembered how he'd taken care of me at his house when I cried. That night had ended all wrong, but I enjoyed being with him. He still made me feel seen.

"I want to share something special with you," I said.

"Okay." He licked his lips. "But I should tell you first that I have to leave by ten tonight. I have a plane to catch back to Seattle."

"I understand. You'll still make your flight." I opened the passenger door of the truck and climbed down, bringing my purse and the bouquet.

Gabe followed me up my porch steps. He watched as I got out the key to my front door. We both entered the house, and he tried to reach for me, but I slipped out of his grasp.

"I'm just going to take these heels off," I said in a breezy voice. "It'll only be a second. You can wait for me in the living room."

He seemed perplexed but stayed in the living room while I brought my purse and bouquet into the bedroom with me. I kicked off my shoes and went into my master bathroom to search for the box of condoms I'd bought back when Clement and I started dating. Eventually, I had an IUD put in, so we didn't need them, but I still had the box. I finally found it under the sink and pulled one out.

When I stood up, I caught a glimpse of myself in the mirror.

Are you really doing this?

I studied my reflection, searching for some obvious change. I'd never known I was capable of experiencing animal lust. Not like this. Not without any intellectual compatibility. I mean, for God's sake, this guy was a football player!

If I didn't know myself, I'd think I'd lost my mind.

I left the bathroom and found my backpack, tucking the condom inside, then wondered if I should change out of my dress. The silky fabric tied behind my neck and then swept over my breasts to cinch at my waist. It was long and flowing with a slit up one leg—not really appropriate for where we were going. But then I remembered the admiring way Gabe kept looking at me in it.

The dress stays.

My sneakers were by my bed, so I sat and put them on. When I was finally ready, I joined Gabe in the living room, where he was perusing my bookshelf.

"Do you enjoy reading?" I asked.

"You have a lot of books about bees," he said, tilting his head to read one of the titles. "*The Mind of a Bee?* Do bees really have minds?"

I pulled sunblock out of my backpack and began lathering it over my arms and shoulders, avoiding the dress's fabric. "Of course they do. Bees are sentient and likely have a rudimentary consciousness. They feel pain. They dream. They solve problems. Bees can count up to four and understand the concept of zero."

He stopped reading my bookshelf. "You're kidding."

"I'm not. They play and have been trained to use tools. They also recognize human faces."

"That's amazing." He watched me with the sunblock and then glanced down at my sneakers. "Are we going someplace?"

I nodded. "I told you I want to share something special with you."

"You did say that," he murmured. "Though I think I might have gotten the wrong impression of what you meant."

When I was finished with the sunblock, I put it away, then I noticed his footwear. "Maybe we should go by your house and get you some sneakers too. I should have thought of that before coming here."

He considered his dress shoes. "Actually, I have a pair in my bag in the truck."

"You do?"

"I take it you want me to put them on?"

I picked up my backpack. "It would be for the best."

We left my house, and I followed him down to his vehicle, waiting while he sat in the back seat and changed shoes. "So what's the big mystery here, Professor? You got to tell me what's going on."

"It's not something I can explain adequately with words."

Once he was done, I motioned for him to follow me. I led him down to my lower backyard.

"Are we visiting your bees again?" he asked. "Because I'm sure you'd like to tell them how you're rethinking all your uncharitable opinions about football players."

I smiled. "Sorry, we're not visiting my bees."

I could tell I had him puzzled and was enjoying it immensely.

We continued walking. Past my beekeeping shed, past my hives. It was late afternoon, so many of my bees would still be out foraging.

I walked up to the gate in back that had been decorated with a Celtic design by some previous owner. In my mind, I'd almost given it a mystical significance. Though, of course, that wasn't possible.

"Where are you taking me?" he asked, eyeing the design on the gate.

"You'll see."

I swung it open and reached for Gabe's hand, and then I led him toward someplace extraordinary.

CHAPTER NINETEEN

~ Gabe ~

"What is this place?" I asked in amazement. We'd been walking through the woods for about fifteen minutes before Theo led me out to a large grassy field filled with wildflowers. I could barely believe my eyes when I saw it. It felt like I was hallucinating.

"It's my secret meadow."

I followed her over to a part that she'd obviously set up for herself. There was a brown plastic Adirondack chair with blue blankets stacked on top and what looked to be a small cooler and a lantern beside it.

She pulled both blankets off the chair, and I went over to help her spread them on the grass. "You need to layer them," she said. "Otherwise, the grass pokes through too much and it makes it hard to get comfortable." She motioned toward the cooler. "I refresh that every few days. There are water bottles and some other snacks in there if you want anything."

I nodded, still in a daze, glancing around at this place that I'd seen in my mind when I first met her. *How is this possible?*

"Is everything okay?" she asked, shielding her eyes from the sun. She'd gone over and sat down on the blankets.

I didn't know what to say. I'd never experienced anything like this in my life.

"You look kind of pale. Do you need some water?"

I took a deep breath. "I'm fine. This place is amazing." I went over to join her on the blankets. She'd kicked off her shoes, so I did the same. "How did you find it?"

"I sort of stumbled upon it."

She shifted around on the blanket to get comfortable. "Maybe I should have changed out of this dress. I hope I don't ruin it. Thank God I put on sunblock."

"I'm glad you didn't change. It looks great on you."

Our eyes met, and she smiled shyly before turning away. "Now you've had the visual experience of this meadow, but there's more."

"There is?"

"First you have to lie down on the blanket with me."

I grinned. "I think I know where this is going, and I approve."

She laughed lightly and then positioned herself, smoothing her dress out so she could lie on her back. I let my eyes drift over her long, slender body, over the curve at her breasts and waist, enjoying myself.

"What are you waiting for?" she asked, patting the blanket.

And so I lay down flat on my back next to her, both of us gazing up at the infinite sky. Blue and cloudless. I couldn't remember the last time I'd really looked at the sky, even though I was outside all the time.

"Now close your eyes. Just take in everything around you."

I did as she asked, closing my eyes and letting myself experience it. Her meadow of wildflowers. And it was different with my eyes closed. Surprisingly rich. I smelled the surrounding greenery mixed with something earthy. A warm breeze blew past, and the sound of grass swayed nearby. Birds chirped and insects buzzed. There was a chorus of sounds, and I couldn't identify them all.

A feeling of comfort and relaxation came over me. All my usual stresses seemed far away.

As we lay there, I became aware of something else. Of Theo beside me. I reached over to take her hand, lacing our fingers together, both of us immersed in this experience.

Days like this didn't come along often in my life, and an instinct told me I'd remember this one for a long time.

Eventually, I opened my eyes, and all the colors came back into sharp focus. "What made you bring me here?" I asked, curious, still feeling relaxed.

"I thought you'd appreciate this place, and I wanted to share it with you."

"Thank you."

"You're the only person I've ever brought here."

"Really?" I watched a bird fly overhead. A large one, probably a hawk or an eagle. I turned my head to look at her. "I want to tell you something that's going to sound strange. But I swear it's true."

"What?"

I watched that bird again. "I've seen this place before. When I first met you, I had a vision of you in a field of wildflowers. It was *this* meadow."

"What do you mean?" She pulled her hand from mine and sat up. "You were spying on me?"

I shook my head. "Not at all. I had a vision in my *mind* where I saw you here." I wondered if I should tell her she was naked in that vision. Probably not. The whole thing was weird enough already.

She considered me. "You're right. That is strange. Do you have visions often?"

"You don't believe me?"

"I'm not saying that. I'm just wondering how often you have these visions."

I closed my eyes again for a moment. "I've never had one. That was the first."

"What do you think it means? It must mean something."

I tucked my arm under my head so I could see her better as we contemplated each other. "I'm not sure."

"Perhaps you had a mystical experience. Even though I don't believe in that sort of thing. This place sometimes feels mystical." Theo gazed out at the tall grass and the flowers everywhere. "It's become my haven."

She was so beautiful. I couldn't pull my eyes away. So natural, everything about her as vivid as the surrounding colors.

"Come here," I said softly.

She shifted her attention to me. And by the expression on her face, I could tell she knew what I wanted.

There wasn't any hesitation at all when she lay down beside me again. I rolled on my side to face her and then gently pushed her onto her back.

"Most likely it's a coincidence," she said, still analyzing. "I must have mentioned it to you without realizing it. That's the only explanation that makes sense."

I could tell she was nervous. She still had her glasses on and fell silent when I reached up and took them off, placing them on the blanket above our heads.

We gazed at each other. Her eyes were as green as the wild grass. She began to say something else, but I brought my mouth down to hers, absorbing her words. I felt her hand move up to stroke my jaw. Just like on the dance floor, she kissed me back with passion. She tasted so good. So right. Like possibilities long closed for me were now opening again, like the rusty padlock on that door might be removed.

My blood grew hot, already rushing to parts of me, and I told myself to slow down. Because I shouldn't be here. I shouldn't be allowing any of this.

I just wanted to kiss her for a little while in this amazing place.

I slid my hands down her body, enjoying her soft curves. Theo's fingers grasped my hair and then the back of my neck, pulling me closer as our mouths tangled.

I rolled on top of her, pressing her into the blanket, and she moaned. That little moan did all sorts of things to me. One of her legs wrapped around my hip, and my dick strained against my zipper. All I could think about was how much I wanted to bury myself inside her, how good that would be for us both.

This is nuts. I should stop before things go too far.

My conscience was at war with my libido.

I tried to kiss her neck but couldn't get to it. "How does this dress come off?" I asked.

"It ties behind my neck, and there's also a zipper."

"Why are women's clothes so complicated?"

She smiled and reached behind her neck. "I can help."

And it was that beautiful smile of hers that finally did me in, forced me to acknowledge the truth. I pulled away from her and sat up, running a hand through my hair as I tried to collect myself.

"Jesus, I'm sorry," I said. "I shouldn't be doing this with you."

Her brows came together. "What do you mean?"

"You just had your heart broken by that idiot. It wouldn't be right for me to take advantage of the situation."

"You're not taking advantage. I like you."

I shook my head. "Theo, you don't want to get involved with me. I've got more skeletons in my closet than a Halloween warehouse."

She sat up beside me. "What does that mean? Besides, I don't care. I want this to happen. I'm very... attracted to you."

"You don't know what you're saying. How can you be attracted to me when you don't even respect me?"

"That's not true. I respect you."

I chuckled. "You think what I do for a living is worthless. Admit it."

She squirmed and bit her lip. "It's true. I'm not a football fan, but I respect you as an individual. I can tell you're a good person."

"Except I'm not a good person." I rubbed my brow. "You don't know me very well. Trust me, I'm an asshole."

She shook her head. "I used to think you were an asshole, but now that I've gotten to know you better, it's the opposite."

I brushed my hand along her cheek and then down to her neck and shoulders, unable to resist touching her. "I don't deserve someone like you. I wish I did."

"Of course you do."

"I have so many things in my life to atone for. I don't want you to be one of them."

She didn't reply and instead reached behind her neck, fiddling with the back of her dress. Before I knew it, she'd untied the top part, letting it drop to reveal a white strapless bra.

"What are you doing? Haven't you heard a word I'm saying?"

Despite the words coming out of my mouth, my hard-on went into the red zone. I couldn't take my eyes away from all that smooth pale skin. Those freckles sprinkled everywhere.

"We shouldn't do this," I muttered, but she was already moving closer. I let her straddle my lap, her sweet scent surrounding me.

"It's just animal lust," she whispered in my ear. "That's all. Don't you deserve that?"

I slid my hand down to her waist, to her hips, squeezing them, pulling her tighter on my lap so she could feel my cock, how hard I was. "So I'm just a body to you, is that it?"

Her eyelids fluttered as we pushed against each other. "Exactly."

But it was a lie. She may have even convinced herself. But with a woman like Theo, on some level, this was going to matter.

"Take my bra off," she said, resting her arms on my shoulders. "Just do it."

I smiled a little. "What did you say before about domineering women?"

"I'm assertive when the situation calls for it."

God, she's something else.

I reached up to her bra and unhooked it. My heart began to

hammer, and my pulse pounded in my ears. Her breasts were small and perfect, with rosy pink nipples.

And then it was like something snapped in me. Took over. Guess it was that animal lust she was talking about. I lifted her onto her knees so I could have access to those breasts, licking and suckling each one while Theo moaned and held me to her.

I brought her down onto my lap again, and we rocked against each other, both of us breathing hard. My dick throbbed. Her fingers went to my shirt, unbuttoning each button until it was open and we were finally pressed skin to skin. And even as I continued to tell myself we shouldn't be doing this, my hands were already trying to find their way under the fabric of her dress.

"I have something," she said. "Let me get it."

"Get what?"

To my dismay, she got up and walked over to her backpack on the chair. I glanced down at my erection pushing against the zipper of my slacks.

When Theo returned, straddling me again, she held up a shiny square foil packet.

My brows rose. "You brought a condom?"

She nodded and smiled, dangling it in the air like it was bait on the end of a fishing line. "I like to plan ahead."

I was a planner myself, but she'd out-planned even me.

We began kissing again and grinding against each other.

I closed my eyes. Theo wanted it. I wanted it. My cock definitely wanted it.

Sorry, conscience. You've been outvoted.

"Are you sure about this?" I asked.

"Of course." She bit my lower lip, lightly tugging on it. "I'm very sure."

My hands were still trying to work their way under all that fabric. Finally, I found her thighs, so soft. And then her panties. My fingers snaked beneath the elastic. She was hot and wet and softer than anything I'd ever felt.

I swallowed, my breath ragged. Theo moaned as I lightly circled her clit.

Jesus, this is too much. Her panties had to go.

"Stand up," I instructed. "Let's take these off you." Because now that I'd decided to ignore my conscience, I was all in. She did as I asked, and I slid her underwear off. White lace panties. "Now the dress."

"It unzips in the back," she said, turning around, and I slid the zipper down.

It fell off her, gathered in a pile around her feet, and like Venus on a half shell, she stepped out of it.

And there she was. Just like my vision.

My mouth went dry.

"Look at you," I murmured. My hands reached out of their own volition, and I slid them down her body, over those long legs. She was a goddess. "Damn, you're stunning."

Theo seemed to accept the compliment, though she also brought her dress over to the chair. I enjoyed watching her, but at the same time, she was out of reach.

"Just leave it," I said. "Come back here."

She walked that short distance toward me.

Fuck.

When she was close enough, I pulled her down, and we began making out again. It was different. Hotter. Neither of us holding back anything.

Before long she was tugging on my zipper, still straddling me. "I think this thing is stuck or something."

"Let me do it," I said, trying to catch my breath.

She lifted, and I unzipped my pants, shoving them off along with my boxers. My cock sprang free, and we both stared at it like a surprise guest to a dinner party.

"Where's that condom?" I asked, my voice deep to my own ears.

She still had it in her hand and opened the pack to pull it out. Bright yellow. "I want to put it on you."

"Why?"

"I just do."

I closed my eyes and tried to breathe. *This woman is going to be the death of me.* "All right, fine."

I leaned back on one hand and kept my other on her leg while gazing at her body. Soon I felt her warm fingers grab hold of me, and I sucked in my breath. She stroked my length and then squeezed the head. I closed my eyes and gave in to the sensation. It felt good. But then she kept stroking and squeezing.

I grabbed her hand. "This party is going to be over before it begins."

"I was just curious. Your penis appears to be larger than Clement's."

"Is this a science project or animal lust?"

Her eyes widened. "Oh, definitely the latter."

I smiled. "Then let's get to the lust part."

She got a determined expression on her face and went back to it. This time, I watched as she finally rolled the condom down my length. It was a tight fit. She wasn't kidding about Clement's insect-sized dick.

I helped her position herself over me and began to sweat. I wanted her so badly, my hands were shaking. If this was animal lust, it was a kind I'd never experienced before. My whole body grew tense with need as she slowly sank down onto me.

CHAPTER TWENTY

~ Theo ~

I gasped as our bodies joined together. This was already the best sex I'd ever had in my life, and we'd barely just started. Gabe's cheeks were flushed, and he looked so handsome even now in the midst of our coupling.

We began to move, and I kept wanting more. My whole body felt alive with sensation.

"Your penis feels extraordinary," I said, trying to catch my breath.

He was breathing hard, too, but chuckled. "I'm glad you think so." His eyes went to my mouth. "Say the word 'cock.'"

"Cock?" But then I understood. "Your cock feels extraordinary."

"Yeah... that's it." He smiled, grabbing my ass as we continued to bring our bodies together. "Now you've got it. You're a quick study, Professor."

It was true. I was a quick study.

"Your pussy feels good too," he whispered, his hot breath against my neck. "Extraordinary."

My breath shook as I took in the complete experience. Sex with this hulking athlete. I wrapped my arms tighter around his neck as a powerful need grew in me. I wanted things from him. Things I was certain only he could give me.

It was scandalous to be out here naked in the late afternoon sunshine. I'd never done anything remotely like this. In the past, I'd always had sex in a bed under the covers, though once in college, I did it with my lab partner in the back of his car.

We continued to move, and it felt so good. Gabe was telling me things, telling me I was amazing and sexy, that he'd wanted me from the moment we met.

Was that true? I wanted to analyze it, but it would have to wait until later. I was too caught up in the sensations of my own body careening toward a climax.

Finally, my breath caught, and I began to moan, grabbing him, biting his shoulder as I got sucked into a vortex. It was exquisite and went on and on.

"Hold on to me," Gabe growled. And then, to my amazement, he lifted us both and brought me down onto my back.

I was still wrapped around him as the sex changed. His thrusts grew powerful, seeking his own release. It felt feral and wild. And I loved every second.

"Kiss me," he demanded, and our mouths crashed together with tongues and teeth.

The whole world seemed to have shifted. Down was up, black was white, and it turned out I was someone who enjoyed hot, animalistic sex. *Who knew?*

Gabe's breath was shaking as his movements grew more urgent. It was exciting—exciting enough that I felt myself sucked into another vortex. This second climax was so intense I yelled. I wasn't even sure what I was yelling. He gave a final powerful thrust and then groaned.

His movements slowed, and we held each other before coming back to ourselves.

I thought he would roll off of me right away, since that's what Clement always did, but Gabe stayed. He kissed my mouth and then showered my neck with kisses. And then he gazed into my eyes, both of us still trying to catch our breaths.

"What did you say when you came the second time?" he asked. "It sounded like 'Release the dogs.'"

"Why would I say that?"

"I don't know."

I tried to remember what I said. I didn't normally yell out in the throes of passion.

He eased himself out of me, and then his warmth and weight were gone as he collapsed onto his back. Sweat was already cooling on us both. "Jesus, that was intense." He swung his arm out in a grand gesture. "Release the dogs!"

I laughed. "I did *not* say that."

"You sure did." He turned to gaze at me and looked so handsome that my breath caught and my insides turned loopy. "It turns out I was right about you."

"Right about me how?"

He nodded, smiling at me like he knew a secret. "Hot and passionate. That's exactly how I predicted you'd be."

"You thought of me like that?"

He lifted his head briefly to strip the used condom off and put it on the grass next to us. "Of course I did. It's one of the reasons you annoyed me so much. Because I was attracted to you."

I was stunned. I shouldn't have been—he *was* here having animalistic sex with me—but I was surprised that he'd felt that way about me when were still enemies.

Rolling on my side to face him, I studied his perfect profile. He'd closed his eyes and seemed very relaxed.

I remembered the day I first met him in person. "What ever happened to your men's cologne? Did you finally pick out a bottle?"

He shook his head. "Nah. I've tabled the whole thing. I'm not sure if a cologne really goes with my brand."

"Your brand?"

"Mmm." He had one arm tucked beneath his head and opened his eyes, motioning to me. "Come here. Put your head on my shoulder."

I did as he requested and tucked myself against his side with one leg draped over him.

We were both quiet, and I closed my eyes, too, listening to the peaceful sounds of the early evening. Gabe was warm and solid. My mind drifted, and I began to reflect over the experience I'd just had. I thought I knew myself pretty well, but it turned out there was always more to learn. That was the great adventure of life. I also thought about the things Gabe had said earlier.

"Why do you think you're an asshole?" I asked, curious. "Tell me the reason."

He tensed beneath me, and then I heard him sigh. "Don't analyze everything, Theo. Just leave it."

"I can't help it. I analyze data for a living."

"So do I."

"You do?"

He snorted. "Do you know how much game film I watch? I'm constantly analyzing our opponents' strengths and weaknesses, not to mention our own."

This was something I didn't know.

I lifted my head so I could rest it on my hand, facing him. "So, what are the things you have to atone for? Is that why you came to my house in the middle of the night before? You seemed upset."

He chuckled. "Damn, you're stubborn. I have trouble sleeping. That's what you saw that night. Just me and my insomnia."

"I don't believe you. There's more."

He turned to face me. "Maybe there is more. But let's not spoil this amazing time here by talking about it."

I reached out to stroke his jaw and realized he was right. This time had been amazing. I didn't want to spoil it. "I'm glad I brought you here."

He grinned. "Me too." When I smiled back, his eyes dropped to my mouth. "You have such an incredible smile."

"Thank you. I've always been self-conscious about the gap between my front teeth. I've thought about fixing it but never seem to get around to it."

He seemed disturbed by this news. "Don't change that gap. It's sexy."

"Really?" I wasn't sure if I would have believed him if he didn't seem so sincere.

His eyes dropped lower to my naked body. "Everything about you is sexy."

I opened my mouth but didn't know what to say.

As if to confirm it, he took my hand and led it down to his penis— er... cock, which was growing stiff.

"You're hard again," I said with surprise.

He smirked. "That's because we're only at halftime. There are two more quarters, and I'm pretty sure this game is going into overtime."

"Is that a football reference?"

He wore a satisfied grin. "It is. Your first lesson. I hope you're paying attention."

Before I knew it, he'd flipped me onto my back and was lying over me. I yelped with laughter. My animal lust was pleased, but my still-functioning brain reminded me of something. "I don't have any more condoms."

He was kissing my neck but stopped. "You only brought one condom?"

"It never occurred to me to bring more. Clement and I never had sex more than once in a row."

"Really?" He seemed stunned by this information.

I nodded.

He shook his head and grinned. "It doesn't matter. There are a lot of other things we can do."

I smiled back, wondering what he had in mind, but then I heard a strange sound in the distance. A sound I'd never heard before in my meadow.

Voices.

I froze. "Did you hear that?" I whispered in alarm. "There's someone here!"

Gabe went still. We both listened, but everything was silent again.

He spoke quietly. "Have you ever seen anyone else while you were out here?"

I shook my head. "Never."

Luckily, we were surrounded by tall grass, but our invisibility also meant we couldn't see who was out there.

Gabe lifted himself off of me and reached for his boxer shorts and pants, pulling them both on as he kept low.

I did the same with my bra and panties. "I need my dress," I said, feeling vulnerable being out here mostly naked.

He scooted over on the blanket, and his reach was long enough that he grabbed it for me.

"Who on earth could be out here?" I said, slipping the dress over my head. I tied the front portion behind my neck as Gabe went on his knees, searching over the grass.

"I don't see anyone."

"We definitely heard them."

He was still searching, standing up now as he buttoned his shirt. "Who owns this land? I take it that it's not yours?"

"It belongs to two brothers who inherited it from their dad." I told him what I'd learned about the property. How the brothers didn't live in Truth Harbor and had put the land up for sale.

"How much land is it?"

I adjusted my dress and then stood up, letting Gabe zip the back for me. "Fifty acres. It's worth a fortune. It's been listed for sale for a long time."

"So we're trespassing on private property?"

"Pretty much. I wonder who it was that we heard." I gazed out at the meadow. He was right. There was no one else here.

"Probably just hikers. Didn't you tell me there was a state forest east of here?"

I nodded, though I felt worry in the pit of my stomach.

"What is it?" He was looking at me and must have noticed my stricken expression.

"I just hope the brothers haven't found a buyer. What if some developers ruin all this by turning it into houses and condos?"

"There's no reason to think that. It was probably just some people hiking through the woods who got off course."

He glanced around at the fading light. "Come on, we should head back."

We both put our shoes on, and Gabe helped me fold the blankets and put them back on the chair. I handed him a tissue, and he wrapped the used condom in it and stuffed it in his pocket to throw away later. He insisted on carrying my backpack, which seemed silly, but he was trying to be chivalrous, so I let him.

We held hands as we walked back through the woods. He was going to have to leave when we got to my house, and I felt a strange pang. Like I was going to miss him.

I knew what this was. He'd made it clear that he didn't want a relationship, and I didn't want one either.

Except I felt good when I was with him.

Clement felt like a distant memory when I was with Gabe.

When we arrived at the house, it was almost dark. He pulled his phone out, and I could tell he was checking the time. "I'm going to have to go, Theo. My flight leaves soon."

"I know."

"Come here." He pulled me in close and kissed me. "I had an incredible time with you today."

I wrapped my arms around him and rested my head on his shoulder. "Thank you for crashing Leah's wedding reception. No one's ever done anything like that for me before."

He stroked my back. "Anytime. I'll be happy to crash future wedding receptions. Just let me know."

I smiled. "And then I'll always have a dance partner."

"Always."

I pulled away from him, wishing he didn't have to leave. I wanted him to stay. "Take care of yourself, Gabe."

"You, too, Theo."

And then I watched as this football player, who couldn't be more different from me, got into his truck and drove off into the night.

CHAPTER TWENTY-ONE

~ Gabe ~

It was nearly midnight when I reached the hotel where the team stayed every year for training camp. I knew I wouldn't see any of the guys in the lobby or bar this late. In fact, I shouldn't have been out here this late either, but it couldn't be helped tonight. This was way past my bedtime.

I had to be up by six tomorrow morning, breakfast at seven, workout with weights at eight, and then a team meeting at nine. It was a lighter day because we had a preseason game tomorrow night against Arizona. As a starter, I'd be on the sidelines. What all this meant was I was only getting six hours of sleep. It was worth it though. The whole day with Theo, all of it had been worth it.

I'd barely gotten inside my room and kicked my shoes off when my phone buzzed. I felt a jolt of excitement, wondering if it might be her. She had my phone number, after all, though she'd never called me.

Except it wasn't Theo. It was Davis. He must have seen a copy of my flight itinerary and knew when I'd arrived in Seattle.

"How did it go?" he asked. "I take it you had no trouble crashing the wedding reception?"

I sat on the bed and pulled my socks off. "None whatsoever. Though the security was tighter than I expected."

"Where are you now?"

"I just got back to the hotel and can't talk long. I gotta hit the sack."

"So how was it? Who was there? Did you meet anybody I should know about?"

It figured that he'd want details. Davis liked to be in the know about everything and was always examining every angle. "To be honest, I didn't pay much attention to the guest list. That's not why I was up there."

I heard him chuckle. "So how was it with the bee biologist? Did you take her to pound town?"

Anger flashed through me. "Her name's *Theo*. And if you want to live to see another sunrise, I suggest you don't speak about her like that ever again."

"Jesus, don't get your knickers in a twist. I assume you had a good time. What exactly is going on between you two? Were you just helping her out of a jam or what?"

I went over to the end of the bed and opened my bag to get my toiletry kit. I needed a shower, but it was late and would have to wait until morning. "Look, I gotta go, Davis."

"So I hired Franklin to dig up some dirt on this guy Miranda's seeing. You'll never believe what she found out about him."

I paused, curious. "What did she find?"

He let his breath out. "Not a fucking thing! Can you believe it? Which, if you ask me, is suspicious as hell."

I laughed and shook my head. "You're crazy. You should be glad she didn't find anything." I dug around for a clean T-shirt and boxers to wear to bed—Bardales Jock Style, of course.

"I mean, who doesn't have *something* in their past? The only thing she could find were some unpaid parking tickets. It doesn't make sense."

I continued to shake my head. "Give it a rest, seriously. You need to get over this obsession."

"It's not an obsession. I'm just looking out for Miranda and Petey's welfare."

"I don't know why you two don't just get back together. She calls you ten times a day as it is."

"Because she wants me to cut back on my hours. How can I do that? She told me I'm only allowed to carry one phone. *One!*" Believe it or not, Davis had three phones. Though, to be fair, one of them was just for Miranda. It was supposed to be his personal line, but she's the only one who ever called him on it. Even I never called him on that number.

"Maybe you should listen to her. I only have one phone."

"Yeah, well, it's not like you're taking multiple calls in the middle of practice or a game, are you?"

He had me there. I grabbed my stuff to head into the bathroom. "I gotta get some sleep."

"That guy's hiding something," Davis said. "I'm sure of it. I'm going to get to the bottom of it."

"I'm hanging up now."

He was still talking when I ended the call. I couldn't help chuckling to myself. Davis was a lunatic, but he was also loyal as hell, and I never doubted he had my back. I couldn't say that about many people in my life.

As I brushed my teeth and did my usual routine getting ready for bed, I thought about Theo. I'd thought about her on the flight, and then I thought about her some more on the drive back from the airport. I may have accused Davis of having an obsession, but I was obsessing myself.

When I got into bed, I could sense my demons were far away.

Whatever mystical effect Theo had on me seemed to be holding strong.

The last thing I thought of before I fell asleep was Theo in her flower-filled meadow, and I was lying right beside her.

———

"Are you coming by the house after the game?" Regina asked on the phone. "Tess already made up the guest bedroom for you."

"Yeah, I'll be there." Preseason ended two weeks ago, and our first game of the season was in Los Angeles this Sunday. I always stayed the night with my sister when we played in LA.

"I told Mateo you were coming. I think he might drop by."

We talked for a little longer, but since I'd be seeing her soon enough, I figured we'd catch up more in person.

It had been over three weeks since Theo and I spent that incredible day together, but we hadn't spoken since. I hadn't been up to Truth Harbor at all. My schedule wouldn't allow it.

I wondered how she was doing. I'd even thought about calling or texting her, but I knew that was opening the door to something. A door I'd probably have trouble closing, since I was already having trouble with it.

The truth was I thought about her all the time, reliving that day in my mind. I even looked her up online. I found her academic page at the university, her picture and the list of classes she taught and the various papers she'd published.

I stared at that picture of her way too much. She was standing outside some place I didn't recognize with a bunch of those square beehives behind her. That wild red hair and that incredible smile.

I'd even read about bees online, curious to understand why she was so captivated by them.

I still remembered that I told her I'd teach her about football.

And I was still carrying that jar of honey with me everywhere.

So, yeah.

I might have been worried about Theo getting involved with me, but it turned out, I should have been worried for myself.

CHAPTER TWENTY-TWO

~ Theo ~

"I still have it," I told Leah after she asked me about her bridal bouquet. Of course, I didn't mention that it was in the back of my junk closet.

It was Sunday, and Leah, Claire, and I were having breakfast together at Bijou's. Isabel was invited, too, though she was running late. Leah got back from her honeymoon a week ago, and we were all meeting to catch up on things.

"You know, I threw that toward you on purpose," Leah said. "But later I realized that was probably really dumb. I'm sorry."

"Why would you think it was dumb?" I asked, picking up my glass of orange juice.

"Well, you know... because you and Clement broke up. And then you were there with Beauty Bardales, so the whole thing was weird."

Claire leaned over to grab the pepper shaker for her eggs. "What-ever happened with Bardales? I know you told me he offered to be your plus-one as a sort of apology for everything that happened between you guys, but are you still seeing him?"

I shook my head and tried to keep my voice light. "That was just a one-time thing."

"You left the reception with him," Claire said. "Where did you guys go?"

"He took me home."

Leah tilted her head. "I'm still wrapping my brain around the fact that you were there with him at all. He seemed like a step down from Clement. I mean, at least Clement never tried to sue you."

I shifted uncomfortably in my chair, still not having told them the truth about what happened with Clement. I couldn't believe I'd let it go this long. Finally, I took a deep breath. "Clement's not so innocent."

"What do you mean?" Leah picked up her coffee mug.

Claire glanced up from her plate. "Did something happen?"

And so I told them the whole story about Clement breaking up with me, how he wanted to explore new relationships, but it turned out he'd already had a relationship in mind with his research assistant, Kendra.

They both looked shocked.

"I can't believe it," Claire said. "Do you think he was cheating with her?"

"I don't know. I certainly hope not. But he obviously didn't want to tell me about her."

"That sucks," Leah said. "I wish you'd told us. We could have been more supportive."

"I'm sorry I wasn't honest. I've felt terrible about it. It was just so humiliating, and then you guys had all these happy things going on, and I didn't want to bring you down."

Claire shook her head. "I should have known something was up. You seemed unnaturally calm about the whole thing. Next time tell us."

"We've all gone through stuff," Leah said. "We'd never judge you. And it wouldn't bring me down to be supportive."

I nodded. "I know. I should have told you both from the start."

"How are you doing now?" Claire asked. "Are you still upset about it?"

I shrugged. "I'm doing okay. Something else happened that's sort of helped me moved past it."

"And what's that?" Leah asked, buttering a slice of toast.

"I slept with Gabe."

"Gabe? Who's that?" Leah stopped buttering and appeared mystified while Claire nearly spat out her coffee.

"Oh my God!" Claire laughed. "I should have guessed the way you guys were going at it on the dance floor!"

Leah was flashing looks between the two of us. "What did I miss here? Going at it? Who was going at it?"

Claire motioned to me. "Theo and Beauty Bardales. They were kissing at your wedding reception."

Leah's eyes widened. "Oh, *wow*. Gabe is Gabriel Bardales? Holy shit! You slept with him?"

I glanced around the restaurant, glad it was noisy and busy.

"I did," I said.

They both stared at me with amazed expressions. It felt fun being the one who was scandalous for a change.

"So how was it?" Claire wanted to know. "Reputation aside, he's gorgeous. Philip said he thought he seemed all right, which is actually high praise coming from Philip."

"It was... pleasant," I said, not sure quite how to put into words one of the most astonishing experiences of my life.

"Pleasant?" Leah made a face. "Taking a warm bath is pleasant. I sure hope it was better than that."

"Oh, it *was*." My face warmed. "It was the best sexual experience I've ever had. Quite extraordinary."

Both of them were grinning and practically cheering.

"You have to tell us more," Claire said eagerly. "Are you going to see him again?"

I shook my head. "Like I said, it was a one-time thing. Neither of us wants a relationship. I just got out of one with Clement."

"Wow, so you and Beauty Bardales were getting busy," Leah said with a sly grin. "And to think I gave him a hard time at the reception. Little did I know. That's one way to forget about Mr. Horned Passulus Beetle."

"I agree," Claire said. "So, what's Bardales like? Or I guess I should call him Gabe. I can't picture you guys having anything in common."

"It's true, we're very different." But as soon as I said it, I realized Gabe and I were different, but we were also oddly in sync. "For some reason we get along."

Leah nodded. "I can actually see it. He's known for being stubborn and focused. You're kind of the same way."

I laughed. It was true.

"Well, at least Clement is definitely in the rearview mirror." Claire picked up her mug of coffee. "So that's a good thing."

"That's usually the first step toward getting over someone. Sleeping with someone new," Leah said. "At least for me."

Claire nodded. "I agree. That helps."

I raised my shoulders. "Well, then I guess I've taken my first step into the future."

After breakfast, I went home and picked up around the house. Eliza, Philip's younger sister, was coming over to help me with some graphic art.

While I'd never sold my honey before, I'd decided recently to start selling it to a local health food store. The owners, Doug and Daphne, tasted my honey at Claire's house and approached me about it some months ago. I'd said no at the time but had since changed my mind. I'd always given my honey away for free, but the reality was it was costing me. Even though I accepted donations, I was still in the red. I paid for all the equipment and jars. If I could sell it in their store, I'd still be able to give honey away, but perhaps I could at least break even.

Hence the graphic art for the labels.

Around noon, I heard a car out front and went to open the door. Eliza was pulling up in her silver Prius.

She waved from inside as she parked in the driveway next to my Jeep.

"Theo! It's great to see you," she called out as she strode jauntily toward the house. Tall and lanky, Eliza always appeared to be moving even when she was standing still.

She wasn't anywhere near as tall as I was, but our height was one of the things we'd bonded over silently when we first met.

As was typical, she wore unusual clothing. I wasn't so much into fashion, but even I noticed how Eliza had a unique style. Today she had on a white T-shirt and cropped jeans. The jeans were covered with what appeared to be clip art drawn with magic markers. I wondered if she'd made them herself. Her shoes were patterned flats with a strap across the top. All in all, Eliza was a colorful, ever-moving blur.

She wore her dark hair in a topknot that bounced excitedly along with the rest of her. Large black sunglasses perched just below it.

"Thank you so much for coming by," I said. "I really appreciate your help with this."

"No problem!" She glanced up at the blue sky. "I heard there's supposed to be a storm today."

I glanced up too. I'd heard the same thing, though the weather in Truth Harbor could be unpredictable.

We entered the house, and I brought her over to the dining room table where I had my computer, some jars of honey, and some of my own ideas drawn out on paper. I offered her something to drink, and she accepted a glass of iced tea.

"Are these your sketches?" she asked, sitting at the table and looking them over.

"Sorry, I'm a terrible artist, but I thought I should get something down."

"You're calling it Theo's Honey?" She glanced at me with striking blue eyes. Her brother Philip had a similar eye color.

I nodded. "Not the most original name, but it was all I could think of."

"I like it actually. Your name is kind of unusual."

"I suppose that's true." I picked up my glass of tea and took a sip.

She studied my sketches some more, tilting her head this way and that, staring at my pitiful stick figure drawings.

"Do you think I could see your beehives and take some photos of them? It might help me come up with a concept."

"Of course. We can walk down there right now if you like."

I led her out through my French doors in back and asked how things were going with her acting career as we walked down the slope.

"It's been busy," she said. "I was an extra on a TV show that filmed in Seattle recently, and I just auditioned for a play up here in Truth Harbor."

She was commuting between both places regularly. She had an apartment in Seattle, then either stayed with her mom or Philip and Claire when she came here.

I couldn't imagine being an actress, but it suited Eliza. Only in her midtwenties, she was quite pretty and seemed glamorous and artsy.

As we approached my hives, she pulled her phone out and began taking lots of photos. I told her we could put suits on and get much closer if she wanted.

I showed her the shed where I kept all my beekeeping equipment, and we both donned suits.

"I never know when inspiration will strike," she said, clicking away with her phone. "Sometimes it's the weirdest thing that will inspire me, so I like to get lots of input."

We put veils on, and I took her over toward my hives. It was late morning, and guard bees were flying nearby. I brought my smoker and opened a hive I hadn't touched in a few weeks.

"Do the bees collect honey all day?" she asked, peering inside. "Are they always busy? Like busy bees?"

I explained how some of the workers were out collecting pollen and nectar all day while others collected propolis and water. "Various workers have different tasks. Many of them also work in the hive to keep it clean and healthy." I gently pulled out a frame near the front and inspected its comb. "The term 'busy bees' is certainly appropriate though."

As Eliza took photos, I continued to check frames and combs, always careful not to crush bees or cause vibrations. I left the center alone for now, since the queen was likely there. I saw some hive beetles on one of the combs, but the bees appeared to be handling the situation. Thankfully, I didn't see any Varroa mites.

Once we were done, Eliza thanked me for showing her the hive. "It's really wild seeing them like that," she said. "I eat honey all the time, but I don't really think about where it comes from."

I nodded. "Of course, most of the food you eat has been pollinated in some fashion."

"That's true, isn't it?"

As we chatted a bit, I noticed it was getting breezy outside. When I glanced up at the sky, it wasn't blue anymore.

"It looks like that storm is coming in," she said. "I should head out. I'm going to a football party this afternoon, and I want to get there before it hits."

This got my attention. "*Football?*"

She nodded. "The Sentries are playing in Los Angeles. It's the first game of the season. A friend of mine from the theater is having a little party."

"I would never have guessed you were a football fan." I was

excited and breathless even saying the word "football." *What's wrong with me?*

She shrugged. "It's fun to watch sometimes. I'm not a fanatic or anything, though I have friends who basically are."

We began walking up toward the house. "Would you like a jar of honey?"

"Really? I'd love one!"

It always delighted people to receive honey.

We went inside, and I grabbed one of the jars off the table for her, then walked her out to her car.

Eliza gave me a quick hug, smelling like fruity perfume. "I'll let you know if inspiration strikes," she said. "I have a good feeling, so I'm pretty sure it will!"

Just before she got into her car, I asked her a question I never thought I'd ask in my life. "Do you know what time that football game starts?"

CHAPTER TWENTY-THREE

~ Theo ~

Eliza told me the game started at one o'clock. It was past that now, and I debated whether I should watch it.

I'd already gone into the kitchen and made myself a peanut butter and honey sandwich for lunch, bringing it into the living room.

Rain pummeled my windows as thunder boomed outside. The storm had arrived with a vengeance.

My laptop sat on the coffee table since I was supposed to be working on my fall lesson plan. The university asked me to teach an online undergraduate course this quarter along with my usual class of graduate students.

Finally, I couldn't stand it anymore.

"I can't believe I'm doing this," I said as I turned on my television and began flipping through channels. It didn't take long to find the live game between Seattle and Los Angeles.

Am I really watching football?

I glanced at my sandwich. I wasn't hungry for lunch, but I was definitely hungry to see Gabe.

I studied the television screen and tried to understand what I was watching. Between the padded uniforms and helmets, it wasn't easy to tell the athletes apart.

It's the numbers. I needed to figure out Gabe's number and team's colors.

I had no idea what they were.

After our wonderful day together, I'd promised myself I wasn't going to look him up online or learn anything more about him. It had been a hard promise to keep. I'd been tempted. Very tempted. But I didn't want to get emotionally involved. This was just supposed to be animal lust between us, and looking him up online would have felt like something else, like maybe I cared about him. Like maybe I even missed him.

It was already hard enough not thinking about him all the time. The irony was that at least I wasn't thinking about Clement anymore.

I sat cross-legged on the couch and opened my computer. Instead of going to the lesson plan for fall, I opened a new tab and typed in *Gabriel Bardales.*

I sucked in my breath as images of him appeared on-screen.

My God.

It was a good thing I hadn't been looking him up online. Something shifted inside me as soon as I saw his picture. Those soulful eyes. With a sharp longing, I remembered that day out in my meadow.

Number seven.

My eyes flashed back up to the screen. That was Gabe's number. Commentators were speaking football jargon that sounded like gibberish. From various angles, camera cutaways showed the giant field and the crowd filling the enormous stadium.

I took it all in with amazement. Football players appeared to be modern-day gladiators.

I tried to make sense of what I saw on-screen as the game progressed, but I didn't get it. Things happened quickly, and none of it made sense. Was it possible that football was more complicated than I thought?

The commentators kept talking. There was a lot of action and then things slowed, and then more action, and then my breath stopped.

Number seven. In a navy-blue-and-white uniform.

"There he is," I murmured to myself.

I couldn't pull my eyes away. It was definitely Gabe. I recognized his walk when he strode out onto the field. My heart pounded. He looked magnificent. I'd never thought football uniforms were sexy, but I might have been wrong about that.

His face appeared in a sidebar on-screen, and the commentators were talking about him. Something about passes and interceptions. Apparently the Sentries had high expectations for him, and Gabe had been mostly fulfilling them. He was expected to lead the team to the playoffs this year—whatever that was.

I kept my eyes on him. He stood behind a row of other men who were crouched over. Somehow the football was thrown to him. I tried to follow it, but it seemed to disappear. Then it reappeared. Things stopped, and then they were starting all over again.

What a strange game.

This was so much different than I expected. I tried to imagine what this must be like for Gabe, surrounded by a stadium of screaming fans. All the people in their homes watching. The pressure.

Crikey.

I'd certainly underestimated him.

My eyes must have left the screen for a moment, because when I looked back, Gabe now had the football tucked in his arm and was trying to run with it. I felt breathless. *Go, Gabe!* I didn't even know what he was doing, but I cheered him on.

Except he didn't get very far. Three players from the other team seemed to appear out of nowhere. He tried to move past them, but—

No!

He was tackled! Not just by one of them but by all *three*.

It was *horrifying*.

These men were *enormous*.

Thunder boomed outside again. My windows rattled.

One of the commentators was yelling, "And Bardales is sacked! Oooh, you know that's gotta hurt... especially on the first—"

My television went blank, and the living room fell silent.

I blinked around in confusion.

The storm knocked out the power!

Wind and rain still howled and pummeled the house.

But what about Gabe?

All I could think about was what I'd just witnessed on-screen. Three enormous men tackling him!

I felt sick to my stomach. Was he seriously injured? How could he *not* be after what I just saw?

My computer's wireless was out, so I had no way to go online. My heart was in my throat as I ran into the kitchen, searching for my phone.

Finally, I found it on the counter.

No service. SOS mode.

I couldn't believe it!

This qualifies as an emergency, doesn't it?

I searched for his number in my contacts. He was still listed as "Jock Ogre." I tried calling, but I knew it wouldn't work. It only allowed 911 calls.

My stomach churned. I felt sick with worry.

So much for unemotional animal lust.

I stared down at the phone in my hand, still showing his contact information. Apparently I'd developed feelings for the jock ogre.

The rest of the afternoon was spent in a blur, pacing the house as the storm raged. This was so far out of my usual experience that I didn't know what to do with myself. I tried to work on my lesson plans but couldn't focus. I tried to read but kept seeing that image in my head of Gabe knocked to the ground and jumped on by three giants.

How could someone even survive that?

This was so frustrating!

Why did the electricity have to go out during every storm? Why did I put off buying a generator? Why did I live on an island with power lines as weak as spaghetti noodles?

I kept checking to see if cellular service was back up, and then finally, at twenty past six, a miracle happened. Those magic bars appeared.

Thank God!

Immediately I brought up Gabe's number on my phone. I wasn't sure what I expected to happen when I called. What if no one answered? What would I do then?

To my surprise, someone answered on the second ring. "Theo? What's wrong? Is everything okay?"

Relief flooded through me. It was Gabe.

"*Me*, I'm fine. I'm calling to see if *you're* okay!"

People were talking in the background of what sounded like a large, busy space.

"Why wouldn't I be okay?"

"Because I saw three giant men knock you to the ground and then throw themselves on you! It was unbelievable. Is that even legal?"

The line went silent, though I could hear all sorts of activity around him.

"Holy shit." He sounded incredulous. "Are you saying you *watched* the game?"

"I watched part of it. The terrifying part. But then the power went out, and I didn't know what happened after that."

Gabe began to laugh.

"I can't believe you're laughing!"

"And I can't believe you watched a football game. It's a damn shame you didn't see the whole thing. We won 27–23."

He sounded extremely cheerful. Not at all like someone who might be secretly putting on a brave front.

"Well, that's... very good. Congratulations."

"Thanks. It's nice to have a win for the first game of the season."

"I'm so happy for you. And I'm also happy to hear you're still breathing."

He chuckled. "I'm okay. I've been sacked worse than that. We lost a few yards but luckily made up for it later."

"Sacked? Is it what they call it when you're tackled?"

"Yeah, when it's the quarterback behind the line of scrimmage. Otherwise, it's just a tackle." I heard him smile through the phone line. "Well, listen to this. Sounds like you're getting your second football lesson, Professor."

"What was my first lesson?"

"Out in the meadow together. I told you about halftime and overtime, remember?"

How could I ever forget? That day had tattooed itself onto my brain. My heart, too, if I was honest. "I remember," I said.

He went quiet. We both did.

"What's the line of scrimmage?" I asked.

Gabe chuckled softly, as if he were guarding secret knowledge. "Wouldn't you like to know? Guess you'll have to wait for your third lesson to find out."

CHAPTER TWENTY-FOUR

~ Gabe ~

This had turned out to be a great day. Winning our first game of the season was fantastic, and then having Theo call felt like the whipped cream, sprinkles, and cherry on top.

She even reminded me of a cherry with her red hair. Both sweet and tart on the inside.

"Actually, I didn't know we were still doing the football lessons," she said. "I wasn't sure if we'd see each other again."

I wanted to see her again, and after hearing her voice, I *had* to see her.

"Hell yeah, we're doing the lessons. How else am I going to make sure you stay open-minded about football?"

"I already told you I'm open-minded."

"We'll see." I'd taken a ten-minute ice bath a short while ago, and now Heidi, one of our team's athletic trainers, came over to check on my left wrist. It was pure luck that I'd grabbed my phone. "Listen, I have to go," I said to Theo. "Can I call you later tonight?"

"Okay... I'll be here. And Gabe?"

"Yeah?"

"I'm glad you're okay."

"Thanks." A warm sense of pleasure rolled through me. I couldn't remember the last time somebody who didn't have a vested interest in my health had worried about me. "I'll talk to you tonight."

I was still grinning when I put my phone down.

"How does the wrist feel?" Heidi asked. "Can you move it around?"

I tested my lower arm and hand, making a fist.

"Who was that on the phone?" Heidi had been with the Sentries for years, so I'd gotten to know her pretty well. She was married to a paramedic and had a young son. "It sounded like someone you were happy to talk to."

I glanced at her, knowing I could be gruff at times. Definitely ill-tempered when we were losing.

"It's... someone special," I admitted. *How can I describe Theo?* "Someone pretty amazing who I hope I get to know better."

She smiled and gave me an approving look. "Good for you, Gabe."

I continued to test my wrist. "It's a little sore but not too bad."

Heidi nodded. "It's likely a mild sprain. Do you want me to give you a brace to wear later, or a bandage?"

I'd already talked to reporters right after the game, but I still had the press room in a little while. Heidi knew there was no way in hell I was going on camera with a brace or a bandage on my wrist.

"Give me the bandage. We'll see if I need it later. I'll try to rest it and check how it feels tomorrow."

When we were done, I showered, got dressed, and made my way over to the press room to be grilled. Luckily, things went smoothly and there were no surprises. Local and national reporters were there, but I was used to it. Afterward, I grabbed my travel bag and headed out to the car our team's travel coordinator had set up for me. She knew my sister lived out here and had scheduled a ride to get me to her house, then another one for the airport tomorrow. There were some Sentries fans out by the gate who wanted autographs, so I stopped and signed a bunch.

By the time we made it past the traffic and I got to Regina and Tess's place in Santa Monica, it was after eight. I was pretty beat, but it was great to see my sister and her wife. It turned out our brother, Mateo, was there, which was nice, since I hadn't seen him in a while either. There were hugs all around. To my dismay, I found out they hadn't eaten dinner yet and were waiting for me.

"It's nearly eight thirty," I said after putting my stuff in the guest bedroom. "You guys should have just eaten without me. I can't believe you waited."

"I know." Mateo rolled his eyes. He was five years younger than me, five inches shorter, and mostly interested in computers and creating graphic novels. "I was ready to eat hours ago, but these two weren't having it."

"I can't believe we lost today," Regina said as we all sat down at the table. "I'm going to have to pretend I don't know who you are when I go into the bar tomorrow. Everyone's going to be pissed about losing."

I shrugged. "What can I say? Your team needs a better defense."

Tess brought out a pitcher of ice water and set it down, eyeing us both. "I already told Regina I'm setting a timer for the amount of football talk allowed over dinner tonight."

We did talk about football, but when the timer went off—Tess wasn't kidding about that—we switched to other topics. I asked how everybody was doing and what was new. Apparently the bar was doing fine, though Regina was having problems hiring all the staff she needed. Tess had gotten the job at the new school. She was enjoying it but wasn't sure about her new principal. It turned out Mateo was publishing his second graphic novel soon, and we were all thrilled for him. I couldn't wait to read it.

It was relaxing to be around everyone. While I didn't necessarily miss Los Angeles, I definitely missed my siblings.

I was grateful nobody mentioned our dad, but of course, then Mateo had to spoil that. He worked with Dad at the store every day, so I should have expected it.

"Are you going to stop by and see Pop?" he asked.

I shook my head. "Nope. I don't see any reason for that."

"He's mellowed a lot. I think you should give him a chance. At least call him."

"Phone works both ways." My father had made it clear he didn't want me in his life, and after spending years trying, I was done.

Mateo sighed and, thankfully, dropped the subject.

We ate and talked for a while longer. By the time we wrapped things up, it was after ten. Tess had to be up early for work, and so did Mateo. I told everyone I was going to bed.

But when I got to the bedroom, I got out my phone to call Theo. It was nearly ten thirty, and I hoped it wasn't too late. I texted her first to check.

Gabe: Sorry, is this too late to call?

I waited, and my pulse jumped when I saw her responding.

Theo: It's not too late. I'm still awake.

I called her, but instead of a regular call, I used FaceTime.

I smiled when Theo appeared on-screen. Her hair was pulled off her face into a bun on top of her head, and she was just as beautiful as I remembered.

"Hi," I said.

She blinked rapidly behind her glasses like she was adjusting to the screen. "I wasn't expecting a video call."

"Is this okay?"

She studied me. "It's fine."

"So, how's the storm?" I asked. "Is your power still out?"

"Actually, it came on a short while ago." She turned to the side, glancing around her room. "I was surprised they got it back up so fast. It sometimes takes days."

"You should have snuck over to my house. I have a generator in the garage."

"That would have come in handy." She appeared to be thinking something over. "Why did you answer your phone when I called earlier asking if something was wrong? Did you know about the storm?"

I shook my head. "It's because you've never called me before." I tucked an extra pillow behind me on the bed and winced a little at my wrist. "It's been a few weeks since we saw each other, so I worried maybe something was wrong." I thought of that night she showed up at my house crying about the brilliant idiot, but I didn't want to bring that up.

"Is your arm okay? You looked like you were in pain for a moment."

Shit. I was hoping she hadn't noticed that. "It's nothing. I sprained my wrist, but it's mild."

"Was it when you got sacked?"

I nodded. "It's no big deal. It already feels better than earlier."

She shook her head and frowned.

"What is it?"

"It's awful that you're constantly facing the threat of injury. How can you justify it? Doesn't it seem reckless?"

I sat up. "It's not reckless. I'm *never* reckless. A lot of people have jobs where they face injury or even worse. Think about cops, or firefighters, or anyone in the military. Not that I'm comparing myself to them. I'm definitely not saving lives. But I'm very lucky. If something happens, we've got world-class doctors right there."

She mulled over my words. "I suppose it's true that any job has its dangers. I remember an entomologist Clement worked with who got quite ill after being bitten by a kissing bug accidentally."

"A kissing bug? That sounds like he got cooties."

"Definitely *not* cooties. They can carry a parasite in their feces that causes Chagas disease. They're members of the Triatominae and are also called vampire bugs." She went on to describe the insect in more detail, telling me its habitat and life cycle, until I finally had to tell her to stop.

"Okay," I said with a chuckle. "I believe you, Professor. I surrender. It's not cooties. Maybe we could change the subject?"

Theo pushed her glasses up on her nose. "Of course. I apologize." She laughed lightly. "I suppose you didn't call me to talk about insects, did you?"

"I can't say that I did."

She smiled and met my eyes. "What would you like to discuss?"

Even though her hair was pulled up, some of those wild curls sprang loose, framing her face. Freckles sprinkled across her nose and cheeks. She was damned cute.

There was a knock on my bedroom door, and I called out, "Come in."

Regina poked her head inside. "Just wanted to say good night. Who are you on the phone with? Is that Davis?"

"It's not Davis. It's a... friend."

"Oh. If it was Davis, I wanted you tell him that I solved The Crossword in ten and Wordle in three today."

"I'm sure he'll be impressed."

Regina grinned. "Good night."

"Good night, Reg."

"Who was that?" Theo asked.

"My sister, Regina. I'm staying at her and her wife's house in Santa Monica."

"I didn't know you had a sister."

I nodded and leaned back on the bed again to get more comfortable, still holding the phone up. "A younger brother too. What about you? Do you have siblings?"

She shook her head. "I'm an only child. My parents were both in their forties when they had me."

I could easily picture that. I'd bet she was around adults a lot growing up. She struck me that way.

"Why was she talking about The Crossword and Wordle?"

"She and Davis have an ongoing competition about who can solve them the fastest. They're both crazy for puzzles. Why? Are you into those?"

She shrugged. "Not really. I solve them for fun sometimes, but only occasionally."

"I've done them occasionally, too, but it always seems like a waste of time."

Theo laughed. "I feel the same way."

We were smiling at each other, and as always, I felt lighter around her. Even on the phone like this.

"What are you doing next week?" I asked on impulse. "I want you to come to Seattle."

She tilted her head. "Seattle?"

"I'm flying back tomorrow and only get one day off a week during the season." I took a breath. "Tuesdays."

"I have to work on Tuesday."

I nodded, trying to hide my disappointment. "I understand." I usually spent my Tuesdays doing errands anyway.

"Classes haven't started yet." She appeared to be deliberating. "I suppose I could call in sick."

I couldn't take my eyes off of her. "Then call in sick," I urged. "I want to see you."

She smiled. The sweetest sunshower. "You're seeing me right now. What do you call this?"

"You know what I mean." A terrible thought occurred to me. "Don't you want to see me?"

It took her a moment, and she seemed to compose herself. I waited and worried. Finally, she nodded. "I want to."

"Yeah?"

"Definitely."

I grinned. The excitement of seeing Theo again vibrated through me, lighting me up like a starlit sky. Something told me the path I was on had changed, and maybe my old story was wrong. Maybe this was my new story.

All I knew was I couldn't wait until Tuesday.

CHAPTER TWENTY-FIVE

~ Theo ~

I hadn't been to Seattle in several months. Occasionally, I came into the city for meetings at the university or to meet a friend, but never to meet a man for animal lust. It sounded so scandalous. So illicit. Like someone else's life. Certainly not mine. I may have developed feelings for Gabe, but they didn't appear to be interfering with my physical attraction to him.

Theo: Am I staying the night on Tuesday? Should I pack a bag?

Gabe: Yes. You're staying the night.

Erotic sparks flew through me. I liked that he was so direct. It was hot. It had sometimes felt like pulling teeth to get a straight answer out of Clement. Even breaking up, it turned out he hadn't been straight with me.

I left on an early ferry and encountered little traffic on the way down to the city. Gabe had given me instructions on how to find his building. Apparently he lived in one of the high-rises downtown.

While the traffic getting to Seattle hadn't been bad, the traffic inside the city was terrible. He told me to call when I arrived in Seattle, so I did.

"Just drive in front of my building and park your car with the valet," he instructed, his deep voice coming through my Jeep's speakers. "Then call me, and I'll come down and get you."

His building has valet parking? I'd never heard of such a thing. "Am I going to have to pay for that?"

I could hear him smile. "I already put your name on my guest list. You won't have to pay anything."

I did as he told me, and as soon as I found his building, I drove in front and allowed the valet to take my car.

I didn't have to call Gabe though. He was already there waiting for me.

"Theo." He held his hand up and grinned.

Oh my goodness. He wore jeans and a navy blue T-shirt that set off his dark hair and eyes. He was absurdly handsome.

Is this really my life?

I walked over to him carrying my bag, and I didn't know what to do. *Am I supposed to hug him or kiss him hello?*

It turned out neither.

"I'm glad you came," he said, meeting my eyes. He reached over to grab my overnight bag.

I followed him into his building, taking in the lobby's chandelier, the marble floors, and what appeared to be a large front desk staff. "This isn't a hotel, is it?"

He smiled. "It's not a hotel."

We walked into an elevator, and I had to admit this experience felt like I was visiting another planet. I wondered if I should have packed a spacesuit and an oxygen tank.

An older lady got in the elevator with us. She smiled and nodded at us, and we smiled back. She got off on a lower floor, but we kept going.

He asked how the ride down from Truth Harbor was, and I told him it was fine. I didn't know why, but I felt nervous. It reminded me of when we first met.

We left the elevator, but then he took me over to another one.

"How many elevators are going to be involved here?" I asked.

There was a flash of white when he laughed. He used a keycard to open the doors. "Just two, I promise. I live in the penthouse."

It was a brief ride up. We entered into a hallway, overlooking the city, with doors on each end.

He nodded to the left. "C'mon, I'm this way."

"Does someone else live down there?"

"The CEO for a software company and his wife own it, but they're not here much. They mostly live in New York."

I nodded as if this were completely normal. To own a penthouse in Seattle worth millions that you rarely bothered to visit.

Finally, he opened the door and led me into his place. Not that I got to see much of it. I tried to look around but didn't get a chance.

"God, I haven't been able to stop thinking about you," Gabe said, pulling me into his arms. He brought his mouth down to mine.

The kiss was fierce and filled with passion. After being startled for a second, I was immediately on board. I threw my arms around his neck, pressing myself flush against his muscular body. His hands roamed my back, pulling me even closer as he deepened the kiss.

Whatever this is, I want more.

I'd never experienced passion like this. Even when Clement came back after being away for months, we were never like this.

Gabe tasted faintly of mint, and when he broke the kiss, his lips moved to my neck. "I've been wanting to do that since we talked on Sunday," he said, breathing hard. "I can't wait to show you what else I've been wanting to do."

"I can't wait either."

He looked into my eyes. "Tell me this isn't one-sided. Tell me you've been thinking about me too."

"I have," I admitted, stroking the back of his neck. "A lot."

His eyes turned heated. "Good."

He took my hand and led me away from the door and into the living room, a luxurious space with a breathtaking view of the city and water—not that I could focus on it. I was too caught up in the way my heart pounded with anticipation. He continued to lead me down a hallway and then to what was obviously his bedroom.

It was richly furnished and offered more views of the skyline, but I barely noticed it, more focused on the large bed that dominated the room.

He pulled me to him. I couldn't believe the way he gazed at me, full of hunger and longing. "Damn," he whispered.

He reached up and took my glasses off, putting them on his night-stand. And then he was back, and we were kissing again. His hands were warm against my skin as he lifted my shirt, pulling it off. Next came my bra. His touch on my breasts sent tingles down my spine as he teased and played with them.

I moaned into his mouth, feeling reckless and out of control. I could barely catch my breath. Nothing in my life had prepared me for these sensations, and yet I knew exactly what I wanted.

Reaching down, I cupped my hand over the hard column beneath his jeans and squeezed. Gabe grunted softly. I shoved his zipper down, then the pants, until finally I found him. Thick and hard.

He hissed softly as I stroked his length. And I loved that. Loved the way his breath was coming fast.

"Oh, wow," I said, watching his face, his eyes half-lidded. I was moved by how affected he was.

We kissed again, and then everything seemed to happen in a blur. Somehow we wound up on the bed, pulling the rest of our clothes off. From a distance, I heard fabric tearing, but I didn't know whose it was.

He lowered himself on top of me, his hardness pressing against my thigh. I pulled him in tighter, desperate to feel him inside of me.

But Gabe seemed to have other ideas as he ran his hands over my body, down my sides, then up to my breasts. He squeezed them gently, and I moaned at the sensation, arching my back.

For a moment, he lifted. I could almost see the desire spread across his face as he studied me.

"You're so beautiful," he whispered.

I turned my head.

"Don't look away," he said. "It's true. Accept it."

I bit my lip and tried to do what he asked. It wasn't easy in the afternoon light. Everything exposed.

It wasn't that I thought I was undesirable. I'd had men desire me. However, all the evidence I'd gathered over the years told me I was not a beauty. Clement had certainly never told me I was beautiful.

"How am I supposed to ignore years of solid data?" I asked him.

Gabe snorted. "Data? I've got your data right here. I'm it."

He always had a way of turning things around.

"You're only one sample."

"I'm the only one who matters, Theo."

He said it with such certainty. Such authority. And he was doing that thing again where I felt seen. Yet I still didn't believe him.

I sucked in my breath when his mouth went down to my breasts again, lavishing them with attention. Then he slid lower to my stomach, and then lower still. He spread my thighs, kissing them, and I tried to steady myself.

It was obvious his intention was to move between my thighs, so I reached for his shoulders, trying to pull him up. "I think I should put a condom on you now."

Those soulful eyes looked up at me. "I want to go down on you first. This beautiful pussy is calling my name."

I nearly choked. "I'd rather you didn't. It's not pleasant for me."

"Not pleasant?"

I nodded. "I don't enjoy it."

He seemed to process this. "I would never want you to do something you didn't enjoy, but can I ask why?"

I sighed and thought of Clement's various attempts. Before him,

I'd been with two other men who'd attempted this, and the experiences hadn't been any better. I had to conclude that this particular sexual act just wasn't for me. "I simply don't like it."

"How about this? Let me try, and if I do something you don't like, I'll change it."

"I doubt that will make any difference. I've already tried that with Clement."

"Give me a chance. Just for a minute. If you tell me to stop, I'll stop."

"Fine." I was annoyed but figured I could tolerate one minute of a misguided tongue poking at me. "You'll stop right away? And that will end this conversation?"

"I promise."

I leaned my head back against the pillow. "All right then, proceed."

Gabe chuckled as I felt him position himself between my thighs. I prepared myself for the usual disappointment. I could never understand why other women liked this so much.

Any second now, the tongue probing would begin. I waited.

Except that wasn't what happened. Something else did.

There was a soft sensation, not on my clitoris but around it.

Huh. This is new.

The sensation continued. A soft swirling around the spot. It was... pleasurable. Quite pleasurable.

Where's the usual jabbing tongue?

I lifted my head to watch with curiosity. It turned out watching made the pleasure even greater. Seeing Gabe, his eyes closed, concentrating. As it continued, my breathing grew rapid. It was difficult to resist this sensation. It was *very* good. Soon the swirling increased, and so did the pressure that had moved onto my clitoris. There were other things going on. It was hard to keep track. He was lightly squeezing and manipulating the top of my vulva.

"My God," I whispered in a daze. This was unreal.

Gabe's eyes opened. They were dark and heated. He watched me and then pulled his mouth away.

A desperate whimper escaped my throat. *Why is he stopping?*

"Shall I continue?" he asked, his voice husky.

I nodded, my breath shallow. "Please continue."

"So polite." He tilted his head, still observing me while touching me lightly. "Let's see if I can push you out of the polite zone."

His mouth was on me again, and it was like a symphony. That's the closest thing I could think of. It was Beethoven. My favorite composer filling a concert hall with multilayered music. It went on and on. Endless. The pleasure building but never going over the edge. And when Gabe pulled away, asking again if he should continue, I couldn't even speak.

"That's more like it," he murmured.

I began to grab and pull his hair. I began to tremble all over. I began to wonder if I could even survive this intensity much longer. There was the sound of a woman moaning and begging, and it was my voice.

When he finally showed mercy and brought me to that crescendo, I screamed at the ecstasy pulsing through me. I'd never climaxed like this in my life. It seemed to go on for an eternity, and when the colors of the room swam into focus again, I felt like a different person. More aware. Changed.

I wanted to examine it, but there wasn't time.

Gabe was all business now. His face was flushed as he quickly moved up on the bed and grabbed something from his nightstand. A condom. He was breathing hard, and I watched as his hands shook putting it on.

He moved over me and pulled my hips down. I grabbed him, wanting this, wanting *him*. As soon he entered me, we both moaned. So good. He took me hard, the bed shaking, the walls rattling. My legs locked around his hips. His teeth bared, panting as he thrust into me again and again. I was myself but someone else too. Someone different. Someone I'd never been before.

"God, Theo," he groaned loudly as he reached his release.

Just like the last time, he didn't pull out right away. Instead, we gazed at each other as he stroked my hair. I felt a kind of wonder move through me, filling me up until I thought it might overflow.

And no matter what happened between me and this football player, for my whole life, I knew I'd never regret it.

CHAPTER TWENTY-SIX

~ Gabe ~

"So that's what people do." Theo's voice was soft. She sounded amazed, gazing out the window at the skyline. "I never knew."

"What people?" I was lying on my side, facing her, propped up on one elbow. The two of us were naked on my bed with sweat cooling on our skin.

"The ones having hot love affairs."

"You mean *us*?"

She turned back to me and didn't say anything for a long moment. We studied each other. I knew I should keep some distance —some semblance of it, at least—but I couldn't even pretend I wasn't sucked into this like a tornado.

"I'm going to be honest with you," she said.

"I thought you were always honest with me."

Theo smiled. That beautiful smile as bright as the sun. And in that moment, she could have asked me anything. She could have asked me to go live with her in a yurt on a mountain in the middle of nowhere and be goat and bee farmers, and I would have agreed to it.

"This is more than animal lust for me," she said. "I seem to have developed feelings for you."

"Yeah." I reached over and lightly traced the edges of her mouth. "Me too."

"I don't even know what this is. You and I are like opposites who have nothing in common. What are we supposed to do?"

I shrugged. "It's chemistry. And who says we have to do anything? Stop analyzing everything."

"I guess you're right." She gave me a look. "Don't you dare fall in love with me."

I scoffed and rolled my eyes. "Listen to you. The arrogance."

"I mean it, Gabe. I just got out of a relationship. I can't handle anything serious."

I nodded and ignored the way my stomach dropped. "Don't worry, I'm not looking for anything serious either." I kept my voice light. What I didn't add was that I never looked for anything serious.

She continued to study me, then got a funny little grin.

"What?"

"How did you learn how to do that so well? You know...." She glanced down at that trimmed red bush that was as bright as the hair on her head.

I pretended confusion. "I don't know what you're talking about."

"You *do* know. But you're not going to tell me. I must say, that was remarkable. I finally understand why Claire and Leah act like it's so great."

"I take it the brilliant idiot was bad at eating pussy?" I couldn't help my self-satisfied smirk. "Not so brilliant after all."

"I did try to instruct him. It may have been my failing."

"Did he follow your instructions?"

She appeared to be thinking this over. "He tried. But I always sensed a certain impatience from him. Clement seemed to think the problem lay mostly with me."

I shook my head in disgust. "I know that breakup hurt you, and I'm sorry for that, but from everything you've told me about him, that jackass actually did you a favor."

"That's likely true." She reached out to stroke my jaw. "What about you? Do you have a Clement in your past?"

I shook my head and told her the truth. "I've dated a number of women but nobody serious. It's not something I've sought out."

"What about all the skeletons you said are knocking around in your closet?"

I shook my head again. That was not something we were going to talk about. And if I didn't stop her, the professor would attack the subject like a lioness with a fresh antelope. "I'm hungry. Do you want to eat something?"

She considered me. "Maybe after."

"After what?"

Theo scooted closer, sliding her leg over my hip. "You know, I have an IUD, so we don't have to worry about pregnancy."

"Is that so?" I was pleased where this conversation was going.

"And I got tested after Clement broke up with me. How about you?"

"I get tested regularly. I'm clean and healthy."

She smiled. "Remember that first football lesson about halftime and overtime? What part are we at now, would you say?"

I grinned, my cock already springing to life again. My hand roamed down her body, over all that smooth skin, to squeeze her ass. "Trust me, this game has barely begun."

EVENTUALLY, we came up for air and left my bedroom. We were standing in the kitchen eating from a bowl of grapes on the counter, waiting for the food I'd ordered to be delivered. It was from a healthy

Thai place over in the U-District that served whole food meals without extra additives.

"All this sexual activity really does burn a lot of calories," Theo mused. "I'm starving."

"Me too," I agreed. "I hope I ordered enough food for the dogs."

"What dogs?" But then she shook her head. "*No*, don't do it!"

I howled like a wolf. "Release the dogs!"

She laughed. "Stop howling like that. I did *not* yell, 'Release the dogs.'"

"You sure as hell did. That's the second time now." I reached for more grapes, chuckling. "That seems to be your mating call. Just like a moose."

She smacked me on the chest. "You're making it up. I know you are."

"I wish I were. How did I get involved with a woman who wants to 'release the dogs' every time we have sex?"

She nibbled on a grape and appeared mystified. "I don't know why I would say such a thing. It makes no sense."

I enjoyed watching her as she stood in my kitchen. With the glasses and the wild red curls, she looked like a sexy mad scientist.

I'd slipped on sweats since I'd be answering the door soon, but Theo only wore one of my T-shirts. It came down to about midthigh, which was the perfect length so I still got to see those amazing long legs of hers.

"So, when's my next football lesson?" she asked. "You never told me about the line of scrimmage."

"You're right." I rubbed my hands together. "It *is* time for your next lesson. So, the line of scrimmage is very important. It's an imaginary line the ball is on to start each play."

She went quiet, thinking this over. "Does it move?"

"Yep. It moves to whatever yard line the ball has moved to at the end of a play. Of course, sometimes it doesn't move at all."

She nodded. "I think I get it. I must say, football is far more complicated than I'd originally thought."

"You don't know the half of it. There are a ton of rules. Hell, there are a bunch of rules just around the line of scrimmage."

The doorbell rang, and I went to answer it.

One of our doormen from downstairs handed me the bag, and I thanked him. When I got back to the kitchen, Theo had already found plates and laid them out so we could dish food out for ourselves.

We ate in the living room on the sofa and talked. It was comfortable. Instead of football, she wanted to know more about my family, about how I grew up. I described a bit of my childhood in California, trying to focus on the good parts.

"What does your dad do for a living?" she asked. "You never mentioned that. Is he into sports like you?"

"He owns a furniture store. His father started it, so it's a family business."

"Really?" She bit into a piece of broccoli. "Did you work there too?"

I nodded, digging my chopsticks into some brown rice. "All three of us did. Mateo still does. I worked when it didn't interfere with football practice, mostly helping with deliveries and moving inventory."

She smiled. "I can totally picture that."

"I enjoyed it. As long as my dad wasn't around."

"You don't get along with your dad?"

I shook my head. "We don't see things the same. He disagreed with me pursuing football the way I did."

"That's too bad. Surely he's proud of you now. You said before that he raised you and your siblings alone, right?"

I picked up my glass of water to take a drink. "He did, though his family helped a lot. My grandparents were always around, and they were great. My parents split up when I was a kid."

"That's a shame. What happened to your mom?"

"She married some rich guy and moved across the country. We hardly ever saw her."

Theo blinked with dismay. "That's terrible. Why would she do that?"

I got back to my meal. "She wanted to be an actress before she met my dad, and then she modeled for a while. Except none of it panned out. She's too impatient. She's one of those people who are never satisfied with what they have."

"I'm really sorry. Are you in contact with her at all?"

I shrugged. "Not really. We talk every once in a while. She's on her fourth or fifth husband now."

"That must have been difficult for all of you when she left."

I ate the last bite of my food and put my plate on the coffee table. "We got through it. What about you? Where are your parents?"

"They're in Oregon. I grew up in Eugene."

Her legs were draped over my lap, and I slid the tips of my fingers lightly over her skin. "And they're still there?"

She nodded and leaned over to put her plate on the table too. "They're retired now, but they were both academics who taught at the university."

I could totally see that. It fit completely with my image of Theo. "What did they teach?"

"My mom was an English professor, and my dad taught history."

"You're kidding." I grinned. "I was a history major."

"Really?" She seemed delighted by this. "That's surprising. I wouldn't have guessed that. Where did you go to school?"

"The Ohio State."

"Ohio? Why there?"

I glanced toward the window out at the view of the water. "It's one of the top football schools in the country."

"I didn't know that. It sounds like an achievement. Did you get a scholarship?"

This conversation was going in the wrong direction. The heaviness had seeped in. I felt it. All my demons that had been magically chased away by Theo were trying to come back.

"Yeah," I heard myself say. "I got a full ride."

"That sounds remarkable." She must have noticed my expression. "Are you okay? Is something wrong?"

I turned my head away and swallowed. "I'm fine."

She reached over and stroked my arm. "Is it talking about your mom? I'm sorry. I didn't know."

I snorted and half laughed. "That's *not* it. Trust me, I got over that ages ago."

"What is it, then?"

A part of me wanted to tell her, to share the whole tragic story. What would Theo say if she knew the truth? Would she think less of me? How could she not?

I turned back to her. "It's nothing. Let's forget about it. Come here," I said, reaching out for her. "Come sit on my lap."

She moved closer and did as I asked, straddling me. I was sitting on the couch with my feet resting on the floor. I let my hands slide beneath the T-shirt to grasp her hips, noticing she'd put her underwear back on.

"We're going to play a little game," I said. "I'm going to tell you what to do, and you're going to follow my instructions. Do you think you can handle that?"

"A game? But what if I don't agree with your instructions?"

"You'll agree with them. That's part of the game."

Theo pouted, and it was cute. I'd never seen her pout before, and I suspected she was trying it out. "How do you know I'll agree?"

"Because I know everything."

She rolled her eyes, and I chuckled to myself. It was fun getting a rise out of her.

Theo opened her mouth, most likely to complain some more, but I shook my head. "That's enough back talk. Are you ready?"

"All right. Fine."

I smiled. "I want you to kiss me."

Her brows went up. "That's your first instruction?"

"It is."

"I can follow that." She leaned forward and brought her soft lips to mine, resting her arms on my shoulders. Our tongues tangled together as the kiss deepened. She tasted sweet and perfect. Tasted like she was made for me.

When the kiss ended, we gazed at each other, our faces close. "Your eyes remind me of that day in our secret meadow," I whispered. "All that wild grass."

"*Our* secret meadow?"

"That's how I think of it. I think of that day a lot," I admitted.

Her expression softened. "So do I."

My hands tightened on her hips. "All right." My voice turned officious. "Enough of that. I want you to kiss me again." I tilted my head to the side. "Do my neck this time."

She moved in closer. I felt those soft curls brush against my face, then her hot breath on the side of my neck. My eyes closed as I took in the sensation. Warm mouth, wet licks, and then soft bites.

I meant this to be a silly game, something to change the subject, but I couldn't believe how much it was turning me on. Way more than I expected. My breathing quickened while my cock jumped to attention.

"How's that?" she whispered in my ear.

"Nice," I said, trying not to sound so aroused.

Theo drew back, and I couldn't resist squeezing her ass as we rocked against each other. A pretty flush spread over her cheeks.

I licked my lips. "All right, take my shirt off next."

Her gaze went down to my body and then back up. Her eyes were heated, and I could tell she was enjoying our game.

She reached down for the hem on each side, and I leaned forward, lifting my arms so she could pull it over my head. She tossed it aside, and I liked the way she studied my upper body with approval. It was a look I'd seen on other women, but coming from Theo, it was an even bigger turn-on.

"What's next?" she asked.

"Kiss my chest," I said in a husky voice. "Especially my nipples."

She slid down, and I opened my thighs to give her space. Then she did as I'd asked. Her mouth moved from my collarbone down to my chest, her hands all over me. And then her mouth was on my right nipple while she played with the left one.

Fuck.

My eyes closed as my blood grew hot.

I began to sweat. Even though I was the one giving instructions, it felt like I'd somehow switched to the weaker position.

This is too much.

Eventually, she worked her way down my chest to my stomach, stopping at the enormous erection now tenting my sweats.

"I can't believe you're this hard again," she said in amazement, running her hand over it.

To be honest, I was amazed too. We'd already had sex three times within a matter of hours. I had great stamina, but even I typically needed *some* recovery time.

She pulled my sweats lower, and I lifted slightly to help her so my cock was freed. She took me in her hand. I secretly hoped she was comparing me to the brilliant idiot's insect dick and noting that I was the winner.

Theo was on her knees in front of me, stroking my length. "What's your next instruction?"

I gazed at her beautiful face, so close. So perfect. Both of us already knew what I was going to say. "Take me in your mouth." The words came out deep and rougher than I intended.

She smiled and then did what I'd instructed. I tried not to close my eyes, but I nearly had to. I'd had women give me head who were practically like professionals, and Theo wasn't like that at all, but somehow this was far more erotic.

It was because she didn't want anything from me. Not a damn thing. Not fame or money, or the prestige of being on my arm. She didn't even *like* football. She was here strictly for *me*. For Gabe. And how many times in my life could I say that about anyone?

I nearly allowed the blow job to go on too long.

"That's enough," I panted, reaching down for her. "Get back up here."

"Do you have more instructions?' she asked, feigning innocence, though there was a hitch in her voice. She sounded breathless.

"Straddle me again."

She did as I asked, moving over me, and I could barely control myself. I kissed her, wanting to use the time to calm myself the fuck down.

Except the kiss turned nuts. The opposite of calm. She was pulling my hair, moaning into my mouth as we devoured each other. Desire and lust barreled through me, forming a tight knot of need.

Finally, I couldn't stop myself and shoved her panties aside. "Now we're going to fuck," I growled as I gripped her hip with one hand and guided myself into her with the other.

She moaned and, without warning, slammed herself down onto me.

It was white-hot.

I didn't even know if she yelled "Release the dogs" when she came. All I could hear was the roaring in my own ears as I poured myself into her. We were like two entities who'd come together to create something different. Something new. Not separate anymore but joined forever.

LATER IN BED, I spooned her as we both gazed out the window at the night sky and the view of the city.

"Can people see us?" Theo asked. "If they had a telescope and were spying?"

I stuck my nose in her hair, inhaling her scent. She smelled like the soap from my shower, and like herself. Sweet as honey. "It's one-way glass. No one can see anything."

She fell silent, but then spoke after a moment. "What time do you have to leave tomorrow for football practice?"

"Early. I'm up at five."

She shifted in bed and then turned around to face me. "I wish this day wasn't over."

"Me too. Can you come down again?"

She bit her lip. "I don't know. I can try. Obviously, I have to work, and then I have classes starting soon."

We gazed at each other. My insides were thorny and complicated, but at the same time, I felt so good. So happy. Light as air. I couldn't deny how much I wanted this.

"Try," I said.

And for the first time in my life, I wished we were at the end of the season and not the beginning, because if it were the end, I'd get to see Theo every day.

CHAPTER TWENTY-SEVEN

~ Theo ~

"So, what do you think?" Eliza asked.

I was stunned and didn't know what to say as I studied the drawings and photos she'd put together for my honey jar labels.

"But these are all pictures of me," I said. "You want to put *my* picture on the jars?"

She nodded. "It's the idea I kept coming back to. You're so pretty and have such a unique look. I figured, why not take advantage of it?"

I stared at her. I almost wanted to ask if Gabe had put her up to this, but that was absurd. They didn't even know each other.

"Let me think about it."

"Sure. No problem."

After she left, I sat and studied the images. There were a few different photos she suggested for the front of the label. A couple of my face head-on and one of me looking from the side, then another one of my profile. I hadn't even noticed her taking this many photos. For the back of the jar, there were more, but in those I was wearing a veil and examining one of the combs from my hives, along with a description of my honey.

I figured I'd ask friends and family what they thought, though I was already certain my parents would love it. I decided to ask Gabe too. He was always direct and honest with me. A trait I appreciated.

So far in the past five weeks, I'd managed to take off two more Tuesdays using vacation days. It was pure luck that it worked out. None of my graduate classes met on Tuesday, and the undergraduate class was online, so I just brought my computer to Seattle and checked messages and answered questions while I was there.

It was ironic that I was basically in another long-distance relationship, though this was nothing like Clement. Or I should say Gabe was nothing like Clement.

The two men couldn't be more different.

I'd let it slip to a few people that we were seeing each other. Claire and Leah, who were delighted for me. I told a friend at work, too, though unfortunately, Gerald overheard me. It turned out he was a big football fan.

"Beauty Bardales?" he kept repeating like one of Claire's squawking parakeets. "You're dating Beauty Bardales?" He seemed shocked.

I wondered if the news would reach Clement's ears. Most of me couldn't care less, but the small spiteful part hoped it did.

"That's right," I said breezily. "We've been seeing each other." I was tempted to tell him we were having a hot, passionate love affair, but the reality of what Gabe and I had was special and private, and none of Gerald's or Clement's business.

While Gabe and I didn't see each other as much as we wanted, we talked on the phone a lot. Despite being so different, we seemed to agree on a surprising number of things. Often we'd take a different route to get there but still reached the same conclusion.

"Where would you ideally want to live?" he asked over the phone Friday night. "City or country?"

"Hmm...." I thought this over. "Both. They each have something to offer. I loved the culture in the city, but I also love the freedom you feel out in the country."

"I agree," he said. "That's why I have a place in the city *and* the country."

"You're very fortunate that way."

"Mountains or ocean?"

"That's easy. Ocean."

He chuckled. "Yeah, me too."

"California boy. Of course you'd say that. So, are you a sucker or a biter?"

"A what?"

"With hard candy, do you suck it or bite it?"

"I bet I know what you are," he teased. "I'll bet you're a biter."

I laughed with surprise. "How did you know that?"

"Because I know everything."

"You're so full of it. So, which one are you?"

He contemplated this. "I'd say I'm a sucker. I like to savor things."

"It's true. I've noticed that you don't like to be hurried. Daydreaming or night dreaming?" I asked.

"Definitely daydreaming. Mostly about you."

My stomach fluttered. "Me too."

"Middle or edge brownies?"

"Hmm... I prefer the crispy edge ones. I like that crunch."

"You're kidding," he said. "I like the gooey middle. It sounds like we're perfect for each other!"

I laughed some more. Amazingly, we could spend hours having these silly conversations. It was a new experience for me. Clement had always been so serious, and we didn't laugh together nearly as much. Gabe usually called right before he went to bed, and that's when we had our talks.

"You know, Davis and Regina are both dying to meet you. I don't know if I can hold Davis off much longer. He has Petey next Tuesday and is threatening to clear his schedule and come by when you're here."

"But I've already met Davis."

"He says that meeting doesn't count because he was acting as my lawyer and not as my friend."

"I wouldn't mind meeting him again. In fact, I'd like that." I was curious about Davis.

"You're definitely coming Tuesday, right?"

"Hopefully, unless Gerald creates a fresh problem." I'd had to cancel my visit last Tuesday and fill in for Gerald at his evening beekeeping extension class since I'd agreed to be the backup. He claimed he was sick, though he came in to work on Wednesday and seemed perfectly healthy.

"Who's Gerald?"

"He's this jerk I work with." I told him how Gerald resented me and had never gotten over my getting the professorship over him. "He's the reason I had to cancel last time. He called in sick but was probably just messing with me."

"Am I going to have to talk with Gerald?"

"That would be hilarious, but I'm handling it." In fact, I'd already asked my colleague Mattie to fill in if Gerald announced another mysterious illness.

"Do you have any football homework for me tonight?"

Smiling, I lay back on my pillow. I'd been trying to watch his games when they were on, though often I'd been forced to grade papers or work on lesson plans at the same time. "I watched the game on Thursday last week," I said. "But I'm still confused about how the scoring works. Can you explain a little more about that? How do teams actually win?"

I could feel him settling in for the question. Gabe *loved* to talk about football. "Well, whoever gets the most points wins, obviously, but there are a number of ways to earn points." He began to describe the difference between a touchdown, a field goal, and a two-point safety. As was typical, there were a lot of rules.

I closed my eyes and listened to his deep voice explain it all. If someone had told me that someday I'd enjoy listening to some jock tell me all about football, I would have thought they were crazy.

Our lessons hadn't just been a one-way street. I'd been teaching him about bees too.

"There are over twenty thousand different types of bees," I explained to him the next night on FaceTime.

"Really? How's that possible?"

"It's a common misconception. People often think of honey bees as the only type, but only about 4 percent of all bees actually make honey."

"You're kidding."

"Also, the majority of bees don't live in hives. Fewer than 3 percent. Most bees either nest together in the ground or are solitary."

Those brown eyes seemed stunned. "That goes against everything I thought I knew."

"It's a good thing you met someone who could clear up all that misinformation for you," I teased.

He asked me some more about my work, and I explained that it centered on *Apis mellifera*. "It's the most well-known honey bee. The one people commonly use to pollinate crops and supply the honey industry."

"So they're like bumble bees?"

I shook my head. "Bumble bees and honey bees are separate and distinct species."

"Whaaat?"

I laughed at his expression. "Bumble bees do make honey, but only enough for themselves. Also, they live in the ground."

"My mind is blown. A whole new world just opened up."

I grinned. I knew he was playing it up for my sake and was only interested in bees because of me, but I still enjoyed it.

"This all reminds me, could you bring a jar of honey down for Davis?"

"Of course," I said. "I'll bring some more for you too. Did you ever eat that first jar I gave you?"

He turned his head to the side, listening. "I think the coaches are actually doing a bed check tonight. I should probably go."

He was staying at a hotel with the rest of the team before the game.

"Good luck tomorrow."

"Are you going to be watching?"

"I will."

"Good." He paused. "I miss you."

"I miss you too."

He smiled, showing off that dimple in his right cheek. "I can't wait to see you on Tuesday."

EVEN THOUGH THIS was only my fourth Tuesday spent with Gabe, I'd gotten comfortable with the valet parking and the two elevators. He met me downstairs as usual and took my bag. But this time he was wearing a brace on his left hand.

"What's that?" I asked, motioning to it with concern. "Are you injured?"

He glanced down at it. "I jammed my thumb. It's no big deal."

"When did this happen?"

He held open the elevator door so we could both enter. "A couple of weeks ago during the game with Detroit."

My jaw dropped in surprise. "You never told me that." We'd spoken multiple times on the phone since then.

He shrugged. "It's my left hand." As if that explained everything.

I reached out and stroked his arm. "Are you really okay?"

"I'm fine. I should warn you, Davis is here. He got here a little while ago." The elevator doors opened, and we walked over to the

one for the penthouse. He looked around stealthily. "I should probably ravish you right now while I have the chance. The odds are
Davis won't leave, even if I drop a million hints."

I smiled. There was no chance he would ravish me in the elevator, because he was concerned about cameras. Apparently that was
the reason he never kissed me hello.

"It's not that I don't want to," he'd told me when I asked him
about it a few weeks ago. "But between the building's security
cameras and every rando walking around with a phone, it's a battle to
keep my privacy."

"What about the dance floor at Leah's wedding reception?"

"Yeah," he admitted. "I lost my head there."

Gabe opened the door to his condo, and right away I heard the
pitter-patter of toenails on hardwood floors running toward us. A cute
little dog wearing a white cable-knit sweater appeared from around
the corner.

"This must be Petey," I exclaimed, bending down to pet him.

Davis appeared right behind the dog, and I glanced up. I recognized him from that night where he acted like I was a beaker full of
nitroglycerin.

"Hello, Theo," he said. "It's nice to see you again."

"You too. Your dog is so sweet."

"He seems to like you," Davis commented.

The dog was already running toward Gabe, who also bent down
to pet him. "How you doing, buddy?"

We headed toward the open space that combined Gabe's kitchen
and living room with the view overlooking Puget Sound. It smelled
like food, and it turned out Davis had brought an early lunch to share.

But first the three of us sat in the living room and talked for a
while. Davis seemed nice enough, and I could tell Gabe was comfortable around him. We'd gone out to dinner during one of my visits and
had run into a couple of his teammates. Gabe had been pleasant and
even cracked jokes, but still with a certain formality. There was none
of that with Davis.

Davis leaned toward me. "So, Gabe tells me one of the things you're working on is understanding Colony Collapse. Is that true?"

I nodded. "In a roundabout way. My colleagues and I study Varroa destructor infestations and whether there's a connection to Colony Collapse Disorder." I talked for a little while, explaining more about my research and that one of the things I focused on was changes in queen laying behavior due to Varroa mites and possible ways to mitigate it. "Colony Collapse Disorder is a separate issue, and a complex one. Thus far, there appear to be a number of likely causes."

I was careful not to go into too much detail. It was a flaw of mine that I could talk about bees and my research to the point of exhausting my audience's interest.

Davis told me a little about his work as a lawyer. I already knew from Gabe that Davis was a workaholic who had four assistants and carried multiple phones. Despite a somewhat boyish appearance, there was a certain calculating air about him. He struck me as someone you'd probably want on your side if you ever had any kind of problem—legal or otherwise.

"What do you say we eat the soup and sandwiches you brought?" Gabe said to Davis, getting up off the couch where he'd been sitting next to me. He headed toward the kitchen. "I hope you remembered no oil or sugar."

"Don't worry, they came from that healthy place you like."

Petey, who'd been sitting on Gabe's lap, came over to me, and I petted him.

"So, I hear you're learning about football from a zero-knowledge base," Davis said to me.

I laughed. "That's one way of putting it, but yes, I am. In fact, I have some new questions," I said, turning toward Gabe in the kitchen.

He was opening the bag of food Davis had brought. "Fire away."

"What's a turnover? I kept hearing that phrase mentioned on Sunday."

Both Gabe and Davis took turns explaining to me that a turnover was when the teams switched possession of the ball for various reasons, including a fumble, interception, or turnover on downs.

"Is a fumble just what it sounds like?" I asked.

"For the most part." Gabe told me how they happen and some of the rules surrounding them, which, of course, were numerous.

"And what are interceptions? I keep hearing those mentioned too."

Gabe got a strange look on his face and shook his head. "You don't need to learn about those. Trust me. In fact, you know what? That's enough football lessons for today."

Davis laughed.

I glanced at him. "What's so funny?"

"An interception is when a pass thrown by the quarterback is caught by a defensive player from the opposing team."

I considered this. "That doesn't sound good for the quarterback."

He smirked. "Definitely *not*."

Gabe banged around in a drawer in the kitchen, looking for something. "Dammit, Davis. Why did you have to go and tell her that? You've led her out of the Garden of Eden into a snake pit."

"Do they happen a lot? Have you had many interceptions?" I asked Gabe.

He scowled, pulling a knife out of the drawer. "No comment."

Davis wore an amused expression. "Quarterbacks *hate* interceptions, and what they hate even more is talking about their own." He grinned. "But yes, Gabe has had ninety-eight interceptions in his career."

There was a choking noise from the kitchen. "Eighty-seven!" a deep voice barked at us.

"Are you *sure*?" Davis asked with an innocent lilt. "Because I thought you were getting awfully close to one hundred."

"Go fuck yourself, Davis."

He chuckled and turned back to me. "As you can see, they're very touchy on the subject."

"He *does* seem quite touchy," I agreed.

"Quarterbacks don't like to acknowledge their interceptions."

Gabe growled. "Don't talk about me like I'm not standing right here! I acknowledge them, but then I move on. You don't win football games being overly cautious. Having said that, let's talk about something else, shall we?"

"Rainbows and unicorns?" Davis offered.

"Sounds perfect."

CHAPTER TWENTY-EIGHT

~ Gabe ~

The three of us ate soup and sandwiches and talked. I could already tell Davis approved of Theo. She was a lot different from my other girlfriends. For starters, Theo was full of opinions and couldn't care less if they contradicted mine. Davis once told me he'd never understood why I always dated such agreeable women. "Don't you get bored?" he asked. "The placidity?" Theo and I agreed on a lot of things, but she never hesitated to tell me when she thought I was wrong.

Also, she was stunningly beautiful. Maybe that was shallow on my part, but I couldn't help myself. If I was honest, she was probably the most beautiful woman I'd ever dated, and I didn't just mean beauty on the outside.

I thought about all the talks we had before I went to bed at night. Listening to her right before I fell asleep completely relaxed me.

Sometimes we'd talk for hours, and I worried I'd be tired the next day, but I never was. Instead, I felt like a million bucks.

A few of my teammates had commented on it, telling me I wasn't as big of an asshole as usual.

"Hey, whatever happened to that next-door neighbor of yours?" Xavier asked after a scrimmage. "With the red hair?"

"Yeah," Carson said. "That crazy woman who chained herself to your house."

I grinned at my two linemen. "I made her my girlfriend."

They both laughed and hooted with approving high fives.

"Damn, dawg. I knew there was something special about that one," Xavier said.

Carson nodded. "A woman like that? No wonder you're not pissed off like you usually are. I'll bet she's wild."

I smiled to myself. Theo *was* wild. She'd never see herself that way, but I saw it. She could be fierce and fearless. Not to mention stubborn. But I enjoyed all of it.

After lunch, Theo and I walked Davis and Petey to the front door.

Davis put his coat on and studied Theo. "So you're the one."

"What do you mean?" she asked.

He didn't reply, but I knew what he meant.

"I didn't see this coming," he said. "Somehow I missed it."

Theo tilted her head. "Missed what, exactly?"

"It's the challenge. I should have seen it the minute you chained yourself to his house, except it seemed crazy at the time." Davis shook his head with concern. He always examined things from so many angles that he liked to think he could predict the future. And I had to admit, oftentimes he could. "I think I'm *slipping*," he said with alarm.

"Don't worry," I said. "You're not slipping. For all you knew, she could have been actually crazy," I pointed out. "Also, you didn't know I had a thing for redheads."

Davis nodded and seemed both relieved and irritated. "That's true. I didn't have all the facts, did I? I was missing a vital piece of information. You should have mentioned that you liked redheads. I can't believe you never told me that."

I shrugged. "It never came up."

Of course, what I didn't tell Davis was that my sister had nailed this thing right from the start. That would have really driven him nuts. He and Regina with their puzzle competitions and who had the fastest brain.

"I almost forgot," Theo said to Davis. "Don't leave yet. I have something for you." She stood up from where she'd been petting Petey and disappeared briefly.

When she returned, she was carrying a jar of honey.

"This is for you." She handed it over.

Davis brightened. "Thank you. I can't wait to taste it. I'm sure it's delicious."

Theo seemed surprised. "You never tried any from the jar I gave Gabe?"

He glanced at me and snorted. "I never got the chance." Luckily, that was all he said.

We both gave Davis a brisk hug and Petey one last pat on the head before the two of them left.

As soon as they were gone, I bent down and picked up Theo, tossing her over my shoulder.

"Aaaah!" she screeched. "What are you *doing*!"

"You'll see."

I carried her through the living room and down the hall toward my bedroom with her laughing and complaining the whole way. Once we got inside the room, I took her over to the bed and dropped her onto it.

Her face was flushed as she giggled. "I can't believe you just did that!"

"I've been wanting to do that since the day we met, remember?"

She nodded, and there was a breathless quality to her voice. "I *do* remember."

I climbed onto the bed and lay over her, caging her in. "Damn, I thought Davis was *never* going to leave."

She smiled and wrapped her body around mine. "You trust him, don't you? I can tell."

"Yeah, I do."

"Does he know about all those skeletons rattling around in your closet?"

"For the most part," I admitted. Theo had been bringing this up more often lately, and it obviously bothered her.

"I tell you everything," she said. "I'm always honest."

"I'm honest with you too."

"But you don't trust me."

"It's not that simple."

Because the more we'd gotten to know each other, it was apparent that Theo wasn't like me. She didn't have anything to hide or be ashamed of from her past. Nothing scandalous. Her biggest scandal was that she'd made up most of the essay and padded what she'd written about herself on her undergraduate college application.

"Everybody pads those things," I said. "That's your biggest scandal?"

"They certainly do not!"

"Sure they do. They're basically like job résumés. What else you got?"

"I shoplifted some makeup when I was in high school."

I rolled my eyes.

"I had sex with my best friend's boyfriend while they were still together."

I turned to her with surprise. "Did you really?"

"No, but I could have! He came on to me, but I turned him down."

I chuckled. "It's okay that you don't have any skeletons. You should be glad."

"Is that why you won't tell me yours?"

I thought about this. "I just don't want you to think less of me, that's all."

"I won't think less of you." She stroked my cheek. "I promise."

But I knew she would.

———

WE SPENT the next few hours in bed. As always, Theo kept me hard like no other woman I'd ever been with. My dick was actually getting *sore*.

"Jesus," I said after our third intense round. "I can't believe I'm saying this, but I think I need a breather."

Theo laughed lightly. She was still on top, straddling me after releasing the dogs. "What do you mean? I'm doing all the work."

"I'm doing *some* of it," I said with indignation.

She ran a hand over my chest and down my arm. "You're the one who's a finely tuned athletic machine. I'm just some bookworm who stares at bugs all day."

"Except I think you've stumbled upon your superpower, and it's got nothing to do with bugs."

She smiled, leaning over me. "You're right. I never knew I enjoyed sex this much."

"Come here," I said, pulling her down so we were skin to skin. I closed my eyes and ran my hands down her silky-smooth body, those soft breasts pressing into me.

Somehow, Theo had become my heart and soul. I didn't know exactly when it happened, but there it was. The sex was crazy good, but the rest of it was crazy good too.

She lifted her head, and the two of us contemplated each other. We did this a lot. Sometimes we'd stop everything and just stare at each other like we were telepathic.

"How's your thumb?" she asked, since I was still wearing the brace on my hand. Her brows drew together. "Why didn't I see you wearing a brace during the game on Sunday?"

"Because I didn't wear it on the field."

"Shouldn't you have?"

I shrugged. "I considered taping it, but I didn't need to."

She frowned and sat up, running her hand down my arm. "I think you're making that up. You're obviously still injured."

"Football's not just a physical game, it's a mental one. I can't afford to look weak."

"It seems reckless to play with an injury and not try to protect it."

I shook my head. "I'm *never* reckless. You know that."

She stroked my arm some more. "I hate this. The hardest part about watching a football game is seeing you get tackled or hurt. It never gets any easier."

"I told you, it's not as bad as it looks. We wear helmets and all that padding for a reason."

She studied me. "You don't know what it's like watching it though."

"It comes with the territory, Theo. It's not something I can change."

"I just don't know how I'm supposed to get used to it."

I went quiet. "You *have* to. This is my *life*."

She took a deep breath, then nodded. "You're right. I'll do my best."

Eventually, we got out of bed and took a shower together. Afterward, we threw some clothes on and decided to go out for dinner. During football season, I ate a strict whole food diet, and luckily, there were a few places in Seattle that were accommodating.

We held hands in the car as I drove us up to a place in Wallingford where I'd eaten a few times. It was a brisk fall evening, and both of us were bundled up in warm coats. Theo's nose and cheeks were pink, and she looked so pretty.

The restaurant was crowded as we waited in front for a table, having requested a booth.

"Excuse me, sir," a server said as he approached us, holding a couple of menus. "Would you be okay sitting in the center? It's just that we're really busy tonight."

The problem was the guy didn't call *me* "sir." He was talking to *Theo.*

"*What* did you just say to her?" I asked, stepping forward. But Theo immediately put her hand on my chest to subdue me.

She turned to the server. "I'm a woman, so please don't call me 'sir.'"

The guy's eyes widened, and at least he seemed mortified. "I'm really sorry! My apologies! I don't know what I was thinking. Maybe I need glasses!"

She nodded. "And yes, a table in the center is acceptable."

We followed him into the restaurant and took a seat. He dropped the menus like they were on fire and sprinted away from us as fast as he could. It was a busy place, and every table and booth around us was full. I felt a few people eyeing me, probably recognizing who I was.

Theo seemed calm as she picked up one of the menus and began to look through it.

I was *not* calm. Because a terrible realization came to me.

"That's happened to you before, hasn't it?"

She put her menu down. "It's my height. Sometimes I get mistaken for a guy." I could tell she was embarrassed, and it pained me to see it. "I told you. No one calls me beautiful but you."

I was dumbfounded. "I don't understand this." My head swam. The world seemed tilted and backward. *Are these people all living in crazy land? Am I the only sane person?*

"You can see now why I have difficulty accepting your version of reality," she said. "I've been living in this one my whole life."

I reached down and grabbed the edge of her chair, dragging it close to mine. And then I leaned over and kissed her.

At first she pulled back and seemed stunned. "What are you doing?"

"I'm kissing my girlfriend, who happens to be incredibly beautiful."

"What about cameras and cell phones and people watching?"

"Fuck 'em," I growled. And then I kissed her again. This time with heat and passion and everything else I felt for her.

When we parted, she put her hand to my cheek. "I don't know what I'm going to do with you, Gabe. You're so wonderful."

I gave her a sly grin and lowered my voice. "You seem to know what to do with me just fine."

She laughed and pushed at my shoulder. Her eyes were bright as she leaned in close again and whispered, "You're right, I do."

WHEN WE GOT BACK to my penthouse that evening, Theo showed me samples of jar labels that a friend of hers had designed for her honey. She'd already mentioned to me how she planned to sell it at a local health food store to help recoup some of her costs.

I looked over each of the labels. A couple of them had drawings of bees, while most of them had pictures of Theo.

"Eliza thinks I should use one with a photo," Theo said. "She thinks I have a unique look and that I should take advantage of it."

I studied the labels some more. Theo looked pretty in all the photos. I especially liked one where her head was turned to the side, but she was still looking at the camera.

"Your friend is right. These photos are great, especially this one." I pointed to my favorite. "You look particularly beautiful."

"Do you really think so? You're not just saying that because of what happened at the restaurant?"

I gave her a look. "I'm saying it because it's the truth."

"Okay." She gazed at me for a long moment. "I believe you."

I unfolded myself from the couch. "Also, I have something I meant to give you earlier." I went into the kitchen and grabbed the black keycard.

"What's this?" she asked after I handed it to her and sat down again.

"It's a keycard to the penthouse elevator."

Her brows went up.

"This way you can come up directly. And if you ever happen to be in the city, you can drop by. Your name's already been added to my permanent guest list."

She studied the black card in her hand. "Who else has one of these?"

"Just Davis and Regina."

"Really? No old girlfriends?"

I shook my head. I'd never given one of these to any woman I'd dated. "Just you, Professor."

I could tell she was pleased. "I might have to drop by on you unannounced sometime. Catch you in the act."

"The act of what?"

"I don't know. We'll see, won't we?" She wore a teasing expression. "Whatever you do with yourself when you're all private and alone."

LATER THAT NIGHT IN BED, as we lay there facing each other, she began to tell me about some of her other experiences. The way she'd been mistreated over her appearance. Names she'd been called since she was a kid. Weirdos following her around. Strangers coming up to her and saying terrible things.

My gut clenched, and it was hard to listen to without feeling a torrent of rage. "I'd burn this whole fucking world to the ground for you. You know that, right? If I thought for one second it would make any difference."

She reached over and stroked my neck. "I know you would."

"I don't even understand it. It makes no sense."

"I'm guessing you've never experienced anything like it. It's different for men. And you're extremely handsome. I'll bet your appearance has never been a detriment. Just the opposite."

"That's not true. I think my dad's always resented me for the way I look."

Her brows drew together. "What do you mean?"

"Regina and Mateo look like him, but I look just like *her*. Like my mom."

"Is that so terrible?"

"Every time he sees me, I think I remind him of what she did to us. There's no other explanation for why he's always been such a jerk to me."

We studied each other. The city lights shone behind her through the large bedroom window, illuminating her pale skin.

"I'm sorry," she said. "That's terrible. I hope it's not true."

I shrugged. "It doesn't matter what's true anymore. I've moved on." I took her hand and laced our fingers. "And now I have you."

The two of us gazed at each other. It felt like I'd spent my whole life searching for her.

If only I'd met her years ago.

"I'm going to tell you something," I said. "And you're not going to like it. In fact, you're probably going to get pissed."

"What?" She stared at me with trepidation.

I licked my lips, half in disbelief over what I was about to admit. "I've fallen in love with you, Theo."

CHAPTER TWENTY-NINE

~ Theo ~

"It's the one thing you told me not to do," Gabe said. "And I don't expect you to say it back. Not unless you feel the same."

I was so stunned I didn't know what I felt. "I wasn't expecting this."

He nodded. "I know you weren't."

We gazed at each other, and my feelings were a tangled knot to unravel.

"Talk to me," he said. "I can feel that brain of yours on its hamster wheel."

How had this football jock come to know me so well? Come to be so important in my life? "It wasn't so long ago that I thought I was in love with Clement."

"Are you still in love with him? You can tell me the truth." His expression was calm, but I'd gotten to know Gabe pretty well, too, and he wasn't calm.

"I'm not in love with Clement. Not anymore. Not after what he did to me."

"Good."

I reached over to touch his jaw. "You're like this force of nature, aren't you? Gale winds. A volcano. An earthquake. That's how you've come into my life."

He smiled at that.

"Nothing gets in your way."

"You can handle me because you're the same."

I always felt seen when I was with Gabe, and I realized this was part of it. He never underestimated me. "I guess it was the way we met," I said. "It established a baseline between us."

"You're probably right."

I liked that I didn't have to explain any of this to him, how he followed my thoughts so easily. "You love a challenge so much. Will you still love me once the challenge is over?"

"Don't kid yourself, Theo." His expression turned earnest. "The challenge between us will *never* be over."

I laughed.

Gabe still held my hand, and his gaze was intense. "Listen, maybe you're not ready for this yet, for what I want with you. But know this much—when you are ready, I'll be here."

THE SOUND of rain and wind pummeled Gabe's bedroom window. You couldn't hear any street noise up this high, but I always noticed the weather was stronger.

"I'm glad I told you," he whispered as he lay over me, moving inside me. "No matter what happens between us, you'll always know I love you."

My pulse pounded with all the sensations he was evoking in me. Not just in my body but in my heart and mind. Everything was ready to spill over. Because even though this was the same between us, it all felt different.

"What happened? I thought this was supposed to be animal lust?"

"Don't worry," he said, pulling out. I sucked in my breath. He flipped me onto my stomach, lifted my hips, and, with a groan, took me from behind. My fist tightened around a pillow as I gasped at the invasion, at the molten heat radiating through me. "It still *is*."

WE PARTED EARLY the next morning like we always did after our Tuesdays together. He left for practice, and I drove back up to Truth Harbor. It was only six o'clock, so I typically made it to the pollinator lab by nine.

It was a long drive and then a ferry ride, so it gave me a lot of time to think.

We'd been affectionate in public since the restaurant last night. Apparently Gabe had decided he didn't care about security cameras or random people's cell phones anymore.

"At some point, the press are going to see us together," he warned me last night after dinner. "They're going to figure out you're my girlfriend."

I shrugged. "I'm just a nobody. Besides, I don't care about pop culture or what people think."

"One of the many amazing things about you."

This morning, as we waited for the valet to bring my car around, Gabe had pulled me in close and kissed me in front of his building. "I love you," he said.

"The floodgates have really opened, haven't they?" I teased.

He grinned. "You're right. I'm going to tell you I love you all the time now. And do you want to know why?" He pulled me in tighter, his voice rumbling in my ear. "Because it pleases me."

Erotic sparks flew through my belly.

I couldn't say I was displeased by any of this. A part of me welcomed it with open arms, because I had strong feelings for Gabe. Stronger even than what I'd felt for Clement.

But is it love?

So much of it was tied to my physical attraction to Gabe. This was new for me. How could I know whether these strong feelings weren't just lust mixed with affection?

I asked Claire and Leah about it when we met for dinner at a Mexican restaurant a few nights later.

"You just *know* when it's love," Leah said. "I know that's not a satisfying answer, but it's the truth."

Claire nodded. "How did you know you were in love with Clement?"

I thought this over. "We had a strong intellectual connection. We could talk about our work endlessly and had a lot of common ground. I always looked forward to seeing him. It felt like we understood each other."

"And you don't have that with Gabe?" she asked.

"We do, to a certain degree." In some ways, Gabe understood me better than Clement. Maybe he didn't understand the nuances of my research, but he certainly understood *me*. "It's different with Gabe. We don't have that same common ground with our work, but on the other hand, we do understand each other. We also challenge each other."

"That doesn't sound so bad," Leah said, spooning some salsa onto her plate. "That's probably where all that passion is coming from."

But is it love? I wondered.

"It sounds like you two have grown really close," Claire said.

I nodded. "We have. I don't think I've ever been this close to a guy before."

Leah took a sip from her beer. "You're probably just overthinking it. Sometimes you just have to let yourself feel it."

I laughed. "That's the same thing Gabe's always telling me. 'Stop analyzing everything. Just let it happen.'"

"I think he's right," Leah said.

Claire looked up from her plate. "I nearly forgot. We're having a little party at our house on Sunday to watch the game. Philip invited some people over. You guys are welcome to come too."

Leah nodded. "Josh is going to be in Seattle with the band all weekend, but I can make it."

"I could probably make it too," I said, dipping a chip into some salsa. "I've never been to a football party."

Claire grinned. "I know. Talk about ironic. You always hated football, and here you are dating an NFL quarterback!"

"It *is* very ironic," I agreed.

"Do you still hate football?" she asked, curious.

I shook my head. "I wouldn't say that. I've been learning a lot about it. There are some aspects I don't like. The physicality of it concerns me, but the game is more nuanced than I originally thought. I'm amazed at how complicated the rules are sometimes."

Claire rolled her eyes. "I know. I can't remember all those rules. And it seems like they change them constantly."

"Do you want us to bring anything on Sunday?" Leah asked.

Claire waved her hand. "Don't bother. Philip invited a number of people, so we decided to have the whole thing catered."

"That makes it easy," Leah said.

"I should warn you." Claire turned to me. "Some people might ask you what Gabe is like since they know you're dating him."

My brows came together. "How would they know that?"

"From that photo in the paper yesterday," she said.

I stared at her in confusion. "What photo?"

Leah and Claire looked at me with surprise.

"You haven't seen it?" Leah asked. "We figured you knew about it."

I shook my head, mystified. "I have no idea what you're talking about."

"Let me see if I can find it on my phone," Claire said, swiping hers open. "It's just a picture with a short blurb."

"It's amazing that no one's mentioned this to you," Leah said.

"I found it!" Claire handed me her phone. "It's in the Seattle About Town section."

I took the phone from her and was surprised to see a photo of Gabe and me holding hands, walking near that restaurant we ate at in Wallingford. It was early evening, but you could see us both clearly in the photo. The accompanying text wasn't long: *Seattle Sentries' quarterback Beauty Bardales was spotted out and about town recently with his beautiful new girlfriend, bee biologist Theodora Stewart.*

I was stunned. I glanced at some of the photos on the rest of the page. It appeared to be a local gossip section. "This photo was just taken on Tuesday. How would they know who I am so quickly?"

"Get used to it," Leah said. "Believe me, I speak from experience. Once the press finds out about you, they figure out everything *fast.*"

When I got home later that night, I tried calling Gabe. It went directly to voice mail. I glanced at the time and realized he was likely on his way to Maryland. He'd said the team was flying out tonight for Sunday's game.

I texted him the link to the picture in the paper, wondering if he'd seen it. Probably not. I also told him I'd be watching the game from Claire's on Sunday, and that it was my first football party, figuring he'd be pleased.

He'd already told me how this game with Baltimore was a big deal, that both teams were favored for the playoffs, and there was a lot of pressure on him. From my observation, Gabe didn't rattle easily, but I could tell he was ultrafocused. The last time we spoke was Wednesday evening, and we didn't talk long.

"I have to go," he'd said. "There's still a ton of stuff I have to work on tonight. Remember, I love you."

I wasn't sure what to say in response. *I care for you deeply* didn't seem like enough. "Be safe," I'd said, since it was usually my biggest concern.

"I always am, Professor."

CLAIRE WASN'T KIDDING when she said people would be asking me about Gabe. I'd arrived at her house for the football party less than an hour ago, and three people had already asked me questions about him.

"Are you really Beauty's girlfriend?" Some woman came up to me out of nowhere. She had long bleached hair, inch-thick makeup, and a giant diamond on her finger.

"Yes, we're dating," I said, irritated with all these nosy people. I was trying to be polite, since I was a guest, but wasn't sure how much more of this I could take.

She was drinking a glass of wine and was obviously inebriated. "God, he's so hot. I'll bet he's great in bed." She leaned closer and lowered her voice. "You can tell me the truth. What's he like? Is he kinky? Does he tie you up?"

I was tempted to dump my bottle of water on her head. Maybe I should have had a glass of wine to dull my senses, but I wasn't much of a drinker. I'd gotten drunk that night at Gabe's, but that was unusual for me.

I pointed across the room. "I believe that extremely handsome man over there is waving at you. He's by the French doors."

"What? Where?" She turned her head, and I managed to slip away.

Leah came up to me and linked her arm with mine. "Having fun yet?"

"Why are people so nosy?"

She shrugged. "I think they just want to live vicariously through you. That's the conclusion I've come to."

Luckily, we found Claire and Philip. They were chatting with Daphne and Doug, the owners of the health food store that would soon be carrying my honey. Eliza was nearby as well, talking to Philip's business partner, Gavin.

I smiled and waved hello to them both.

Claire and Philip's home, Sullivan House, was a beautiful hundred-year-old mansion right by the water in Truth Harbor. Claire had actually grown up here. The main living area was the size of a small ballroom, and they had set it up with extra couches and a giant screen to broadcast the game. And even though it was supposed to be casual, there were servers walking around offering people appetizers and glasses of wine and beer.

"For my first football party, this seems quite fancy," I said.

Claire laughed. "I was ready to roast weenies, but Philip invited some bigwigs from his poker game, so the weenie roast was off."

Once the game started, I discovered it was a different experience watching football with a group of fans. People constantly yelled and cursed at the television. Everybody seemed to have an opinion over every aspect and felt compelled to voice it.

It was strange and startling. I was used to watching these games alone in my living room while I graded papers.

Mostly, I focused on Gabe when he was on-screen and blocked everybody else out.

Claire and Leah were chatting about a book the three of us were reading.

"I just love the main character," Leah said. "What an adventurous life."

"I know," Claire agreed. "I can't imagine being a mistress, a spy, and a snake charmer all at the same time."

Meanwhile, on the television screen, Gabe had just gotten the ball and was running with it. People around us started to yell.

Leah and Claire stopped talking and watched.

He managed to dodge two defensive players from the other team as he headed in for a touchdown. I watched with bated breath. Everyone around me was screaming their heads off. Even the sportscasters describing it were excited. My heart beat faster, willing him to make it.

And he did!

The entire room erupted in a cheer.

The sportscasters were yelling, "Touchdown for the Sentries!"

But then something happened.

Without warning, some guy from the other team, who'd been following close, jumped on Gabe and knocked him to the ground, even though they were in the end zone.

Everyone around me started yelling.

"What the fuck's he doing?"

"Is that sonofabitch blind?"

"That's going to be a fifteen-yard penalty!"

All I could do was stare at the screen in a panic. I knew it was against the rules for a player to tackle another player after they'd scored a touchdown. Gabe once told me that after a touchdown, you were exhausted and vulnerable to injury.

The commentators kept talking about a foul and saying a defensive end named Travis Ward had tackled quarterback Gabriel Bardales after he scored.

I watched as this Ward guy got off of Gabe, but Gabe wasn't moving.

"Oh my God," I whispered.

The whole room around me had quieted as it became apparent that Gabe wasn't getting up.

CHAPTER THIRTY

~ Theo ~

The sportscasters were jabbering endlessly, showing the tackle on a replay window, while I watched in what felt like slow-motion horror as a bunch of medical personnel ran out onto the field. Very quickly, there was a crowd around Gabe.

Is he unconscious? Is he breathing?

My eyes were glued to the screen as I sat on the edge of the couch, sick to my stomach with panic.

"Oh my God," I kept repeating. "What's happening? Is he okay?"

I felt everyone in the room glancing in my direction. Claire took my hand and held it tight. Leah put her arm around me.

"They've got a first-class medical team there," Philip said. "They'll take care of him, Theo."

As I watched all these doctors surrounding Gabe on the field, I kept thinking about our last phone conversation, the way he'd said "I love you" and the way he'd been saying it to me over and over.

I should have said it back! What was I thinking?

Because it was crystal clear now.

I'm deeply in love with Gabe.

With all my stupid analyzing, I'd analyzed myself right out of the truth. Gabe was the best thing that had ever happened to me. I'd felt more alive since I'd met him. I felt more like myself when I was with him.

We'd opened up a whole new world for each other.

The idea of something happening to him was too terrible to even contemplate.

What if he never gets to hear me say I love him?

Everyone in the room continued to watch the screen as a bunch of people still surrounded Gabe on the field.

My phone buzzed on the table in front of me, and I grabbed it. It was Davis.

"What's happening, Davis? I'm scared to death."

"He's going to be okay, Theo."

"Are you sure? How do you know that?" I glanced around the room as everyone watched me on the phone, then returned my attention to the television. Everything felt disjointed and wrong.

"I just talked to one of the team's athletic trainers," he said. "Gabe's definitely conscious."

"He is? Then why isn't he getting up?"

"I don't know, but that's what they're trying to figure out." There was a beeping noise. "That's my other line. I have to go. I need to talk to Regina, but I wanted you to know I'm here. He's going to be okay."

He hung up.

My eyes went to the screen, and then we all watched as the crowd around Gabe stepped away. They'd brought a stretcher out for him. Apparently he didn't need it, though, because he was being helped to his feet.

Relief flooded through me like a raging river. *Thank God.* His helmet was off, and he put his hand up and waved to all the fans in the stadium. People cheered, and everyone in the room with me cheered and clapped as well.

I put my hands over my face and cried.

HE CALLED me from the locker room. "I'm okay, Theo. I can't talk long, but I wanted you to know I'm fine. I just had the wind knocked out of me, that's all."

"Thank God you're okay!" I was so relieved to hear his voice. "I'm so glad. What happened?"

"That motherfucker hit me right after I scored! He better get ejected from the game!" He sounded furious. I heard him talking to somebody else who was there. "Yeah, *good*. Baltimore is getting a fifteen-yard penalty, and they're ejecting that sonofabitch."

"Why weren't you able to get up?"

"I just had trouble breathing for a minute. But I'm fine now. Seriously."

We talked a little more, but he said he needed to call Regina really quick too.

"Have you spoken to Davis?" I asked.

"Yeah, for like two seconds. I guess he'd already talked to one of the trainers and knew I was okay."

We hung up, and I was beyond relieved that he was all right.

The irony was that after everything, Gabe played during the last quarter, and the Sentries won. I was on pins and needles the whole time, but he seemed fine. They beat Baltimore by twelve points.

Everyone around me was cheering and yelling when it was all over.

I didn't cheer and yell. Instead, I felt emotionally wrung out.

I WAS STILL in an emotional state when I got to work on Monday and discovered how the Seattle paper figured out I was Gabe's girlfriend. Apparently Gerald told them.

"So let me get this straight," I said to Gerald, standing in his office. "A reporter called here asking about my personal life, and you decided to tell them who I'm dating?"

"I didn't think it was a secret," he said in an innocent tone.

"It's not a secret, but it's still personal. Why didn't you just take a message and let *me* talk to them?"

He shrugged. "What does it matter? Besides, I think you were in class, *Professor* Stewart."

And there it was, the jealousy I was beyond sick of.

"Are you ever going to get past my being chosen for this professorship over you?"

He stiffened, and I could tell it surprised him to be confronted so directly.

"I've had enough of all your backstabbing and trying to undermine me," I said. "You must be extremely unhappy here. Maybe you should consider getting a job elsewhere."

"Are you threatening me?"

"Of course not. But why waste yourself in a place you don't want to be?"

Gerald went silent. He pushed his glasses up on his nose, and I thought he wasn't going to say anything more, but then he spoke. "They never should have given it to you. The only reason they did is because you're a woman. It's not fair."

I shook my head in frustration. This wasn't the first time I'd dealt with misogyny. Unfortunately, the field of entomology was dominated by men and could be quite the boys club.

"I've been here way longer than you," he said, his voice taking on a whiny quality. "You're younger than me. It's obvious that *I* should have gotten that professorship. Not you!"

"Funny that. I'm younger, and I haven't been here as long, and yet somehow I've managed to publish more. Maybe you should spend less time complaining and more time on the things that matter." What I didn't say was that I brought more passion to my work than I'd ever seen in Gerald's.

"It's not complaining when I'm trying to improve things!"

"You spent hours writing letters to the dean because you were unhappy with how the parking spots are arranged. Is that really the best use of your time?"

He glared at me.

"And I know you went behind my back to the chair, saying I was an embarrassment to the department, that I was unfit. How did that work out for you?"

Gerald's face turned bright red, and his features scrunched with fury. "I can see now why Clement dumped you. You're a beast! A big, tall, ugly bitch!"

I blinked in shock at the ferocious insult. In the past, I would have taken it to heart. I would have fought back, but deep down, I still would have believed that's what I was. But not anymore. I had Gabe to thank for that.

"Actually, I know exactly what I am," I said with a laugh. "I'm not a beast. And I'm a big, tall, *beautiful* bitch!"

CHAPTER THIRTY-ONE

~ Gabe ~

I t was Monday night, and I'd gotten home so late that I'd fallen directly into bed. I was drifting in and out of sleep with my usual insomnia when the doorbell rang.

What the fuck? What time is it?

I grabbed my phone. It was nearly midnight.

It rang again, and I got up. I slept in the nude when I was home, so I threw on some shorts and a T-shirt.

Is it the front desk? Is there a problem?

When I got to the door, I didn't even bother with the peephole and just swung it open.

The next thing I knew, a tall, gorgeous redhead was hurling herself at me. She threw her arms around my neck and wrapped her long legs around my waist.

"Theo?" I laughed, kicking the door shut. "What the hell are you doing here?"

"I'm surprising you," she said, kissing me.

I kissed her back, our tongues dueling together, playing with each other. Already I felt lighter and better now that she was here.

"Did I catch you in the act?" she asked, smiling at me.

"You sure did. The act of sleeping."

She laughed, but then her expression changed, turning serious. "Oh my God, Gabe, I was *so* scared."

I understood right away. "I know you were, baby."

We hugged each other, and neither of us spoke for a while. I closed my eyes and held her tight. This woman who I knew was the love of my life.

"I don't know what I'd do if something happened to you," she whispered.

"It's okay."

She drew back to look at me. "I should have told you. I'm so stupid!"

"Told me what?"

She quieted. "That I love you."

"Oh, that."

"Yes, *that*." She considered me and then tilted her head. "Did you already know?"

I nodded. "Yeah, I pretty much did."

She seemed amazed. "How did you know?"

"Because I know everything." Theo rolled her eyes, and I smiled. "I also knew that once you stopped analyzing it, you'd finally figure it out for yourself."

She stroked the back of my neck. "I really love you."

"I love you too."

"You're sure you're okay? There isn't anything you're not telling me, is there?"

"I'm definitely okay."

"Thank God."

She rested her head on my shoulder, her legs still wrapped

around my waist, and I carried her through my penthouse toward my bedroom.

I put her on the bed and lay over her, and for the longest time, we gazed at each other. Neither of us spoke as I began to undress her. She helped me by kicking off her shoes, lifting so I could pull off her hoodie, and then raising her arms to slide off her bra.

Even though I was the one who'd taken a hit, I knew Theo had taken one too. And that while I felt fine, she was still hurting.

"It was terrible," she said when we both lay skin to skin. "I've never been afraid like that."

"I know," I whispered. "But everything's okay now."

She nodded, and I used all my powers to soothe her, to turn her on, to excite her, to make her feel anything but that hurt.

I kissed her all over, my mouth moving over her breasts, teasing and playing with her nipples until she was grabbing my head, squirming against me.

I trailed my mouth lower over her stomach, then lower still. She sighed when I used every trick I'd ever learned to bring her to the brink of climax over and over again.

My cock felt heavy and almost painfully hard, but I ignored it. Theo's breathing was fast and quiet. I could always tell when she'd had enough. She grabbed my hair when I finally pushed her over the edge, moaning so loud and long that it nearly brought me there myself.

I moved up, panting. A stiff breeze would have probably done me in, but I grabbed her hips.

"Gabe," she breathed.

"I got you," I rasped. "It's just you and me." And then I took her with a groan. She was so perfect. So right. Always.

Afterward, we lay beside each other, and I drew lazy circles on her back. "Are you going to tell your bees about us?" I asked. "Tell them we're in love?"

"I already have."

"When?"

"Today before I came here. I told them we love each other, and that if it hadn't been for them, we might have never even met."

I smiled. "That's true."

"I went out to our secret meadow too."

"How's it doing?"

"Chilly and rainy, but still wonderful."

"I can't wait to be there with you again."

She sighed. "Me too."

I thought about how lucky I was. It wasn't because of football. It wasn't because millions of people knew who I was. It wasn't fame or money. None of that.

It was because of Theo. She loved *me*.

IT WAS LATE. So late. And even though we'd worn each other out physically, neither of us seemed ready to sleep.

We'd both grown quiet, contemplative, lying together in a tangle of damp sheets. I watched light reflections from the city flicker across the wall.

"I have a son," I said, my voice breaking the silence in my bedroom.

She turned to me, and I could tell I'd surprised her, probably shocked her. I dreaded this conversation, but at the same time, it had to happen. It wouldn't be right for her not to know exactly what she was getting into with me.

"He's twelve," I said. "He lives in Los Angeles with his mom and her husband."

"What's his name?" She sounded calm.

"Christopher."

She shifted onto her stomach to face me. "So, this is the skeleton in your closet? The cause of your insomnia?"

I nodded. There was more, but I figured this was enough for now.

"Are you in contact with him?"

I shook my head. "I haven't seen him since he was six months old."

She went silent then whispered, "*God*. I'm *so* sorry, Gabe."

I turned to her and fingered the curls brushing her shoulder. It shouldn't have surprised me that she would instantly get this, that she would know how much it hurt me that I hadn't been a part of his life.

"Who's his mom?" she asked.

"The girlfriend of my best friend in high school."

"And where is *he* now?"

Jesus. Theo had already found her way to the heart of it. She never failed to amaze me.

"He's dead."

She reached over and took my hand, and we laced our fingers. It was dark, but with the city lights I could still make out her features.

"What happened?"

"He died in an accident the summer after high school." I didn't go into more detail than that. "I came back from college after my freshman year, and maybe it was our shared grief, I don't know, but we started seeing each other. We got involved." I went quiet for a moment. "I didn't even know Gemma was pregnant until after I left to go back to school in Ohio."

Theo gazed at me, listening intently.

"I came back right away when she told me. But she didn't want that." I fell silent, remembering it, the helplessness I felt. "Her family stepped in after he was born. They're well off financially, and at the time, I was just a college student. They pushed me out." There was no other way to describe it.

"They didn't want you involved in Christopher's life?" Theo asked.

I snorted. "Not at all."

"But you were still his dad."

I nodded. And here was the horrible part. "I let them. I let them push me out."

Theo went quiet this time, and I wondered what was going through her mind.

"Still not thinking less of me?" I asked in a dry voice. I swallowed, praying I wasn't going to lose her over this.

"Why?" she asked. "Why would you do that?"

"Because I was young and stupid. All I could think about was football. I'd spent my whole life focused on one thing. So I stayed in Ohio, graduated with honors, and became a first round draft pick for San Francisco."

"San Francisco?"

I nodded. "I played with them for three years before being traded to the Sentries."

"And then what?"

"And then nothing. I tried to push my way back in, but it was too late. By that point, Gemma had gotten married, and her husband, Julian, had become Christopher's father. She wanted me to let Julian adopt him, so I did. It seemed like the right thing to do at the time. After that they wanted nothing from me. Not even my money, because by then I had plenty."

Theo didn't say anything, just listened.

"I sent them money for Christopher anyway. Davis set it up for me. That's how we met. I also started having Franklin keep tabs on things to make sure Christopher was okay."

"Who's Franklin?"

"She's Davis's private investigator. He uses her for a lot of stuff. I get these reports every year that tell me how he's doing." I smiled. "And the good news is he's doing great. Julian is a good guy. Christopher seems happy and healthy. What more could I want for him?"

Theo nodded. "I'm glad he's doing well. Does he know about you?"

"I have no idea. I'm not in contact with Gemma at all."

"Are you content with that?"

I took a deep breath. "Not really, though I've spent a lot of years trying to convince myself that I am."

"I think all kids want to know their parents."

"What are you saying?"

"I'm saying maybe you should consider meeting him."

I glanced behind Theo to the night sky, trying to find some solace in it. "It's not like I've never thought about it. I've thought about it a lot, actually. I just don't want to mess things up for him. It sounds like he has a happy and stable life. What if he doesn't want to know me?"

"Maybe he should decide that for himself. Twelve years is old enough."

I chewed my lower lip. "You don't think it's selfish that I want to get to know him after all this time? He's going to ask me where I've been all these years."

"Tell him the truth."

I shook my head. "I don't know."

"How could having one more person in his life who loves him be bad?"

Coincidentally, I had a meeting that same day with Davis to get my yearly report from Franklin. I told Theo I had to go out and why.

"What's in these reports?" she asked, sitting at the kitchen counter holding a mug of coffee.

"I can show it to you when I get back. It just tells me about Christopher's life, and a little about his interests and friends."

"So she spies on him?"

"It's nothing invasive," I said. "And maybe it sounds bad, but I just want to make sure he's all right."

She nodded. "I get it. When it comes down to it, he's still your son."

We'd slept in until ten, taken a shower together, and were having breakfast. Fruit and oatmeal with Theo's honey drizzled on it for me while she had buttered toast.

"I won't be gone that long," I said, finishing my oatmeal and going over to kiss her goodbye. "Make yourself at home."

It was a rainy November day as I headed to the heart of downtown, to the tall glass tower that housed Davis's office. Even though he was a partner in a law firm, he was so eccentric—and brought in so much damn money—that they'd basically given him his own floor.

I arrived five minutes early for our meeting, but Beth, one of his assistants, escorted me in right away. As usual it smelled like fresh popcorn. Davis had a popcorn machine and a fridge filled with drinks and other snacks right outside his office. A lot of his clients were athletes, and apparently we were all kids at heart, because even I couldn't resist the popcorn machine half the time.

He got up from his desk and gave me a quick hug. "Damn, Gabe. I'm glad to see you're still in one piece."

"Thanks. Me too."

Instead of heading back to his desk, we went and sat on the couches near the window with a dizzying view of Seattle. Beth asked me if I wanted anything, but I told her, "No, thanks," and she left.

We talked for a bit as we waited for Franklin. Davis was still obsessing about Miranda and the boyfriend.

"I think the guy's in the witness protection program," he announced.

I rolled my eyes. "Give me a break." But then I looked at him. "Are you serious?"

"Or maybe he's a former member of some black ops group."

"Did Franklin finally find something?"

He snorted. "Fuck no. Not a damn thing. *Nothing.* Can you believe it? This guy is the most boring, milquetoast asshole who ever walked the face of the earth." He wore a disgusted expression.

I shook my head and chuckled. Davis was used to people like *me.* People who had their secrets. Clearly he didn't know what to do with someone who had nothing to hide.

"Laugh all you want, but I think it's creepy," Davis said.

"You *would.*"

"It doesn't matter anyway." He glanced out the window, keeping his voice light. "It looks like Miranda and I are getting back together."

I tilted back and slapped my hand to my forehead. "Thank *God!* When did this happen?"

He laughed. "We're still officially in negotiations, but things are moving along nicely."

"Negotiations, huh?" Miranda ran a successful interior decorating firm and was as feminine as they come but, in some ways, could be as tough as Davis. "That must be fun."

He smiled. "It *is*, actually."

Davis's office door opened, and Franklin entered. She spotted us and came over carrying the familiar manila envelope she gave me every year.

Speaking of milquetoast, it was a look Franklin fostered to brilliant perfection. A full-figured woman in her midfifties with shoulder-length brown hair, glasses, and nondescript clothing, she looked like someone's harmless mom or grandmother. Davis told me she was the best private investigator he'd ever worked with, bar none. In fact, he'd called her a genius more than once.

With her generic appearance, Franklin could blend in anywhere. I always thought her only "tell," if you wanted to call it that, was if you took the time to look past those mud-brown glasses, her eyes were bright blue and full of intelligence. She never missed a thing.

"Nothing unusual to report," she said, smiling and handing me the envelope. "From what I can tell, he's a great kid, Gabe."

"Thank you." I took it from her. "I appreciate you doing this for me."

"My pleasure."

I knew Davis paid her a fortune and worried constantly that some other law firm would try to poach her. So far she'd remained loyal.

We chatted a little. She was a football fan and told me she was glad to see I was okay after the game last Sunday.

After she left, I put the envelope on the table in front of us and turned to Davis. "I told Theo about Christopher."

He didn't seem surprised. "What did she say?"

"She thinks I should see if he wants to be in contact with me."

Davis paused, and I could see the wheels in his head turning. He smoothed down the sapphire-blue tie he wore with his immaculate gray suit. "As your lawyer, I should advise you that you could be opening yourself to a myriad of problems that neither of us can predict, including the press finding out."

I nodded and glanced over at the envelope on the table. I knew there'd be a single picture of Christopher inside. At my request, Franklin took only one, since my goal wasn't to spy on him but to make sure he was okay. But that single picture was one of the highlights of my year.

Davis leaned forward. "Having said all that, as your friend, my advice is different."

I turned back to him.

"I think Theo is right. I've seen how much you've struggled with this over the years. You should see if Christopher wants that contact."

"Has Gemma's lawyer ever said anything?" I asked. "Do you know what she's told him about me?"

He shook his head. "I haven't heard anything, but if you want me to, I can reach out and see if the family is open to it." He paused. "Obviously they could say no."

I nodded. "I understand."

"We could still pursue it even then, but it would be different. Far more complicated."

"Let's just reach out and see what Gemma says."

CHAPTER THIRTY-TWO

~ Theo ~

"Why is there a jar of my honey wrapped in two T-shirts inside your travel bag?" I asked. I was looking for a nail file in his toiletry kit and had pulled it out, mystified.

Gabe glanced up at me from the bed where he was watching game film on his iPad and taking notes. Something he did a lot.

He'd already told me all about the meeting with Davis earlier and had shown me the information Franklin gave him about Christopher. There was a photo of him. He was a handsome kid. He looked more like Gemma, Gabe said, though I could see he had Gabe's coloring.

I knew he'd been worried about telling me he had a son, but I didn't hold it against him. He'd made some mistakes when he was young, but it sounded like he'd done everything he could to fix them, to make sure Christopher was all right.

"Uh...." Gabe wore a strange expression.

"It looks like it's never been opened," I said, examining the jar.

There was already an opened jar of honey in his kitchen that I'd used on my buttered toast this morning. I'd noticed that Gabe used it freely.

Realization dawned on me. "Wait, is this that first jar I gave you?"

"What are you doing for Thanksgiving?" he asked, putting his iPad down. "We have our bye week, so I've got the time off. Regina and Tess are flying up, and I'm going to invite Davis and Miranda since they're back together. I want to do it at the house in Truth Harbor."

I went over and sat next to him on the bed. "You're changing the subject."

He glanced down at the jar in my hand and still wore that odd expression. Finally, I realized what it was.

Embarrassment.

Gabe reached over, took the jar from me, and placed it on his nightstand.

"I never knew you were so sentimental," I said, pleased to learn something new about him.

He shrugged and seemed oddly shy, glancing off to the side. "I guess so. About some things."

"I like that you're sentimental." I leaned over and kissed him. "It's sweet."

He snorted and then, without warning, grabbed me and tossed me onto my back while I shrieked with laughter. "What are you *doing?*"

Gabe lay over me and grinned. "I got your 'sweet and sentimental' right here," he said, reaching for my hand and pressing it over the zipper of his jeans.

I smiled. "Not always such a tough guy, are you? I enjoy seeing your soft underbelly."

"It's not going to be soft for long."

And he was right. I could already feel his cock stirring beneath my fingers. "You're changing the subject again."

"But it's your favorite subject," he murmured, kissing my neck, bringing up goose bumps all over.

My breath quickened as my eyes fell shut. "I think it just might be."

I undid the button on his jeans and shoved the zipper down. He was already thick and hard.

"Are you ready to be fucked, Professor?" he whispered, watching me as I stroked him with my hand. "Because it's going to be *good*."

"Are you sure you can handle me?" I teased. "I'm a lot."

He balanced himself on his arms, gazing down. "It's true, you are."

We studied each other, and I felt seen just like always.

Then he stripped my jeans and underwear off and was back, both of us still half dressed. The sex *was* good. Slow and sensual, our eyes locked on each other the whole time.

"Have you ever had anything like this with anyone before?" I asked afterward as we both came down from the erotic high. We hadn't talked much about his past relationships, and I was curious. "Were you in love with Gemma?"

"I liked her, but I wasn't in love with her. I haven't been in love much in my life."

"Me either."

We were both lying on our backs, and he reached down for my hand. "Just one more way we're perfect for each other."

"You know, after seeing that photo of us together in the paper, I looked you up online. I couldn't find many photos of you with other women." There were like two, and the angle made it hard to see.

"That's because I'm always discreet."

"Did that photo of the two of us together bother you?"

"No." Then he turned his head to look at me. "Did it bother *you*?"

"I couldn't care less."

He nodded. "Good. Because that probably won't be the last one. Actually, I was thinking recently. Do you want to come to a game?"

I raised my brows and considered this. "I've never been to a football game."

"Yeah, I know. It's definitely time to change *that*."

It turned out the wives and girlfriends of the Sentries players had their own seating area inside the football stadium. After arriving, I flashed the special pass Gabe had given me and was escorted to join the other women.

Being inside a football stadium felt surreal.

Talk about modern-day gladiators. The stadium was filled with thousands of fans, and there were giant screens showing the action on the field. I had the strangest sensation that I was out of time and place. That I could just as easily have been in ancient Rome, seated with all the wives and family members of those gladiators.

Some of the women were friendly to me, though several were standoffish. I figured it was a clique I wasn't a part of. It didn't help that I didn't really fit in. Most of them wore heels and stylish clothing, whereas I just had my usual jeans and sneakers.

"You're Beauty's girlfriend?" a few of them asked me, and I told them that, yes, I was Gabe's girlfriend.

They told me who their boyfriends or husbands were, and I recognized many of the names. I was polite and tried to ask the right questions, but to be honest, I wasn't at my best in these types of social situations. I reverted back to my nerdy high school self—the outcast who never fit in with the popular girls.

I could tell there were a few who didn't know what to make of me, and there was someone named Brooke who basically glared at me. In fact, I thought I recognized her from that party Gabe threw when I was chained to his house.

"Don't mind her," a very pretty woman with dark skin and large brown eyes said, sitting in the empty chair next to me. "Brooke's just jealous. She's dating Cooper, but everyone knows she has the hots for Bardales."

I nodded, glancing at Brooke again, who was still throwing daggers my way. I didn't know what to say to this. A lot of women were attracted to Gabe. He once showed me a huge bag of fan mail he'd received. Quite a few of the letters came from women. Some of them claimed their undying love, and some even included naked pictures of themselves.

"I'm Dawn," she said, holding her hand out to me. "My husband is George Daniels. He's a wide receiver."

"Oh!" I smiled and shook it. "I know who that is. Gabe speaks very highly of him."

We chatted for a bit, and it was a relief to meet someone who was so friendly and down-to-earth.

The game went on for over three hours, and, as always, I worried about Gabe's safety.

"How do you do it?" I asked Dawn. "How do you not worry all the time when they're on the field?"

"Oh, I *do* worry," she said. "Trust me, I worry like crazy sometimes."

"How can you stand it?"

"Because I remind myself that playing in the NFL has been George's dream his whole life. How many of us get to live our dreams?"

After the game, as I was headed out from the special seating area, it surprised me to see a number of reporters gathered nearby. What surprised me even more was that some of them were calling me by name.

"Theodora Stewart! Is it true you're Beauty Bardales's girlfriend?"

"Did you really start dating him after chaining yourself to his house?"

At first I ignored them, but then it occurred to me that this might be useful. "It's true," I said, turning toward a couple of reporters. "I'm dating Gabriel Bardales, and it's also true I chained myself to his house. Would you like to know why?"

They grinned at me, eager to shove their microphones in my face, hoping to hear something juicy. "To get his attention?" they asked. "It sure looks like it worked!"

By now there were three reporters in front of me holding out microphones with cameramen next to them.

"I was there for my bees." And then I told these reporters all about honey bees and how important they were for our environment.

They kept trying to interrupt me with silly questions, asking me how long Gabe and I had dated and was it serious, or what did I think his chances were of leading the Sentries to the Super Bowl. It was quite absurd. Did they really think I was qualified to discuss football? And that I'd even consider discussing my personal life?

"Please avoid using pesticides on *all* flowering plants," I said, looking directly into each camera. I held my finger up. "Or, at the very least, please read the labels on them to make sure they're bee safe. Do you know how many millions of honey bees die every year from pesticide poisoning?"

Some of the reporters began to get that desperate look I recognized from when my audience wanted to escape.

"Remember, honey bees are vital to our food crops," I said quickly before they cut me off. "*You* can make a difference!"

CHAPTER THIRTY-THREE

~ Gabe ~

"Don't fuck this up," Regina said to me. It was Thanksgiving, and we were alone in the kitchen getting dessert for everyone still sitting at the table. "She's good for you."

"I know."

Regina pointed a triangular spatula at me. "She's smart, and she's not going to let you get away with jack shit."

I snorted. "Believe me, I know that too."

Regina and Tess had flown up yesterday and were staying in my guesthouse while Davis and Miranda were staying in one of the guest bedrooms in the main house. And even though Theo lived right next door, she was staying in my bed with me.

Regina gave me a sly grin after she pulled the pumpkin pie out from the fridge. "You always liked those smart girls in school."

Did I? I thought back to when I was a kid.

It was true. I did.

I grabbed plates and the pecan pie Theo and I had picked up from a local bakery yesterday. We brought everything out to the dining room, where there was a lively discussion going on about Truth Harbor's origins as a pirate town.

"Regina and I have always loved pirate stuff," Tess said to me as I placed the pecan pie on the table for everyone. "I can't believe you never told us about the origins of this place."

"You guys should definitely do some exploring while you're here," Theo told them. "There's even a pirate museum. It's really fun."

"That sounds great," Regina agreed.

They were staying for the weekend. Davis and Miranda were headed back to the city tomorrow, and I had to leave on Saturday since we had a game on Monday.

"I enjoyed your short interview with the press last week," Davis said to Theo as he spooned whipped cream onto his pecan pie. "Very educational about bees."

"I enjoyed it as well," I said with a grin. It had been entertaining as hell watching Theo talk about bees while all those reporters frantically tried to get her to change the subject.

"I was amazed they actually aired it," Davis continued. "Though I've heard people are fascinated by you two."

Theo and I glanced at each other.

"They are?" I asked. "Where did you hear that?"

Davis smiled. "You know me. I have my sources."

Huh. I wasn't sure what to make of that.

"Who decorated your house, Gabe?" Miranda asked as she dug a fork into a piece of pumpkin pie. I hadn't seen her in a while, not since she and Davis had broken up. She was a pretty woman with a curvy body and long blonde hair. She usually wore a lot of pink and pastel colors, and today was no exception.

I glanced at Davis, who was smirking with amusement.

"I did," I said. My decorating skills left something to be desired. I'd bought a big leather couch and chairs along with a flat-screen for the great room. My priorities were gym equipment and beds for rooms that needed them. A sparse office. And not much beyond that. Regina had been nice enough to help me stock the kitchen the first time she came up.

"It's quite... rustic," Miranda said, glancing around. "It reminds me of a frat house. The basketball hoop in the living room is an interesting choice."

I pointed my thumb at Davis. "Hey, *he* helped me decorate." No way was I taking all the blame for this. "In fact, I think that basketball hoop was his idea."

"It's true," Davis said, turning to her. "I did help, but I didn't have *you* to consult. He decorated it while we were apart."

"You could have still consulted me," she said, swallowing a bite of pie.

"My pride wouldn't let me, darling."

"You poor thing." She reached over and took his hand. The two of them gazed at each other, and it was obvious they were happy to be together again. Petey was happy, too, as he slept contentedly on the nearby dog pillow they'd brought for him. The whole thing made me feel like I was in a Cary Grant movie.

"Thank goodness I'm here now." Miranda looked around some more. "The house itself is stunning, but you're definitely not showing it to its potential."

"I'm sure you're right," I said, eating some pecan pie—a one-day indulgence. "What do you suggest I do?"

Everyone joined in on the discussion about how they thought I should decorate my house. It was amusing, to say the least. Regina thought I needed pinball machines. Tess thought I needed houseplants. Davis said I should hang up football memorabilia, to which Miranda surprisingly agreed. "But only in your office," she clarified.

Theo didn't comment at all. We kept glancing at each other, our eyes lingering. She sat beside me, and I snuck my hand under the table to hold hers like we were teenagers.

Yesterday, after going into town for groceries, we'd managed to sneak off to our secret meadow. It had been cold and damp, and all the wildflowers were gone, but it was still amazing. And it was still *our* place as we snuggled together on a stack of blankets, gazing at the shifting gray clouds above us.

"Should I ravish you now?" I'd asked, the two of us wrapped in each other's arms for warmth.

"How about you ravish me later in front of the fireplace in your nice, warm bedroom."

I chuckled and squeezed her tight. "I was hoping you'd say that."

"Look." She pointed upward at a lone bird circling the sky.

It was an eagle. We watched it glide beneath the clouds.

"I wonder what it's like to be so high. So free," she said. "Can you imagine?"

We continued to watch it, both of us up there soaring with it in spirit.

After Thanksgiving dinner, Davis, Regina, and I settled ourselves in the great room to watch the second football game of the day. Miranda, Tess, and Theo stayed for part of it, then left to go hang out and talk somewhere else.

Later that night, when I went upstairs to join Theo in the bedroom, she was sitting on the bed wearing one of her long T-shirts with her laptop open.

"Tess told me your dad is getting married," she said. "You never mentioned that."

I shrugged out of my jeans and hung them over a chair, figuring I'd wear them again. "That's because I just found out myself."

"Do you happen to know who he's marrying?"

I shook my head. "No clue. Regina says she's met her and likes her. My dad and I haven't spoken in almost two years."

"I wonder if you should call him. Maybe it's time to bury the hatchet."

I gave her a look as I searched through my drawer for clean boxers. "I think you know how I feel about that."

"You always tell me I'm pigheaded, but you are too."

I shrugged. "I've never denied it."

"Who's Tyler?"

I paused. "Where did you hear that name?"

"I overheard Regina talking to Tess. She said you and Davis clowning around together sometimes reminds her of Tyler."

"That's not true," I muttered. Davis was nothing like Tyler. Tyler had been reckless, whereas Davis was just the opposite.

"So who is he?"

I pulled out a clean T-shirt and boxers from the drawer. Most of my demons had been slumbering since Theo entered my life, but now it felt like they'd guzzled a case of energy drinks and were ready to rock. "He was my best friend from high school. The one who died."

"I'm sorry. I didn't know."

I kept my face neutral, though my insides were churning.

She studied me, and I waited with dread for Theo to get interested, for the scientist to start analyzing the last skeleton that was trying to punch its way out of my closet. I wondered if she sensed my emotions.

"Do you want to tell me about him?"

"Not tonight. Maybe another time."

I felt her deliberating and hoped she didn't push it. Finally, she nodded. "Tess says Regina is really happy that you're reaching out to Gemma about Christopher."

I let out a quiet sigh of relief. "Yeah, she is." Regina had gotten nearly weepy when I told her I hoped to establish a relationship with him. And my sister *never* got weepy. Apparently having a nephew who she'd never seen or spoken to had been harder on her than I thought.

"I want to ask you something, Gabe."

I glanced up at the tone of her voice. "What?"

Theo closed her laptop and set it on the nightstand. "Would you like to come with me to my parents' house for Christmas?"

My brows shot up.

She took in my expression. "Is it too much too soon? I'll understand if it is. We've only been dating four months. I've told them about you, though, and they're curious."

I put down the T-shirt and boxers and came over to her on the bed. "It's not too much too soon," I said, taking her hand. "I think it's great. I'd love to meet them."

"You would?"

I nodded, pleased that she wanted this. I'd meant what I said before, that when she was ready for what I wanted, I'd be here. And what I wanted from Theo was something serious and lasting.

"I'll probably only be able to stay a night or two," I warned. "It's still football season, but I have Christmas Day off this year."

She smiled. "That's okay. It's enough."

LIKE EVERY YEAR, the month of December was intense. There was a lot of pressure with every game, especially since we were favored to make it to the playoffs. The schedule was grueling, and I worked harder than I ever had in my life. And when I wasn't working, I tried to spend every spare second I could with Theo. We managed to attend a couple of team Christmas parties together, and I got the impression that Davis was right. People seemed fascinated with our relationship.

I had mixed feelings about this. While I was used to being in the spotlight, I wasn't used to having someone I cared about being in the spotlight with me. I worried it might distress Theo. Not that it seemed to at all. I should have known she was tougher than that. Any time a reporter stuck a microphone in our faces, I was happy to tell them I was only here to win football games, then stand back and let Theo do her thing. It was fun to watch. Especially because as hard as the press tried to get her off the subject of bees, she could *not* be deterred.

She told me that her department chair was thrilled with all the positive publicity and that they'd been getting a lot of support and interest at the university's pollinator lab where she worked.

I wondered if I'd hear about any of this from the GM or even the Sentries' owner, but they didn't seem to have a problem with it either.

The day before Christmas Theo and I headed down to her parents' place in Eugene. I was nervous about meeting them, but they turned out to be nice people. Neither of them were into football, but they didn't seem to hold my career choice against me. Her dad was pleased that I'd been a history major, and I enjoyed talking to them both. I was completely in love with their daughter, and I suspected they saw it, and could also see how happy Theo was with me.

Everything seemed to be going great. By the end of the month, the Sentries were locked in for the playoffs. Postseason started in January, and the timing worked out that the whole team had New Year's Eve and New Year's Day off.

As a result, I was able to make it to a New Year's Eve dinner Theo had with her friends every year. Being a harbor town, there were a few swanky seafood restaurants along the water in Truth Harbor, and we met at one to ring in the new year.

For the first time in my life, I was happy and in love, and headed for the Super Bowl. The coming year looked like it was going to be smooth sailing.

CHAPTER THIRTY-FOUR

~ Theo ~

In the three years that I'd dated Clement, he'd only made it back to Truth Harbor *once* for New Year's Eve. So most of the time, while people around me were cheering and kissing each other as they rang in the year, I was usually the lone outsider.

Well, not this New Year's Eve. This time I wasn't on the fringes.

"5... 4... 3... 2... 1—Happy New Year!"

Everybody cheered and clapped. Gabe swept me into his arms. He felt strong and solid. Like my future. Like everything in my life was finally coming together exactly how it was supposed to.

"I love you," he said after we kissed. "This is our year, Theo."

I smiled. "It is. And I love you too."

The elegant restaurant we'd gone to had the best seafood in town, along with a live band that played swinging rockabilly. It was the largest group we'd ever had for our New Year's Eve dinner. To think it used to be just Claire, Leah, and me. Now it included Philip and

Josh. Dean—Josh's best friend. Eliza was there, along with a fellow actor she was dating. Isabel and her new boyfriend came. Leah's brother, Lars, stopped by our table to say hello. Even Gavin—Philip's business partner—showed up with his supermodel girlfriend, though I couldn't help noticing the way his eyes were constantly on Eliza.

We danced, toasted with champagne, and nibbled on delicious prawn appetizers all night. The party didn't break up until around one thirty.

"There's one last thing I need to do," I told Gabe after we arrived at my house. While I enjoyed his Spanish castle, I'd insisted we stay at my place tonight for a change.

"What's that?"

"I have to tell my bees it's a new year."

He yawned, leaning against the doorframe. His cheeks were flushed, and he looked handsome standing under the porch light in his black wool peacoat. "Can't you just tell them tomorrow?"

"Come on," I said, after tucking my purse under a chair on on the porch and grabbing his hand. I was still a little tipsy from drinking champagne. "It won't take long. It's a tradition. I do it every new year after midnight."

He laughed. "All right, fine. Let's go talk to some bees."

We headed down into my lower yard, still holding hands. Luckily, I had solar lights set up, so it wasn't pitch-black. I hadn't even changed my shoes and was still wearing a pair of peep-toed platform pumps. I'd painted my toenails dark red for the holidays.

"Do we need to put on those bee suits again?" Gabe asked.

I shook my head. "It's not necessary. I'm not opening any hives."

As we approached my bees, I let go of Gabe's hand so I could move in closer. Bees didn't hibernate during the winter, and I knew inside each hive they'd formed a winter cluster around their queen to keep everyone warm.

My ritual every year was the same one I'd been doing since I was a little girl. I'd stand behind each hive and quietly tell the bees inside that it was a new year, and it was going to be a good one.

I could feel Gabe standing back, watching with interest as I spoke to each beehive. Even though this whole thing was odd, I'd gotten the impression that he liked the quirkier aspects of my personality.

"It's a new year," I said quietly when I finally got to the last hive in the row, repeating what I'd said to all the others. "And it's going to be a *good* year."

Before leaving, I walked around to check the front of each hive. On one of them, I noticed some leaves and twigs were blocking the entrance. Even though bees didn't forage in the winter, some of them still left the hive to keep it clean, and of course, the undertaker bees had to remove the dead ones from inside.

Without thinking, I reached down and brushed the leaves and other debris away. I wasn't sure what possessed me, since I was never careless like that. In the dark, I could barely make out the movement of any bees nearby.

"Ow!" I yelped as a familiar burning pain pricked my ring finger. I quickly jerked my hand away.

"What's wrong?" Gabe asked, moving toward me. "Is everything okay?"

"Stay back. I've been stung."

"Are you all right?"

I cursed with irritation. It had been over a year since a bee had stung me. I walked quickly toward him, holding my finger up. "Come on, we better move away."

We both strode up the hill. Glancing back, I didn't see any angry bees following us. It was night and winter, so that worked in our favor.

"Do you have a credit card?" I asked Gabe.

"Uh, sure." He gave me a quizzical look but reached into his back pocket for his wallet.

"It's the best way to remove the stinger," I explained. "I'll need the light from your phone too."

"You don't want to go inside the house and do this?"

I sniffed and shook my head. It was cold out, but I knew from past experiences that it was best to get the stinger out right away. "You don't want too much venom in your system," I explained. "It can make the reaction worse."

He handed me the credit card and held his phone up with the flashlight on over my hand as I tried to scrape the stinger out.

"Dammit," I muttered. "I can see it right there."

"Do you want me to try?"

"I can do it." I worked at it for another minute before I finally got it out.

"Your hand is turning red," he said with alarm. "Is that normal?"

I nodded. "For me it is. Wherever I'm stung, the area typically gets red and swollen. In fact, I should go put some ice on it." I felt my finger burning.

He turned his phone's flashlight off, and we headed the rest of the way to the house. I was annoyed with myself for being so careless. What was I thinking? Obviously I'd panicked one of the guard bees enough that she stung me.

Gabe kept glancing over, and I could tell he was worried.

"It's okay," I said. "I've been stung lots of times. It's unpleasant, but that's all. In fact, I think I've built up some immunity over the years, because my reactions have lessened."

Once we got inside the house, he immediately went to my freezer and began searching through it while I washed my finger with soap and water. "You don't have any ice packs?"

I sat on one of my kitchen chairs, drying my hands. "No. Just hand me a bag of frozen peas."

He did as I asked and then stood beside me. "I have some ice packs at my house. Maybe I should go grab a couple."

I glanced up at him and realized he was icing body parts all the time. Of course he had ice packs. "It's not necessary. This will do just fine."

"Can I get you anything else?"

I smiled. Gabe was like a mother hen. "I'm okay. Really." I

yawned and looked over at the clock on the stove. It was almost two in the morning. "We should probably go to bed."

He nodded. "Yeah, we should."

"There is one more thing you can help me with," I said, still holding the frozen peas on my hand. "You can help me undress."

Gabe grinned. "*That* I'm happy to do."

MY BED WAS ONLY A QUEEN, and Gabe looked comically large in it. It also had a pink, girlish flowered duvet, which only added to the effect that he was a visiting giant.

"I'm buying you a California king," he said, fluffing a pillow for his head. "This bed is ridiculous."

"It would never fit in my room."

He glanced around my bedroom that was less than half the size of either of his. "We'll *make* it fit."

I rolled my eyes and laughed as I climbed in beside him. He'd helped me undress and change into a T-shirt since I couldn't use my right hand effectively. He also switched out the bag of frozen peas for a baggie of ice wrapped in a dish towel.

"Let me see your hand," he said.

I took the ice off and held it up. My entire hand was red, and my ring and pinky fingers were swollen.

"Jesus. Does it hurt?"

"It burns, but this isn't that bad."

"Are you going to be able to sleep? Maybe you should take something for the pain."

I yawned again, using my left hand to cover my mouth. "I'll be fine. If it keeps bothering me, I'll get some ibuprofen."

"Wake me up, and I'll get it for you."

"I'm not going to wake you up! It's just a little bee sting."

"Except it's not little." He glanced at my hand again. "You're sure that's normal, huh?"

I nodded and closed my eyes. It felt cozy being in my bed with him, his big warm body beside me. "It's fine. Could you turn the light off?"

He reached around to my nightstand and plunged us into darkness.

I must have been really tired because I fell asleep right away. My dreams were strange. I began to dream that my throat was itchy, and I was trying to scratch it. But the itch only seemed to get worse. In fact, it was getting so bad that I was having trouble swallowing.

I woke up with a loud gasp. "Oh my God," I croaked.

Gabe was sleeping beside me, and I grabbed his arm to shake him awake. "What's going on?" he mumbled.

I put my hand up to my throat, which felt itchy and tight. My chest felt tight too. Panic flooded my veins. "Something's wrong," I wheezed, barely able to get the words out.

He jerked awake and fumbled with the lamp on my nightstand. The space around my bed filled with light. He turned to me with alarm. "Are you okay?"

I shook my head, trying to stop my panic. I knew what this was, and it terrified me. I couldn't believe it was happening.

Gabe vaulted off the bed and grabbed his phone from the nightstand. My heart pounded in my ears as I took wheezing breaths. From a distance, I heard him talking to someone and realized he was calling 911.

"What's your house number?" He turned to me, frantic.

I tried to speak, but I couldn't say it.

He sprinted from the room, still talking on the phone, telling them the street we both lived on and that a bee had stung me a short while ago.

I knelt on the bed with my hands splayed. I tried to concentrate on breathing, to stay calm somehow and not let the panic take over.

Gabe reappeared. He was holding the phone to his ear with one hand and a piece of mail in the other. "They're on their way, Theo. Hold on tight, okay?"

I nodded, still wheezing and struggling for every breath, staring at the flower print of my duvet, my whole body drenched in sweat.

He was at my side and began to say calming things. Telling me to take slow breaths, that the paramedics would be here soon, that I was going to be okay. I could tell he was trying to keep the panic out of his voice.

I closed my eyes and tried to breathe, to calm my racing heart, to push my fear away. Something strange was happening, and the edges of my vision grew dim. The terror increased, overwhelming me, and then finally I realized I couldn't stop it—I was losing consciousness.

CHAPTER THIRTY-FIVE

~ Gabe ~

I'd had moments in my life that scared the shit out of me, but nothing compared to this. Not even close.

When the paramedics arrived, I sprinted outside, ready to drag them into the house, but they were fast and efficient, and I quickly realized the best thing was to stay out of their way.

They asked me questions, and I immediately told them about the bee sting. Just as the ambulance had pulled up to the house, Theo lost consciousness, and for one terrifying moment, I didn't know if she was alive or dead. Thankfully, the epinephrine shot they gave her seemed to help her breathe right away, and she began to blink and wake up. They put an oxygen mask on her face, transferred her to a stretcher, and left in the ambulance. I rushed back inside the house and quickly threw on a shirt and sweatpants since I was still only wearing boxer shorts. I stuffed some of her clothes, shoes, and her glasses into a backpack and raced to the hospital.

A horrible thought kept going through my head, playing on an endless loop, and it only increased my fear.

What if I hadn't been here?

What if she'd been stung while she was alone and unable to call for help?

They wanted to keep her in the ER overnight just to make sure she was out of the woods. I could tell this experience had seriously frightened her because Theo didn't even argue. Not one word. Instead, she looked scared and exhausted. Everyone encouraged her to get some rest.

While she slept, I called her parents in Eugene to let them know what happened. It was five in the morning, and no one wants to get a call at that hour, but I assured them she was okay. They'd dealt with the anaphylactic shock from the bee sting. Theo was going to be fine.

Not surprisingly, her parents freaked out and said they were coming up to Truth Harbor immediately, as soon as they could get a flight. I told them I'd let Theo know when she woke up.

I sat beside her in a chair by the bed and watched her sleep. Her freckles stood out in stark contrast against her pale skin. I wanted to hold her hand, to touch her, but I didn't want to wake her up. Instead, I watched her chest move slow and steady like it was supposed to.

Thank God.

Images from earlier kept crowding my head. Theo struggling for every breath. Theo limp and not breathing at all. The horror that she could have died right in front of me and I would have been helpless to prevent it was overwhelming.

I leaned forward in the chair and pinched the bridge of my nose, trying to stay calm. My whole body was shaking. I forced myself to take deep breaths.

Dammit. I needed to keep my shit together.

Somewhere in the early morning, still sitting in the chair, I must have passed out from exhaustion. I woke up to a doctor walking past me to check on Theo, who was awake and sitting up in the hospital bed. I immediately went to her side and took her hand.

"How are you feeling?" he asked her.

"Okay, but tired."

He nodded. "You'll probably feel some fatigue for the next few days as your body recovers from the anaphylaxis. You're very lucky the paramedics arrived when they did." He glanced at a computer, tabbing to a different screen. "It looks like your blood work came back positive for bee venom allergy."

She nodded but didn't say anything. Theo was always so vivid, but at the moment, she seemed worn out. It was as if all her normal zest for life had been drained away.

"Let's keep you for a little longer, but you should be okay to go home later today. Be sure to set up an appointment and see your doctor."

Once he left, I squeezed her hand. "I'm glad you're doing better. You really scared me."

She glanced up, and I'd never seen her so dejected.

"Hey, what's wrong? Aren't you feeling better?"

But she only shook her head and closed her eyes. It was like the weight of the world was pressing down on her.

"Talk to me, Theo," I said, my panic rising again.

"What am I going to *do*?" she wailed, her eyes filling with tears. "This is my worst nightmare. I'm severely allergic to *bees*!"

If I had to, I could usually find something to say in any situation. Despite constantly barking orders at my offensive line, I was also yelling encouragements. Except I couldn't think of a single thing to say here. There was nothing encouraging about this situation.

"This is my life's work," she said. She took her glasses off, wiping her cheeks. "I can't believe this is happening."

"Maybe you could switch gears and work with a different type of insect or pollinator."

"That's like you switching to soccer or basketball. How would that feel?"

I squeezed her hand. "You're right, but we'll figure it out."

By the time they discharged Theo from the hospital, it was almost one. Before we left, they gave her an epinephrine pen and showed her how to use it. They also told her she should consider buying a second pen, that it was best to have a backup.

She spoke to her parents before we left the hospital, and they were relieved she was fine. She tried to tell them they didn't need to fly up, but they were already on their way.

I was glad they were coming. They'd be able to keep an eye on Theo. Especially since I was supposed to head back to Seattle tonight.

While Theo talked to her parents, I decided, to hell with it. I called our head coach and told him I wouldn't be at practice tomorrow, that I had an emergency. He didn't answer his phone, so I left a voice mail. I knew this wouldn't go over well. We had our first game for the playoffs in less than a week.

Once we got back to Theo's house, the mood between us was weird and somber. I was beyond relieved she was okay, and I tried to focus on that, but unfortunately, this had brought up some bad memories for me.

We mostly hung out on the couch and watched movies. She was still icing her hand. At some point, I got up and made us sandwiches, but Theo barely even touched hers. She seemed despondent.

"Do you want to talk?" I asked. "Maybe between the two of us we can figure out a solution."

She stared at the television, looking miserable. "There's nothing to figure out."

I felt totally helpless. It wasn't a feeling I was used to, and I hated it. Not knowing what else to do, I just held her close. We were like two survivors clinging to a life raft in a stormy sea.

As it grew later in the day, I still hadn't heard from Coach Mallory. I figured I'd call Ryan, our GM, next, then our offensive coach, and then go down the list until I finally spoke to someone, but Theo stopped me.

"I'm fine now," she said. "You don't need to babysit me. I want you to go back to Seattle."

"It's not babysitting. I'm worried about you."

She nodded. "I know you are, but I'm tough, remember?"

But she didn't look tough. She looked pale and fragile. Anybody would be after what she'd just gone through.

She rested her hand on my arm. "I need some time alone to process this. And my parents will be here any minute."

"You wouldn't walk down to your hives while you were processing this, right?"

She went silent. "Of course not."

"I know this is terrible for you," I said, turning to her and kissing her softly. "I love you. I'll support you in any way I can."

She leaned against me, and I stroked her wild curls. "I know," she whispered.

I spent the rest of my week with the team getting ready for our wild card game against Pittsburgh on Saturday and worrying about Theo. Davis called me before the game, and I told him what happened. Even he was at a loss for words. He was a fixer, but this couldn't be fixed.

"At least she's all right physically," he said. "That's what you have to focus on."

"Believe me, I know." It's what I'd been trying to focus on. Though the memory of her struggling to breathe and losing consciousness was never going to leave me. For one moment, I thought I'd lost her, and that soul-deep terror was branded into me forever.

I'd been calling and texting Theo every day, but her responses were sporadic. She told me how she hadn't gone into the lab all week. Winter classes hadn't started yet, and her parents were still there, though they were headed back to Eugene soon.

Physically, it sounded like she was fine, but emotionally, I could tell it was bad. I already knew how she kept everything bottled up inside. I felt helpless, not knowing what to do.

It was frustrating as hell.

Despite everything, we won our game against Pittsburgh. Everybody was ecstatic. I was happy about the win, but it was colored by everything else going on. The team celebrated Monday night in Seattle at a local restaurant, and I joined them. Mostly so I didn't look like an asshole. While I was there, I got a text from Theo.

Theo: I just arrived in Seattle. I have some good news.

It was a relief to hear from her, and it was a happy surprise that she'd driven down. I texted back and told her I was at a restaurant downtown celebrating our win.

Gabe: I can leave now and meet you at my place.

Theo: That's okay. I'll come to where you're celebrating. Where are you?

I sent her the place's name and location.

Gabe: Let me know when you arrive, and I'll meet you out front.

It didn't take long for her to text me that she was here. I'd been chatting with Carson and Xavier, and they were both excited to meet her.

"I expect you both to behave," I said to them as I got up to go get her.

"Don't worry, dude. We'll be good," Carson said with a grin.

I made my way through the crowd of people to find Theo standing out front. She had on jeans, brown boots, and a puffy green vest. It was cold outside, and her cheeks and nose were pink. As always, she was stunning.

Mostly, I was happy that her mood had lightened considerably. It was a big change from when I last saw her. She smiled, and that wide, bright smile of hers did me in.

"Hey, you," I said with a grin. I kissed her and then grabbed her hand. "Come on back."

Carson and Xavier were both waving us over, and I brought Theo to join them at the table.

I introduced them to her over the noise and the music. "These are two of my offensive linemen. And if you can believe it, they're also both from my neighborhood in California."

Theo shook each of their hands. "It's nice to meet you."

"I can't believe I'm finally meeting the bee professor," Xavier said in awe. "You're famous."

"I am?"

He nodded and grinned. "Hell yeah. You're the boss with the press. Those bee interviews are tight."

She laughed. "Good to know."

Carson leaned forward with an earnest expression. "I even told my grandma to stop using pesticides on her flower garden. She stopped right away. She said she didn't know they killed bees."

Theo smiled and touched his arm. "I'm very glad to hear that. Please thank her for me."

A server came by, asking us if we wanted anything to drink. The place was hopping, everyone celebrating the win. People were dancing and having a great time. Daniels, our wide receiver, arrived with his wife, Dawn, and they both came over to join us. Theo and Dawn hugged hello. I knew they'd become friendly.

I tried to ask Theo what her good news was, but she shook her head. "I'll tell you about it later," she said over the music.

"Do you want to dance?" I asked.

She nodded enthusiastically, and we joined the crowd. Theo still hopped around shooting lasers and pistols like Annie Oakley, but I'd noticed she'd added some new moves—King Tut strutting that turned into a cat clawing the air when "Mr. Brightside" from The Killers started.

We spent the next couple of hours dancing and having fun with everyone. I wasn't usually this social but had discovered I enjoyed it when I was with her.

Once it got late, we said good night to people and left. Since we'd come in separate vehicles, she followed me to my building downtown.

I couldn't wait to get her upstairs, to be alone with her. I didn't even realize how bad my need was until I started kissing her in the elevator.

"What about the security cameras?" Theo asked, her face close to mine.

"Fuck 'em." I leaned in again.

Once we were inside my place, I was all over her. It was all I could do to control myself. Like all the fear and panic I'd experienced from almost losing her were unleashed.

We were kissing and stripping our clothes off, headed toward my bedroom, but didn't even make it. I couldn't wait. I pushed her against the wall in the hallway, my cock hard and straining.

"Don't you want a bed?" she asked, breathless.

"I want *you*."

We gazed at each other, and then she reached down, slipped her fingers beneath the elastic of my boxers, and took me in hand. "I want you too."

I swallowed hard. Inhaled the scent of her skin, so close. So familiar. Desire and despair clashed as they both raged through my veins.

"I almost lost you," I whispered, choking on the words. "Do you know that?"

She went quiet. "I know."

We continued to gaze at each other, and then it was like something inside me burst free. I kissed her again, but I also shoved her panties aside and took her right there against the wall. It wasn't elegant. It wasn't refined. It was rough and desperate, and I barely recognized the noises I made in my throat as I invaded her.

Theo held me tight, gasping and moaning with every thrust. I felt like an animal, not like myself at all. I should have been gentle after everything that happened, but instead, I felt selfish and greedy.

"It was *terrible*," I said, my voice hoarse as the beginnings of a climax overtook me. I shook my head and fought it off. I didn't want it. I wanted to be joined like this with Theo forever. Except the climax moved through me like a wrecking ball, and then I groaned because I couldn't stop myself from surrendering to it.

"Gabe, are you okay?" she asked, hugging me tight afterward. She stroked my back as I began to shake all over, crying.

"*So* terrible," I whispered.

CHAPTER THIRTY-SIX

~ Theo ~

It was the middle of the night, and we'd lit candles and were taking a bath together in Gabe's giant tub. He tried to hide it, but I could tell he was still crying.

I'd never seen him so distraught. What happened to me had been terrifying, and I should have known it was terrifying for him too. He'd obviously been holding it all in.

I lathered soap in my hands and smoothed them over his powerful chest, his arms resting on the sides of the tub. He looked so strong. Like a superhero. My very own gladiator. And he acted so tough all the time that it was easy to forget he wasn't a superhero, that he was just a man with weaknesses like the rest of us.

Gabe sniffed and ran a hand down his face, wiping away tears.

Those dark, soulful eyes watched me as I continued to soap him up. He remained silent. And I didn't comment on the crying because

I knew he didn't want me to. Instead, I took care of him. Scrubbed him and then used a washcloth to rinse off the soap.

"I should be doing this for *you*." His voice sounded hoarse as it filled the confines of his bathroom.

"Hush" was all I said as I continued to wash him.

He closed his eyes, and I reached for the soap again. It was one of the honey and lavender-scented bars I'd brought from home. A fellow beekeeper made them, and they smelled divine. Candlelight flickered across the walls. The large bathroom window looked out onto the inky waters of Puget Sound. The only noises were me splashing water and my hands on Gabe's skin.

"I've been thinking about something," I said after a while, running soap along his leg.

He glanced at me and wiped his eyes with the thumb and two fingers of his hand. "Yeah, what's that?"

"During the second quarter of the game last Sunday, I noticed you faked a handoff to the running back. Was a play-action pass really the best thing there?"

Gabe blinked at me.

"I wonder if it would have been smarter to just do a running play."

He stared at me in amazement. "Holy shit," he whispered. "I've created a monster."

I shrugged and tried to hide my smile as I reached for the washcloth. "You pretty much have."

"Get over here right now," he demanded, reaching for me with a grin.

"We're splashing water everywhere!" I shrieked, letting him pull me onto his lap so I was straddling his thighs. Water rocked out of the sides of the tub.

I felt his hands on my back and then sliding down to grasp my hips. "How long did you work on that?"

I smiled, resting my arms on his shoulders, and leaned in close. "I wanted to surprise you," I said. "Did you like it?"

"So you're going to start telling me how to play football, huh?"

"You know me. I just might." And then I leaned in and kissed him. He tasted so perfect. His lips and tongue were wet and warm, tangling with mine. We deepened the kiss as desire ignited within us both.

"I've never done it in a bathtub," I said, already breathless.

"Really?"

"It's true." Gabe and I had done it in his shower lots of times, but I'd never had sex in a bathtub with anyone. Probably because the tubs were always too small.

"I'd say it's time we fix that," he murmured.

He was lightly caressing between my thighs, circling my clit. But I was the one who positioned myself over him and slowly sank down.

We both moaned at how good it was. The glow of candlelight flickered around us, making it seem more intimate. He molded my breasts and lightly pinched my nipples, doing everything just the way I liked. We'd gotten to know each other's bodies so well.

I gripped the edges of the tub behind him as our movements picked up pace. "Touch me," I begged. And he did. One hand on my hip, the other exactly where I needed it. I began to yell as powerful waves of ecstasy overtook me.

Gabe wasn't far behind, the two of us consumed in each other. Insulated from the world outside. Finally, he groaned and shuddered against me, driving himself deep.

I lay against his shoulder, trying to catch my breath, while he buried his face in my neck.

"Hey, look at me," he whispered.

I pulled back slightly. "What?"

"I love you, Theo."

"I love you too."

"You're *it* for me. You're my always."

AFTER THE BATH, we dried ourselves and then padded barefoot and naked into his kitchen for water, which we both drank greedily.

"Are you hungry?" he asked, wiping his mouth with the back of his hand. He went over and opened the fridge, staring inside.

I leaned back with my glass and watched him. Gabe standing there in nothing but his birthday suit was a view worth admiring. It was certainly true that he had the perfect body to sell T-shirts and underwear. He was right about his brand.

Putting my glass on the counter, I went over and slid my arm around him as we stared into the fridge together, contemplating what to eat.

"There's fruit," he suggested. "Or I could make us omelets. Or what about those wraps?" He pointed to a stack of prepared whole food meals he had delivered weekly during football season.

"Are there any of the Mexican ones left?"

He nodded and reached inside. "Hell yeah. Those are my favorite." He took three wraps out and stuck them in the microwave.

"You're not using the oven?"

Even though he owned one, Gabe had an aversion to microwaves. He said meals didn't taste as good heated in them. "Nah, that'll take too long."

As always, there was a basket of avocados ripening on his counter. He told me that avocados were his favorite food. And, I had to admit, he seemed to eat them with practically everything. I even saw him eat spaghetti with avocado on top once.

When the wraps were done, Gabe put two on a plate for himself and one for me. The wraps were huge. It always amazed me how much food he could eat. He opened each wrap and stuffed them with avocado slices before closing them up again.

I'd gotten out a jar of salsa, and we stood there in the middle of the night completely naked, devouring our food. It was delicious.

"You never told me your good news," he said, leaning against the counter, spooning salsa onto a wrap.

I swallowed a bite and smiled. "It looks like this bee allergy isn't going to be as big of a deal as I thought."

His brows drew together. "How's that?"

"I had a meeting with the chair of our department and the dean. We figured out a way that I wouldn't have to have exposure to live bees." I then explained how I'd already worked with a hive that was encased in glass, and they were going to set up a few more for me. Whatever frames I was collecting data from could simply be moved at my request. "That's mostly what I work on. I also dissect dead bees, and I already wear gloves for that, so that won't be an issue."

"Damn, that's fantastic. I'm glad to hear it. What about your beehives at home?"

I took a deep breath. This was the tricky part. I knew Gabe wasn't going to be crazy about what I had to say next. "I'm going to keep the hives at my house."

"What do you mean?" He looked confused. "How is that possible?"

I took a small bite and put my wrap on the plate. "It isn't necessary to get rid of my beehives," I said evenly. "I'll just wear a suit, veil, and gloves whenever I need to access them. And, of course, I'll always carry an EpiPen."

He stopped chewing and stared at me. "And what if you get stung by a bee?"

"I won't. I'll be careful."

Gabe put his burrito down and shook his head. "That's nuts, Theo. You told me yourself that you've had bees get inside your veil without knowing how they managed it."

"Like I said, I'll be very careful."

"That's not good enough."

"Of course it is."

"It's not, and you *know* it."

"Well, it's going to have to be, because I'm not getting rid of my *bees!*" I didn't mean to raise my voice, but I couldn't help it. All the frustration and anger I'd been feeling all week came rushing back. I was sure my face was turning red.

He stared at me, incredulous. "Are you fucking kidding me? You nearly *died* from a bee sting! Am I the only one remembering that?"

I tried to stay calm. The terror of not being able to breathe and then blacking out was hardly something I could forget. "Of course I remember."

He was shaking his head, agitated and angry. "It's foolish and dangerous. You're purposefully putting yourself in harm's way!"

"Oh, and *you're* not?"

"What are you talking about?"

"I've spent the past four months watching you get tackled and pummeled every week. Every time I see you, you're wearing a bandage, or a brace, or icing some new body part."

"Don't turn this around. It's not the same thing at all."

"It's exactly the same thing." I couldn't believe we were having this argument standing naked in his kitchen. "Every time you walk on that football field, there's a chance you could be seriously injured. You could be paralyzed. You could even *die*."

He scoffed. "Give me a break. I've been playing football my whole life."

"And what about brain damage and CTE? You think I haven't read those studies? Because I've read them all!" My voice sounded shrill and high-pitched. "And that danger is *very* real."

"I've read them, too, but that's not going to happen to me."

"Why? Because you're so invincible?"

"This is bullshit!" He slapped the counter. "Stop turning this around. This isn't about me."

"You're nothing but a hypocrite," I said. "You expect me to accept the real danger you put yourself in every week without a care but then act like my keeping beehives is reckless."

"Because it *is*!" he roared. "It's reckless, and I won't allow it!"

"You won't *allow* it?" I asked in amazement. "Who do you think you are?"

Gabe blinked rapidly, breathing hard. "I mean it, Theo. I won't let you keep those beehives."

I rolled my eyes. "Give me a break. Maybe you haven't noticed, but I'm not part of your offensive line. I don't have to take orders from you."

He shook his head, his face flushed. "Don't push me on this. I won't let you do something so irresponsible."

"It's not irresponsible! I'm a grown woman, and I'll do what I want. You can't stop me."

"I can, and I will. Have you forgotten how we met?"

"What do you mean?" But then a terrible realization dawned on me.

He nodded, his face stern. "I'll sue you again, and I'll force you to remove them if I have to."

My mouth dropped open. "*What?* You'd do that?"

"To keep you safe, I'd do anything. You should know that by now."

"My God," I whispered, light-headed with shock. "We've come full circle, haven't we?"

CHAPTER THIRTY-SEVEN

~ Gabe ~

"You'd really do that to me?" Theo's face was pale. "You'd *sue* me again? You'd try to control me like that?"

"I don't want to do it," I clarified. "But I can't stand by and watch you put yourself at risk. I won't allow that."

She was shaking her head, and her shocked expression changed to something else. To fury. "Go *fuck* yourself, Gabe!"

"Theo...."

But she turned on her heels and stalked out of the kitchen. I watched those long legs and that perky ass stride across my living room and then disappear down the hall.

I couldn't believe this situation. She'd nearly *died*, and if she thought I was going to let that happen again on my watch, she was wrong. Years ago, I'd made the mistake of standing by and doing nothing when a person I cared about was reckless. Never again.

I stood there for a moment in the kitchen with my hands on the counter, still processing this crazy argument. Then I headed for the bedroom. Surely I could talk some sense into her. Theo was a scientist. I couldn't believe she was behaving so irrationally.

When I got there, to my surprise, she was already dressed.

"What are you doing?"

She glared up at me, shoving her boots on with a jerky movement. "What does it look like I'm doing? I'm *leaving*."

"It's the middle of the night. Let's talk about this."

"There's nothing to talk about." She gave me a skewering look. "And to think you said you stopped being a bully."

I grabbed a pair of clean gray boxer briefs and pulled them on. "Don't be ridiculous. I'm not bullying you."

"Ha! I'll be the judge of whether I'm being bullied or not." She stood up, then went over and grabbed her overnight bag, the one she always brought with her.

"Theo, I love you. This is—"

"You *love* me? So that's why you're going to sue me? That's why you want to take away my—" Her voice hitched. "—my *bees*?"

"I don't *want* to take them away. You know I would never hurt you. But you're not thinking clearly."

She shook her head. "I'm leaving. Get out of my way."

I was standing in front of her, but I didn't move.

"Get out of my way!"

I gazed at her. Those tortoiseshell glasses and those wild red curls. If I wanted to, I could stop her, could make her talk to me, but I wasn't that kind of man. So I stepped aside and let her shove past me.

And then I just stood there dumbfounded and listened as my front door opened and slammed shut.

———

SHE JUST NEEDS *time to cool off. She'll come to her senses.* There was no way anyone else in her life would be on board with this crazy decision to keep her bees.

I stalked around my penthouse, replaying our argument in my head. It was by far the worst fight we'd ever had. We argued occasionally, usually about dumb stuff. Nothing this serious.

Eventually, I went to bed and tried to sleep. Of course, my demons were back like an invading army. *Fuck you*, I told them all. *Go screw yourselves.* They could torture me all they wanted over past mistakes, but they sure as hell couldn't stop me from preventing future ones.

I spent the next day running errands, studying game film, and trying not to think about Theo. *She accuses me of thinking I'm invincible, but she's the one not facing reality.*

On Wednesday morning, I was up at five thirty for an early meeting with Coach Mallory. Everyone was hyperfocused. We'd won the wild card round and were determined to win the division. In the past, I'd used football as a crutch, as a way to avoid thinking about things I didn't want to examine too closely. But I wasn't doing that anymore. I was focused on the game, but I was facing everything else head-on.

I called and texted Theo every spare moment I had. And being as pigheaded as she was, she refused to answer me.

Gabe: How long is this fight going to go on? I love you. I miss you. I want to release the dogs with you.

Nothing.

I tried leaving voice messages. "I haven't told Davis to do anything yet. I know you want to keep your bees. I get it. Believe me, if I had to give up football, I'd be losing my shit too. But talk to me, okay?"

Still nothing.

"I don't know what to do," I told Davis on the phone late Sunday night. I was at the airport headed home after we beat Denver in the divisional game. There was a lot of excitement in the air, and the press had been chasing us after our win. "She won't answer any of my texts or phone calls. I'm going up to Truth Harbor on Tuesday, even though I'll have to come back the same day."

"Do you still want me to hold off on any legal action about her bees?"

"Don't do anything yet." It wasn't like I *wanted* to sue Theo. What I wanted was for her to see reason. "Have you heard anything back from Gemma?"

"Not yet. I spoke to her lawyer. I suspect they're just taking some time to think things over."

I nodded. "That makes sense." I'd told Davis to make it clear that I didn't want to intrude on Gemma's family, but they were probably still worried. "I wonder if I should talk to Gemma myself."

"I can pass that on. Maybe set up a phone call."

I nodded. "Let's do that. How are things with you?" I asked him.

"Excellent. Miranda and I have been discussing whether Petey needs a sibling."

I was stunned into silence. "A... *baby*?"

Davis laughed. "Another dog."

I grinned. "Whew. Hopefully he won't get jealous."

"That's our biggest concern."

The speaker overhead announced our gate was opening. "I have to go. Our flight is boarding."

"You guys are flying commercial?"

The Sentries had a private plane, which the team usually used to fly everyone to games, but it wasn't always available on the return. "Yeah, can you believe it?"

I got off the phone and boarded the flight. At least the team's owner had bought out the entire first class section for us. And, luckily, I was also able to get an aisle seat.

As I sat down, I noticed one of the flight attendants looked familiar.

"Hi, Gabe," she said, coming over to me with a big smile. "I can't believe I finally got you on one of my flights. And congratulations on the win today."

"Thank you, I appreciate that." I remembered her now. She was one of the women who came to my impromptu party back when Theo was still chained to my house.

"It's Brooke," she said. "In case you've forgotten."

"I remember."

"Can I get you anything?" She leaned close enough that I could smell her perfume. "Anything at all?"

"I'm good for now. Thanks."

Once we were in the air, I leaned back and tried to relax. There was still excitement in the air, but everyone was also exhausted. It had been a close game.

Brooke kept coming by frequently to chat, trying to flirt with me. She kept making lots of eye contact and leaning in. I kept mentioning my girlfriend, hoping she'd take the hint and cool her heels.

"Your girlfriend is a professor, right?" she asked.

I nodded. "She's a bee biologist."

"I met her when she came to one of the Sentries' games a couple of months ago."

I took a drink from my water bottle. "Is that right?"

"Speaking of which." She leaned in close again. "I hope this isn't too forward of me to ask."

Uh-oh. I hoped she wasn't going to try to show me her new tattoo or any pierced body part. It always amazed me how insistent some women were, even when I made it clear I wasn't interested.

"Do you think you could help me get some tickets to the conference championship game next Sunday? My family is flying up from California to visit, and they're huge football fans."

"Tickets?" I asked with relief. "Sure, no problem." At least she wasn't asking me to go into the bathroom and autograph her breasts. Not that I'd do it, but sometimes those conversations got annoying and awkward. "I can help you with that."

"Oh, good. Let me give you my number."

I pulled my phone out and entered it. I told her I'd call and let her know but that it shouldn't be an issue.

Once I got back to my penthouse, I tried texting and calling Theo again, even though it was late.

"I don't know if you saw the game today, but I wanted to hear your opinion about that double pass during the third quarter." I grinned, remembering how she'd surprised me that night. "I miss you. I love you. I want to live by the ocean with you and eat the gooey middle brownies while you eat the crispy outer ones."

I hung up and waited, staring at my phone. For something. *Anything.*

Her silent treatment had gone on so long that I was getting worried.

I GOT lucky with the timing of the ferry on Tuesday and arrived in Truth Harbor by ten in the morning. First thing I did was drive by Theo's house. Her driveway was empty, and the porch light was on. I walked up to the front door and rang the bell, but it was obvious no one was home. I peered through the front window. Everything looked the same, except no sign of Theo.

Turning around, I headed back to my SUV, figuring she was most likely at work.

I'd never been to her workplace before and had to use my phone to find it. The pollinator lab was housed in a university building on some acreage just outside of town that looked like a large warehouse.

There was a front lobby area, but there wasn't anyone there to help me, so I wandered through the building myself. I kept getting whiffs of coffee from somewhere. There were various signs with arrows for lecture halls, beehives, the pollinator lab, and faculty offices.

I figured I'd head to the lab first. But once I arrived, I couldn't enter. The door was locked. It required a keycard to open it. At least there was a large window and I could see inside, except there was no sign of Theo. I peered through the glass with curiosity to see where she spent so much time. It looked like a regular lab with computers, microscopes, and a lot of other equipment. I also saw one of the glass beehives she'd been talking about.

"Can I help you?"

I turned to find a woman with shoulder-length dark hair standing next to me wearing a white lab coat. "Yeah, hi. I'm looking for Theo."

Her brows went up, and I watched as she took in my size and seemed to put two and two together. She grinned. "You're Gabe, aren't you?"

"I am."

She nodded. "It's nice to meet you. I'm Mattie, a friend and colleague of Theo's."

"It's nice to meet you too. Is she around? I don't see her anywhere."

"I haven't seen her this morning yet, but I just got back from vacation and arrived late. She's probably in her office."

Mattie pointed down the hallway I just came from and gave me directions. I thanked her. The faculty offices were just past what looked to be a number of empty classrooms. Finally, I found one with her name on the door.

Theodora Stewart, PhD, Professor, Entomology Department.

I knocked, but there was no answer, so I turned the knob. To my surprise it was unlocked. Her office was empty with the lights off, and I flicked them on. I lingered for a moment, walking around, taking it in. There was a computer, books, and a few whimsical bee items, including a wooden bee puzzle. Her window looked out onto a wooded area.

There was a framed picture on her desk that caught my attention, and I picked it up. It was a photo of the two of us. A silly selfie we'd taken a while back. We'd been goofing around and had drawn curly mustaches on each other's faces with a black marker.

I smiled, remembering it. We kept calling each other "Monsieur," and I pretended to speak fake French, which Theo found particularly hilarious for some reason. She'd nearly peed herself laughing.

I kept staring at the picture of us. We were so good together. I'd never felt so at ease with anyone.

So where the heck is she? And why isn't she answering my messages?

I left her office and searched around some more. Some guy in one of the offices nearby had his door open, so I knocked on it lightly. "Excuse me, do you know where I can find Theo?"

He had his back to me, but when he turned in his chair and saw me, his jaw dropped. *"What?"* he squeaked, staring at me.

"I'm looking for Theo. Have you seen her around today?"

"I haven't." He shoved his black glasses up on his nose. "She's taking a leave of absence."

My eyes widened. "She is? For how long?"

The guy seemed so nervous that I figured he must be a Sentries fan. It was weird, though, because he almost seemed afraid of me. "I'm not sure." He was balding on top, with a comb-over, and had a dark goatee. "She wasn't here at all last week. I think someone mentioned she was going out of town."

"Did she say where she was going?"

He quickly shook his head. "I wouldn't know that." He seemed to be calming down a little. "You're Beauty Bardales."

I nodded. "That's right."

"Do you think I could get your autograph?"

I didn't say anything. I wasn't sure why, but something made me turn my head to look at the name on his open office door.

Gerald Jones, PhD, Associate Professor, Entomology Department.

I stared at it for a beat. "Your name's Gerald?" I asked, turning back to him.

He nodded and squirmed in his chair. "Yes... uh, yes, it is."

So this was the asshole who'd been hassling Theo, who was jealous of her. And I could see it too. He was exactly the kind of guy who complained about everything and only did the bare minimum to get by.

Gerald didn't just seem nervous, he seemed petrified, and I had to wonder if there was more going on here than what Theo had told me.

I was tempted to tell Gerald to stay the fuck away from her, but I knew she'd be even more pissed at me than she already was if she found out.

Instead, I narrowed my eyes and gave him my hardest glare. The same one I used on the field when I was growling at my offensive line, demanding results. The same one I'd tested on Theo when we first met, and she didn't even flinch.

Well, this guy was flinching all over the place. It looked like he was scared shitless. I pointed at him and, in a menacing tone, said two words, "Watch yourself."

He turned as white as a sheet of paper.

I left with a little smile on my face.

I GOT BACK to my car and sat for a minute. Theo had taken a leave of absence from the university. My stomach churned with worry. This wasn't good news.

Where could she have gone?

I drove by her house again, hoping she'd magically appear. Everything looked the same as when I was there a couple of hours ago. I decided the next step was to ask her friends if they'd spoken to her.

I didn't have Claire's number, but I'd hired her maid service a couple of times and knew she had an office in town, so I looked it up.

It was a small, tidy space just off Main Street with the name Maids of Truth done in a superhero-styled font on the window.

When I entered I asked the receptionist if I could speak to Claire.

She blinked a few times, taking in my height. "Is she expecting you?"

"Just tell her Gabe is here."

A few minutes later, Claire came out and seemed surprised to see me. "Gabe? Do you need a maid? You could have just called or gone online to set it up."

"I'm here about Theo. I'm trying to get a hold of her."

She seemed taken aback. "What do you mean? Can't you just call her?"

I shook my head. "I've tried that. It's been two weeks now, and she won't speak to me. Apparently she's taken a leave of absence from the university and has left town."

By the expression on Claire's face, she clearly had no idea what I was talking about. "Come on back," she said, and I followed her into her office.

She closed the door. There was a desk, but she ignored it and sat in a chair near a stack of boxes filled with cleaning supplies. The place smelled like lemons. I took the couch next to her.

"What exactly is going on?" Claire asked.

I hesitated. I wasn't used to talking about my personal life like this, but it was obvious I didn't have a choice, so I told her what happened.

"Wait a minute." She looked confused after I explained about the fight we'd had. "You're going to sue Theo over her beehives again?"

"I know it sounds bad, but I don't have a choice. She nearly *died* right in front of me from that bee sting, and she won't listen to reason."

Claire seemed shocked. "It was *that* bad?"

I nodded. "Didn't she tell you?"

"She told me and Leah that she was stung and had an allergic reaction but said it wasn't that big of a deal. That it wasn't going to affect her work or anything else."

"Trust me. It was a *very* big deal."

"And now she won't speak to you?"

"She won't respond to me at all. Have you heard from her?"

Claire shook her head. "Not really. The three of us were supposed to have lunch last week, but she texted and said she couldn't make it, that she'd be out of town."

"Did she say where she was going?"

"She didn't. I just assumed it was for work, but it sounds like it wasn't."

I leaned back on the couch. "Will you let me know if you do hear from her? At least let me know she's okay?"

"Of course. I'll tell Leah too."

I gave Claire my number, thanked her, and left. Not knowing what else to do, I drove back to Theo's house. I parked my SUV in the driveway and just sat there.

The only people I hadn't tried yet were her parents. I hesitated, mainly because I didn't want to drag them into the middle of our argument. Theo would hate that. I had her dad's number, so I called it. There was no answer, but I left a short voice mail explaining that I was trying to get a hold of her, and if he could call me back, I'd appreciate it.

It was cold when I got out of my car. I zipped up my jacket and headed down into her backyard. Maybe I could find some clue as to what was going on.

I passed her beehives and then headed out through the back gate toward our secret meadow. She'd once told me that she camped out there occasionally, and a part of me hoped maybe that's where I'd find her.

But she wasn't there. There was still a chair and some of her blankets wrapped in a plastic bag. The cooler was still there. But no sign of Theo.

I sat in the chair for a little while, remembering that vision I'd had of her out here when we first met. I'd never had a mystical experience like that before and wished I'd have another one. One that would explain all this and tell me what to do.

Theo had a way about her that always drew me in. I remembered that first night when she'd snuck onto my property and we'd played catch in my backyard. Later, I'd discovered footage on my security camera of her sticking her tongue out and flipping the bird with both hands. It had been hilarious.

God, I miss her.

Finally, I got up and headed toward her house. Instead of leaving, when I got to her backyard, I walked around her beehives. They still looked like filing cabinets to me. The hives were quieter than they were in the summer months, with fewer bees buzzing nearby.

I thought about how much honey bees meant to Theo, how she'd spent her whole life studying them, and how even just the thought of having them ripped away must be incredibly difficult. Maybe she hated me for it. She was obviously blaming me.

"Theo is always talking to you ladies... and to you dudes in there too," I said, speaking to her beehives. "'Telling the bees the important things,' as she would say. Well, now *I'm* telling you something important. I love this woman, your keeper, and I can't risk her life over you."

And as I stood there in the middle of her hives, talking to her bees, a terrible understanding washed over me. It was staring me right in the face. *Fuck.* I couldn't believe I didn't see it sooner.

Theo had stopped answering my calls or texts. She'd stopped responding to me altogether, and now I couldn't find her anywhere.

How could I have been so blind?

The plain truth was that she'd left me and wasn't coming back. She'd disappeared from my life.

Just like her bees when they'd had enough.

Theo had absconded.

CHAPTER THIRTY-EIGHT

~ Theo ~

It hadn't been easy ignoring all of Gabe's messages. He could be extremely charming, and we had so many secret jokes and such intimate knowledge of each other that he was using it all against me.

I nearly answered him a couple of times, but then I remembered what he said. That he wasn't going to *allow* me to keep my bees.

Allow me!

No one was going to *allow* me to do anything.

I set my own path in life.

Finally, I forced myself to stop listening to his messages and deleted his texts before I could read them. I didn't want the temptation.

I never should have watched the first game of the playoffs. Somehow, I couldn't resist, but then I accidentally caught part of an interview with Gabe afterward. My eyes wouldn't leave the screen. He answered questions about the game and then looked directly into the camera. "We really released the dogs during the second half," he said with a grin. He looked so handsome, showing off that dimple on his right cheek, and, of course, he was talking to *me*. Our secret joke.

I'd turned off the television so fast you'd have thought I was being electrocuted.

I had to take slow, deep breaths to calm myself after that. My throat felt tight, not because of any allergy but because this emotional attachment I had to Gabe was overpowering.

I discovered it was very difficult to let go of my feelings for him. Obviously I'd fallen in love, and even though I'd decided that was no longer acceptable, these feelings weren't going away. But how could I be with a man who wanted to control me, even if he claimed it was for my own good?

The answer is I can't.

It had been two weeks now, and he was still leaving messages and texts.

"I know you've *absconded*," he said to me in a recent voice mail. "I finally understand. You've left me. But, Theo, know this. I love you. And I'll *always* love you." There was an anguish in his voice that made my stomach ache. It brought back the memory of that night when he'd broken down crying. My heart clenched and my eyes stung. But I wasn't going to cry. *I won't!*

Of course, he was right. I *had* absconded. It figured that he'd get that. That he'd see it, because he always saw me.

When is he going to stop leaving these messages!

I felt like throwing my phone at the wall. I shouldn't have listened to it in the first place. I missed him, and I wished I didn't.

These past two weeks had been extremely difficult. Initially, after the university agreed to let me take a temporary leave of absence, I'd gone down to my parents' house in Eugene.

They were happy to see me, and I slept in my old bedroom like always. I told them I'd broken up with Gabe and that I just needed some personal time. I didn't tell them the reason why we'd broken up.

They were glad when they heard that I'd still be able to work at the pollinator lab, and they obviously assumed I'd be finding a new home for my bees. I didn't tell them anything different, and the subject didn't come up until the second week I was there.

"Have you contacted any beekeepers about moving your hives yet?" my dad asked me one morning over breakfast. He was holding a cup of coffee and reading the news on his iPad.

"I haven't," I said, eating some buttered toast without honey. My doctor told me to avoid it. I was also supposed to make an appointment to go in for allergy tests and treatment.

"Your leave of absence is ending soon. Maybe the hives can be removed before you return home. At least it's winter, so that should make things easier."

I didn't reply. He was right. Winter was definitely the best time to move bees since the colony was intact and not out flying.

"I'm not so sure about giving up my beehives."

"What do you mean?" My dad looked at me. My mom looked over too.

"I know that's the logical conclusion after what happened," I said, "but I don't think it's necessary."

"You can't be serious." My mom's expression turned to concern. "Of course it's necessary. I understand this is heartbreaking for you, but it's too risky to keep them."

"I agree." My dad put his coffee and iPad down. "It's not a smart decision. What if you were stung again?"

"I'll just carry a couple of epinephrine pens in my backpack and have them nearby."

"And what if you forget?" he asked. "Or what if something goes wrong? A bee gets inside your house? Or inside your veil or suit?"

"Then I'll handle it." My parents were staring at me like I was nuts. "I don't understand why this is such a big deal. It's not like I'm getting stung every day. It doesn't happen that often, and if I'm super careful, it likely won't happen at all."

My mom shook her head. "This is extremely foolish behavior. I can't believe you're even contemplating it."

We spent the next two hours arguing. Round and round. Unfortunately, I accidentally let it slip that Gabe was planning to sue me again to force me to remove my hives, and that's why we'd broken up.

"He's right," my dad said with a stern expression. "What you're doing *is* irresponsible! Your stubbornness is getting in the way of your common sense."

I put my hands over my face in frustration and tried to calm myself. Bees were an integral part of my life, a part of my identity even. I moved my hands away. "I've had beehives since I was a child. If there's one thing I know how to handle, it's bees."

My mom leaned forward on the table. "Of course you do, but this is different. We always supported your interest, but we never would have allowed you to have hives as a child if you'd been allergic to bee venom!"

Finally, I shook my head and stood up. "I'm sorry, but I can't discuss this anymore."

Both of them looked up at me, and I could see how worried they were.

"Please at least think about what we're saying," my dad said.

My mom reached for my hand. "Yes, please think carefully about this decision. Do your research."

Finally, I nodded. Mostly so we could stop talking about it.

I packed up and left the next day because I knew how they were. In fact, they were already sending me articles and studies about honey bees and anaphylaxis.

Instead of going home, I drove up the Oregon coast. My roommate in college lived on some acreage outside of Cannon Beach, and I stopped by to visit her. She and her husband offered for me to stay a few days, and I took them up on it.

I couldn't hide out forever. My leave of absence was ending soon, and I needed to get back to the lab and to my classes.

And, yes, to my bees.

"Beauty Bardales was here looking for you while you were gone." It was Gerald's whiny voice over my shoulder. He was standing in the doorway to my office. "You should know that he threatened me and that I plan to write a letter to the chair about it since he's *your* boyfriend. In fact, I'm considering taking legal action against him."

I'd been back to work less than two hours and was at my computer going through a mountain of emails. Gerald's intrusion was the last thing I needed.

"What are you talking about?"

"Just what I said. Beauty Bardales pushed his way into my office looking for you. He was very rude! And then he threatened me."

"Why would he do that?"

He snorted and crossed his arms so they rested on his paunchy belly. "*You* obviously told him to!"

I tilted my head, perplexed. I had told Gabe very little about Gerald, and I definitely never told him that he'd called me a "beast" or an "ugly bitch." God knew what Gabe would have done then. I'd considered telling Michael, our department chair, what Gerald said to me but decided I had better things to do with my time. "What did he say to you?"

"Like I said, he threatened me. He's enormous. I was afraid for my life!"

"But what did he actually say?"

Gerald sniffed. "He told me to watch myself."

"That doesn't sound very threatening."

"Oh, it *was*. It was the *way* he said it."

I rolled my eyes and got up. "Get out of my office, Gerald."

He waggled his finger at me. "This isn't the end of it, I assure you. I can't believe you're involved with a monster like that. He wouldn't even sign an autograph for me—"

I closed the door with Gerald still spewing complaints on the other side.

Afterward, I sat back down and gazed out the window. So Gabe had come by here. I should have guessed he'd do that, though I wondered when he'd managed it. I doubted he had a moment to spare with the playoffs happening.

I didn't mean to look at the sports section, but somehow it popped up on my phone. The Sentries had won the divisional round last Sunday and were scheduled to play New York this Saturday for the conference championship.

I had no intention of watching it.

Thursday afternoon, I met Claire and Leah for lunch. I hadn't spoken to them since before my leave of absence. I told them that I'd broken up with Gabe, but I couldn't believe their reaction. All they wanted to talk about was if it was true that I was keeping my beehives. When I explained that he was planning to sue me again, I thought they'd be on *my* side. But they both defended *him*! I could barely believe it.

"You're defending the guy who's planning a lawsuit against me?" I asked, incredulous. "The guy who's trying to control me?"

"We're defending the guy who's trying to save your life," Leah said. "Because you're not thinking clearly."

I rolled my eyes. *Not this again.* It felt like no one understood anything. "Trust me, I can handle myself around bees. It's one thing I'm *very* good at."

Claire nodded. "We don't doubt that, but is it true you had a severe allergic reaction? Gabe told me you almost died."

"You were talking to Gabe?"

She nodded. "He came by Maids of Truth. He's really worried about you."

I couldn't believe this. I tried to explain myself to them, but it was clear they weren't getting it. *How is this happening? It's like everyone is against me.*

When I finally got back to my house, I tried to put it out of my mind. I was tired of people telling me I was being unreasonable, that I was too stubborn for my own good.

Instead, it was time to visit my bees.

I HAD two EpiPens in my backpack as I headed into my lower yard wearing jeans and two thick long-sleeved shirts.

My heart pounded as I walked down the hill toward my beehives, and I tried to calm myself. The expression that bees could smell fear was basically true. Bees could detect fear pheromones from people and animals and viewed it as a threat.

I was never afraid of my bees. I was always calm around them. I always moved slowly and methodically, and it was the main reason I seldom got stung.

Once I got to the lower yard, I opened my shed and put on a bee suit, a veil, and a pair of gloves. The smell of honey was pungent, and the walls of the shed were lined with all the jars I planned to start selling soon.

I grabbed my smoker and my hive tool and kept telling myself that everything was fine. This was just a normal day.

But as I approached the first hive, my heart was still pounding. It didn't help that I kept getting a flashback of the last time I was here with Gabe. That was a terrifying night, and the truth was, if he hadn't been here with me, I probably would have died.

I saw a few bees flying around the entrance to the hive I planned to open. Mostly I was just checking that they had enough food and there were no immediate problems I needed to be aware of.

I'd done this hundreds of times—probably a thousand, if you counted all the times I'd opened up a beehive as a child—so why was I nervous?

I swallowed and tried to breathe slowly through my nose.

Before opening the hive, I used smoke to settle everyone down. Once it was open, I inspected a couple of frames and could see that

TRUTH ABOUT NERDS & BEES 309

everything looked good. There was plenty of food. Most of the bees were clustered around the queen, keeping her warm. It was exactly as it should be.

The whole time, I could hear my heart hammering, could hear my breath inside my veil as if I were wearing a space suit. My nervous system felt keyed up and on the edge of panic. I'd always enjoyed examining my hives, but now I felt like an astronaut on a dangerous mission.

As quickly as I could, I closed everything again. A number of bees were out of the hive and bumping against me to warn me away. They probably smelled my fear. I smoked them some more so they couldn't warn the others.

Initially, I'd planned to tell them about Gabe and me, that we'd broken up and the reason why, but I didn't.

I didn't because all I could think about was getting away from these bees.

CHAPTER THIRTY-NINE

~ Gabe ~

I knew I was being an asshole. We'd been running plays and scrimmages all day, getting ready for the game on Saturday, and I was yelling at everyone. I kept getting nervous looks from my teammates. Guys the size of a two-story house were tiptoeing around my hair-trigger mouth.

It didn't help that I hadn't been sleeping for shit.

And it wasn't my usual insomnia. It was Theo. Since I couldn't let myself feel sad about her absconding, I was angry.

"Everything all right?" Coach Mallory asked, coming over to me. "Might want to dial down that attitude."

I had my helmet off and was drinking a bottle of water. "Yeah, you're right. I'll cool it." I wiped my forehead and felt bad for being such a dick.

We'd been having team meetings every morning to discuss strategy, analyzing every game played this season, going over weaknesses and strengths in fine detail. Everyone was pumped and ready for Saturday.

I was so immersed that I was eating, sleeping, and dreaming football. Except I was also dreaming about Theo.

She kept invading my thoughts. In the same way I analyzed game film, I was analyzing our relationship, especially my part in it. It wasn't easy to admit, but somehow I'd screwed up. I'd chased her away. It was the last thing I'd ever want to do, but she didn't abscond for no reason.

Had I been too heavy-handed? Too blunt? Too ill-tempered?

Was I really supposed to go along with her keeping her beehives? Because there was no way I could go along with that.

Regina called me Thursday evening to wish me well with the game on Saturday, and I thanked her.

"Any word from Theo?" she asked. I'd already told her everything that happened with the bee sting, and that we'd broken up.

"Nothing."

"I told you not to fuck this up, and you fucked it up anyway."

I snorted. "Thanks, Reg. I appreciate you rubbing it in."

"I've been giving all this some thought. Does she know about Tyler?"

I went quiet. "Not really. She knows about Gemma, obviously." It was a miracle that Theo didn't think less of me after hearing about Christopher and the selfish way I'd bungled things years ago. I worried her hearing about Tyler would be too much. Not that it mattered now.

"That was a mistake. You should have told her."

"What difference would it make? I'd still do whatever it takes to keep her safe. There's no way I'm going to allow her to put herself in danger with those beehives, even if she hates me for it."

Regina paused. "*Allow* her? Please tell me that's *not* what you said."

I shrugged and glanced over at my travel bag packed for tomorrow. The team was staying at a hotel before the championship game. "I might have."

I could actually feel my sister rolling her eyes. "This is why I'm *so* glad I'm not into men. How would you feel if some girlfriend told you they weren't going to *allow* you to play football because it's too dangerous?"

"I wouldn't put up with it, obviously." My stomach dropped as I realized exactly what she was trying to say.

"No woman is going to put up with it either. Especially someone like Theo. Are you forgetting that she *chained* herself to your house? She's a fighter. And since she doesn't know about Tyler, she has no context for your behavior."

I rubbed my forehead. "What the hell am I supposed to do?"

"Talk to her."

"How? I don't even know where she is."

I'd heard from her dad a few days ago. He told me Theo had been staying with them but left. It sounded like she might still be in Oregon visiting a friend. It heartened me to hear that both of her parents were against her keeping those bees.

"Figure it out."

I took a deep breath. If only Theo would quit ignoring me.

"So, listen," Regina said. "I got an offer on the bar, and I think I'm going to accept it."

My brows shot up. "I thought you weren't planning to sell." Over the years, she'd received several offers on her bar, but never seriously entertained any of them.

"It's a *really* good offer. Tess and I have been thinking about making a change for a while now."

"What kind of change?"

"Initially, we weren't sure, but now we are. We want to move to Truth Harbor."

I laughed with surprise. "You're kidding." I knew she and Tess had fallen in love with the small town, which, along with all the pirate stuff, had a funky, artsy vibe.

"Tess will still teach, and I was thinking of maybe opening a coffee shop or a café."

"For lesbians?" Her bar in LA was a lesbian bar.

"Probably not. I figured I'd keep it artsy but mainstream."

"Interesting."

We talked a little longer, and she said she'd let me know more when they had some of the specifics worked out.

"Davis could probably hook you up with a lawyer in LA to go over the paperwork," I said. Regina and Davis texted each other their puzzle scores, but I wasn't sure how much they talked beyond that.

"That's a good idea. I'll give him a call."

We hung up, and I stared at my phone, still thinking about Theo. My missing her was always worse this time of the night since it's when we had our talks. I thought about that jar of honey in my travel bag. The one I was still carrying around like a lovesick fool.

Before I could stop myself, I opened a text message to her.

Gabe: I miss you. I love you. I'm sorry for everything.

I stared at the screen, willing some kind of response.

Regina was right. I never should have ordered Theo to do anything. Even if it was for her own good. I was so blinded by my fear of losing her that I'd forgotten who I was dealing with. I should have tried another way, because Theo would *never* put up with that.

THE CONFERENCE CHAMPIONSHIP started out like any normal game, but it quickly spun into a fiasco. After having thrown only two interceptions the entire season, I somehow threw two of them in the first half alone.

And it wasn't just me. Everything was falling apart. Our offense was struggling. I wound up getting sacked in the second quarter. We weren't moving the ball effectively and were barely converting on third down. Unfortunately, our defense wasn't much better and had missed tackles and blown coverages.

In the end, we lost 16–21.

So that was it. A crushing disappointment for the whole team, especially since we'd worked so hard.

I felt numb going through all the postgame interviews and press conferences. The year had started out so promising, and now it felt like it had all slipped through my fingers. Everything felt wrong.

And even though losing the championship and not making it to the Super Bowl was bad, if I was honest, losing Theo was still far worse.

AFTER ALL THE postseason player evaluations and all the other expectations on me were pushed aside, I basically stayed holed up in my penthouse, brooding. I didn't want to see anybody. Too busy licking my wounds.

To my further annoyance, Brooke kept calling me. After getting her those championship tickets, she had my phone number. At first I was polite, making it clear I wasn't interested, but finally I just blocked her. In the past, a woman like Brooke would have been exactly my type, but it was hard to even imagine that now.

Davis came by with Petey a couple of times and we hung out, but I was lousy company. At least Davis and Miranda were still back together and doing well, so I was happy for him.

To my surprise, Theo texted me a few days after our championship loss.

Theo: I'm sorry you guys didn't make it to the Super Bowl. I know how much that meant to you.

I stared at the message and felt a small spark of hope. It was the first time I'd heard from her in weeks. I knew she was back home because Claire had told me.

Gabe: Thanks, I appreciate it. Can we talk?

Theo: There's nothing to talk about.

I really only had one question for her. It was the only thing that really mattered, so I asked it.

Gabe: Do you still love me?

I waited for her to say no, and if she did, that would be the end. She'd never have to hear from me again.

But she didn't say no. She didn't say anything.

Days went by, and I waited. Any normal person would have let this go. Would have given up. Would have accepted defeat.

But not me.

I began to call her again. She never answered, but I'd leave long, rambling messages telling her about my day. I'd tell her what was happening with Davis or Regina. Sometimes I'd just sit in bed at night, stare out the window, and describe the colored lights of the Seattle skyline.

I didn't tell her about Tyler, but I told her I wished I'd communicated better, and that I was sorry I had ever tried to control her. I told her I wasn't suing her, and that I realized it was wrong of me to even threaten her with it.

As usual, she didn't reply.

For all I knew, she was deleting every single message.

I also began to think about something Regina had said to me. About how Theo and I first met.

I called Claire one day and asked her to tell me honestly what was happening with Theo. Had she moved on? Was she happy?

"Honestly, I think she's kind of lost, Gabe. She doesn't have her bees anymore."

"What do you mean?"

"She decided to give them away to a local beekeeper."

"Damn, I had no idea." Even though a part of me was relieved, because I lay awake at night worrying about her getting stung, I also knew how devastating that must have been for her.

I couldn't believe she didn't tell me.

That's when I made a decision. If I went up there and knocked on her door, she'd turn me away, so something else needed to be done.

Theo once went to extreme circumstances to get my attention. It was time for me to do the same.

CHAPTER FORTY

~ Theo ~

"There's a strange man chained to the front of your house," Eliza said, looking out my living room window as she sipped a glass of lemonade. She tilted her head. "Oh, wait. It's Beauty Bardales."

My head jerked up. "*What?*"

Since I only worked half days on Friday, Eliza had come over to help me move my jars of honey. We'd been in my lower yard the past few hours, loading them from my bee shed into a wheelbarrow and then stacking them in my dining room. My beehives might be gone, but I still had hundreds of jars of honey I'd committed to selling. Eliza had been nice enough to come over and help me cart them up so we could start labeling them.

She nodded and took another sip of lemonade. "Yep, that's definitely him."

I scrambled off my chair so fast I nearly knocked it over. When I got to the window, all the breath left my lungs. I felt light-headed.

It was Gabe.

There was a chain around his waist that attached him to one of the posts of my front porch.

I stared at him, flabbergasted.

Has he lost his mind?

I strode toward the door and yanked it open, then marched outside to where Gabe was sitting on my front steps. He was drinking a green smoothie, still sucking on the straw when he looked up at me with those big, soulful eyes.

All my feelings for him came rushing back. It was dizzying. "What do you think you're doing?"

He stopped sucking the straw. "What's it look like? I'm trying to get your attention. You've been ignoring all my messages."

My mouth fell open. I glanced down at the chain he had around his waist. It was 5/8-inch steel. The same kind I'd used.

He stroked it like a new pet snake. "Recognize it? Heavy gauge steel. Straight from the Professor Stewart playbook."

"All I need is an angle grinder to cut it off of you. You know that, right?"

"Good luck finding one of those."

I eyed him warily. "What do you mean?"

"With Davis's help, I managed to secure every single angle grinder within a hundred miles." He smirked and sucked on his smoothie again. "The benefits of being rich."

I threw my hands up. "Fine, then I'll call the sheriff. And the press too. I'm sure they'd love a story like this."

He shrugged. "That's your prerogative."

"I can't believe you're doing this."

"I'm here because you never answered my question. Do you want to answer it now?"

"What question?"

He put his smoothie down. "You know which one."

I quickly looked away. I *did* know. But I wasn't going to answer it. I could just lie and tell him I didn't love him anymore. But why should I have to lie?

"I'm calling the sheriff," I said, turning on my heels and heading back to the house.

Once inside, I closed the door and leaned against it, trying to catch my breath. Trying not to let the hurricane of emotions take over. I didn't want Gabe here. I wanted him to *leave*.

Eliza came and stood beside me. "He's here for you, isn't he?"

I nodded.

She smiled. "That's so romantic."

"Romantic?" I scoffed. "There's nothing romantic about it."

I pushed away from the door and went back to the window again. He was still sitting out there, leaning against the side of my porch, relaxed and comfortable, looking at his phone. And, what's more, he hadn't changed one bit. If anything, he was even more handsome than I remembered.

I turned away from the window. I had told Gabe I was going to call the sheriff, but I didn't.

"Are you ready to start labeling those jars?" I asked Eliza.

"Of course. That's why I'm here."

We both sat at the dining room table and started attaching "Theo's Honey" labels to the front and back of each jar. Ironically, I'd gone with the photo of myself that Gabe had liked best.

"So what's going on between you and your brother's business partner?" I asked as a way to distract myself from the interloper on my porch. "I thought I sensed something during New Year's Eve."

"Gavin?" Eliza got a strange look on her face. "I don't know what you mean," she said pressing a label onto a jar of honey. "He's my brother's best friend. He has a girlfriend. Didn't you see that super-model he was with?"

"Of course, I saw her." Although Gavin had tried to hide it, I mostly saw the way he looked at Eliza and it was definitely different than the way he looked at the supermodel.

"He's eleven years older than me. I've known him forever. Nothing's going on between us."

I shrugged. "Okay. I guess I was wrong."

Eliza began to tell me about the play she was doing with a small theater group in town. It was clear she wanted to change the subject. She described auditioning for one of the lead parts and how excited she was when they called her back and told her she'd gotten it.

As she talked, I thought about all the phone calls I'd gotten from Gabe. The voice mails he'd left. He'd started sending them again after he'd asked me if I still loved him.

I should have just lied.

But I didn't want to start lying. I'd never lied to Gabe. He was the one person I'd always been honest with, no matter what.

I wasn't sure why I didn't delete all those new messages from him. They sat on my phone like a ticking time bomb. I'd even been tempted to listen to a few but then stopped myself.

There were a lot of jars to put labels on. It was still hard to believe my hives were with a new beekeeper and this was the last of my honey. It had broken my heart to ask my friend Karl if he'd take my bees. But it was necessary. I couldn't care for them anymore. My fear was too overwhelming, and my bees deserved better.

"Have you started getting treated for your allergy yet?" Eliza asked me.

"Not yet, but soon," I said. I'd been putting it off. My doctor told me that with treatment, I might be less allergic after a couple of years. "I know I should, but I find the whole thing depressing."

"Why is that? My mom had treatment for hers, and apparently it's helped a lot. Though she still carries an EpiPen just in case."

"Your mom has a bee allergy?"

Eliza shook her head. "Shellfish, but it was like yours. It came on suddenly and out of the blue."

"I didn't know that."

She nodded. "It happened about five years ago." We heard a car outside, and both of us glanced toward the living room window. "I wonder if he's still out there."

I rolled my eyes. "I hope not."

Out of curiosity, I got up and peeked outside. To my amazement, there was a blue car parked in my driveway, and some delivery guy was handing Gabe a bag of food from Bijou's Café.

"This is unbelievable." I turned to Eliza. "I'll be right back."

"Actually"—she stood up, stretching her back—"do you mind if we finish the rest of these another day? I didn't realize how late it was getting. I have rehearsals tonight."

"Oh, of course, certainly! Don't let me keep you. I really appreciate all of your help."

Eliza grabbed her purse—a big funky cross-body bag made of purple velvet. I walked her outside, and we both crossed my porch to where Gabe was sitting, eating a burger and fries.

"Hi, Eliza," Gabe said, stuffing a fry in his mouth. "It's nice to see you again."

"You too," she said with a smile, taking in the chain around his waist. She glanced back at me and then at him. "Somebody should write a book about you two. You have a very interesting relationship."

Gabe laughed. "Maybe somebody will."

I snorted. "Over my dead body."

Eliza grinned and then waved to us both as she walked over to her Prius, got inside, and drove away.

I stood there and watched, though I didn't know why. I should have just gone back inside the house.

After she left, Gabe turned to me. "Do you want a french fry?" he asked, holding up the bag.

"I can't believe you had food delivered."

"I got hungry."

"I also can't believe you're eating a burger and fries."

He appeared quizzical. "Why's that?"

"I've only ever seen you eat super-healthy stuff."

He shrugged. "Once football season is over, I let myself indulge." He was still holding up the bag. "Are you sure you don't want one?"

"No, thanks." I stood up straight and tried to appear unaffected by his presence. Except I wasn't unaffected. "What is it you hope to accomplish here exactly?"

"I want to talk to you."

I crossed my arms. "So talk."

He motioned to the step beside him. "Come sit down next to me." And though his tone wasn't seductive, that's what I heard.

I should have left, but I couldn't resist letting my eyes trail over his broad shoulders and down to that muscular chest. Images of all the hot, sensual sex we used to have flashed through my mind. Sometimes when I visited him in Seattle, we never even got out of bed.

My animal lust, which had been asleep, woke up and was body-slamming the door to be let out.

I sniffed. My arms were still crossed. "I can hear you just fine from where I'm standing."

He leaned back and took another bite of his burger, chewing. "I came here so you could apologize to me."

I uncrossed my arms and stared at him with amazement. "*Seriously?* You want *me* to apologize to *you?*"

He nodded and picked up a drink I hadn't noticed before. It looked like a milkshake. "You disappeared. I haven't heard from you in weeks. Is that a way to treat a person?" He sucked on the straw of his shake.

I couldn't believe the nerve of him.

He swallowed. "Also, it's rude of you to delete all my messages."

"I haven't deleted all of your messages." Then I was annoyed with myself because I shouldn't have admitted that. I'd forgotten how crafty Gabe could be.

He smiled, obviously pleased with himself that he'd gotten that out of me. "You haven't?"

"Not *yet*."

"Did you listen to any of them?" He was acting casual, but I knew him and could tell he was keenly interested in my answer.

"Not a single one."

"Ouch."

"I'm just telling the truth."

"The truth isn't always easy, is it?"

Our eyes met, and I wondered what he meant by that remark.

We kept looking at each other. I remembered how often we used to do that. Sometimes we'd stop everything and just stare at each other. Gabe used to call it our telepathy.

"I'm sorry about your bees, Theo."

I held my hand up and turned my head. "*Don't.*"

"I'm actually sorry about a lot of things."

"You made a mistake coming here," I told him. "This relationship between us is over."

There was a flash of pain in his eyes, but then it turned to arrogance. "So, have you called the sheriff yet?"

"Just because I haven't doesn't mean I won't." I turned and went back to my house. I paused at the doorway and looked over my shoulder. "You should go home, Gabe. Seriously. You're wasting your time."

THE NEXT MORNING, I woke up, and Gabe was still out there. Though he must have gone home at some point because he was wearing different clothes—blue athletic sweats with a white stripe down each leg and a gray T-shirt.

To my amazement, he was doing push-ups with that chain wrapped around his waist right on my front porch. I couldn't believe it. It was mesmerizing to watch. He made it look so effortless with those huge biceps.

It was like Gabe TV. I knew I should stop watching him, but my animal lust was purring loudly and ignoring my rational brain.

Finally, I forced myself to turn away. *So he's still extremely appealing. What else is new?* I went into the kitchen and made myself coffee. I had papers to grade and decided to work on those first.

In the past, I would have gone down to check on my bees on a Saturday morning. Not necessarily to open hives but just to observe their activity. My bees had always been a comfort to me. I could watch them for hours.

Without their presence, my house and yard felt so different. So empty.

I tried to ignore Gabe out there doing who knows what. Probably jumping jacks or backflips. I was surprised he hadn't brought a football with him to spin in the air.

After getting through most of the papers I needed to grade, I switched to working on an article about my research at the pollinator lab, going over my findings on queen laying habits and the Varroa destructor. As I stared at my computer screen, I heard voices outside. When I got up and looked through my living room window, I saw Claire out there talking to Gabe. She was handing him a bag of what looked like takeout.

"What's going on?" I demanded to know, walking outside to join them.

Claire smiled at me. "Oh, hey. I was just bringing Gabe some Thai food for lunch."

I blinked at her. "You're *feeding* him?"

"I get cranky when I'm hungry," he said with a pout, opening the bag. "You know that. I need a lot of calories."

"Did you bring *me* any Thai food?" I asked Claire, staring at her empty hands. "I love Thai food too."

"Sorry, I didn't." She turned to Gabe. "I have to get back to the house. Amelia's been teething lately and is really out of sorts. Just let Leah know what you want for dinner."

"Leah's bringing him *dinner*?" I was incredulous. "I thought you guys were supposed to be on *my* side."

Claire turned to me and smiled. "Trust me, Theo. We *are* on your side."

After she left, I watched Gabe enjoying his *pad see ew*. "What have you done to my friends?"

He shrugged. "Apparently they like me."

I stared at him. His wavy dark hair had grown longer in back. I remembered how its softness, in contrast to the hardness of the rest of him, had always pleased me so much.

A terrible wave of longing crashed over me. I missed him fiercely. *Why did he have to go and ruin it between us?*

"How's our meadow doing?" he asked, using his chopsticks to grab a piece of broccoli. "Have you been out there at all?"

I shook my head, not trusting myself to speak.

He must have sensed my emotion because he glanced up at me with concern. "What is it? Are you okay?"

"I'm going back inside now. Enjoy your lunch."

It was the middle of the night, and I was restless, staring at the ceiling, unable to sleep. I'd managed to ignore Gabe the rest of the day and hadn't looked out that living room window even once. Except now my brain was overanalyzing like always. I got up, slipped my glasses on, and went to peek out my front window.

To my amazement, Gabe was still there chained to my porch. So persistent. I had to give him that. This gladiator, who'd taken it upon himself to guard me. To be my champion.

I put my robe and my wool-lined slippers on and opened the front door.

Gabe turned to me with surprise. His usual cockiness was gone, and he seemed contemplative.

I walked over to the steps, hesitated for a moment, but then sat down on the opposite side of the same step he was on.

It was chilly out and had rained earlier. The ground smelled like wet pavement. I pulled my robe in tighter.

Neither of us spoke for a while, and it reminded me of that night he'd come here when he was out of sorts. When we barely knew each other.

"So, how are you handling not making it to the Super Bowl?" I asked, breaking the silence. "I imagine it's been difficult."

He glanced at me. "It's been rough. I'm not going to lie. It was disappointing to come so far and then lose. I'm not used to losing."

I nodded. Gabe liked a challenge, but it helped that he won most challenges.

His gaze was still on me. "Although *nothing* has been as terrible as losing you, Theo."

My stomach tightened at his words, and I turned my head away.

"How about you?" he asked. "How has it been without your bees? That's got to be hard."

I swallowed and tried to keep my voice steady. "It hasn't been easy."

"When did you move them?"

"About two weeks ago. My friend Karl, a fellow beekeeper, came and got them. He's been a beekeeper longer than I've been alive, so I know they'll be well cared for."

"I'm sorry you had to go through that." His voice was low and sincere.

I closed my eyes and remained silent for a long moment trying to control my emotions. "What do you want from me, Gabe?"

"I want you to come back."

I turned to look at him.

His eyes were intense. "You once told me you had a hive that absconded, but then you found them again and brought them home. You said they thrived."

"That was years ago...." I couldn't believe he remembered that story.

"We can thrive again too. I'm sure of it. You and me."

I considered this. "What you want and what I want might not be compatible."

"That's not true. I know I made mistakes. After you were stung, I was terrified of losing you. I would have done anything to prevent that from happening again."

"By threatening legal action against me? I'm supposed to be okay with that?"

He shook his head. "No, you're never supposed to be okay with that."

I stared at him. At that handsome face I still loved. My heart ached. I wished he hadn't come back here. It was too difficult seeing him again.

"My reaction was over the top. I'm sorry, Theo. You have no idea how much. But you don't know everything. There's a reason I lost it like that."

"What reason?"

Gabe took a deep breath and leaned his head against the wooden post. His eyes met mine. "Do you think you can handle one more skeleton?"

CHAPTER FORTY-ONE

~ Gabe ~

"It's about Tyler, isn't it?" she asked.

I nodded, not surprised that she'd figured that out.

"I always had a feeling there were things about him you weren't telling me."

I repositioned the chain on my waist so it wasn't digging into my back. "I met him during my freshman year of high school, when his family moved to Long Beach. He was this blond surfer guy who was as obsessed with football as I was, so naturally, we hit it off." I remembered the way Tyler had appeared out of the blue at school one day and how our friendship grew. "Because he was new, I kind of took him under my wing. Eventually, I became our team's quarterback, and he became our wide receiver, so that cemented things even more. He was an incredible athlete. In fact, he got a full scholarship to college just like I did."

"So football was the basis for your friendship?"

I nodded. "Partly. He was popular and fun to be around. We hung out a lot. The problem was he was a risk taker. On the field. Everywhere. He was always on the edge of getting in trouble or getting caught doing something he shouldn't. I tried to look out for him, but he could be reckless. My dad hated him."

She listened, remaining still.

"He thought Tyler was a bad influence on me. It made the problems between us even worse." I stretched my legs out and stared down at my sneakers, remembering all the arguments my dad and I used to have, feeling like shit about them, and wishing things had been different.

Theo tilted her head. Her eyes looked dark in the shadow from her porch light. "You never told me any of that."

"I know." I could smell the night air around us. "It was a past I didn't want to think about. Tyler came up with a lot of crazy stuff. I tried to be the voice of reason, and sometimes he'd listen, but most of the time he wouldn't. He was my best friend, you know? And so, like an idiot, I usually went along with his dumb ideas."

"That doesn't sound like you."

"That's because I've learned from my mistakes."

"How was he reckless? What did he do?"

I snorted. "What *didn't* he do? He was always pushing the edge. Rock climbing without ropes, jumping off bridges, surfing at midnight, picking fights with people he shouldn't. Even playing football—he always took too many chances."

"And you did that stuff too?"

"Believe it or not, I did. Not so much with football but everything else. Occasionally, I'd try to stop him from doing something really stupid, especially if he was drinking. But usually I went along with it. That's actually how he died." I fell silent. It was a hard truth to admit, but if I had been more of a hardass, Tyler would still be alive. "It was an accident that happened the summer after high school. We were at this girl's party celebrating our football scholarships. She had a swimming pool in her backyard, and some people were jumping off the roof into the water. Tyler and I were doing it—a bunch of us were—except Tyler started getting really drunk. I tried to stop him, but I should have tried harder. He jumped off the roof, misjudged the distance, and landed on the cement wrong."

Theo's expression turned sympathetic. "That's terrible. I'm really sorry, Gabe."

"I could have prevented it. I *should* have."

"He doesn't sound like someone who listened to reason."

"Friends look out for each other. I was always looking out for him. I should have dragged him off that roof if I had to. It's my fault."

"Not from what you've said. That doesn't sound like it's your fault."

But I knew she was wrong. I'd gone over that night in my head so many times. There were a bunch of us on that roof. We were joking around with each other. I told Tyler he was wasted and shouldn't jump anymore, and he started saying, "Okay, Mom." But I should have forced him to stop, even if it would have pissed him off.

"I let my best friend die. What kind of asshole does that make me?" I shook my head in disgust. "And then a year later, I got his girlfriend pregnant."

"Are you *trying* to convince me that you're an asshole?"

I chuckled without humor. "I guess I just want you to have all the facts. And now you do."

"I think I get it. So that's why you were ready to sue me to get rid of my bees," she said, mulling it over. "It makes sense."

"It's why I freaked out. I'm sorry."

"You wanted to save me even if I was furious at you, because you didn't save him."

"If you're going to psychoanalyze me, then yeah, I'd say that's basically it."

She went quiet after that. I didn't say anything either, the two of us lost in our own thoughts. I was nervous about what she thought of me after hearing all this. There was a reason I never talked about it.

Theo finally spoke. "I'm glad you told me everything."

It was late, and I could tell she was tired. Nevertheless, I thought she was as beautiful as ever.

I took a deep breath, afraid to ask the burning question but wanting the answer. "Are you ever coming back?"

"I don't know." But then she turned and held my gaze. "Maybe."

———

IT WASN'T A YES, *but it wasn't a no either,* I told myself as I walked back to my house later feeling optimistic—the most optimistic since I'd arrived.

Coming here and chaining myself to Theo's front porch was a Hail Mary pass, but it wouldn't be the first time in my life I'd thrown one of those. I hoped telling her everything had been the right move. Because it was all I had left. It could very easily go the other way, and she might decide it was too much, that she wanted a clean break from me and all my skeletons.

I hoped not.

She didn't say no.

And because I was optimistic, I went to bed that night and slept for the first night in a long time.

———

BY NINE THE NEXT MORNING, I was back on Theo's porch again. And even though I didn't usually work out on Sundays, I loosened the chain and did some push-ups and sit-ups, mostly to get some energy out. I was used to being active all day, and it wasn't easy sitting for hours.

When I was done, I took a breather. I'd only had a bowl of oatmeal with honey for breakfast and was still hungry, so I pulled my phone out and ordered some food to be delivered.

To my delight, as I waited, Theo came outside and joined me on the top porch step. She wore jeans, those yellow sneakers, and her green hoodie. Her bright red curls were pulled back into a short ponytail. She looked so pretty, and she smelled good, like the honey and lavender soap she liked. It brought back memories of how much I loved her skin.

"Good morning," I said, trying not to show how affected I was by her.

She smiled. "You're still here."

"You know me. Stubborn till the end."

A guy driving a red Toyota pulled into Theo's driveway. He got out carrying a bag of food and a couple of drinks.

"Did you order food *again*?" she asked with amazement as the guy approached us. "If I'd eaten this much while I was chained to your house, I would have gained twenty pounds."

I shrugged. "What can I say? It's breakfast. Plus, emotional angst makes me hungry." I took the bag and the two drinks from the guy.

"Hey, you're Beauty Bardales, aren't you?" he asked me.

"I am."

"Damn, dude. This is awesome. Do you think I could get your autograph?"

"Sure. Do you have a pen?" He pulled one out from his front pocket and handed it to me, and I tore off part of the delivery bag to write on. "What's your name?" I asked.

"Cory."

I signed it, *To Cory, Thanks for the delivery. Beauty Bardales.* I felt Theo watching me. Part of me hoped this was impressing her, but I knew it wasn't. The professor wasn't impressed by the types of things other people were. Also, she'd seen me sign autographs before.

Instead of leaving as expected, Cory—a short, overweight guy in his midtwenties, who looked like he'd never touched a football in his life—proceeded to lecture me on every single mistake he thought I'd made during the conference championship game.

It was unbelievable. I tried to keep my face as neutral as possible.

The guy leaned forward, his foot perched on the edge of a step, his hands waving around like he was teaching me something. "Now your biggest mistake during the third quarter was passing the ball to Gomez when Morgan was wide open. I mean, damn, dude, how could you not have seen that? A blind monkey would have seen it!" Cory's phone pinged, and he pulled it out of his pocket. "Oops, looks like I've got another delivery. I better split. Nice talking to you. Thanks for the autograph!"

To my relief, he finally left.

I felt Theo's eyes on me. "You handled that very well."

I gave her one of the drinks. "Everybody's a Monday morning quarterback," I muttered.

"What's this?" she asked, glancing down at the drink I just handed her.

"I know you don't like green smoothies, so I got you a strawberry mango one."

Her eyes widened. "You did? You got me a smoothie?"

I nodded.

"How did you know I'd come out here?"

"I didn't, but I hoped. My other plan was to ring your doorbell, leave the smoothie on your welcome mat, and then run and hide in the bushes while you drank it."

Theo laughed. "Did you get me breakfast too?" She peered into the bag of food.

"Sadly, I didn't. But I'm happy to share my pancakes and scrambled eggs with you."

"Well, that's no way to impress a lady." She sucked on the straw. "At least you get points for the smoothie."

I grinned. This was so familiar. Theo and me with our usual banter.

In the end, she accepted a blueberry pancake and leaned against the porch to eat it with her fingers. "So, I heard you came by my work looking for me while I was on my leave of absence."

I forked some eggs into my mouth and nodded. "Yeah, I did."

"I also heard you talked to Gerald. He said you threatened him. Is that true?"

"No."

"He said he was scared for his life, and that he might take legal action against you."

I chuckled. "Really? That would be entertaining. I hope he does." Davis would swat that guy like a fly.

"I don't need you to fight my battles for me."

I glanced over at her. "I know that."

She appeared skeptical. "Do you?"

"Of course." I ate my eggs and was working on some toast, saving the pancakes for Theo in case she wanted more. "Let me ask you something though. Did you tell me everything that happened between you and that Gerald guy?"

She averted her eyes, which was exactly as I'd suspected.

"What did you leave out?"

Theo smoothed a hand over her jeans and shook her head. "It was no big deal. Nothing I couldn't handle."

"Tell me anyway."

"He just said some things."

"Like what?"

She gazed at me with those eyes the color of wild grass. "He called me a big, tall, ugly bitch. And a beast."

I froze, holding my toast in midair.

"I handled it," she said. "In fact, it's because of *you* that his insult meant nothing to me."

I began to imagine all the ways I was going to torture Gerald. It would be slow and painful and humiliating. I'd get Davis and Franklin involved, too, and Gerald better pray he didn't have a single secret to hide. And all of this would be *after* I beat the shit out of him.

Theo waved a hand in front of my face. "Earth to Gabe, are you hearing me?"

I snapped out of my fantasy. "What did you say?"

"I said he's not worth a second thought, trust me. He's just a small man with a big mouth. Nobody at the pollinator lab likes him. I doubt he has a single friend in the entire entomology department."

"He shouldn't get away with talking to you like that. Have you reported it?"

She shook her head. "In the past, his insult would have hurt me, but not anymore. I know I'm not ugly or a beast, no matter what anybody says." She smiled. "You showed me that I'm beautiful, Gabe. Because of you, I've become immune to the Geralds of the world."

If there was anything she could have said that would make me feel like a million bucks, that was it. The only thing better would have been if she told me she was coming back.

"I love you, Theo. And you're right. You are beautiful."

She was still smiling. "I know."

I put my container of food down. I wanted to take her in my arms.

It was right then that a car pulled up in front of her house. We both turned to look at it. Some guy got out of the back seat. He wore beige cargo pants, a lightweight gray jacket, and was carrying a travel bag.

As he walked toward the house, I glanced at Theo. She'd gone completely still and her mouth hung open.

I was going to ask who this was but didn't get the chance.

"*Clement?*"

My gaze cut back to the guy, and my stomach dropped. *So this is the brilliant idiot.*

As Clement approached us, I saw he didn't know what to make of all this. Theo and I sitting out here together while I was chained to her house. But then I saw something else. That he grasped the situation pretty quickly. He definitely knew who I was, and I could tell he had a good guess about why I was out here. He held my eyes for a moment before turning to Theo.

"Hi, Theo," he said. "I was hoping you'd be here."

She was blinking rapidly, and it disturbed me to see her so upset. You didn't get this upset over someone you didn't have feelings for anymore.

"It's a Sunday! Where else would I be?"

He nodded. "Well, I'm glad you're here. Can we talk?"

Theo's mouth was still open as she stared at him. I wondered if she was going to introduce us.

Instead, Clement turned to me and held his hand out. "I'm Clement."

"Gabe," I said, shaking it with a firm grip. My expression remained stern.

"I just flew in from Belize City," he said, turning back to Theo. "It took me fifteen hours to get here. Do you think we can at least talk inside the house?"

I willed Theo to say no.

Instead, she threw her hands in the air. "Fine. We'll talk in the house." She stood up. "But you're not staying, so don't get any ideas."

Clement glanced at me again, and my stomach churned as I watched him follow her inside. They closed the door behind them.

Fuck.

I sat there, straining to hear anything they were saying through the closed door, but I couldn't hear a damn thing. Any second now, I expected Theo to throw Clement out on his ass. In fact, I was hoping she'd open the door and ask me to do it for her, because I'd be happy to oblige.

Except that wasn't what happened.

A whole hour passed while I sat there. I thought I heard voices a few times, but I couldn't be sure.

When another hour passed, a sense of overwhelming dread came over me. The brilliant idiot wasn't getting tossed out. That much was clear. He also wasn't what I expected. I'd pictured some scrawny egghead who didn't know up from down, but this wasn't that guy. I should have realized Theo wouldn't have fallen in love with someone like that.

I already knew they had a lot in common. They were both academics. Both entomologists. They could probably talk for hours about beetles and bees.

But does he love her as much as I do?

No fucking way. Of that, I was certain.

I wondered how long I should stay out here. Eventually, it was going to be pointless.

I can't believe she'd take him back.

But then I remembered the way she cried over him that night at my house.

Later she told me she didn't love him anymore, but maybe that wasn't true. Or maybe seeing him again brought back all her old feelings.

As I sat there with more time passing, and Clement didn't emerge from that house, it felt like I was getting sucked into a deep black hole. I wasn't sure how I was ever going to claw my way out.

Finally, I got up, unchained myself, and left.

CHAPTER FORTY-TWO

~ Theo ~

"So you really are involved with that football player," Clement said, glancing out the window. He came into my living room and took a seat on the couch, putting his bag down. "I heard about it, but I didn't believe it was true."

I stood there, watching him with annoyance. "Why didn't you believe it was true?"

He snorted. "You and some jock? Seriously? I figured you had better taste than that."

"Get out, Clement. I mean it." I went over and grabbed his bag, ready to toss it outside. "You can leave right now."

"Hey, stop." He took his bag back from me. "Look, I'm sorry if I insulted you and what's-his-name." He motioned toward the porch. "I had a long flight, and I'm not feeling so great."

"What are you even doing here?"

He sighed and relaxed back on the couch again. I remembered

that sound. Sitting in front of me, I remembered a lot of things about Clement. Especially that he'd dumped me.

"I made a mistake, Theo. I never should have broken up with you." He rubbed his forehead. "I don't know what I was thinking."

I stared at him in amazement. "What happened? Did Kendra kick you out? Or maybe you discovered she wasn't as fascinating as you thought."

"What?" He looked confused. "What's Kendra got to do with this?"

I rolled my eyes. "You can drop the innocent act. I know you left me for her. I just wish you would have at least had the guts to be honest about it."

But Clement seemed bewildered. "I didn't leave you for Kendra. Where did you get an idea like that?"

"That's what Gerald told me."

"Gerald? I haven't spoken to that guy in ages. I never liked him. And I've certainly never been involved with Kendra."

"You haven't?" Now it was my turn to be bewildered. Had Gerald been lying to me? "He told me you were living in Belize with Kendra and that you two were romantically involved. This was right after you broke up with me."

Clement shook his head. "I don't know why he told you that, but none of it's true."

I lowered myself in a chair, trying to wrap my head around this. *So this whole time I believed a lie?* "Then why did you break up with me?"

"You honestly thought I could be with Kendra? With a woman who says 'okey dokey' twenty-five times a day? Who comes to work smelling like tequila? Who still doesn't know a *Coleoptera* from an *Orthoptera*?"

I remembered all the ways Clement used to complain about her.

"The only reason she was my assistant is because the university forced her on me. She's some donor's daughter. You *know* that."

"Yes, well, she's also cute and blonde. And you broke up with me for no reason, so at the time, it wasn't that hard to believe you were with her."

He snorted. "I thought you knew me better than that. And if I was so into blondes, I wouldn't have been with you."

"If it wasn't another woman, then why *did* you break up with me?"

Clement didn't reply, instead he glanced to the side at all the jars of honey stacked and labeled in my dining room. "Are you selling your honey? When did you start doing that?"

"Answer my question." I was already getting annoyed, remembering all of Clement's avoidance tactics. Gabe's bluntness was like a breath of fresh air.

He leaned back, went silent, but then looked at me. "It's true. I was interested in someone else. That's why I broke up with you."

I *knew* it. "So Gerald's lie wasn't that far off."

"I never cheated on you, Theo. And the reason I didn't tell you about it was because I didn't want to hurt your feelings."

"Who is she?"

"She's a professor at one of the universities in Peru. We met at a conference I went to down there."

I nodded. I remembered that conference.

"Nothing happened. Not at the conference or while you and I were together. But she emailed me a few times. And then when I moved to Belize City, she came out to visit me."

"And that's when you got involved?"

He nodded. "We dated for a little while. But there's no reason to hold that against me. You were obviously involved with that jock outside. By the way, why is he chained to your house?"

"None of your business."

He smirked. But then got a strange expression on his face. "Can I use your restroom?"

"I suppose. Go ahead."

Clement got up and ran down the hall to the bathroom.

While he was gone, I sat and tried to absorb all of this. The way Gerald had so boldly lied.

Why should it surprise me?

The irony was that if he hadn't lied, there was a good chance I might have never gotten involved with Gabe. It was the lie that drove me to sneak onto Gabe's property that night when he first kissed me.

Clement reappeared from the bathroom, holding his stomach. He took a seat on the couch again. "I'm not feeling so great. I think I accidentally had a drink with ice made from tap water in it before I left Belize."

"I'm sorry to hear that. You can't stay here though, Clement."

"Could I at least get a glass of water?"

I got up from the couch to get it for him.

"Thanks," he said when I came back and handed it over.

I sat back in the chair.

"I heard about your bee allergy," he said after drinking some water. "Everyone was talking about it."

I nodded. It was definitely the sort of thing that would have made news in the entomology circles we were a part of.

"Did you really have to get rid of all your hives? You couldn't have figured out a way to keep them?"

"I had an allergic reaction that nearly killed me. If Gabe hadn't been here, I would have died."

Clement put his glass down on the coffee table. "But now you have an EpiPen, right? Maybe you just need to be a little tougher."

Anger flashed through me. "So what are you saying? I'm weak because I want to avoid another episode of anaphylaxis?"

"That's not what I'm saying. It just seems a little hasty is all."

I thought about the lengths Gabe went through to try to stop me from keeping my bees. He was willing to let me hate him as long as I was safe.

"Why did you come here, Clement?"

He studied me. "I've missed you, Theo. I still love you."

I didn't respond.

"Aren't you going to say anything?"

"What happened to this woman you were involved with from Peru?"

He waved his hand. "That's over. It didn't last long. There was too much drama. She was always angry about something. It made me realize how good we were together, how compatible you and I are."

It was true. Clement and I had been compatible. We seldom argued.

"To be honest, it was just lust with her," he continued. "I found her attractive physically, but I've come to realize that's overrated."

"And you don't find me attractive physically?"

"Of course I do. But that's always been secondary with us. I want to be together with you again. In fact, let's get married. I realize I screwed that up too. I should have married you when I had the chance. Even my family thought so."

"They did?"

He nodded.

"It sounds like you have it all figured out." I thought about this strange situation I was currently in—two men wanting me at the same time. It was one I'd never experienced before in my life. "Except there's a problem with your plan."

Clement's stomach made a loud gurgling noise. "Excuse me." He got up and ran out of the living room.

He was gone quite a while. I got up and looked out the front window. Gabe was still out there chained to the porch, looking at his phone. I was just about to go outside and tell him that Clement was leaving soon when he called me loudly from the bathroom.

I rolled my eyes. *Now what?*

"Do you have any diarrhea medication?" he asked through the closed door.

"I might," I said. "Let me check."

I went into my master bathroom and looked in the basket under the sink, where I kept all my cold remedies and other medications. There was a big, unopened bottle of pink liquid. I grabbed it and went back to the other bathroom, Clement still inside.

"I found some."

"Oh thank God. Hang on a second."

I waited and grimaced as I heard a lot of farting noises and groaning as his bowels evacuated.

"I'm just going to leave this outside the door," I said, not wanting to hear any more.

"No, don't go! Just give me another minute."

I couldn't believe this situation. What was the etiquette when an old boyfriend showed up and had explosive diarrhea in your bathroom?

I waited a little longer, and just when I was ready to put the medication on the floor and leave, I heard the toilet flush and then the sink running.

Finally, Clement opened the door, still drying his hands with a towel.

Yuck. I needed a cartoon clothespin for my nose. The smell was extremely unpleasant.

I handed him the bottle of diarrhea medication.

"Thank you," he said. I had to admit, he didn't look good. Pale and sweaty.

We left the bathroom area and were halfway down the hall when Clement made a moaning noise, then turned around and ran back.

"Theo," he called out to me in a helpless voice.

I went back to the bathroom and discovered he was lying on the floor in a ball, grimacing and holding his stomach again.

"Should I call an ambulance?" I asked with alarm. "Or take you to the ER?"

He shook his head. "I've had this before. It's traveler's diarrhea. Lots of painful cramps and loose stools, but it's not life-threatening. Though it certainly *feels* like it."

I watched as he took deep breaths when another wave of cramps hit him.

"Is there a remedy?" I asked.

He waited a few moments to answer me, obviously in pain. "Just time and lots of liquids to avoid dehydration. Could you get me some more water, or do you have any electrolyte drinks?"

I didn't have any electrolyte drinks, so I trudged back out to the living room, grabbed Clement's water glass, and filled it again.

Before walking back to the bathroom, I decided to tell Gabe what was going on.

"Theo!" Clement yelled. "I need something to drink!"

I ignored him. I figured as loud as he was yelling, he couldn't be *that* sick.

But when I open the front door, Gabe wasn't there anymore. He was gone, and so was the chain.

I stepped outside and looked around the yard, then studied the empty space on my porch with concern. I hadn't told Gabe I was coming back definitively, but surely he must have figured out which way I was leaning, right?

Unless he didn't.

Unless he thought Clement spending two hours inside my house meant we were getting back together again.

"Theo!" It was Clement's loud mouth.

When I got to the bathroom, he was sitting against the wall with his head back and his eyes closed, still pale and sweaty.

"Here's your water," I said, stepping inside my bathroom that he'd stunk up.

Clement opened his eyes and accepted the glass. He took a few sips and put it down.

"What did you mean earlier?" he asked. He picked up the bottle of diarrhea medication and tore off the protective seal. "When you said I had it all figured out, but there was a problem with my plan? What problem?"

I watched as Clement took the cap off the medication, ignored the cup that came with it, and took a swig of pink liquid directly from the bottle.

"What are you doing?" I asked, irritated. "You should have used the cup. Now I'm going to have to get a new bottle."

He shrugged and glanced at it in his hand. "Whatever. I'll buy you another one. Who cares?"

He was right, and it wasn't that big of a deal, but I felt unreasonably angry. "The problem with your plan," I said, "is that I don't love you anymore."

He turned to look at me. His irises were blue or gray depending on the light. I used to love that changing color, but now I couldn't picture myself loving any eye color but brown.

"Don't tell me you're in love with that football player."

"I understand why you came here, Clement. But we're not getting back together."

He blinked at me like I was speaking Martian. "There's no way you're in love with that dumb jock. What could you possibly have in common with him?"

"More than you'd imagine. And he's not dumb."

He scoffed. "I don't believe it."

"Believe whatever you want. But when it comes to choosing between you and Gabe, there's no comparison. I'd always choose Gabe."

"Give me a break. Then why is he chained to your house? I'm guessing you guys are having some kind of problem."

I nodded. "We were, but it's been resolved. In fact, you coming here has helped me see that even more clearly."

"You're serious, aren't you?"

"I am. And I'm also serious when I say you can't stay here. You have to leave."

He seemed flabbergasted. "You want me to *leave?* Are you kidding? I'm sick as hell. Look at me. I'm a mess."

"At least it's not life-threatening. Unlike anaphylaxis. Maybe you just need to be a little tougher, Clement."

He glared at me.

I left the bathroom and went out to the living room, grabbing my computer. Taking a seat in the dining room, I went online and reserved a room for Clement at a local hotel. I had to go back to the bathroom to get his credit card.

After that was done, I lay on the couch with my phone, put my earbuds in, and began listening to all those messages Gabe had left me.

I closed my eyes. I'd forgotten how much I loved his voice.

Occasionally, I got up to check on Clement, who was still in the bathroom, and still had diarrhea. I had decided not to throw him out immediately. I wasn't completely heartless.

After a couple of hours, and when Clement's bowels seemed to have calmed down, I drove him to the hotel.

"You're going to regret this, Theo," he said, reaching inside for his travel bag as I was dropping him off.

"I don't believe I will."

"Eventually, you'll run out of things to talk about with that football jock, and then what?"

I shrugged. "Then I guess we'll have lots of hot sex."

The expression on Clement's face before I drove off was priceless.

CHAPTER FORTY-THREE

~ Theo ~

It was Monday morning, and luckily, someone had canceled, so I was able to get in for an appointment with my doctor right away.

"I understand why we're doing the allergy test for bee venom," she said to me as we talked inside the exam room. "But you also want to be tested for shellfish allergy?"

I nodded. "I do."

"Is there a reason you think you might have a shellfish allergy?"

"Not really," I said. "But I hope so."

She laughed. "That's the first time I've ever heard that before."

After leaving the room, she came back a short while later with a nurse. I had an exam gown on and remained still for them as they did the allergy test on my back.

"All right, let's give that about twenty minutes," my doctor said, taking her gloves off. "We'll see if you have a reaction to either of those."

I knew this was a serious long shot. All the evidence pointed to me being allergic to bee venom, including a positive test result from my blood work at the ER. But Eliza had gotten me thinking after she told me about her mom. After all, we'd been eating seafood all night on New Year's Eve.

Also, I did some research last night after dropping off Clement at the hotel, and I'd discovered something interesting. It turned out that about 20 to 30 percent of blood tests for bee allergy showed a false positive if the person had been stung by a bee within the last couple of years. Which, of course, I had.

I was on pins and needles as I sat there with a magazine, waiting for my results. I tried very hard not to get my hopes up. The odds were strong that I was allergic to bees. What's more, the test area on my back felt quite itchy, and I wasn't sure which test was causing the itch or if I was imagining it altogether.

Eventually, my doctor came into the room again and stared at my back for a long moment.

"Well," she said. "This is interesting."

"What is it?" I tried frantically to look over my shoulder, but of course, I couldn't see anything.

"You appear to be showing signs of a shellfish allergy but not bee venom allergy."

My breath stopped at those words. I nearly collapsed with relief. It was difficult to speak, but I finally managed, "Are you... sure?"

She squeezed my arm with excitement. She knew I was a bee biologist. "That's what I'm seeing, Theo. But let's increase the test, okay? We want to be absolutely certain. Can you stay longer?"

I nodded. "Of course!"

I stayed at the clinic for the next three hours as they added increasingly larger amounts of both bee venom and shellfish to the test sites on my back.

In the end, the results were clear and definitive.

I had developed a severe allergic reaction to shellfish.

I was *not* allergic to bee venom.

I DIDN'T CALL anybody right away. Instead, I sat in my car in the parking lot of the clinic and cried. It felt like a miracle. Like divine intervention.

Finally, I pulled myself together, and the first person I called was Karl, the fellow beekeeper and friend who'd been kind enough to accept all my hives and had moved them onto his property.

I started crying again on the phone with him as I told him my results. As someone who'd been keeping hives for almost forty years and probably knew more about bees than I did, he'd understand the depths of my relief.

"Well, damn, Theo," he said, chuckling with delight. "This is some great news. You better get over here right away and tell your bees they're coming home."

AFTER GOING to Karl's and telling my bees the wonderful news, I headed to my house, hoping I'd see Gabe on my front porch. He wasn't there this morning when I left, and now he still wasn't there. As a result, I was certain that he'd gotten the wrong idea about me and Clement.

I parked my car, but instead of going inside the house, I decided to walk over to Gabe's and talk to him. This wasn't a conversation to be had over the phone.

When I got there, the gate was closed, so I rang the intercom. To my surprise, Regina answered.

"Hey, Theo. I'll let you in."

I heard a buzzing sound and then a click as the side door opened. A curved road led me up toward Gabe's house until finally I was standing on the steps of his Spanish castle. His truck was sitting in the driveway.

Regina was already there at the door, and we hugged each other hello.

"So I heard you and Tess are moving to Truth Harbor," I said, following her into the house. I'd learned this from listening to Gabe's messages yesterday.

"We are. Tess still has school, but after selling my bar, I figured I'd come up and start checking things out."

"You guys are going to love it here. It's a great place to live."

We talked a little more, and she told me how excited she and Tess were about moving, and how they'd already been looking at houses online. I couldn't resist telling her about my bee allergy results. She screeched with excitement and hugged me again.

"That's amazing, Theo! Gabe must be thrilled for you. You guys should go out and celebrate."

"Actually, I came over here looking for him so I could tell him the good news in person."

Her brows rose. "I thought he was at your house, still chained to your front porch."

"I haven't seen him since yesterday."

"Really? I saw him this morning. But if he's not at your house, I don't know where he could be. Let me try calling him."

I followed her into the kitchen so she could get her phone. She called, but there was no answer.

"His truck's in the driveway," she said, mystified. "Maybe he went for a walk?"

Then it dawned on me. "Actually, it's okay. I know exactly where he went."

I left and went back to my house, but rather than go inside, I headed down to my lower yard. I passed by the empty space where my beehives used to be, but instead of an overwhelming sadness, I felt joy knowing they'd be returning home soon.

When I got to our meadow, I didn't see Gabe at first. But then I found him, hidden by the tall grass.

He'd spread the blankets on the ground and was lying on his back, gazing up at the sky. He must have heard me coming because he turned his head and sat up.

"Theo? What are you doing here?"

"I'm looking for you. You weren't chained to my porch this morning. Are you already slacking off?"

Gabe didn't even crack a smile. Instead, he lay down on his back again. "I finally got the message that you didn't want me there anymore."

I stood over him but then knelt on the blankets. "Scoot over. Make room for me."

He gave me a strange look. "You want to lie out here with me?"

"I do."

Gabe didn't budge at first, and I wondered if he was going to. "Fine."

He scooted over, and soon we were both lying on our backs and gazing up at the sky. It wasn't quite spring yet and was still cool out. The white clouds were soft streaks against the blue behind them.

Neither of us spoke, and it reminded me of the first time we were out here together. The day it went from being not just *my* meadow but *our* meadow.

"So, it turns out Clement never left me for Kendra," I said. "It was a lie concocted by Gerald. Can you believe it?"

"Really? You must be thrilled."

"Clement wants me back."

"Of course he does."

"He wants to marry me."

I felt Gabe shift and go still beside me. "What did you tell him?"

"I told him that if there was a competition between you and him, that you'd win every time."

"What?" He lifted himself onto his elbows and turned to me. "What are you saying?"

I gazed up at him and smiled. "I'm coming back to you."

He stared at me. "You *are?*"

I nodded. "Definitely."

Gabe searched my face and then sat up all the way. "What about Clement? You guys were in that house together for hours."

I sat up, too, and then told him how Clement got sick with diarrhea and stank up my whole bathroom. "He couldn't get off the toilet. It was unbelievable. I was afraid to go in there afterward and had to spray the entire room with disinfectant."

He laughed. "Okay, I think I get the picture." He was grinning at me. "Where's he at now?"

"I dropped him off at a hotel last night."

"Damn, Theo. I thought you'd gone back to him. You really like scaring the shit out of me, don't you?"

I reached over and stroked his jaw. "Not particularly. I have some other news too. I found out something incredible." And then I told him about the allergy tests this morning and how it turned out I was allergic to shellfish and not bee venom.

His jaw dropped. "You're *kidding.*"

I smiled and my eyes filled with tears again. "I'm bringing my bees home tonight. Karl and his son are going to help me move them back."

"I'm helping too."

I nodded. "I'd like that."

Gabe gazed at me, and I could see his eyes were getting weepy. He reached up and wiped them with his palm. "I can't believe any of this. I was lying out here feeling sorry for myself, and then you show up and make everything perfect. Just like you always do."

"Maybe it's this place." I glanced around at our secret meadow. "In a way, it really does seem magical here."

"You're right. It does." He was watching me, and I recognized that hungry expression. "Come here, right now." He reached out for me, bringing me onto his lap so I was straddling him.

Then he kissed me. It had been so long since we'd kissed. He tasted wonderful, like every desire I'd ever had. Every part of me was purring, not just my animal lust.

"Damn, Theo, I love you so much."

"I love you."

His arms tightened around my waist. "I can't believe you've come back to me, that you're really here."

I stroked his neck and held him close. "In some ways, I don't think I ever left you, Gabe. Even after absconding, deep down, a part of me always hoped you'd find me and bring me home."

EPILOGUE

~ Gabe ~

I was sitting out here in our meadow feeling sorry for myself. It wasn't like me, and I was usually ready for battle, but I'd gone back into brooding mode. After Clement arrived and didn't leave her house, I thought I'd lost Theo for good, and I didn't think my heart could take it. I found myself at the bottom of a deep black pit.

I'd brought the jar of honey out here with me. The one I'd been carrying around everywhere like an idiot. At first, I was going to smash it on a rock, but then decided I was going to throw it out as far as I could into the meadow so I'd never have to see it again.

Of course, I didn't do either of those things.

Instead, I just sat there with it. I held it up to the light and studied that sweet golden liquid. I'd never forget when she handed me that jar, because in that moment, somehow, *we* began. Eventually, I tucked it into the nearby grass so it was protected, and then I lay down on the blankets and stared up at the sky, wondering how I was ever going to get over her.

I was pretty sure I never would.

But then something amazing happened. Theo found me.

In the same way her bees were coming home to her, she'd come home to me. She pulled me out of that black pit and brought light into my life like she always did.

And now, four months later, we were sitting out in our meadow again.

A lot had happened in that time.

Theo, of course, told everyone the good news that she wasn't allergic to bee venom after all. They were thrilled for her. We threw a "bee" party to celebrate. Seafood was *not* on the menu.

Regina and Tess had both moved to Truth Harbor. Tess applied for a teaching position with the school district, and Regina was scouting locations for her café. They were currently renting a house but were looking to buy.

I finally spoke to Gemma a few months ago. We had a nice conversation, and I assured her that I wasn't trying to cause her family any trouble. I just wanted to get to know Christopher. I flew down to LA and finally met him for the first time in May. We spent the day together. It was a little awkward initially, but it turned out he'd been wanting to meet me too. Christopher wasn't into football but played on a baseball team. What he was most interested in was computers. He was kind of a geek and reminded me a lot of Mateo. Our meeting went so well that I was flying down again in a couple of weeks.

Davis and Miranda were still together and recently adopted a sibling for Petey—another Chihuahua they named Tommy. They worried there might be jealousy issues, but so far, Petey had accepted his younger brother without a hitch. Petey and Tommy were always the best-dressed boys at the dog park.

I received a wedding invitation from my dad, and after some deliberation, Theo and I flew down to California to attend. Surprisingly, I liked my new stepmom, Sheila, quite a bit. And my dad was the happiest I'd ever seen him. He was gracious toward Theo and seemed delighted to meet her. It was the first time my dad and I had spoken in over two years, and I decided I was willing to open the door to having a relationship.

Claire and Leah were both doing well. Claire told us she and Phillip were thinking about having another baby. Leah and Josh were also doing great. Josh's band, East Echo, started a North American tour recently, and Leah flew out to visit him at some of the stops.

Eliza started a new play. It was with the largest theater in town, and while it wasn't the lead, it was an excellent supporting role.

Theo finally started selling her honey, and it brought in just enough money to cover her hive expenses. The best part was when you walked through her lower backyard these days, the place was alive with the buzz of honey bees.

After giving it some thought, we decided to cover my guesthouse swimming pool with a white tent and netting during the warmer months. A simple solution to keep bees away that has worked pretty well.

As for me, I'd finally made peace with the past and said goodbye to my demons. It was a long time coming, but I'd slayed them all, and basically slept like a baby every night.

The biggest news was that I asked Theo to marry me recently, and she said yes. We hadn't set a date yet but would probably do it next summer, unless I could convince her to elope with me instead.

For now, we were enjoying the warm July day by having a picnic in our secret meadow. The place was filled with wildflowers again, just like the first time we'd come here together.

"So, what's the big surprise?" Theo asked. It was the reason I wanted to have a picnic out here. I'd told her I had a surprise for her.

"Would you like a glass of wine first?" I asked.

She laughed and glanced around. "It's the middle of the day on a Saturday. Why not?"

I uncorked the red wine and poured us each a glass. I also pulled out some of the food we'd picked up in town for our picnic.

"I heard a strange rumor at work the other day," Theo said, taking a sip of wine.

I put some cheese on a cracker and popped it in my mouth. "Oh yeah? What's that?"

"It was about Gerald. Remember him?"

"Of course."

"Well, you know how the university moved him to work in their archive building out in the middle of nowhere?"

I nodded and offered her a cracker with cheese, but she declined, so I ate it myself.

"The rumor is he was moved out there because some anonymous person gave the college a generous donation. It came with the stipulation that for one year, Gerald had to work alone in a dark, windowless basement."

I ate another cracker. "That's a pretty weird rumor."

She was watching me closely. "It is, isn't it?"

"As far as rumors go, that's the craziest one I've ever heard." I took a sip of my wine. "Lucky for Gerald it wasn't ten years."

"It *is* far-fetched," she admitted. "And the truth is everyone's delighted he's gone. I never realized how much I dreaded talking to him every day."

"It sounds like it's all good then. Are you ready for my surprise?"

She nodded, and I could tell I'd piqued her curiosity.

I reached over for the backpack we'd brought with us and pulled out a large manila envelope. "This is for you," I said, handing it to her. "Well, I guess it's really for both of us."

She put her glass down. "What is it?"

"Open it and see."

I watched as Theo pulled the stack of papers from the envelope and began looking through them.

"I don't understand," she said slowly, but then she stopped and stared at me in disbelief. "Is this what I think it is?"

I nodded and waved my arm out. "I bought our secret meadow. Just sign the papers and you'll be co-owner."

Theo blinked at me in shock. "This must have cost a fortune! I can't accept a gift like this!"

I shrugged. "All right, fine. Hand it back if you don't want it."

She hugged the papers to her chest. "I didn't say I don't want it."

"We'll be married soon anyway. What's the difference?"

"I can't believe you bought it." She turned her head to gaze out at the meadow. In that moment, a bee chose to fly over and land on a nearby wildflower. Talk about perfect timing.

"No developer will ever touch this land, Theo. Just think of it like that. It'll stay the way it is now for a very long time."

"Gabe, you're remarkable. How did you know I wouldn't be able to refuse a gift like this?"

"Because I know everything."

She rolled her eyes like always, and, of course, I laughed.

Theo put the papers down and then crawled around the picnic basket to climb into my lap.

I slid my hands down to her hips and grinned. "It looks like we're already getting to the good stuff."

She smiled and then kissed me. "Everything with you is the good stuff."

I brought my mouth to her ear. "You taught me all about nerds and bees. Now I'm going to return the favor, Professor." I nuzzled her neck and felt her shiver against me. "I'm going to teach you all about the birds and the bees."

The End

AUTHOR NOTE

Some of you may have noticed the two word spelling for "honey bee" in the book. It's not the typical spelling. In most cases, it's spelled "honeybee."

Entomologists spell it as two words. As I understand it, this is to keep the language precise since there are many different types of bees. They do the same thing with certain other insect spellings as well. For example, an entomologist would spell housefly as "house fly." Being that my heroine is an entomologist, I chose to go with the two word spelling. I believe Theo would approve.

AFTERWORD

Hello,

Thank you for reading Theo and Gabe's story! Book 4 in the series will be TRUTH ABOUT YOU & ME —Eliza and Gavin.

If you'd like to read more about Theo and Gabe, be sure to grab their Bonus Epilogue by typing BookHip.com/HBXXRZG into any browser.

I love hearing from my readers. If you have any comments or thoughts you'd liked share feel free to email me at andrea@andreasimonne.com.

To hear about new releases first, be sure to sign up for my newsletter at andreasimonne.com.

If you enjoyed reading about Theo and Gabe, I hope you'll tell a friend about it, or be kind enough to leave a review or rating.

With so many book choices out there, thank you for choosing mine.

xo,
Andrea

ACKNOWLEDGMENTS

When I first got the idea for this book, I wondered whether I could pull it off. I knew nothing about bees or football. Zip. I had a zero-knowledge base, as Davis would say.

I worried the book would be a struggle to write and hoped the idea wasn't too far fetched. A bee biologist and a quarterback? What was I thinking? But then I started to write and something surprising happened. The book flowed. Heck, it didn't just flow, it *poured* out of me. Theo and Gabe sprang to life, and I could barely keep up with them. It was like those two strong willed people couldn't be stopped. At the same time I was doing tons of research and learning everything I could about bees and football. I became a mini expert.

I laughed, cheered, and cried as I wrote about Theo and Gabe. They became like two of my closest friends. In fact, my son and I were discussing an aspect about bees the other day, and I sighed and said, "If only Theo were here she could explain it to us." (He gave me a funny look like, "Uh, okay, Mom!")

So I'm thankful I got to tell their story. In the book *Big Magic* by Elizabeth Gilbert, she talks about how story ideas sometimes land on authors and they can choose whether to write them or not. Well, I'm grateful this one landed on me. (Just like a bee!)

I want to thank my beta readers Jamie, Nancy, Barb, Stephanie and Zoey for reading the first draft. I appreciate all your comments, ladies. You definitely helped make the book the best it could be. I also want to thank the beta readers from Hot Tree who were kind enough to give me their thoughts and point out what they enjoyed and what could be improved.

My editor Kristin did her usual amazing job. I feel lucky to have someone so talented correcting my books. I'm thankful to her and everyone at Hot Tree for their support over the years.

As always my friend Susan did the final proofread and found mistakes no one else had. No book is perfect, but I'm grateful to have her keen eye helping to find the flaws in mine.

I also want to thank Mark, and especially my friend, Pattie, for their knowledge about football. Pattie, you need to write a football romance! (I know you're surprised I'm calling you out here. But you know you do.) I appreciate all the help I received in better understanding the game. Any football mistakes in the book are definitely my own.

I'm very grateful to Alma and David for graciously answering my many questions about beekeeping. I appreciated their patience and knowledge. And their beehives are amazing.

My husband John gets bonus points for being the best sounding board ever and for listening to my endless chatter about bees, bee venom, bee allergies, honey, quarterbacks, football game schedules, interceptions, and the list goes on....

Last but not least, I want to thank *you*, my readers. For keeping me inspired, and for all your kind words about my books.

xo,

Andrea

SWEET LIFE IN SEATTLE SERIES

I hope you'll check out the first book from my series Sweet Life in Seattle.

He's left her for another woman. Could it get any worse? The mistress is thirteen years older.

Order YEAR OF LIVING BLONDE today!

ALSO BY ANDREA SIMONNE

Sweet Life in Seattle series

Year of Living Blonde

Return of the Jerk

Some Like It Hotter

Object of My Addiction

Too Much Like Love

About Love series

Truth About Men & Dogs

Truth About Cats & Spinsters

Truth About Nerds & Bees

Other

Fire Down Below

ABOUT THE AUTHOR

Andrea Simonne grew up as an army brat and discovered she had a talent for creating personas at each new school. The most memorable was a surfer chick named "Ace" who never touched a surfboard in her life, but had an impressive collection of puka shell necklaces. Andrea still enjoys creating personas though now they occupy her books. She's an Amazon best seller in romantic comedy and contemporary romance, and author of the series Sweet Life in Seattle and About Love. She currently makes her home in the Pacific Northwest with her husband and two sons.

She loves hearing from her readers! You can find her on the web at www.andreasimonne.com.

Email: authorsimonne@gmail.com.

Made in the USA
Las Vegas, NV
02 June 2024

90631568R00218